THE DRAGON GRIAULE

THE
DRAGON
GRIAULE

LUCIUS
SHEPARD

Subterranean Press 2012

First Edition

ISBN
978-1-59606-456-0

Subterranean Press
PO Box 190106
Burton, MI 48519

www.subterraneanpress.com

TABLE OF CONTENTS

THE MAN WHO PAINTED THE DRAGON GRIAULE

Other than the Sichi Collection, Cattanay's only surviving works are to be found in the Municipal Gallery at Regensburg, a group of eight oils-on-canvas, most notable among them being Woman with Oranges. *These paintings constitute his portion of a student exhibition hung some weeks after he had left the city of his birth and traveled south to Teocinte, there to present his proposal to the city fathers; it is unlikely he ever learned of the disposition of his work, and even more unlikely that he was aware of the general critical indifference with which it was received. Perhaps the most interesting of the group to modern scholars, the most indicative as to Cattanay's later preoccupations, is the* Self-Portrait, *painted at the age of twenty-eight, a year before his departure.*

The majority of the canvas is a richly varnished black in which the vague shapes of floorboards are presented, barely visible. Two irregular slashes of gold cross the blackness, and within these we can see a section of the artist's thin features and the shoulder panel of his shirt. The perspective given is that we are looking down at the artist, perhaps through a tear in the roof, and that he is looking up at us, squinting into the light, his mouth distorted by a grimace born of intense concentration. On first viewing the painting, I was struck by the atmosphere of tension that radiated from it. It seemed I was spying upon a man imprisoned within a shadow having two golden bars, tormented by the possibilities of light beyond the walls. And though this may be the reaction of the art historian, not the less knowledgeable and therefore more trustworthy response of the gallery-goer, it also seemed that this imprisonment was self-imposed, that he could have easily escaped his confine; but that he had realized a feeling of stricture was an essential fuel to his ambition, and so had chained himself to this arduous and thoroughly unreasonable chore of perception...

—FROM *MERIC CATTANAY:*
THE POLITICS OF CONCEPTION
BY READE HOLLAND, PH.D.

1

IN 1853, IN A COUNTRY far to the south, in a world separated from this one by the thinnest margin of possibility, a dragon named Griaule dominated the region of the Carbonates Valley, a fertile area centering upon the town of Teocinte and renowned for its production of silver, mahogany, and indigo. There were other dragons in those days, most dwelling on the rocky islands west of Patagonia—tiny, irascible creatures, the largest of them no bigger than a swallow. But Griaule was one of the great Beasts who had ruled an age. Over the centuries he had grown to stand 750 feet high at the midback, and from the tip of his tail to his nose he was six thousand feet long. (It should be noted here that the growth of dragons was due not to caloric intake, but to the absorption of energy derived from the passage of time.) Had it not been for a miscast spell, Griaule would have died millennia before. The wizard entrusted with the task of slaying him—knowing his own life would be forfeited as a result of the magical backwash—had experienced a last-second twinge of fear, and, diminished by this ounce of courage, the spell had flown a mortal inch awry. Though the wizard's whereabouts were unknown, Griaule had remained alive. His heart had stopped, his breath stilled, but his mind continued to seethe, to send forth the gloomy vibrations that enslaved all who stayed for long within range of his influence.

This dominance of Griaule's was an elusive thing. The people of the valley attributed their dour character to years of living under his mental shadow, yet there were other regional populations who maintained a harsh face to the world and had no dragon on which to blame the condition; they also attributed their frequent raids against the neighboring states to Griaule's effect, claiming to be a peaceful folk at heart—but again, was this not human nature? Perhaps the most certifiable proof of Griaule's primacy was the fact that despite a standing offer of a fortune in silver to anyone who could kill him, no one had succeeded. Hundreds of plans had been put forward, and all had failed, either through inanition or impracticality. The archives of Teocinte were filled with schematics for enormous steam-powered swords and other such improbable devices, and the architects of these plans had every one stayed too long in the valley and become part of the disgruntled populace. And so they went on with their lives, coming and going, always returning, bound to the valley, until one spring day in 1853, Meric Cattanay arrived and proposed that the dragon be painted.

He was a lanky young man with a shock of black hair and a pinched look to his cheeks; he affected the loose trousers and shirt of a peasant, and waved his arms to make a point. His eyes grew wide when listening, as if his brain were bursting with illumination, and at times he talked incoherently about "the conceptual statement of death by art." And though the city fathers could not be sure, though they allowed for the possibility that he simply had an unfortunate manner, it seemed he was mocking them. All in all, he was not the sort they were inclined to trust. But, because he had come armed with such a wealth of diagrams and charts, they were forced to give him serious consideration.

"I don't believe Griaule will be able to perceive the menace in a process as subtle as art," Meric told them. "We'll proceed as if we were going to illustrate him, grace his side with a work of true vision, and all the while we'll be poisoning him with the paint."

The city fathers voiced their incredulity, and Meric waited impatiently until they quieted. He did not enjoy dealing with these worthies. Seated at their long table, sour-faced, a huge smudge of soot on the wall above their heads like an ugly thought they were sharing, they reminded him of the Wine Merchants Association in Regensburg, the time they had rejected his group portrait.

"Paint can be deadly stuff," he said after their muttering had died down. "Take Vert Veronese, for example. It's derived from oxide of chrome and barium. Just a whiff would make you keel over. But we have to go about it seriously, create a real piece of art. If we just slap paint on his side, he might see through us."

The first step in the process, he told them, would be to build a tower of scaffolding, complete with hoists and ladders, that would brace against the supraorbital plates above the dragon's eye; this would provide a direct route to a seven-hundred-foot-square loading platform and base station behind the eye. He estimated it would take eighty-one-thousand board feet of lumber, and a crew of ninety men should be able to finish construction within five months. Ground crews accompanied by chemists and geologists would search out limestone deposits (useful in priming the scales) and sources of pigments, whether organic or minerals such as azurite and hematite. Other teams would be set to scraping the dragon's side clean of algae, peeled skin, any decayed material, and afterward would laminate the surface with resins.

"It would be easier to bleach him with quicklime," he said. "But that way we lose the discolorations and ridges generated by growth and age, and I think what we'll paint will be defined by those shapes. Anything else would look like a damn tattoo!"

There would be storage vats and mills: edge-runner mills to separate pigments from crude ores, ball mills to powder the pigments, pug mills to mix them with oil. There would be boiling vats and calciners—fifteen-foot-high furnaces used to produce caustic lime for sealant solutions.

"We'll build most of them atop the dragon's head for purposes of access," he said. "On the fronto-parietal plate." He checked some figures.

"By my reckoning, the plate's about three hundred and fifty feet wide. Does that sound accurate?"

Most of the city fathers were stunned by the prospect, but one managed a nod, and another asked, "How long will it take for him to die?"

"Hard to say," came the answer. "Who knows how much poison he's capable of absorbing? It might just take a few years. But in the worst instance, within forty or fifty years, enough chemicals will have seeped through the scales to have weakened the skeleton and he'll fall in like an old barn."

"Forty years!" exclaimed someone. "Preposterous!"

"Or fifty." Meric smiled. "That way we'll have time to finish the painting." He turned and walked to the window and stood gazing out at the white stone houses of Teocinte. This was going to be the sticky part, but if he read them right, they would not believe in the plan if it seemed too easy. They needed to feel they were making a sacrifice, that they were nobly bound to a great labor. "If it does take forty or fifty years," he went on, "the project will drain your resources. Timber, animal life, minerals. Everything will be used up by the work. Your lives will be totally changed. But I guarantee you'll be rid of him."

The city fathers broke into an outraged babble.

"Do you really want to kill him?" cried Meric, stalking over to them and planting his fists on the table. "You've been waiting centuries for someone to come along and chop off his head or send him up in a puff of smoke. That's not going to happen! There is no easy solution. But there is a practical one, an elegant one. To use the stuff of the land he dominates to destroy him. It will *not* be easy, but you *will* be rid of him. And that's what you want, isn't it?"

They were silent, exchanging glances, and he saw that they now believed he could do what he proposed and were wondering if the cost was too high.

"I'll need five hundred ounces of silver to hire engineers and artisans," said Meric. "Think it over. I'll take a few days and go see this dragon of yours…inspect the scales and so forth. When I return, you can give me your answer."

The city fathers grumbled and scratched their heads, but at last they agreed to put the question before the body politic. They asked for a week in which to decide and appointed Jarcke, who was the mayoress of Hangtown, to guide Meric to Griaule.

THE VALLEY EXTENDED seventy miles from north to south, and was enclosed by jungled hills whose folded sides and spiny backs gave rise to the idea that beasts were sleeping beneath them. The valley floor was cultivated into fields of bananas and cane and melons, and where it was not cultivated, there were stands of thistle palms and berry thickets and the occasional giant fig brooding sentinel over the rest. Jarcke and Meric tethered their horses a half-hour's ride from town and began to ascend a gentle incline that rose into the notch between two hills. Sweaty and short of breath, Meric stopped a third of the way up; but Jarcke kept plodding along, unaware he was no longer following. She was by nature as blunt as her name—a stump beer-keg of a woman with a brown weathered face. Though she appeared to be ten years older then Meric, she was nearly the same age. She wore a gray robe belted at the waist with a leather band that held four throwing knives, and a coil of rope was slung over her shoulder.

"How much farther?" called Meric.

She turned and frowned. "You're standin' on his tail. Rest of him's around back of the hill."

A pinprick of chill bloomed in Meric's abdomen, and he stared down at the grass, expecting it to dissolve and reveal a mass of glittering scales.

"Why don't we take the horses?" he asked.

"Horses don't like it up here." She grunted with amusement. "Neither do most people, for that matter." She trudged off.

Another twenty minutes brought them to the other side of the hill high above the valley floor. The land continued to slope upward, but more gently than before. Gnarled, stunted oaks pushed up from thickets of chokecherry, and insects sizzled in the weeds. They might have been walking on a natural shelf several hundred feet across; but ahead of them, where the ground rose abruptly, a number of thick greenish-black columns broke from the earth. Leathery folds hung between them, and these were encrusted with clumps of earth and brocaded with mold. They had the look of a collapsed palisade and the ghosted feel of ancient ruins.

"Them's the wings," said Jarcke. "Mostly they's covered, but you can catch sight of 'em off the edge, and up near Hangtown there's places where you can walk in under 'em…but I wouldn't advise it."

"I'd like to take a look off the edge," said Meric, unable to tear his eyes away from the wings; though the surfaces of the leaves gleamed in the strong sun, the wings seemed to absorb the light, as if their age and strangeness were proof against reflection.

Jarcke led him to a glade in which tree ferns and oaks crowded together and cast a green gloom, and where the earth sloped sharply downward. She lashed her rope to an oak and tied the other end around Meric's waist. "Give a yank when you want to stop, and another when you want to be hauled up," she said, and began paying out the rope, letting him walk backward against her pull.

Ferns tickled Meric's neck as he pushed through the brush, and the oak leaves pricked his cheeks. Suddenly he emerged into bright sunlight. On looking down, he found his feet were braced against a fold of the dragon's wing, and on looking up, he saw that the wing vanished beneath a mantle of earth and vegetation. He let Jarcke lower him a dozen feet more, yanked, and gazed off northward along the enormous swell of Griaule's side.

The scales were hexagonals thirty feet across and half that distance high; their basic color was a pale greenish gold, but some were whitish, draped with peels of dead skin, and others were overgrown by viridian moss, and the rest were scrolled with patterns of lichen and algae that resembled the characters of a serpentine alphabet. Birds had nested in the cracks, and ferns plumed from the interstices, thousands of them lifting in the breeze. It was a great hanging garden whose scope took Meric's breath away—like looking around the curve of a fossil moon. The sense of all the centuries accreted in the scales made him dizzy, and he found he could not turn his head, but could only stare at the panorama, his soul shriveling with a comprehension of the timelessness and bulk of this creature to which he clung like a fly. He lost perspective on the scene—Griaule's side was bigger than the sky, possessing its own potent gravity, and it seemed completely reasonable that he should be able to walk out along it and suffer no fall. He started to do so, and Jarcke, mistaking the strain on the rope for a signal, hauled him up, dragging him across the wing, through the dirt and ferns, and back into the glade. He lay speechless and gasping at her feet.

"Big 'un, ain't he," she said, and grinned.

After Meric had gotten his legs under him, they set off toward Hangtown; but they had not gone a hundred yards, following a trail that wound through the thickets, before Jarcke whipped out a knife and hurled it at a raccoon-sized creature that leaped out in front of them.

"Skizzer," she said, kneeling beside it and pulling the knife from its neck. "Calls 'em that 'cause they hisses when they runs. They eats snakes, but they'll go after children what ain't careful."

Meric dropped down next to her. The skizzer's body was covered with short black fur, but its head was hairless, corpse-pale, the skin wrinkled as if it had been immersed too long in water. Its face was squinty-eyed, flat-nosed, with a disproportionately large jaw that hinged open to expose a nasty set of teeth.

"They's the dragon's critters," said Jarcke. "Used to live in his bung-hole." She pressed one of its paws, and claws curved like hooks slid forth. "They'd hang around the lip and drop on other critters what wandered in. And if nothin' wandered in…" She pried out the tongue with her knife—its surface was studded with jagged points like the blade of a rasp. "Then they'd lick Griaule clean for their supper."

Back in Teocinte, the dragon had seemed to Meric a simple thing, a big lizard with a tick of life left inside, the residue of a dim sensibility; but he was beginning to suspect that this tick of life was more complex than any he had encountered.

"My gram used to say," Jarcke went on, "that the old dragons could fling themselves up to the sun in a blink and travel back to their own world, and when they come back, they'd bring the skizzers and all the rest with 'em. They was immortal, she said. Only the young ones came here 'cause later on they grew too big to fly on Earth." She made a sour face. "Don't know as I believe it."

"Then you're a fool," said Meric.

Jarcke glanced up at him, her hand twitching toward her belt.

"How can you live here and *not* believe it!" he said, surprised to hear himself so fervently defending a myth. "God! This…" He broke off, noticing the flicker of a smile on her face.

She clucked her tongue, apparently satisfied by something. "Come on," she said. "I want to be at the eye before sunset."

THE PEAKS OF Griaule's folded wings, completely overgrown by grass and shrubs and dwarfish trees, formed two spiny hills that cast a shadow over Hangtown and the narrow lake around which it sprawled. Jarcke said the lake was a stream flowing off the hill behind the dragon, and that it drained away through the membranes of his wing and down onto his shoulder. It was beautiful beneath the wing, she told him. Ferns and waterfalls. But it was reckoned an evil place. From a distance the town looked picturesque—rustic cabins, smoking chimneys. As they approached, however, the cabins resolved into dilapidated shanties with missing boards and broken windows; suds and garbage and offal floated in the shallows of the lake. Aside from a few men idling on the stoops, who squinted at Meric and nodded glumly at Jarcke, no one was about. The grass-blades stirred in the breeze, spiders scuttled under the shanties, and there was an air of torpor and dissolution.

Jarcke seemed embarrassed by the town. She made no attempt at introductions, stopping only long enough to fetch another coil of rope from one of the shanties, and as they walked between the wings, down through the neck spines—a forest of greenish gold spikes burnished by the lowering sun—she explained how the townsfolk grubbed a livelihood from Griaule. Herbs gathered on his back were valued as medicine and charms, as were the peels of dead skin; the artifacts left by previous Hangtown generations were of some worth to various collectors.

"Then there's scalehunters," she said with disgust. "Henry Sichi from Port Chantay'll pay good money for pieces of scale, and though it's bad luck to do it, some'll have a go at chippin' off the loose 'uns." She walked a few paces in silence. "But there's others who've got better reasons for livin' here."

The frontal spike above Griaule's eyes was whorled at the base like a narwhal's horn and curved back toward the wings. Jarcke attached the ropes to eyebolts drilled into the spike, tied one about her waist, the other about Meric's; she cautioned him to wait, and rappelled off the side. In a moment she called for him to come down. Once again he grew dizzy as he descended; he glimpsed a clawed foot far below, mossy fangs jutting from an impossibly long jaw; and then he began to spin and bash against the scales. Jarcke gathered him in and helped him sit on the lip of the socket.

"Damn!" she said, stamping her foot.

A three-foot-long section of the adjoining scale shifted slowly away. Peering close, Meric saw that while in texture and hue it was indistinguishable from the scale, there was a hairline division between it and the surface. Jarcke, her face twisted in disgust, continued to harry the thing until it moved out of reach.

"Call 'em flakes," she said when he asked what it was. "Some kind of insect. Got a long tube that they pokes down between the scales and sucks the blood. See there?" She pointed off to where a flock of birds was wheeling close to Griaule's side; a chip of pale gold broke loose and went tumbling down to the valley. "Birds pry 'em off, let 'em bust open, and eats the innards." She hunkered down beside him and after a moment asked, "You really think you can do it?"

"What? You mean kill the dragon?"

She nodded.

"Certainly," he said, and then added, lying, "I've spent years devising the method."

"If all the paint's goin' to be atop his head, how're you goin' to get it to where the paintin's done?"

"That's no problem. We'll pipe it to wherever it's needed."

She nodded again. "You're a clever fellow," she said; and when Meric, pleased, made as if to thank her for the compliment, she cut in and said, "Don't mean nothin' by it. Bein' clever ain't an accomplishment. It's just somethin' you come by, like bein' tall." She turned away, ending the conversation.

Meric was weary of being awestruck, but even so he could not help marveling at the eye. By his estimate it was seventy feet long and fifty feet high, and it was shuttered by an opaque membrane that was unusually clear of algae and lichen, glistening, with vague glints of color visible behind it. As the westering sun reddened and sank between two distant hills, the membrane began to quiver and then split open down the center. With the ponderous slowness of a theater curtain opening, the halves slid apart to reveal the glowing humor. Terrified by the idea that Griaule could see him, Meric sprang to his feet, but Jarcke restrained him.

"Stay still and watch," she said.

He had no choice—the eye was mesmerizing. The pupil was slit and featureless black, but the humor…he had never seen such fiery blues and crimsons and golds. What had looked to be vague glints, odd refractions of the sunset, he now realized were photic reactions of some sort. Fairy rings of light developed deep within the eye, expanded into spoked shapes, flooded the humor, and faded—only to be replaced by another and another. He felt the pressure of Griaule's vision, his ancient mind, pouring through him, and as if in response to this pressure, memories bubbled up in his thoughts. Particularly sharp ones. The way a bowlful of brush water had looked after freezing over during a winter's night—a delicate, fractured flower of murky yellow. An archipelago of orange peels that his girl had left strewn across the floor of the studio. Sketching atop Jokenam Hill one sunrise, the snow-capped roofs of Regensburg below pitched at all angles like broken paving stones, and silver shafts of the sun striking down through a leaden overcast. It was as if these things were being drawn forth for his inspection. Then they were washed away by what also seemed a memory, though at the same time it was wholly unfamiliar. Essentially it was a landscape of light, and he was plunging through it, up and up. Prisms and lattices of iridescent fire bloomed around him, and everything was a roaring fall into brightness, and finally he was clear into its white furnace heart, his own heart swelling with the joy of his strength and dominion.

It was dusk before Meric realized the eye had closed. His mouth hung open, his eyes ached from straining to see, and his tongue was glued to his palate. Jarcke sat motionless, buried in shadow.

"Th…" He had to swallow to clear his throat of mucus. "This is the reason you live here, isn't it?"

"Part of the reason," she said. "I can see things comin' way up here. Things to watch out for, things to study on."

She stood and walked to the lip of the socket and spat off the edge; the valley stretched out gray and unreal behind her, the folds of the hills barely visible in the gathering dusk.

"I seen you comin'," she said.

A WEEK LATER, after much exploration, much talk, they went down into Teocinte. The town was a shambles—shattered windows, slogans painted on the walls, glass and torn banners and spoiled food littering the streets—as if there had been both a celebration and a battle. Which there had. The city fathers met with Meric in the town hall and informed him that his plan had been approved. They presented him a chest containing five hundred ounces of silver and said that the entire resources of the community were at his disposal. They offered a wagon and a team to transport him and the chest to Regensburg and asked if any of the preliminary work could be begun during his absence.

Meric hefted one of the silver bars. In its cold gleam he saw the object of his desire—two, perhaps three years of freedom, of doing the work he wanted and not having to accept commissions. But all that had been confused. He glanced at Jarcke; she was staring out the window, leaving it to him. He set the bar back in the chest and shut the lid.

"You'll have to send someone else," he said. And then, as the city fathers looked at each other askance, he laughed and laughed at how easily he had discarded all his dreams and expectations.

> *It had been eleven years since I had been to the valley, twelve since work had begun on the painting, and I was appalled by the changes that had taken place. Many of the hills were scraped brown and treeless, and there was a general dearth of wildlife. Griaule, of course, was most changed. Scaffolding hung from his back; artisans, suspended by webworks of ropes, crawled over his side; and all the scales to be worked had either been painted or primed. The tower rising to his eye was swarmed by laborers, and at night the calciners and vats atop his head belched flame into the sky, making it seem there was a mill town*

in the heavens. At his feet was a brawling shantytown populated by prostitutes, workers, gamblers, ne'er-do-wells of every sort, and soldiers: the burdensome cost of the project had encouraged the city fathers of Teocinte to form a regular militia, which regularly plundered the adjoining states and had posted occupation forces to some areas. Herds of frightened animals milled in the slaughtering pens, waiting to be rendered into oils and pigments. Wagons filled with ores and vegetable products rattled in the streets. I myself had brought a cargo of madder roots from which a rose tint would be derived.

It was not easy to arrange a meeting with Cattanay. While he did none of the actual painting, he was always busy in his office consulting with engineers and artisans, or involved in some other part of the logistical process. When at last I did meet with him, I found he had changed as drastically as Griaule. His hair had gone gray, deep lines scored his features, and his right shoulder had a peculiar bulge at its midpoint— the product of a fall. He was amused by the fact that I wanted to buy the painting, to collect the scales after Griaule's death, and I do not believe he took me at all seriously. But the woman Jarcke, his constant companion, informed him that I was a responsible businessman, that I had already bought the bones, the teeth, even the dirt beneath Griaule's belly (this I eventually sold as having magical properties).

"Well," said Cattanay, "I suppose someone has to own them."

He led me outside, and we stood looking at the painting.

"You'll keep them together?" he asked.

I said, "Yes."

"If you'll put that in writing," he said, "then they're yours."

Having expected to haggle long and hard over the price, I was flabbergasted; but I was even more flabbergasted by what he said next.

"Do you think it's any good?" he asked.

Cattanay did not consider the painting to be the work of his imagination; he felt he was simply illuminating the shapes that appeared on Griaule's side and was convinced that once the paint was applied, new shapes were produced beneath it, causing him to make constant changes. He saw himself as an artisan more than a creative artist. But to put his question into perspective, people were beginning to flock from all over the world and marvel at the painting. Some claimed they saw intimations of the future in its gleaming surface; others underwent transfiguring experiences; still others— artists themselves—attempted to capture something of the work on canvas, hopeful of establishing reputations merely by being competent copyists of Cattanay's art. The painting was nonrepresentational in character, essentially a wash of pale gold spread across the dragon's side; but buried beneath the laminated surface were a myriad tints of iridescent color that, as the sun passed through the heavens and the light bloomed and faded, solidified into innumerable forms and figures that seemed to flow back and forth. I will not try to categorize these forms, because there was no end to them; they were as varied as the conditions under which they were viewed. But I will say that on the morning I met with Cattanay, I—who was the soul of the practical man, without a visionary bone in my body—felt as though I were being whirled away into the painting, up through geometries of light, latticeworks of rainbow color that built the way the edges of a cloud build, past orbs, spirals, wheels of flame...

—FROM *THIS BUSINESS OF GRIAULE*
BY HENRY SICHI

2

THE HAD BEEN SEVERAL WOMEN in Meric's life since he arrived in the valley; most had been attracted by his growing fame and his association with the mystery of the dragon, and most had left for the same reasons, feeling daunted and unappreciated. But Lise was different in two respects. First, because she loved Meric truly and well; and second, because she was married—albeit unhappily—to a man named Pardiel, the foreman of the calciner crew. She did not love him as she did Meric, yet she respected him and felt obliged to consider carefully before ending the relationship. Meric had never known such an introspective soul. She was twelve years younger than he, tall and lovely, with sun-streaked hair and brown eyes that went dark and seemed to turn inward whenever she was pensive. She was in the habit of analyzing everything that affected her, drawing back from her emotions and inspecting them as if they were a clutch of strange insects she had discovered crawling on her skirt. Though her penchant for self-examination kept her from him, Meric viewed it as a kind of baffling virtue. He had the classic malady and could find no fault with her. For almost a year they were as happy as could be expected; they talked long hours and walked together on those occasions when Pardiel worked double shifts and was forced to bed down by his furnaces, they spent the nights making love in the cavernous spaces beneath the dragon's wing.

It was still reckoned an evil place. Something far worse than skizzers or flakes was rumored to live there, and the ravages of this creature were blamed for every disappearance, even that of the most malcontented laborer. But Meric did not give credence to the rumors. He half believed Griaule had chosen him to be his executioner and that the dragon would never let him be harmed; and besides, it was the only place where they could be assured of privacy.

A crude stair led under the wing, handholds and steps hacked from the scales—doubtless the work of scalehunters. It was a treacherous passage, six hundred feet above the valley floor; but Lise and Meric were secured by ropes, and over the months, driven by the urgency of passion, they adapted to it. Their favorite spot lay fifty feet in (Lise would go no farther; she was afraid even if he was not), near a waterfall that trickled over the leathery folds, causing them to glisten with a mineral brilliance. It was eerily beautiful, a haunted gallery. Peels of dead skin hung down from the shadows like torn veils of ectoplasm; ferns sprouted from the vanes, which were thicker than cathedral columns; swallows curved through the black air. Sometimes, lying with her hidden by a tuck of the wing, Meric would think the beating of their hearts was what really animated the place, that the instant they left, the water ceased flowing and the swallows vanished. He had an unshakable faith in the transforming power of their affections, and one morning as they dressed, preparing to return to Hangtown, he asked her to leave with him.

"To another part of the valley?" She laughed sadly. "What good would that do? Pardiel would follow us."

"No," he said. "To another country. Anywhere far from here."

"We can't," she said, kicking at the wing. "Not until Griaule dies. Have you forgotten?"

"We haven't tried."

"Others have."

"But we'd be strong enough. I know it!"

"You're a romantic," she said gloomily, and stared out over the slope of Griaule's back at the valley. Sunrise had washed the hills to crimson, and even the tips of the wings were glowing a dull red.

"Of course I'm a romantic!" He stood, angry. "What the hell's wrong with that?"

She sighed with exasperation. "You wouldn't leave your work," she said. "And if we did leave, what work would you do? Would—"

"Why must everything be a problem in advance!" he shouted. "I'll tattoo elephants! I'll paint murals on the chests of giants, I'll illuminate whales! Who else is better qualified?"

She smiled, and his anger evaporated.

"I didn't mean it that way," she said. "I just wondered if you could be satisfied with anything else."

She reached out her hand to be pulled up, and he drew her into an embrace. As he held her, inhaling the scent of vanilla water from her hair, he saw a diminutive figure silhouetted against the backdrop of the valley. It did not seem real—a black homunculus—and even when it began to come forward, growing larger and larger, it looked less a man than a magical keyhole opening in a crimson-set hillside. But Meric knew from the man's rolling walk and the hulking set of his shoulders that it was Pardiel; he was carrying a long-handled hook, one of those used by artisans to maneuver along the scales.

Meric tensed, and Lise looked back to see what had alarmed him. "Oh, my God!" she said, moving out of the embrace.

Pardiel stopped a dozen feet away. He said nothing. His face was in shadow, and the hook swung lazily from his hand. Lise took a step toward him, then stepped back and stood in front of Meric as if to shield him.

Seeing this, Pardiel let out an inarticulate yell and charged, slashing with the hook. Meric pushed Lise aside and ducked. He caught a brimstone whiff of the calciners as Pardiel rushed past and went sprawling, tripped by some irregularity in the scale. Deathly afraid, knowing he was no match for the foreman, Meric seized Lise's hand and ran deeper under the wing. He hoped Pardiel would be too frightened to follow, leery of the creature that was rumored to live there; but he was not. He came after them at a measured pace, tapping the hook against his leg.

Higher on Griaule's back, the wing was dimpled downward by hundreds of bulges, and this created a maze of small chambers and tunnels so low that they had to crouch to pass along them. The sound of their breathing and the scrape of their feet were amplified by the enclosed spaces, and Meric could no longer hear Pardiel. He had never been this deep before. He had thought it would be pitch-dark; but the lichen and algae adhering to the wing were luminescent and patterned every surface, even the scales beneath them, with whorls of blue and green fire that shed a sickly radiance. It was as if they were giants crawling through a universe whose starry matter had not yet congealed into galaxies and nebulas. In the wan light, Lise's face—turned back to him now and again—was teary and frantic; and then, as she straightened, passing into still another chamber, she drew in breath with a shriek.

At first Meric thought Pardiel had somehow managed to get ahead of them; but on entering he saw that the cause of her fright was a man propped in a sitting position against the far wall. He looked mummified. Wisps of brittle hair poked up from his scalp, the shapes of his bones were visible through his skin, and his eyes were empty holes. Between his legs was a scatter of dust where his genitals had been. Meric pushed Lise toward the next tunnel, but she resisted and pointed at the man.

"His eyes," she said, horror-struck.

Though the eyes were mostly a negative black, Meric now realized they were shot through by opalescent flickers. He felt compelled to kneel beside the man—it was a sudden, motiveless urge that gripped him, bent him to its will, and released him a second later. As he rested his hand on the scale, he brushed a massive ring that was lying beneath the shrunken fingers. Its stone was black, shot through by flickers identical to those within the eyes, and incised with the letter *S*. He found his gaze was deflected away from both the stone and the eyes, as if they contained charges repellent to the senses. He touched the man's withered arm; the flesh was rock-hard, petrified. But alive. From that brief touch he gained an impression of the man's life, of gazing for centuries at the same patch of unearthly fire, of a mind gone beyond mere madness into a perverse rapture, a meditation upon some foul principle. He snatched back his hand in revulsion.

There was a noise behind them, and Meric jumped up, pushing Lise into the next tunnel. "Go right," he whispered. "We'll circle back toward the stair." But Pardiel was too close to confuse with such tactics, and their flight became a wild chase, scrambling, falling, catching glimpses of Pardiel's smoke-stained face, until finally—as Meric came to a large chamber—he felt the hook bite into his thigh. He went down, clutching at the wound, pulling the hook loose. The next moment Pardiel was atop him; Lise appeared over his shoulder, but he knocked her away and locked his fingers in Meric's hair and smashed his head against the scale. Lise screamed, and white lights fired through Meric's skull. Again his head was smashed down. And again. Dimly, he saw Lise struggling with Pardiel, saw her shoved away, saw the hook raised high and the foreman's mouth distorted by a grimace. Then the grimace vanished. His jaw dropped open, and he reached behind him as if to scratch his shoulder blade. A line of dark blood eeled from his mouth and he collapsed, smothering Meric beneath his chest. Meric heard voices. He tried to dislodge the body, and the effects drained the last of his strength. He whirled down through a blackness that seemed as negative and inexhaustible as the petrified man's eyes.

SOMEONE HAD PROPPED his head on their lap and was bathing his brow with a damp cloth. He assumed it was Lise, but when he asked what had happened, it was Jarcke who answered, saying, "Had to kill him." His head throbbed, his leg throbbed even worse, and his eyes would not focus. The peels of dead skin hanging overhead appeared to be writhing. He realized they were out near the edge of the wing.

"Where's Lise?"

"Don't worry," said Jarcke. "You'll see her again." She made it sound like an indictment.

"Where is she?"

"Sent her back to Hangtown. Won't do you two bein' seen hand in hand the same day Pardiel's missin'."

"She wouldn't have left…" He blinked, trying to see her face; the lines around her mouth were etched deep and reminded him of the patterns of lichen on the dragon's scale. "What did you do?"

"Convinced her it was best," said Jarcke. "Don't you know she's just foolin' with you?"

"I've got to talk to her." He was full of remorse, and it was unthinkable that Lise should be bearing her grief alone; but when he struggled to rise, pain lanced through his leg.

"You wouldn't get ten feet," she said. "Soon as your head's clear, I'll help you with the stairs."

He closed his eyes, resolving to find Lise the instant he got back to Hangtown—together they would decide what to do. The scale beneath him was cool, and that coolness was transmitted to his skin, his flesh, as if he were merging with it, becoming one of its ridges.

"What was the wizard's name?" he asked after a while, recalling the petrified man, the ring and its incised letter. "The one who tried to kill Griaule…"

"Don't know as I ever heard it," said Jarcke. "But I reckon it's him back there."

"You saw him?"

"I was chasin' a scalehunter once what stole some rope, and I found him instead. Pretty miserable sort, whoever he is."

Her fingers trailed over his shoulder—a gentle, treasuring touch. He did not understand what it signaled, being too concerned with Lise, with the terrifying potentials of all that had happened; but years later, after things had passed beyond remedy, he cursed himself for not having understood.

At length Jarcke helped him to his feet, and they climbed up to Hangtown, to bitter realizations and regrets, leaving Pardiel to the birds or the weather or worse.

It seems it is considered irreligious for a woman in love to hesitate or examine the situation, to do anything other than blindly follow the impulse of her emotions. I felt the brunt of such an attitude—people judged it my fault for not having acted quickly and decisively one way or another. Perhaps I was overcautious. I do not claim to be free of blame, only innocent of sacrilege. I believe I might have eventually left Pardiel—there was not enough in the relationship to sustain happiness for either of us. But I had good reason for cautious examination. My husband was not an evil man, and there were matters of loyalty between us.

I could not face Meric after Pardiel's death, and I moved to another part of the valley. He tried to see me on many occasions, but I always refused. Though I was greatly tempted, my guilt was greater. Four years later, after Jarcke died—crushed by a runaway wagon—one of her associates wrote and told me Jarcke had been in love with Meric, that it had been she who had informed Pardiel of the affair, and that she may well have staged the murder. The letter acted somewhat to expiate my guilt, and I weighed the possibility of seeing Meric again. But too much time had passed, and we had both assumed other lives. I decided against it. Six years later, when Griaule's influence had weakened sufficiently to allow emigration, I moved to Port Chantay. I did not hear from Meric for almost twenty years after that, and then one day I received a letter, which I will reproduce in part:

"...My old friend from Regensburg, Louis Dardano, has been living here for the past few years, engaged in writing my biography. The narrative has a breezy feel, like a tale being told in a tavern, which—if you recall my telling you how this all began—is quite appropriate. But on reading it, I am amazed my life has had such a simple shape. One task, one passion. God, Lise! Seventy years old, and I still dream of you. And I still think of what happened that morning under the wing. Strange, that it has taken me all this time to realize it was not Jarcke, not you or I who was culpable, but Griaule. How obvious it seems now. I was leaving, and he needed me to complete the expression on his side, his dream of flying, of escape, to grant him

*the death of his desire. I am certain you will think I have leaped to
this assumption, but I remind you that it has been a leap of forty
years' duration. I know Griaule, know his monstrous subtlety. I can
see it at work in every action that has taken place in the valley since
my arrival. I was a fool not to understand that his powers were at the
heart of our sad conclusion.*

*"The army now runs everything here, as no doubt you are aware.
It is rumored they are planning a winter campaign against Regensburg. Can you believe it! Their fathers were ignorant, but this genera-
tion is brutally stupid. Otherwise, the work goes well and things are as
usual with me. My shoulder aches, children stare at me on the street,
and it is whispered I am mad..."*

—FROM *UNDER GRIAULE'S WING*
BY LISE CLAVERIE

3

ACNE-SCARRED, LEAN, ARROGANT, MAJOR HAUK
was a very young major with a limp. When Meric had entered, the major
had been practicing his signature—it was a thing of elegant loops and
flourishes, obviously intended to have a place in posterity.

As he strode back and forth during their conversation, he paused frequently to admire himself in the window glass, settling the hang of his
red jacket or running his fingers along the crease of his white trousers.
It was the new style of uniform, the first Meric had seen at close range,
and he noted with amusement the dragons embossed on the epaulets. He
wondered if Griaule was capable of such an irony, if his influence was sufficiently discreet to have planted the idea for this comic-opera apparel in
the brain of some general's wife.

"...not a question of manpower," the major was saying, "but of..." He
broke off, and after a moment cleared his throat.

Meric, who had been studying the blotches on the backs of his hands, glanced up; the cane that had been resting against his knee slipped and clattered to the floor.

"A question of materiel," said the major firmly. "The price of antimony, for example..."

"Hardly use it anymore," said Meric. "I'm almost done with the mineral reds."

A look of impatience crossed the major's face. "Very well," he said; he stooped to his desk and shuffled through some papers. "Ah! Here's a bill for a shipment of cuttlefish from which you derive..." He shuffled more papers.

"Syrian brown," said Meric gruffly. "I'm done with that, too. Golds and violets are all I need anymore. A little blue and rose." He wished the man would stop badgering him; he wanted to be at the eye before sunset.

As the major continued his accounting, Meric's gaze wandered out the window. The shantytown surrounding Griaule had swelled into a city and now sprawled across the hills. Most of the buildings were permanent, wood and stone, and the cant of the roofs, the smoke from the factories around the perimeter, put him in mind of Regensburg. All the natural beauty of the land had been drained into the painting. Blackish gray rain clouds were muscling up from the east, but the afternoon sun shone clear and shed a heavy gold radiance on Griaule's side. It looked as if the sunlight were an extension of the gleaming resins, as if the thickness of the paint were becoming infinite. He let the major's voice recede to a buzz and followed the scatter and dazzle of the images; and then, with a start, he realized the major was sounding him out about stopping the work.

The idea panicked him at first. He tried to interrupt, to raise objections; but the major talked through him, and as Meric thought it over, he grew less and less opposed. The painting would never be finished, and he was tired. Perhaps it was time to have done with it, to accept a university post somewhere and enjoy life for a while.

"We've been thinking about a temporary stoppage," said Major Hauk. "Then if the winter campaign goes well..." He smiled. "If we're not visited by plague and pestilence, we'll assume things are in hand. Of course we'd like your opinion."

Meric felt a surge of anger toward this smug little monster. "In my opinion, you people are idiots," he said. "You wear Griaule's image on your shoulders, weave him on your flags, and yet you don't have the least comprehension of what that means. You think it's just a useful symbol…"

"Excuse me," said the major stiffly.

"The hell I will!" Meric groped for his cane and heaved up to his feet. "You see yourselves as conquerors. Shapers of destiny. But all your rapes and slaughters are Griaule's expressions. His will. You're every bit as much his parasites as the skizzers."

The major sat, picked up a pen, and began to write.

"It astounds me," Meric went on, "that you can live next to a miracle, a source of mystery, and treat him as if he were an oddly shaped rock."

The major kept writing.

"What are you doing?" asked Meric.

"My recommendation," said the major without looking up.

"Which is?"

"That we initiate stoppage at once."

They exchanged hostile stares, and Meric turned to leave; but as he took hold of the doorknob, the major spoke again.

"We owe you so much," he said; he wore an expression of mingled pity and respect that further irritated Meric.

"How many men have you killed, Major?" he asked, opening the door.

"I'm not sure. I was in the artillery. We were never able to be sure."

"Well, I'm sure of my tally," said Meric. "It's taken me forty years to amass it. Fifteen hundred and ninety-three men and women. Poisoned, scalded, broken by falls, savaged by animals. Murdered. Why don't we—you and I—just call it even."

THOUGH IT WAS a sultry afternoon, he felt cold as he walked toward the tower—an internal cold that left him light-headed and weak. He tried to think what he would do. The idea of a university post seemed less appealing away from the major's office; he would soon grow weary of worshipful students and in-depth dissections of his work by jealous academics. A man hailed him as he turned into the market. Meric waved but did not stop, and heard another man say, "That's *Cattanay*?" (That ragged old ruin?)

The colors of the market were too bright, the smells of charcoal cookery too cloying, the crowds too thick, and he made for the side streets, hobbling past one-room stucco houses and tiny stores where they sold cooking oil by the ounce and cut cigars in half if you could not afford a whole one. Garbage, tornadoes of dust and flies, drunks with bloody mouths. Somebody had tied wires around a pariah dog—a bitch with slack teats; the wires had sliced into her flesh, and she lay panting in an alley mouth, gaunt ribs flecked with pink lather, gazing into nowhere. She, thought Meric, and not Griaule, should be the symbol of their flag.

As he rode the hoist up the side of the tower, he fell into his old habit of jotting down notes for the next day. What's that cord of wood doing on level five? Slow leak of chrome yellow from pipes on level twelve. Only when he saw a man dismantling some scaffolding did he recall Major Hauk's recommendation and understand that the order must already have been given. The loss of his work struck home to him then, and he leaned against the railing, his chest constricted and his eyes brimming. He straightened, ashamed of himself. The sun hung in a haze of iron-colored light low above the western hills, looking red and bloated and vile as a vulture's ruff. That polluted sky was his creation as much as was the painting, and it would be good to leave it behind. Once away from the valley, from all the influences of the place, he would be able to consider the future.

A young girl was sitting on the twentieth level just beneath the eye. Years before, the ritual of viewing the eye had grown to cultish proportions; there had been group chanting and praying and discussions of the experience. But these were more practical times, and no doubt the young men and women who had congregated here were now manning administrative desks somewhere in the burgeoning empire. They were the ones about whom Dardano should write; they, and all the eccentric characters who had played roles in this slow pageant. The gypsy woman who had danced every night by the eye, hoping to charm Griaule into killing her faithless lover—she had gone away satisfied. The man who had tried to extract one of the fangs—nobody knew what had become of him. The scalehunters, the artisans. A history of Hangtown would be a volume in itself.

The walk had left Meric weak and breathless; he sat down clumsily beside the girl, who smiled. He could not remember her name, but she came often to the eye. Small and dark, with an inner reserve that reminded him of Lise. He laughed inwardly—most women reminded him of Lise in some way.

"Are you all right?" she asked, her brow wrinkled with concern.

"Oh, yes," he said; he felt a need for conversation to take his mind off things, but he could think of nothing more to say. She was so young! All freshness and gleam and nerves.

"This will be my last time," she said. "At least for a while. I'll miss it." And then, before he could ask why, she added, "I'm getting married tomorrow, and we're moving away."

He offered congratulations and asked her who was the lucky fellow.

"Just a boy." She tossed her hair, as if to dismiss the boy's importance; she gazed up at the shuttered membrane. "What's it like for you when the eye opens?" she asked.

"Like everyone else," he said. "I remember…memories of my life. Other lives, too." He did not tell her about Griaule's memory of flight; he had never told anyone except Lise about that.

"All those bits of souls trapped in there," she said, gesturing at the eye. "What do they mean to him? Why does he show them to us?"

"I imagine he has his purposes, but I can't explain them."

"Once I remembered being with you," said the girl, peeking at him shyly through a dark curl. "We were under the wing."

He glanced at her sharply. "Tell me."

"We were…together," she said, blushing. "Intimate, you know. I was very afraid of the place, of the sounds and shadows. But I loved you so much, it didn't matter. We made love all night, and I was surprised because I thought that kind of passion was just in stories, something people had invented to make up for how ordinary it really was. And in the morning even that dreadful place had become beautiful, with the wing tips glowing red and the waterfall echoing…" She lowered her eyes. "Ever since I had that memory, I've been a little in love with you."

"Lise," he said, feeling helpless before her.

"Was that her name?"

He nodded and put a hand to his brow, trying to pinch back the emotions that flooded him.

"I'm sorry." Her lips grazed his cheek, and just that slight touch seemed to weaken him further. "I wanted to tell you how she felt in case she hadn't told you yourself. She was very troubled by something, and I wasn't sure she had."

She shifted away from him, made uncomfortable by the intensity of his reaction, and they sat without speaking. Meric became lost in watching how the sun glazed the scales to reddish gold, how the light was channeled along the ridges in molten streams that paled as the day wound down. He was startled when the girl jumped to her feet and backed toward the hoist.

"He's dead," she said wonderingly.

Meric looked at her, uncomprehending.

"See?" She pointed at the sun, which showed a crimson silver above the hill. "He's dead," she repeated, and the expression on her face flowed between fear and exultation.

The idea of Griaule's death was too large for Meric's mind to encompass, and he turned to the eye to find a counterproof—no glints of color flickered beneath the membrane. He heard the hoist creak as the girl headed down, but he continued to wait. Perhaps only the dragon's vision had failed. No. It was likely not a coincidence that work had been officially terminated today. Stunned, he sat staring at the lifeless membrane until the sun sank below the hills; then he stood and went over to the hoist. Before he could throw the switch, the cables thrummed—somebody heading up. Of course. The girl would have spread the news, and all the Major Hauks and their underlings would be hurrying to test Griaule's reflexes. He did not want to be there when they arrived, to watch them pose with their trophy like successful fishermen.

It was hard work climbing up to the fronto-parietal plate. The ladder swayed, the wind buffeted him, and by the time he clambered onto the plate he was giddy, his chest full of twinges. He hobbled forward and leaned against the rust-caked side of a boiling vat. Shadowy in the twilight, the great furnaces and vats towered around him, and it seemed this system of fiery devices reeking of cooked flesh and minerals was the actual machinery of Griaule's thought materialized above his skull. Energyless, abandoned. They had been replaced by more efficient equipment down below, and it had been—what was it?—almost five years since they were last used. Cobwebs veiled a pyramid of firewood; the stairs leading to the rims of the vats were crumbling. The plate itself was scarred and coated with sludge.

"Cattanay!"

Someone shouted from below, and the top of the ladder trembled. God, they were coming after him! Bubbling over with congratulations and plans for testimonial dinners, memorial plaques, specially struck medals. They would have him draped in bunting and bronzed and covered with pigeon shit before they were done. All these years he had been among them, both their slave and their master, yet he had never felt at home. Leaning heavily on his cane, he made his way past the frontal spike—blackened by years of oily smoke—and down between the wings to Hangtown. It was a ghost town, now.

Weeds overgrowing the collapsed shanties; the lake a stinking pit, drained after some children had drowned in the summer of '91. Where Jarcke's home had stood was a huge pile of animal bones, taking a pale shine from the half-light. Wind keened through the tattered shrubs.

"Meric!" "Cattanay."

The voices were closer.

Well, there was one place where they would not follow.

The leaves of the thickets were speckled with mold and brittle, flaking away as he brushed them. He hesitated at the top of the scalehunters' stair. He had no rope. Though he had done the climb unaided many times, it had been quite a few years. The gusts of wind, the shouts, the sweep of the valley and the lights scattered across it like diamonds on gray velvet—it all seemed a single inconstant medium. He heard the brush crunch behind him, more voices. To hell with it! Gritting his teeth against a twinge of pain in his shoulder, hooking his cane over his belt, he inched onto the stair and locked his fingers in the handholds. The wind whipped his clothes and threatened to pry him loose and send him pinwheeling off. Once he slipped; once he froze, unable to move backward or forward. But at last he reached the bottom and edged upslope until he found a spot flat enough to stand.

The mystery of the place suddenly bore in upon him, and he was afraid. He half turned to the stair, thinking he would go back to Hangtown and accept the hurly-burly. But a moment later he realized how foolish a thought that was. Waves of weakness poured through him, his heart hammered, and white dazzles flared in his vision. His chest felt heavy as iron. Rattled, he went a few steps forward, the cane pocking the silence. It was too dark to see more than outlines, but up ahead was the fold of wing where he and Lise had sheltered. He walked toward it, intent on revisiting it; then he remembered the girl beneath the eye and understood that he had already said that goodbye. And it was goodbye—that he understood vividly. He kept walking. Blackness looked to be welling from the wing joint, from the entrances to the maze of luminous tunnels where they had stumbled onto the petrified man. Had it really been the old wizard, doomed by magical justice to molder and live on and on? It made sense. At least it accorded with what happened to wizards who slew their dragons.

"Griaule?" he whispered to the darkness, and cocked his head, half-expecting an answer. The sound of his voice pointed up the immensity of the great gallery under the wing, the emptiness, and he recalled how vital a habitat it had once been. Flakes shifting over the surface, skizzers, peculiar insects fuming in the thickets, the glum populace of Hangtown, waterfalls. He had never been able to picture Griaule fully alive—that kind of vitality was beyond the powers of the imagination. Yet he wondered if by some miracle the dragon were alive now, flying up through his golden night to the sun's core. Or had that merely been a dream, a bit of tissue glittering deep in the cold tons of his brain? He laughed. Ask the stars for their first names, and you'd be more likely to receive a reply.

He decided not to walk any farther—it was really no decision. Pain was spreading through his shoulder, so intense he imagined it must be glowing inside. Carefully, carefully, he lowered himself and lay propped on an elbow, hanging on to the cane. Good, magical wood. Cut from a hawthorn atop Griaule's haunch. A man had once offered him a small fortune for it. Who would claim it now? Probably old Henry Sichi would snatch it for his museum, stick it in a glass case next to his boots. What a joke! He decided to lie flat on his stomach, resting his chin on an arm—the stony coolness beneath acted to muffle the pain. Amusing, how the range of one's decision dwindled. You decided to paint a dragon, to send hundreds of men searching for malachite and cochineal beetles, to love a woman, to heighten an undertone here and there, and finally to position your body a certain way. He seemed to have reached the end of the process. What next? He tried to regulate his breathing, to ease the pressure on his chest. Then, as something rustled out near the wing joint, he turned on his side. He thought he detected movement, a gleaming blackness flowing toward him...or else it was only the haphazard firing of his nerves playing tricks with his vision. More surprised than afraid, wanting to see, he peered into the darkness and felt his heart beating erratically against the dragon's scale.

    It's foolish to draw simple conclusions from complex events, but I suppose there must be both moral and truth to this life, these events. I'll leave that to the gadflies. The historians, the social scientists, the expert apologists for reality. All I know is that he had a fight with his girlfriend over money and walked out. He sent her a letter saying he had gone south and would be back in a few months with more money than she could ever spend. I had no idea what he'd done. The whole thing about Griaule had just been a bunch of us sitting around the Red Bear, drinking up my pay—I'd sold an article—and somebody said, "Wouldn't it be great if Dardano didn't have to write articles, if we didn't have to paint pictures that color-coordinated with people's furniture or slave at getting the gooey smiles of little nieces and nephews just right?" All sorts of improbable moneymaking schemes were put forward. Robberies, kidnappings. Then the idea of swindling the city fathers of Teocinte came up, and the entire plan was fleshed out in minutes. Scribbled on napkins, scrawled on sketchpads. A group effort. I keep trying to remember if anyone got a glassy look in their eye, if I felt a cold tendril of Griaule's thought stirring my brains. But I can't. It was a half-hour's sensation, nothing more. A drunken whimsy, an art-school metaphor. Shortly thereafter, we ran out of money and staggered into the streets. It was snowing—big wet flakes that melted down our collars. God, we were drunk! Laughing, balancing on the icy railing of the University Bridge. Making faces at the bundled-up burghers and their fat ladies who huffed and puffed past, spouting steam and never giving us a glance, and none of us—not even the burghers—knowing that we were living our happy ending in advance...

—FROM *THE MAN WHO PAINTED
THE DRAGON GRIAULE*
BY LOUIS DARDANO

THE SCALEHUNTER'S BEAUTIFUL DAUGHTER

For Bob, Karol, and Timalyne Frazier

One

NOT LONG AFTER THE CHRISTLIGHT of the world's first
morning faded, when birds still flew to heaven and back, and even the
wickedest things shone like saints, so pure was their portion of evil, there
was a village by the name of Hangtown that clung to the back of the dragon Griaule, a vast mile-long beast who had been struck immobile yet not
lifeless by a wizard's spell, and who ruled over the Carbonales Valley, controlling in every detail the lives of the inhabitants, making known his will
by the ineffable radiations emanating from the cold tonnage of his brain.
From shoulder to tail, the greater part of Griaule was covered with earth
and trees and grass, from some perspectives appearing to be an element of
the landscape, another hill among those that ringed the valley; except for

sections cleared by the scalehunters, only a portion of his right side to the haunch, and his massive neck and head remained visible, and the head had sunk to the ground, its massive jaws halfway open, itself nearly as high as the crests of the surrounding hills. Situated almost eight hundred feet above the valley floor and directly behind the fronto-parietal plate, which overhung the place like a mossy cliff, the village consisted of several dozen shacks with shingled roofs and walls of weathered planking, and bordered a lake fed by a stream that ran down onto Griaule's back from an adjoining hill; it was hemmed in against the shore by thickets of chokecherry, stands of stunted oak and hawthornes, and but for the haunted feeling that pervaded the air, a vibrant stillness similar to the atmosphere of an old ruin, to someone standing beside the lake it would seem he was looking out upon an ordinary country settlement, one a touch less neatly ordered than most, littered as it was with the bones and entrails of skizzers and flakes and other parasites that infested the dragon, but nonetheless ordinary in the lassitide that governed it, and the shabby dress and hostile attitudes of its citizenry.

Many of the inhabitants of the village were scalehunters, men and women who scavenged under Griaule's earth-encrusted wings and elsewhere on his body, searching for scales that were cracked and broken, chipping off fragments and selling these in Port Chantay, where they were valued for their medicinal properties. They were well paid for their efforts, but were treated as pariahs by the people of the valley, who rarely ventured onto the dragon, and their lives were short and fraught with unhappy incident, a circumstance they attributed to the effects of Griaule's displeasure at their presence. Indeed, his displeasure was a constant preoccupation, and they spent much of their earnings on charms that they believed would ward off its evil influence. Some wore bits of scale around their necks, hoping that this homage would communicate to Griaule the high regard in which they held him, and perhaps the most extreme incidence of this way of thinking was embodied by the nurture given by the widower Riall to his daughter Catherine. On the day of her birth, also the day of his wife's death, he dug down beneath the floor of his shack until he reached Griaule's back, laying bare a patch of golden scale some six feet long and five feet wide, and from that day forth for the next eighteen years he forced her to sleep upon the scale, hoping that the dragon's essence would seep into her and so she would be protected against his wrath. Catherine complained at first about this isolation, but she came to enjoy the dreams that visited her, dreams of flying, of otherworldly climes (according to legend, dragons were native to another universe to which they traveled by flying into the sun); lying there sometimes, looking up through the plank-shored tunnel her father had dug, she would feel that she was not resting on a solid surface but was receding from the earth, falling into a golden distance.

Riall may or may not have achieved his desired end; but it was evident to the people of Hangtown that propinquity to the scale had left its mark on Catherine, for while Riall was short and swarthy (as his wife had also been), physically unprepossessing in every respect, his daughter had grown into a beautiful young woman, long-limbed and slim, with fine golden hair and lovely skin and a face of unsurpassed delicacy, seeming a lapidary creation with its voluptuous mouth and sharp cheekbones and large, eloquent eyes, whose irises were so dark that they could be distinguished from the pupils only under the strongest of lights. Not alone in her beauty did she appear cut from different cloth from her parents; neither did she share their gloomy spirit and cautious approach to life. From earliest childhood she went without fear to every quarter of the dragon's surface, even into the darkness under the wing joints where few scalehunters dared go; she believed she had been immunized against ordinary dangers by her father's tactics, and she felt there was a bond between herself and the dragon, that her dreams and good looks were emblems of both a magical relationship and consequential destiny, and this feeling of invulnerability—along with the confidence instilled by her beauty—gave rise to a certain egocentricity and shallowness of character. She was often disdainful, careless in the handling of lovers' hearts, and though she did not stoop to duplicity—she had no need of that—she took pleasure in stealing the men whom other women loved. And yet she considered herself a good woman. Not a saint, mind you. But she honored her father and kept the house clean and did her share of work, and though she had her faults, she had taken steps—half-steps, rather—to correct them. Like most people, she had no clear moral determinant, depending upon taboos and specific circumstances to modify her behavior, and the "good," the principled, was to her a kind of intellectual afterlife to which she planned some day to aspire, but only after

she had exhausted the potentials of pleasure and thus gained the experience necessary for the achievement of such an aspiration. She was prone
to bouts of moodiness, as were all within the sphere of Griaule's influence, but generally displayed a sunny disposition and optimistic cast of
thought. This is not to say, however, that she was a Pollyanna, an innocent.
Through her life in Hangtown she was familiar with treachery, grief, and
murder, and at eighteen she had already been with a wide variety of lovers. Her easy sexuality was typical of Hangtown's populace, yet because
of her beauty and the jealousy it had engendered, she had acquired the
reputation of being exceptionally wanton. She was amused, even somewhat
pleased, by her reputation, but the rumors surrounding her grew more
scurrilous, more deviant from the truth, and eventually there came a day
when they were brought home to her with a savagery that she could never
have presupposed.

Beyond Griaule's frontal spike, which rose from a point between his
eyes, a great whorled horn curving back toward Hangtown, the slope of the
skull flattened out into the top of his snout, and it was here that Catherine
came one foggy morning, dressed in loose trousers and a tunic, equipped
with scaling hooks and ropes and chisels, intending to chip off a sizeable
piece of cracked scale she had noticed near the dragon's lip, a spot directly
above one of the fangs. She worked at the piece for several hours, suspended by linkages of rope over Griaule's lower jaw. His half-open mouth
was filled with a garden of evil-looking plants, the calloused surface of his
forked tongue showing here and there between the leaves like nodes of red
coral; his fangs were inscribed with intricate patterns of lichen, wreathed
by streamers of fog and circled by raptors who now and then would plum-
met into the bushes to skewer some unfortunate lizard or vole. Epiphytes
bloomed from splits in the ivory, depending long strings of interwoven
red and purple blossoms. It was a compelling sight, and from time to time
Catherine would stop working and lower herself in her harness until she
was no more than fifty feet above the tops of the bushes and look off into
the caliginous depths of Griaule's throat, wondering at the nature of the
shadowy creatures that flitted there.

The sun burned off the fog, and Catherine, sweaty, weary of chipping,
hauled herself up to the top of the snout and stretched out on the scales,

resting on an elbow, nibbling at a honey pear and gazing out over the valley with its spiny green hills and hammocks of thistle palms and the faraway white buildings of Teocinte, where that very night she planned to dance and make love. The air became so warm that she stripped off her tunic and lay back, bare to the waist, eyes closed, daydreaming in the clean spring-time heat. She had been drifting between sleep and waking for the better part of an hour, when a scraping noise brought her alert. She reached for her tunic and started to sit up; but before she could turn to see who or what had made the sound, something fell heavily across her ribs, taking her wind, leaving her gasping and disoriented. A hand groped her breast, and she smelled winy breath.

"Go easy, now," said a man's voice, thickened with urgency. "I don't want nothing half of Hangtown ain't had already."

Catherine twisted her head, and caught a glimpse of Key Willen's lean, sallow face looming above her, his sardonic mouth hitched at one corner in a half-smile.

"I told you we'd have our time," he said, fumbling with the tie of her trousers.

She began to fight desperately, clawing at his eyes, catching a handful of his long black hair and yanking. She threw herself onto her stomach, clutching at the edge of a scale, trying to worm out from beneath him; but he butted her in the temple, sending white lights shooting through her skull. Once her head had cleared, she found that he had flipped her onto her back, had pulled her trousers down past her hips and penetrated her with his fingers; he was working them in and out, his breath coming hoarse and rapid. She felt raw inside, and she let out a sharp, throat-tearing scream. She thrashed about, tearing at his shirt, his hair, screaming again and again, and when he clamped his free hand to her mouth, she bit it.

"You bitch! You...goddamn..." He slammed the back of her head against the scale, climbed atop her, straddling her chest and pinning her shoulders with his knees. He slapped her, wrapped his hand in her hair, and leaned close, spittle flying to her face as he spoke. "You listen up, pig! I don't much care if you're awake...One way or the other, I'm gonna have my fun." He rammed her head into the scale again. "You hear me? Hear me?" He straightened, slapped her harder. "Hell, I'm having fun right now."

"Please!" she said, dazed.

"Please?" He laughed. "That mean you want some more?" Another slap. "You like it?"

Yet another slap.

"How 'bout that?"

Frantic, she wrenched an arm free, in reflex reaching up behind her head, searching for a weapon, anything, and as he prepared to slap her again, grinning, she caught hold of a stick—or so she thought—and swung it at him in a vicious arc. The point of the scaling hook, for such it was, sank into Key's flesh just back of his left eye, and as he fell, toppling sideways with only the briefest of outcries, the eye filled with blood, becoming a featureless crimson sphere like a rubber ball embedded in the socket. Catherine shrieked, pushed his legs off her waist and scrambled away, encumbered by her trousers, which had slipped down about her knees. Key's body convulsed, his heels drumming the scale. She sat staring at him for a long seamless time, unable to catch her breath, to think. But swarms of black flies, their translucent wings shattering the sunlight into prisms, began landing on the puddle of blood that spread wide as a table from beneath Key's face, and she became queasy. She crawled to the edge of the snout and looked away across the checkerboard of fields below toward Port Chantay, toward an alp of bubbling cumulus building from the horizon. Her chest hollowed with cold, and she started to shake. The tremors passing through her echoed the tremor she had felt in Key's body when the hook had hit into his skull. All the sickness inside her, her shock and disgust at the violation, at confronting the substance of death, welled up in her throat and her stomach emptied. When she had finished she cinched her trousers tight, her fingers clumsy with the knot. She thought she should do something. Coil the ropes, maybe. Store the harness in her pack. But these actions, while easy to contemplate, seemed impossibly complex to carry out. She shivered and hugged herself, feeling the altitude, the distances. Her cheeks were feverish and puffy; flickers of sensation—she pictured them to be iridescent worms—tingled nerves in her chest and legs. She had the idea that everything was slowing, that time had flurried and was settling the way river mud settles after the passage of some turbulence. She stared off toward the dragon's horn.

Someone was standing there. Coming toward her, now. At first she watched the figure approach with a defiant disinterest, wanting to guard her privacy, feeling that if she had to speak she would lose control of her emotions. But as the figure resolved into one of her neighbors back in Hangtown—Brianne, a tall young woman with brittle good looks, dark brown hair and an olive complexion—she relaxed from this attitude. She and Brianne were not friends; in fact, they had once been rivals for the same man. However, that had been a year and more in the past, and Catherine was relieved to see her. More than relieved. The presence of another woman allowed her to surrender to weakness, believing that in Brianne she would find a fund of natural sympathy because of their common sex.

"My God, what happened?" Brianne kneeled and brushed Catherine's hair back from her eyes. The tenderness of the gesture burst the dam of Catherine's emotions, and punctuating the story with sobs, she told of the rape.

"I didn't mean to kill him," she said. "I…I'd forgotten about the hook."

"Key was looking to get killed," Brianne said. "But it's a damn shame you had to be the one to help him along." She sighed, her forehead creased by a worry line. "I suppose I should fetch someone to take care of the body. I know that's not…"

"No, I understand…it has to be done." Catherine felt stronger, more capable. She made as if to stand, but Brianne restrained her.

"Maybe you should wait here. You know how people will be. They'll see your face,"—she touched Catherine's swollen cheeks—"and they'll be prying, whispering. It might be better to let the mayor come out and make his investigation. That way he can take the edge off the gossip before it gets started."

Catherine didn't want to be alone with the body any longer, but she saw the wisdom in waiting and agreed.

"Will you be all right?" Brianne asked.

"I'll be fine…but hurry."

"I will." Brianne stood; the wind feathered her hair, lifted it to veil the lower half of her face. "You're sure you'll be all right?" There was an odd undertone in her voice, as if it were really another question she was asking, or—and this, Catherine thought, was more likely—as if she were thinking ahead to dealing with the mayor.

Catherine nodded, then caught at Brianne as she started to walk away. "Don't tell my father. Let me tell him. If he hears it from you, he might go after the Willens."

"I won't say a thing, I promise."

With a smile, a sympathetic pat on the arm, Brianne headed back toward Hangtown, vanishing into the thickets that sprang up beyond the frontal spike. For awhile after she had gone, Catherine felt wrapped in her consolation; but the seething of the wind, the chill that infused the air as clouds moved in to cover the sun, these things caused the solitude of the place and the grimness of the circumstance to close down around her, and she began to wish she had returned to Hangtown. She squeezed her eyes shut, trying to steady herself, but even then she kept seeing Key's face, his bloody eye, and remembering his hands on her. Finally, thinking that Brianne had had more than enough time to accomplish her task, she walked up past the frontal spike and stood looking out along the narrow trail that wound through the thickets on Griaule's back. Several minutes elapsed, and then she spotted three figures—two men and a woman— coming at a brisk pace. She shaded her eyes against a ray of sun that had broken through the overcast, and peered at them. Neither man had the gray hair and portly shape of Hangtown's mayor. They were lanky, pale, with black hair falling to their shoulders, and were carrying unsheathed knives. Catherine couldn't make out their faces, but she realized that Brianne must not have set aside their old rivalry, that in the spirit of vengeance she had informed Key's brothers of his death.

Fear cut through the fog of shock, and she tried to think what to do. There was only the one trail and no hope that she could hide in the thickets. She retreated toward the edge of the snout, stepping around the patch of drying blood. Her only chance for escape would be to lower herself on the ropes and take refuge in Griaule's mouth; however, the thought of entering so ominous a place, a place shunned by all but the mad, gave her pause. She tried to think of alternatives, but there were none. Brianne would no doubt have lied to the Willens, cast her as the guilty party, and the brothers would never listen to her. She hurried to the edge, buckled on the harness and slipped over the side, working with frenzied speed, lowering in ten and fifteen foot drops. Her view of the mouth lurched and veered—a panorama of bristling leaves and head-high ferns, enormous fangs hooking up from the jaw and pitch-dark emptiness at the entrance to the throat. She was fifty feet from the surface when she felt the rope jerking, quivering; glancing up, she saw that one of the Willens was sawing at it with his knife. Her heart felt hot and throbbing in her chest, her palms were slick. She dropped half the distance to the jaw, stopping with a jolt that sent pain shooting through her spine and left her swinging back and forth, muddle-headed. She began another drop, a shorter one, but the rope parted high above and she fell the last twenty feet, landing with such stunning force that she lost consciousness.

She came to in a bed of ferns, staring up through the fronds at the dull brick-colored roof of Griaule's mouth, a surface festooned with spiky dark green epiphytes, like the vault of a cathedral that had been invaded by the jungle. She lay still for a moment, gathering herself, testing the aches that mapped her body to determine if anything was broken. A lump sprouted from the back of her head, but the brunt of the impact had been absorbed by her rear end, and though she felt pain there, she didn't think the damage was severe. Moving cautiously, wincing, she came to her knees and was about to stand when she heard shouts from above.

"See her?"

"Naw...you?"

"She musta gone deeper in!"

Catherine peeked between the fronds and saw two dark figures centering networks of ropes, suspended a hundred feet or so overhead like spiders with simple webs. They dropped lower, and panicked, she crawled on her belly away from the mouth, hauling herself along by gripping twists of dead vine that formed a matte underlying the foliage. After she had gone about fifty yards she looked back. The Willens were hanging barely a dozen feet above the tops of the bushes, and as she watched they lowered out of sight. Her instincts told her to move deeper into the mouth, but the air was considerably darker where she now knelt than where she had landed—a grayish green gloom—and the idea of penetrating the greater darkness of Griaule's throat stalled her heart. She listened for the Willens and heard slitherings, skitterings, and rustles. Eerie whistles that, although soft, were complex and articulated. She imagined that these were not the cries of tiny creatures but the gutterings of breath in a huge throat, and she had a terrifying sense of the size of the place, of her own relative insignificance. She couldn't bring herself to continue in deeper, and she made her way toward the side of the mouth, where thick growths of ferns flourished in the shadow. When she reached a spot at which the mouth sloped upward, she buried herself among the ferns and kept very still.

Next to her head was an irregular patch of pale red flesh, where a clump of soil had been pulled away by an uprooted plant. Curious, she extended a forefinger and found it cool and dry. It was like touching stone or wood, and that disappointed her; she had, she realized, been hoping the touch would affect her in some extreme way. She pressed her palm to the flesh, trying to detect the tic of a pulse, but the flesh was inert, and the rustlings and the occasional beating of wings overhead were the only signs of life. She began to grow drowsy, to nod, and she fought to keep awake. But after a few minutes she let herself relax. The more she examined the situation, the more convinced she became that the Willens would not track her this far; the extent of their nerve would be to wait at the verge of the mouth, to lay siege to her, knowing that eventually she would have to seek food and water. Thinking about water made her thirsty, but she denied the craving. She needed rest far more. And removing one of the scaling hooks from her belt, holding it in her right hand in case some animal less cautious than the Willens happened by, she pillowed her head against the pale red patch of Griaule's flesh and was soon fast asleep.

Two

MANY OF CATHERINE'S DREAMS OVER the years had seemed sendings rather than distillations of experience, but never had she had one so clearly of that character as the dream she had that afternoon in Griaule's mouth. It was a simple dream, formless, merely a voice whose words less came to her ear than enveloped her, steeping her in their meanings, and of them she retained only a message of reassurance, of security, one so profound that it instilled in her a confidence that lasted even after she waked into a world gone black, the sole illumination being the gleams of reflected firelight that flowed along the curve of one of the fangs. It was an uncanny sight, that huge tooth glazed with fierce red shine, and under other circumstances she would have been frightened by it; but in this instance she did not react to the barbarity of the image and saw it instead as evidence that her suppositions concerning the Willens had been correct. They had built a fire near the lip and were watching for her, expecting her to bolt into their arms. But she had no intention of fulfilling their expectations. Although her confidence flickered on and off, although to go deeper into the dragon seemed irrational, she knew that any other course offered the certainty of a knife stroke across the neck. And, too, despite the apparent rationality of her decision, she had an unshakable feeling that Griaule was watching over her, that his will was being effected. She had a flash vision of Key Willen's face, his gaping mouth and blood-red eye, and recalled her terror at his assault. However, these memories no longer harrowed her. They steadied her, resolving certain questions that—while she had never asked them—had always been there to ask. She hadn't been to blame in any way for the rape, she had not tempted Key. But she saw that she had left herself open to tragedy by her aimlessness, by her reliance on a vague sense of destiny to give life meaning. Now it appeared that her destiny was at hand, and she understood that its violent coloration might have been different had *she* been different, had she engaged the world with energy and not with a passive attitude. She hoped that knowing all this would prove important, but she doubted that it would, believing that she had gone too far on the wrong path for any degree of knowledge to matter.

It took all her self-control to begin her journey inward, feeling her way along the side of the throat, pushing through ferns and cobwebs, her hands encountering unfamiliar textures that made her skin crawl, alert to the burbling of insects and other night creatures. On one occasion she was close to turning back, but she heard shouts behind her, and fearful that the Willens were on her trail, she kept going. As she started down an incline, she saw a faint gleam riding the curve of the throat wall. The glow brightened, casting the foliage into silhouette, and eager to reach the source, she picked up her pace, tripping over roots, vines snagging her ankles. At length the incline flattened out, and she emerged into a large chamber, roughly circular in shape, its upper regions lost in darkness; upon the floor lay pools of black liquid; mist trailed across the surface of the pools, and whenever the mist lowered to touch the liquid, a fringe of yellowish red flame would flare up, cutting the shadows on the pebbled skin of the floor and bringing to light a number of warty knee-high protuberances that sprouted among the pools—these were deep red in color, perforated around the sides, leaking pale threads of mist. At the rear of the chamber was an opening that Catherine assumed led farther into the dragon. The air was warm, dank, and a sweat broke out all over her body. She balked at entering the chamber; in spite of the illumination, it was a less human place than the mouth. But once again she forced herself onward, stepping carefully between the fires and, after discovering that the mist made her giddy, giving the protuberances a wide berth. Piercing whistles came from above. The notion that this might signal the presence of bats caused her to hurry, and she had covered half the distance across when a man's voice called to her, electrifying her with fear.

"Catherine!" he said. "Not so fast!"

She spun about, her scaling hook at the ready. Hobbling toward her was an elderly white-haired man dressed in the ruin of a silk frock coat embroidered with gold thread, a tattered ruffled shirt, and holed satin leggings. In his left hand he carried a gold-knobbed cane, and at least a dozen glittering rings encircled his bony fingers. He stopped an arm's length away, leaning on his cane, and although Catherine did not lower her hook, her fear diminished. Despite the eccentricity of his appearance, considering the wide spectrum of men and creatures who inhabited Griaule, he seemed comparatively ordinary, a reason for caution but not alarm.

"Ordinary?" The old man cackled. "Oh yes, indeed! Ordinary as angels, as unexceptional as the idea of God!" Before she had a chance to wonder at his knowledge of her thoughts, he let out another cackle. "How could I not know them? We are every one of us creatures of his thought, expressions of his whim. And here what is only marginally evident on the surface becomes vivid reality, inescapable truth. For here,"—he poked the chamber floor with his cane—"here we live in the medium of his will." He hobbled a step closer, fixing her with a rheumy stare. "I have dreamed this moment a thousand times. I know what you will say, what you will think, what you will do. He has instructed me in all your particulars so that I may become your guide, your confidant."

"What are you talking about?" Catherine hefted her hook, her anxiety increasing.

"Not 'what,'" said the old man. "Who." A grin split the pale wrinkled leather of his face. "His Scaliness, of course."

"Griaule?"

"None other," The old man held out his hand. "Come along now, girl. They're waiting for us."

Catherine drew back.

The old man pursed his lips. "Well, I suppose you could return the way you came. The Willens will be happy to see you."

Flustered, Catherine said, "I don't understand. How can you know..."

"Know your name, your peril? Weren't you listening? You are of Griaule, daughter. And more so than most, for you have slept at the center of his dreams. Your entire life has been prelude to this time, and your destiny will not be known until you come to the place from which his dreams arise...the dragon's heart." He took her hand. "My name is Amos Mauldry. Captain Amos Mauldry, at your service. I have waited years for you...years! I am to prepare you for the consummate moment of your life.

I urge you to follow me, to join the company of the Feelys and begin your preparation. But," he shrugged—"the choice is yours. I will not coerce you more than I have done...except to say this. Go with me now, and when you return you will discover that you have nothing to fear of the Willen brothers."

He let loose of her hand and stood gazing at her with calm regard. She would have liked to disregard his words, but they were in such accord with all she had ever felt about her association with the dragon, she found that she could not. "Who," she asked, "are the Feelys?"

He made a disparaging noise. "Harmless creatures. They pass their time copulating and arguing among themselves over the most trivial of matters. Were they not of service to Griaule, keeping him free of certain pests, they would have no use whatsoever. Still, there are worse folk in the world, and they do have moments in which they shine." He shifted impatiently, tapped his cane on the chamber floor, "You'll meet them soon enough. Are you with me or not?"

Grudgingly, her hook at the ready, Catherine followed Mauldry toward the opening at the rear of the chamber and into a narrow, twisting channel illuminated by a pulsing golden light that issued from within Griaule's flesh. This radiance, Mauldry said, derived from the dragon's blood, which, while it did not flow, was subject to fluctuations in brilliance due to changes in its chemistry. Or so he believed. He had regained his lighthearted manner, and as they walked he told Catherine he had captained a cargo ship that plied between Port Chantay and the Pearl Islands.

"We carried livestock, breadfruit, whale oil," he said. "I can't think of much we didn't carry. It was a good life, but hard as hard gets, and after I retired...well, I'd never married, and with time on my hands, I figured I owed myself some high times. I decided I'd see the sights, and the sight I most wanted to see was Griaule. I'd heard he was the First Wonder of the World...and he was! I was amazed, flabbergasted. I couldn't get enough of seeing him. He was more than a wonder. A miracle, an absolute majesty of a creature. People warned me to keep clear of the mouth, and they were right. But I couldn't stay away. One evening—I was walking along the edge of the mouth—two scalehunters set upon me, beat and robbed me. Left me for dead. And I would have died if it hadn't been for the Feelys."

He clucked his tongue. "I suppose I might as well give you some of their background. It can't help but prepare you for them…and I admit they need preparing for. They're not in the least agreeable to the eye." He cocked an eye toward Catherine, and after a dozen steps more he said, "Aren't you going to ask me to proceed?"

"You didn't seem to need encouragement," she said.

He chuckled, nodding his approval. "Quite right, quite right." He walked on in silence, his shoulders hunched and head inclined, like an old turtle who'd learned to get about on two legs.

"Well?" said Catherine, growing annoyed.

"I knew you'd ask," he said, and winked at her. "I didn't know who they were myself at first. If I had known I'd have been terrified. There are about five or six hundred in the colony. Their numbers are kept down by childbirth mortality and various other forms of attrition. They're most of them the descendants of a retarded man named Feely who wandered into the mouth almost a thousand years ago. Apparently he was walking near the mouth when flights of birds and swarms of insects began issuing from it. Not just a few, mind you. Entire populations. Wellsir, Feely was badly frightened. He was sure that some terrible beast had chased all these lesser creatures out, and he tried to hide from it. But he was so confused that instead of running away from the mouth, he ran into it and hid in the bushes. He waited for almost a day…no beast. The only sign of danger was a muffled thud from deep within the dragon. Finally his curiosity over- came his fear, and he went into the throat." Mauldry hawked and spat. "He felt secure there. More secure than on the outside, at any rate. Doubtless Griaule's doing, that feeling. He needed the Feelys to be happy so they'd settle down and be his exterminators. Anyway, the first thing Feely did was to bring in a madwoman he'd known in Teocinte, and over the years they recruited other madmen who happened along. I was the first sane person they'd brought into the fold. They're extremely chauvinistic regarding the sane. But of course they were directed by Griaule to take me in. He knew you'd need someone to talk to." He prodded the wall with his cane. "And now this is my home. More than a home. It's my truth, my love. To live here is to be transfigured."

"That's a bit hard to swallow," said Catherine.

"Is it, now? You of all those who dwell on the surface should under-stand the scope of Griaule's virtues. There's no greater security than that he offers, no greater comprehension than that he bestows."

"You make him sound like a god."

Mauldry stopped walking, looking at her askance. The golden light waxed bright, filling in his wrinkles with shadows, making him appear to be centuries old. "Well, what do you think he is?" he asked with an air of mild indignation. "What else could he be?"

Another ten minutes brought them to a chamber even more fabulous than the last. In shape it was oval, like an egg with a flattened bottom stood on end, an egg some 150 feet high and a bit more than half that in diameter. It was lit by the same pulsing golden glow that had illumi-nated the channel, but here the fluctuations were more gradual and more extreme, ranging from a murky dimness to a glare approaching that of full daylight. The upper two thirds of the chamber wall were obscured by stacked ranks of small cubicles, leaning together at rickety angles, a geom-etry lacking the precision of the cells of a honeycomb, yet reminiscent of such, as if the bees that constructed it had been drunk. The entrances of the cubicles were draped with curtains, and lashed to their sides were ropes, rope ladders, and baskets that functioned as elevators, several of which were in use, lowering and lifting men and women dressed in a style similar to Mauldry: Catherine was reminded of a painting she had seen depicting the roof warrens of Port Chantay; but those habitations, while redolent of poverty and despair, had not as did these evoked an impres-sion of squalid degeneracy, of order lapsed into the perverse. The lower portion of the chamber (and it was in this area that the channel emerged) was covered with a motley carpet composed of bolts of silk and satin and other rich fabrics, and seventy or eighty people were strolling and reclin-ing on the gentle slopes. Only the center had been left clear, and there a gaping hole led away into yet another section of the dragon; a system of pipes ran into the hole, and Mauldry later explained that these carried the wastes of the colony into a pit of acids that had once fueled Griaule's fires. The dome of the chamber was choked with mist, the same pale stuff that had been vented from the protuberances in the previous chamber; birds with black wings and red markings on their heads made wheeling flights in and out of it, and frail scarves of mist drifted throughout. There was a sickly sweet odor to the place, and Catherine heard a murmurous rustling that issued from every quarter.

"Well," said Mauldry, making a sweeping gesture with his cane that included the entire chamber. "What do you think of our little colony?"

Some of the Feelys had noticed them and were edging forward in small groups, stopping, whispering agitatedly among themselves, then edging forward again, all with the hesitant curiosity of savages; and although no signal had been given, the curtains over the cubicle entrances were being thrown back, heads were poking forth, and tiny figures were shinnying down the ropes, crowding into baskets, scuttling downward on the rope ladders, hundreds of people beginning to hurry toward her at a pace that brought to mind the panicked swarming of an anthill. And on first glance they seemed alike as ants. Thin and pale and stooped, with sloping, nearly hairless skulls, and weepy eyes and thick-lipped slack mouths, like ugly children in their rotted silks and satins. Closer and closer they came, those in front pushed by the swelling ranks at their rear, and Catherine, unnerved by their stares, ignoring Mauldry's attempts to soothe her, retreated into the channel. Mauldry turned to the Feelys, brandishing his cane as if it were a victor's sword, and cried, "She is here! He has brought her to us at last! She is here!"

His words caused several of those at the front of the press to throw back their heads and loose a whinnying laughter that went higher and higher in pitch as the golden light brightened. Others in the crowd lifted their hands, palms outward, holding them tight to their chests, and made little hops of excitement, and others yet twitched their heads from side to side, cutting their eyes this way and that, their expressions flowing between belligerence and confusion, apparently unsure of what was happening. This exhibition, clearly displaying the Feelys' retardation, the tenuousness of their self-control, dismayed Catherine still more. But Mauldry seemed delighted and continued to exhort them, shouting, "She is here," over and over. His outcry came to rule the Feelys, to orchestrate their movements. They began to sway, to repeat his words, slurring them so that their response was in effect a single word, "Shees'eer, Shees'eer," that reverberated through the chamber, acquiring a rolling echo, a hissing sonority, like the rapid breathing of a giant.

The sound washed over Catherine, enfeebling her with its intensity, and she shrank back against the wall of the channel, expecting the Feelys to break ranks and surround her; but they were so absorbed in their chanting, they appeared to have forgotten her. They milled about, bumping into one another, some striking out in anger at those who had impeded their way, others embracing and giggling, engaging in sexual play, but all of them keeping up the chorus of shouts.

Mauldry turned to her, his eyes giving back gleams of the golden light, his face looking in its vacuous glee akin to those of the Feelys, and holding out his hands to her, his tone manifesting the bland sincerity of a priest, he said, "Welcome home."

Three

CATHERINE WAS HOUSED IN TWO rooms halfway up the chamber wall, an apartment that adjoined Mauldry's quarters and was furnished with a rich carpeting of silks and furs and embroidered pillows; on the walls, also draped in these materials, hung a mirror with a gem-studded frame and two oil paintings—this bounty, said Mauldry, all part of Griaule's hoard, the bulk of which lay in a cave west of the valley, its location known only to the Feelys. One of the rooms contained a large basin for bathing, but since water was at a premium—being collected from points at which it seeped in through the scales—she was permitted one bath a week and no more. Still, the apartment and the general living conditions were on a par with those in Hangtown, and had it not been for the Feelys, Catherine might have felt at home. But except in the case of the woman Leitha, who served her meals and cleaned, she could not overcome her revulsion at their inbred appearance and demented manner. They seemed to be responding to stimuli that she could not perceive, stopping now and then to cock an ear to an inaudible call or to stare at some invisible disturbance in the air. They scurried up and down the ropes to no apparent purpose, laughing and chattering, and they engaged in mass copulations at the bottom of the chamber. They spoke a mongrel dialect that she could barely understand, and they would hang on ropes outside her apartment, arguing, offering criticism of one another's dress and behavior, picking at the most insignificant of flaws and judging them according to an intricate code whose niceties Catherine was unable to master. They would follow her wherever she went, never sharing the same basket, but descending or ascending alongside her, staring, shrinking away if she turned her gaze upon them. With their foppish rags, their jewels, their childish pettiness and jealousies, they both irritated and frightened her;

there was a tremendous tension in the way they looked at her, and she had the idea that at any moment they might lose their awe of her and attack.

She kept to her rooms those first weeks, brooding, trying to invent some means of escape, her solitude broken only by Leitha's ministrations and Mauldry's visits. He came twice daily and would sit among the pillows, declaiming upon Griaule's majesty, his truth. She did not enjoy the visits. The righteous quaver in his voice aroused her loathing, reminding her of the mendicant priests who passed now and then through Hangtown, leaving bastards and empty purses in their wake. She found his conversation for the most part boring, and when it did not bore, she found it disturbing in its constant references to her time of trial at the dragon's heart. She had no doubt that Griaule was at work in her life. The longer she remained in the colony, the more vivid her dreams became and the more certain she grew that his purpose was somehow aligned with her presence there. But the pathetic condition of the Feelys shed a wan light on her old fantasies of a destiny entwined with the dragon's, and she began to see herself in that wan light, to experience a revulsion at her fecklessness equal to that she felt toward those around her.

"You are our salvation," Mauldry told her one day as she sat sewing herself a new pair of trousers—she refused to dress in the gilt and satin rags preferred by the Feelys. "Only you can know the mystery of the dragon's heart, only you can inform us of his deepest wish for us. We've known this for years."

Seated amid the barbaric disorder of silks and furs, Catherine looked out through a gap in the curtains, watching the waning of the golden light. "You hold me prisoner," she said. "Why should I help you?"

"Would you leave us, then?" Mauldry asked. "What of the Willens?"

"I doubt they're still waiting for me. Even if they are, it's only a matter of which death I prefer, a lingering one here or a swift one at their hands."

Mauldry fingered the gold knob of his cane. "You're right," he said. "The Willens are no longer a menace."

She glanced up at him.

"They died the moment you went down out of Griaule's mouth," he said. "He sent his creatures to deal with them, knowing you were his at long last."

Catherine remembered the shouts she'd heard while walking down the incline of the throat. "What creatures?"

"That's of no importance," said Mauldry. "What is important is that you apprehend the subtlety of his power, his absolute mastery and control over your thoughts, your being."

"Why?" she asked. "Why is that important?" He seemed to be struggling to explain himself, and she laughed. "Lost touch with your god, Mauldry? Won't he supply the appropriate cant?"

Mauldry composed himself. "It is for you, not I, to understand why you are here. You must explore Griaule, study the miraculous workings of his flesh, involve yourself in the intricate order of his being."

In frustration, Catherine punched at a pillow. "If you don't let me go, I'll die! This place will kill me. I won't be around long enough to do any exploring."

"Oh, but you will." Mauldry favored her with an unctuous smile. "That, too, is known to us."

Ropes creaked, and a moment later the curtains parted, and Leitha, a young woman in a gown of watered blue taffeta, whose bodice pushed up the pale nubs of her breasts, entered bearing Catherine's dinner tray. She set down the tray. "Be mo', ma'am?" she said. "Or mus' I later c'meah." She gazed fixedly at Catherine, her close-set brown eyes blinking, fingers plucking at the folds of her gown.

"Whatever you want," Catherine said.

Leitha continued to stare at her, and only when Mauldry spoke sharply to her, did she turn and leave.

Catherine looked down disconsolately at the tray and noticed that in addition to the usual fare of greens and fruit (gathered from the dragon's mouth) there were several slices of underdone meat, whose reddish hue appeared identical to the color of Griaule's flesh. "What's this?" she asked, poking at one of the slices.

"The hunters were successful today," said Mauldry. "Every so often hunting parties are sent into the digestive tract. It's quite dangerous, but there are beasts there that can injure Griaule. It serves him that we hunt them, and their flesh nourishes us." He leaned forward, studying her face. "Another party is going out tomorrow. Perhaps you'd care to join them. I can arrange it if you wish. You'll be well protected."

Catherine's initial impulse was to reject the invitation, but then she thought that this might offer an opportunity for escape; in fact, she realized that to play upon Mauldry's tendencies, to evince interest in a study of the dragon, would be a wise move. The more she learned about Griaule's geography, the greater chance there would be that she would find a way out.

"You said it was dangerous...How dangerous?"

"For you? Not in the least. Griaule would not harm you. But for the hunting party, well...lives will be lost."

"And they're going out tomorrow?"

"Perhaps the next day as well. We're not sure how extensive an infestation is involved."

"What kind of beast are you talking about?"

"Serpents of a sort."

Catherine's enthusiasm was dimmed, but she saw no other means of taking action. "Very well. I'll go with them tomorrow."

"Wonderful, wonderful!" It took Mauldry three tries to heave himself up from the cushion, and when at last he managed to stand, he leaned on his cane, breathing heavily. "I'll come for you early in the morning."

"You're going, too? You don't seem up to the exertion."

Mauldry chuckled. "It's true, I'm an old man. But where you're concerned, daughter, my energies are inexhaustible." He performed a gallant bow and hobbled from the room.

Not long after he had left, Leitha returned. She drew a second curtain across the entrance, cutting the light, even at its most brilliant, to a dim effusion. Then she stood by the entrance, eyes fixed on Catherine. "Wan' mo' fum Leitha?" she asked.

The question was not a formality. Leitha had made it plain by touches and other signs that Catherine had but to ask and she would come to her as a lover. Her deformities masked by the shadowy air, she had the look of a pretty young girl dressed for a dance, and for a moment, in the grip of loneliness and despair, watching Leitha alternately brightening and merging with gloom, listening to the unceasing murmur of the Feelys from without, aware in full of the tribal strangeness of the colony and her utter lack of connection, Catherine felt a bizarre arousal. But the moment passed, and she was disgusted with herself, with her weakness, and angry at Leitha and this degenerate place that was eroding her humanity. "Get out," she said coldly, and when Leitha hesitated, she shouted the command, sending the girl stumbling backwards from the room. Then she turned onto her stomach, her face pressed into a pillow, expecting to cry, feeling the pressure of a sob building in her chest; but the sob never manifested, and she lay there, knowing her emptiness, feeling that she was no longer worthy of even her own tears.

BEHIND ONE OF the cubicles in the lower half of the chamber was hidden the entrance to a wide circular passage ringed by ribs of cartilage, and it was along this passage the next morning that Catherine and Mauldry, accompanied by thirty male Feelys, set out upon the hunt. They were armed with swords and bore torches to light the way, for here Griaule's veins were too deeply embedded to provide illumination; they walked in a silence broken only by coughs and the soft scraping of their footsteps. The silence, such a contrast from the Feelys' usual chatter, unsettled Catherine, and the flaring and guttering of the torches, the apparition of a backlit pale face turned toward her, the tingling acidic scent that grew stronger and stronger, all this assisted her impression that they were lost souls treading some byway in Hell.

Their angle of descent increased, and shortly thereafter they reached a spot from which Catherine had a view of a black distance shot through with intricate networks of fine golden skeins, like spiderwebs of gold in a night sky. Mauldry told her to wait, and the torches of the hunting party moved off, making it clear that they had come to a large chamber; but she did not understand just how large until a fire suddenly bloomed, bursting into towering flames: an enormous bonfire composed of sapling trunks and entire bushes. The size of the fire was impressive in itself, but the immense cavity of the stomach that it partially revealed was more impressive yet. It could not have been less than two hundred yards long, and was walled with folds of thin whitish skin figured by lacings and branchings of veins, attached to curving ribs covered with even thinner skin that showed their every articulation. A quarter of the way across the cavity, the floor declined into a sink brimming with a dark liquid, and it was along a section of the wall close to the sink that the bonfire had been lit, its smoke billowing up toward a bruised patch of skin some fifty feet in circumference with a tattered rip at the center. As Catherine watched the entire patch began to undulate. The hunting party gathered beneath it, ranged around the bonfire, their swords raised. Then, with ponderous slowness a length of thick white tubing was extruded from the rip, a gigantic worm that lifted its blind head above the hunting party, opened a mouth fringed with palps to expose a dark red maw and emitted a piercing squeal that touched off echoes and made Catherine put her hands to her ears. More and more of the worm's body emerged from the stomach wall, and she marveled at the courage of the hunting party, who maintained their ground. The worm's squealing became unbearably loud as smoke enveloped it; it lashed about, twisting and probing at the air with its head, and then, with an even louder cry, it fell across the bonfire, writhing, sending up showers of sparks. It rolled out of the fire, crushing several of the party; the others set to with their swords, hacking in a frenzy at the head, painting streaks of dark blood over the corpse-pale skin. Catherine realized that she had pressed her fists to her cheeks and was screaming, so involved was she in the battle. The worm's blood spattered the floor of the cavity, its skin was charred and blistered from the flames, and its head was horribly slashed, the flesh hanging in ragged strips. But it continued to squeal, humping up great sections of its body, forming an arch over groups of attackers and dropping down upon them. A third of the hunting party lay motionless, their limbs sprawled in graceless attitudes, the remnants of the bonfire— heaps of burning branches—scattered among them; the rest stabbed and sliced at the increasingly torpid worm, dancing away from its lunges. At last the worm lifted half its body off the floor, its head held high, silent for a moment, swaying with the languor of a mesmerized serpent. It let out a cry like the whistle of a monstrous tea kettle, a cry that seemed to fill the cavity with its fierce vibrations, and fell, twisting once and growing still, its maw half-open, palps twitching in the register of some final internal function.

The hunting party collapsed around it, winded, drained, some leaning on their swords. Shocked by the suddenness of the silence, Catherine went a few steps out into the cavity, Mauldry at her shoulder. She hesitated, then moved forward again, thinking that some of the party might need tending. But those who had fallen were dead, their limbs broken, blood showing on their mouths. She walked alongside the worm. The thickness of its body was three times her height, the skin glistening and warped by countless tiny puckers and tinged with a faint bluish cast that made it all the more ghastly.

"What are you thinking?" Mauldry asked.

Catherine shook her head. No thoughts would come to her. It was as if the process of thought itself had been cancelled by the enormity of what she had witnessed. She had always supposed that she had a fair idea of Griaule's scope, his complexity, but now she understood that whatever she had once believed had been inadequate, and she struggled to acclimate to this new perspective. There was a commotion behind her. Members of the hunting party were hacking slabs of meat from the worm. Mauldry draped an arm about her, and by that contact she became aware that she was trembling.

"Come along," he said. "I'll take you home."

"To my room, you mean?" Her bitterness resurfaced, and she threw off his arm.

"Perhaps you'll never think of it as home," he said. "Yet nowhere is there a place more suited to you." He signaled to one of the hunting party, who came toward them, stopping to light a dead torch from a pile of burning branches.

With a dismal laugh, Catherine said, "I'm beginning to find it irksome how you claim to know so much about me."

"It's not you I claim to know," he said, "though it has been given me to understand something of your purpose. But,"—he rapped the tip of his cane against the floor of the cavity—"he by whom you are most known, him I know well."

Four

CATHERINE MADE THREE ESCAPE ATTEMPTS during the next two months, and thereafter gave up on the enterprise; with hundreds of eyes watching her, there was no point in wasting energy. For almost six months following the final attempt she became dispirited and refused to leave her rooms. Her health suffered, her thoughts paled, and she lay abed for hours, reliving her life in Hangtown, which she came to view as a model of joy and contentment. Her inactivity caused loneliness to bear in upon her. Mauldry tried his best to entertain her, but his mystical obsession with Griaule made him incapable of offering the consolation of a true friend. And so, without friends or lovers, without even an enemy, she sank into a welter of self-pity and began to toy with the idea of suicide. The prospect of never seeing the sun again, of attending no more carnivals at Teocinte…it seemed too much to endure. But either she was not brave enough or not sufficiently foolish to take her own life, and deciding that no matter how vile or delimiting the circumstance, it promised more than eternal darkness, she gave herself to the one occupation the Feelys would permit her: the exploration and study of Griaule.

Like one of those enormous Tibetan sculptures of the Buddha constructed within a tower only a trifle larger than the sculpture itself, Griaule's unbeating heart was a dimpled golden shape as vast as a cathedral and was enclosed within a chamber whose walls left a gap six feet wide around the organ. The chamber could be reached by passing through a vein that had ruptured long ago and was now a wrinkled brown tube just big enough for Catherine to crawl along it; to make this transit and then emerge into that narrow space beside the heart was an intensely claustrophobic experience, and it took her a long, long while to get used to the process. Even after she had grown accustomed to this, it was still difficult for her to adjust to the peculiar climate at the heart. The air was thick with a heated stinging scent that reminded her of the brimstone stink left by a lightning strike, and there was an atmosphere of imminence, a stillness and tension redolent of some chthonic disturbance that might strike at any moment. The blood at the heart did not merely fluctuate (and here the fluctuations were erratic, varying both in range of brilliance and rapidity of change); it circulated—the movement due to variations in heat and pressure—through a series of convulsed inner chambers, and this eddying in conjunction with the flickering brilliance threw patterns of light and shadow on the heart wall, patterns as complex and fanciful as arabesques that drew her eye in. Staring at them, Catherine began to be able to predict what configurations would next appear and to apprehend a logic to their progression; it was nothing that she could put into words, but watching the play of light and shadow produced in her emotional responses that seemed keyed to the shifting patterns and allowed her to make crude guesses as to the heart's workings. She learned that if she stared too long at the patterns, dreams would take her, dreams notable for their vividness, and one particularly notable in that it recurred again and again.

The dream began with a sunrise, the solar disc edging up from the southern horizon, its rays spearing toward a coast strewn with great black rocks that protruded from the shallows, and perched upon them were sleeping dragons; as the sun warmed them, light flaring on their scales, they grumbled and lifted their heads and with the snapping sound of huge sails filling with wind, they unfolded their leathery wings and went soaring up into an indigo sky flecked with stars arranged into strange constellations, wheeling and roaring their exultation…all but one dragon, who flew only a brief arc before becoming disjointed in mid-flight and dropping like a stone into the water, vanishing beneath the waves. It was an awesome thing to see, this tumbling flight, the wings billowing, tearing, the fanged mouth open, claws grasping for purchase in the air. But despite its beauty, the dream seemed to have little relevance to Griaule's situation. He was in no danger of falling, that much was certain. Nevertheless, the frequency of the dream's recurrence persuaded Catherine that something must be amiss, that perhaps Griaule feared an attack of the sort that had stricken the flying dragon. With this in mind she began to inspect the heart, using her hooks to clamber up the steep slopes of the chamber walls, sometimes hanging upside down like a blond spider above the glowing, flickering organ. But she could find nothing out of order, no imperfections—at least as far as she could determine—and the sole result of the inspection was that the dream stopped occurring and was replaced by a simpler dream in which she watched the chest of a sleeping dragon contract and expand. She could make no sense of it, and although the dream continued to recur, she paid less and less attention to it.

Mauldry, who had been expecting miraculous insights from her, was depressed when none were forthcoming. "Perhaps I've been wrong all these years," he said. "Or senile. Perhaps I'm growing senile."

A few months earlier, Catherine, locked into bitterness and resentment, might have seconded his opinion out of spite; but her studies at the heart had soothed her, infused her both with calm resignation and some compassion for her jailers—they could not, after all, be blamed for their pitiful condition—and she said to Mauldry, "I've only begun to learn. It's likely to take a long time before I understand what he wants. And that's in keeping with his nature, isn't it? That nothing happens quickly?"

"I suppose you're right," he said glumly.

"Of course I am," she said. "Sooner or later there'll be a revelation. But a creature like Griaule doesn't yield his secrets to a casual glance. Just give me time."

And oddly enough, though she had spoken these words to cheer Mauldry, they seemed to ring true.

She had started her explorations with minimal enthusiasm, but Griaule's scope was so extensive, his populations of parasites and symbiotes so exotic and intriguing, her passion for knowledge was fired and over the next six years she grew zealous in her studies, using them to compensate for the emptiness of her life. With Mauldry ever at her side, accompanied by small groups of the Feelys, she mapped the interior of the dragon, stopping short of penetrating the skull, warned off from that region by a premonition of danger. She sent several of the more intelligent Feelys into Teocinte, where they acquired beakers and flasks and books and writing materials that enabled her to build a primitive laboratory for chemical analysis. She discovered that the egg-shaped chamber occupied by the colony would—had the dragon been fully alive—be pumped full of acids and gasses by the contraction of the heart muscle, flooding the channel, mingling in the adjoining chamber with yet another liquid, forming a volatile mixture that Griaule's breath would—if he so desired—kindle into flame; if he did not so desire, the expansion of the heart would empty the chamber. From these liquids she derived a potent narcotic that she named brianine after her nemesis, and from a lichen growing on the outer surface of the lungs, she derived a powerful stimulant. She catalogued the dragon's myriad flora and fauna, covering the walls of her rooms with lists and charts and notations on their behaviors. Many of the animals were either familiar to her or variants of familiar forms. Spiders, bats, swallows, and the like. But as was the case on the dragon's surface, a few of them testified to his otherworldly origins, and perhaps the most curious of them was Catherine's metahex (her designation for it), a creature with six identical bodies that thrived in the stomach acids. Each body was approximately the size and color of a worn penny, fractionally more dense than a jellyfish, ringed with cilia, and all were in a constant state of agitation. She had at first assumed the metahex to be six creatures, a species that traveled in sixes, but had begun to suspect otherwise when—upon killing one for the purposes of dissection—the other five bodies had also died. She had initiated a series of experiments that involved menacing and killing hundreds of the things, and had ascertained that the bodies were connected by some sort of field—one whose presence she deduced by process of observation—that permitted the essence of the creature to switch back and forth between the bodies, utilizing the ones it did not occupy as a unique form of camouflage. But even the metahex seemed ordinary when compared to the ghostvine, a plant that she discovered grew in one place alone, a small cavity near the base of the skull.

None of the colony would approach that region, warned away by the same sense of danger that had afflicted Catherine, and it was presumed that should one venture too close to the brain, Griaule would mobilize some of his more deadly inhabitants to deal with the interloper. But Catherine felt secure in approaching the cavity, and leaving Mauldry and her escort of Feelys behind, she climbed the steep channel that led up to it, lighting her way with a torch, and entered through an aperture not much wider than her hips. Once inside, seeing that the place was lit by veins of golden blood that branched across the ceiling, flickering like the blown flame of a candle, she extinguished the torch; she noticed with surprise that except for the ceiling, the entire cavity—a boxy space some twenty feet long, about eight feet in height—was fettered with vines whose leaves were dark green, glossy, with complex veination and tips that ended in minuscule hollow tubes. She was winded from the climb, more winded—she thought—than she should have been, and she sat down against the wall to catch her breath; then, feeling drowsy, she closed her eyes for a moment's rest. She came alert to the sound of Mauldry's voice shouting her name. Still drowsy, annoyed by his impatience, she called out, "I just want to rest a few minutes!"

"A few minutes?" he cried. "You've been there three days! What's going on? Are you all right?"

"That's ridiculous!" She started to come to her feet, then sat back, stunned by the sight of a naked woman with long blond hair curled up in a corner not ten feet away, nestled so close to the cavity wall that the tips of leaves half-covered her body and obscured her face.

"Catherine!" Mauldry shouted. "Answer me!"

"I…I'm all right! Just a minute!"

The woman stirred and made a complaining noise.

"Catherine!"

"I said I'm all right!"

The woman stretched out her legs; on her right hip was a fine pink scar, hook-shaped, identical to the scar on Catherine's hip, evidence of a childhood fall. And on the back of the right knee, a patch of raw, puckered skin, the product of an acid burn she'd suffered the year before. She was astonished by the sight of these markings, but when the woman sat up and Catherine understood that she was staring at her twin—identical not only in feature, but also in expression, wearing a resigned look that she had glimpsed many times in her mirror—her astonishment turned to fright. She could have sworn she felt the muscles of the woman's face shifting as the expression changed into one of pleased recognition, and in spite of her fear, she had a vague sense of the woman's emotions, of her burgeoning hope and elation.

"Sister," said the woman; she glanced down at her body, and Catherine had a momentary flash of doubled vision, watching the woman's head decline and seeing as well naked breasts and belly from the perspective of the woman's eyes. Her vision returned to normal, and she looked at the woman's face...*her* face. Though she had studied herself in the mirror each morning for years, she had never had such a clear perception of the changes that life inside the dragon had wrought upon her. Fine lines bracketed her lips, and the beginnings of crow's-feet radiated from the corners of her eyes. Her cheeks had hollowed, and this made her cheekbones appear sharper; the set of her mouth seemed harder, more determined. The high gloss and perfection of her youthful beauty had been marred far more than she had thought, and this dismayed her. However, the most remarkable change—the one that most struck her—was not embodied by any one detail but in the overall character of the face, in that it exhibited character, for—she realized—prior to entering the dragon it had displayed very little, and what little it had displayed had been evidence of indulgence. It troubled her to have this knowledge of the fool she had been thrust upon her with such poignancy.

As if the woman had been listening to her thoughts, she held out her hand and said, "Don't punish yourself, sister. We are all victims of our past."

"What are you?" Catherine asked, pulling back. She felt the woman was a danger to her, though she was not sure why.

"I am you." Again the woman reached out to touch her, and again Catherine shifted away. The woman's face was smiling, but Catherine felt the wash of her frustration and noticed that the woman had leaned forward only a few degrees, remaining in contact with the leaves of the vines as if there were some attachment between them that she could not break.

"I doubt that." Catherine was fascinated, but she was beginning to be swayed by the intuition that the woman's touch would harm her.

"But I am!" the woman insisted. "And something more, besides."

"What more?"

"The plant extracts essences," said the woman. "Infinitely small constructs of the flesh from which it creates a likeness free of the imperfections of your body. And since the seeds of your future are embodied by these essences, though they are unknown to you, I know them...for now."

"For now?"

The woman's tone had become desperate. "There's a connection between us…surely you feel it?"

"Yes."

"To live, to complete that connection, I must touch you. And once I do, this knowledge of the future will be lost to me. I will be as you… though separate. But don't worry. I won't interfere with you, I'll live my own life." She leaned forward again, and Catherine saw that some of the leaves were affixed to her back, the hollow tubes at their tips adhering to the skin. Once again she had an awareness of danger, a growing apprehension that the woman's touch would drain her of some vital substance.

"If you know my future," she said, "then tell me…will I ever escape Griaule?"

Mauldry chose this moment to call out to her, and she soothed him by saying that she was taking some cuttings, that she would be down soon. She repeated her question, and the woman said, "Yes, yes, you will leave the dragon," and tried to grasp her hand. "Don't be afraid. I won't harm you."

The woman's flesh was sagging, and Catherine felt the eddying of her fear.

"Please!" she said, holding out both hands. "Only your touch will sustain me. Without it, I'll die!"

But Catherine refused to trust her.

"You must believe me!" cried the woman. "I am your sister! My blood is yours, my memories!" The flesh upon her arms had sagged into billows like the flesh of an old woman, and her face was becoming jowly, grossly distorted. "Oh, please! Remember the time with Stel below the wing…you were a maiden. The wind was blowing thistles down from Griaule's back like a rain of silver. And remember the gala in Teocinte? Your sixteenth birthday. You wore a mask of orange blossoms and gold wire, and three men asked for your hand. For God's sake, Catherine! Listen to me! The major…don't you remember him? The young major? You were in love with him, but you didn't follow your heart. You were afraid of love, you didn't trust what you felt because you never trusted yourself in those days."

The connection between them was fading, and Catherine steeled herself against the woman's entreaties, which had begun to move her more than a little bit. The woman slumped down, her features blurring, a horrid sight, like the melting of a wax figure, and then, an even more horrid sight, she smiled, her lips appearing to dissolve away from teeth that were themselves dissolving.

"I understand," said the woman in a frail voice, and gave a husky, glutinous laugh. "Now I see."

"What is it?" Catherine asked. But the woman collapsed, rolling onto her side, and the process of deterioration grew more rapid; within the span of a few minutes she had dissipated into a gelatinous grayish white puddle that retained the rough outline of her form. Catherine was both appalled and relieved; however, she couldn't help feeling some remorse, uncertain whether she had acted in self-defense or through cowardice had damned a creature who was by nature no more reprehensible than herself. While the woman had been alive—if that was the proper word—Catherine had been mostly afraid, but now she marveled at the apparition, at the complexity of a plant that could produce even the semblance of a human. And the woman had been, she thought, something more vital than mere likeness. How else could she have known her memories? Or could memory, she wondered, have a physiological basis? She forced herself to take samples of the woman's remains, of the vines, with an eye toward exploring the mystery. But she doubted that the heart of such an intricate mystery would be accessible to her primitive instruments. This was to prove a self-fulfilling prophecy, because she really did not want to know the secrets of the ghostvine, leery as to what might be brought to light concerning her own nature, and with the passage of time, although she thought of it often and sometimes discussed the phenomena with Mauldry, she eventually let the matter drop.

Five

THOUGH THE TEMPERATURE NEVER CHANGED, though neither rain nor snow fell, though the fluctuations of the golden light remained consistent in their rhythms, the seasons were registered inside the dragon by migrations of birds, the weaving of cocoons, the birth of millions of insects at once; and it was by these signs that Catherine—nine years after entering Griaule's mouth—knew it to be autumn when she fell in love. The three years prior to this had been characterized by a slackening of her zeal, a gradual wearing down of her enthusiasm for scientific knowledge, and this tendency became marked after the death of Captain Mauldry from natural causes; without him to serve as a buffer between her and the Feelys, she was overwhelmed by their inanity, their woeful aspect. In truth, there was not much left to learn. Her maps were complete, her specimens and notes filled several rooms, and while she continued her visits to the dragon's heart, she no longer sought to interpret the dreams, using them instead to pass the boring hours. Again she grew restless and began to consider escape. Her life was being wasted, she believed, and she wanted to return to the world, to engage more vital opportunities than those available to her in Griaule's many-chambered prison. It was not that she was ungrateful for the experience. Had she managed to escape shortly after her arrival, she would have returned to a life of meaningless frivolity; but now, armed with knowledge, aware of her strengths and weaknesses, possessed of ambition and a heightened sense of morality, she thought she would be able to accomplish something of importance. But before she could determine whether or not escape was possible, there was a new arrival at the colony, a man whom a group of Feelys—while gathering berries near the mouth—had found lying unconscious and had borne to safety.

The man's name was John Colmacos, and he was in his early thirties, a botanist from the university at Port Chantay who had been abandoned by his guides when he insisted on entering the mouth and had subsequently been mauled by apes that had taken up residence in the mouth. He was lean, rawboned, with powerful, thick-fingered hands and fine brown hair that would never stay combed. His long-jawed, horsey face struck a bargain between homely and distinctive, and was stamped with a perpetually inquiring expression as if he were a bit perplexed by everything he saw, and his blue eyes were large and intricate, the irises flecked with green and hazel, appearing surprisingly delicate in contrast to the rest of him.

Catherine, happy to have rational company, especially that of a professional in her vocation, took charge of nursing him back to health—he had suffered fractures of the arm and ankle, and was badly cut about the face; and in the course of this she began to have fantasies about him as a lover. She had never met a man with his gentleness of manner, his lack of pretense, and she found it most surprising that he wasn't concerned with trying to impress her. Her conception of men had been limited to the soldiers of Teocinte, the thugs of Hangtown, and everything about John fascinated her. For awhile she tried to deny her feelings, telling herself that she would have fallen in love with almost anyone under the circumstances, afraid that by loving she would only increase her dissatisfaction with her prison; and, too, there was the realization that this was doubtless another of Griaule's manipulations, his attempt to make her content with her lot, to replace Mauldry with a lover. But she couldn't deny that under any circumstance she would have been attracted to John Colmacos for many reasons, not the least of which was his respect for her work with Griaule, for how she had handled adversity. Nor could she deny that the attraction was mutual. That was clear. Although there were awkward moments, there was no mooniness between them; they were both watching what was happening.

"This is amazing," he said one day, while going through one of her notebooks, lying on a pile of furs in her apartment. "It's hard to believe you haven't had training."

A flush spread over her cheeks. "Anyone in my shoes, with all that time, nothing else to do, they would have done no less."

He set down the notebook and measured her with a stare that caused her to lower her eyes. "You're wrong," he said. "Most people would have fallen apart. I can't think of anybody else who could have managed all this. You're remarkable."

She felt oddly incompetent in the light of this judgment, as if she had accorded him ultimate authority and were receiving the sort of praise that a wise adult might bestow upon an inept child who had done well for once. She wanted to explain to him that everything she had done had been a kind of therapy, a hobby to stave off despair; but she didn't know how to put this into words without sounding awkward and falsely modest, and so she merely said, "Oh," and busied herself with preparing a dose of brianine to take away the pain in his ankle.

"You're embarrassed," he said. "I'm sorry...I didn't mean to make you uncomfortable."

"I'm not...I mean, I..." She laughed. "I'm still not accustomed to talking."

He said nothing, smiling.

"What is it?" she said, defensive, feeling that he was making fun of her.

"What do you mean?"

"Why are you smiling?"

"I could frown," he said, "if that would make you comfortable."

Irritated, she bent to her task, mixing paste in a brass goblet studded with uncut emeralds, then molding it into a pellet.

"That was a joke," he said.

"I know."

"What's the matter?"

She shook her head. "Nothing."

"Look," he said, "I don't want to make you uncomfortable...I really don't. What am I doing wrong?"

She sighed, exasperated with herself. "It's not you," she said. "I just can't get used to you being here, that's all."

From without came the babble of some Feelys lowering on ropes toward the chamber floor.

"I can understand that," he said. "I..." He broke off, looked down and fingered the edge of the notebook.

"What were you going to say?"

He threw back his head, laughed. "Do you see how we're acting? Explaining ourselves constantly…as if we could hurt each other by saying the wrong word."

She glanced over at him, met his eyes, then looked away.

"What I meant was, we're not that fragile," he said, and then, as if by way of clarification, he hastened to add: "We're not that…vulnerable to one another."

He held her stare for a moment, and this time it was he who looked away and Catherine who smiled.

If she hadn't known she was in love, she would have suspected as much from the change in her attitude toward the dragon. She seemed to be seeing everything anew. Her wonder at Griaule's size and strangeness had been restored, and she delighted in displaying his marvelous features to John—the orioles and swallows that never once had flown under the sun, the glowing heart, the cavity where the ghostvine grew (though she would not linger there), and a tiny chamber close to the heart lit not by Griaule's blood but by thousands of luminous white spiders that shifted and crept across the blackness of the ceiling, like a night sky whose constellations had come to life. It was in this chamber that they engaged in their first intimacy, a kiss from which Catherine—after initially letting herself be swept away—pulled back, disoriented by the powerful sensations flooding her body, sensations both familiar and unnatural in that she hadn't experienced them for so long, and startled by the suddenness with which her fantasies had become real. Flustered, she ran from the chamber, leaving John, who was still hobbled by his injuries, to limp back to the colony alone.

She hid from him most of that day sitting with her knees drawn up on a patch of peach-colored silk near the hole at the center of the colony's floor, immersed in the bustle and gabble of the Feelys as they promenaded in their decaying finery. Though for the most part they were absorbed in their own pursuits, some sensed her mood and gathered around her, touching her, making the whimpering noises that among them passed for expressions of tenderness. Their pasty doglike faces ringed her, uniformly sad, and as if sadness were contagious, she started to cry. At first her tears seemed the product of her inability to cope with love, and then it seemed she was crying over the poor thing of her life, the haplessness of her days inside the body of the dragon; but she came to feel that her sadness was one with Griaule's, that this feeling of gloom and entrapment reflected his essential mood, and that thought stopped her tears. She'd never considered the dragon an object deserving of sympathy, and she did not now consider him such; but perceiving him imprisoned in a web of ancient magic, and the Chinese puzzle of lesser magics and imprisonments that derived from that original event, she felt foolish for having cried. Everything, she realized, even the happiest of occurrences, might be a cause for tears if you failed to see it in terms of the world that you inhabited; however, if you managed to achieve a balanced perspective, you saw that although sadness could result from every human action, that you had to seize the opportunities for effective action which came your way and not question them, no matter how unrealistic or futile they might appear. Just as Griaule had done by finding a way to utilize his power while immobilized. She laughed to think of herself emulating Griaule even in this abstract fashion, and several of the Feelys standing beside her echoed her laughter. One of the males, an old man with tufts of gray hair poking up from his pallid skull, shuffled near, picking at a loose button on his stiff, begrimed coat of silver-embroidered satin.

"Cat'rine mus' be easy sweetly, now?" he said. "No mo' bad t'ing?"

"No," she said. "No more bad thing."

On the other side of the hole a pile of naked Feelys were writhing together in the clumsiness of foreplay, men trying to penetrate men, getting angry, slapping one another, then lapsing into giggles when they found a woman and figured out the proper procedure. Once this would have disgusted her, but no more. Judged by the attitudes of a place not their own, perhaps the Feelys were disgusting; but this was their place, and Catherine's place as well, and accepting that at last, she stood and walked toward the nearest basket. The old man hustled after her, fingering his lapels in a parody of self-importance, and, as if he were the functionary of her mood, he announced to everyone they encountered, "No mo' bad t'ing, no mo' bad t'ing."

Riding up in the basket was like passing in front of a hundred tiny stages upon which scenes from the same play were being performed—pale figures slumped on silks, playing with gold and bejeweled baubles—and gazing around her, ignoring the stink, the dilapidation, she felt she was looking out upon an exotic kingdom. Always before she had been impressed by its size and grotesqueness; but now she was struck by its richness, and she wondered whether the Feelys' style of dress was inadvertent or if Griaule's subtlety extended to the point of clothing this human refuse in the rags of dead courtiers and kings. She felt exhilarated, joyful; but as the basket lurched near the level on which her rooms were located, she became nervous. It had been so long since she had been with a man, and she was worried that she might not be suited to him…then she recalled that she'd been prone to these worries even in the days when she had been with a new man every week.

She lashed the basket to a peg, stepped out onto the walkway outside her rooms, took a deep breath and pushed through the curtains, pulled them shut behind her. John was asleep, the furs pulled up to his chest. In the fading half-light, his face—dirtied by a few days' growth of beard—looked sweetly mysterious and rapt, like the face of saint at meditation, and she thought it might be best to let him sleep; but that, she realized, was a signal of her nervousness, not of compassion. The only thing to do was to get it over with, to pass through nervousness as quickly as possible and learn what there was to learn. She stripped off her trousers, her shirt, and stood for a second above him, feeling giddy, frail, as if she'd stripped off much more than a few ounces of fabric. Then she eased in beneath the furs, pressing the length of her body to his. He stirred but didn't wake, and this delighted her; she liked the idea of having him in her clutches, of coming to him in the middle of a dream, and she shivered with the apprehension of gleeful, childish power. He tossed, turned onto his side to face her, still asleep, and she pressed closer, marveling at how ready she was, how open to him. He muttered something, and as she nestled against him, he grew hard, his erection pinned between their bellies. Cautiously, she lifted her right knee atop his hip, guided him between her legs and moved her hips back and forth, rubbing against him, slowly, slowly, teasing herself with little bursts of pleasure. His eyelids twitched, blinked open, and he stared at her, his eyes looking black and wet, his skin stained a murky gold in the dimness. "Catherine," he said, and she gave a soft laugh, because her name seemed a power the way he had spoken it. His fingers hooked into the plump meat of her hips as he pushed and prodded at her, trying to find the right angle. Her head fell back, her eyes closed, concentrating on the feeling that centered her dizziness and heat, and then he was inside her, going deep with a single thrust, beginning to make love to her, and she said, "Wait, wait," holding him immobile, afraid for an instant, feeling too much, a black wave of sensation building, threatening to wash her away.

"What's wrong?" he whispered. "Do you want…"

"Just wait…just for a bit." She rested her forehead against his, trembling, amazed by the difference that he made in her body; one moment she felt buoyant, as if their connection had freed her from the restraints of gravity, and the next moment—whenever he shifted or eased fractionally deeper—she would feel as if all his weight were pouring inside her and she was sinking into the cool silks.

"Are you all right?"

"Mmm." She opened her eyes, saw his face inches away and was surprised that he didn't appear unfamiliar.

"What is it?" he asked.

"I was just thinking."

"About what?"

"I was wondering who you were, and when I looked at you, it was as if I already knew." She traced the line of his upper lip with her forefinger. "Who are you?"

"I thought you knew already."

"Maybe…but I don't know anything specific. Just that you were a professor."

"You want to know specifics?"

"Yes."

"I was an unruly child," he said. "I refused to eat onion soup, I never washed behind my ears."

His grasp tightened on her hips, and he thrust inside her, a few slow, delicious movements, kissing her mouth, her eyes.

"When I was a boy," he said, quickening his rhythm, breathing hard between the words, "I'd go swimming every morning. Off the rocks at Ayler's Point…it was beautiful. Cerulean water, palms. Chickens and pigs foraging. On the beach."

"Oh, God!" she said, locking her leg behind his thigh, her eyelids fluttering down.

"My first girlfriend was named Penny…she was twelve. Redheaded. I was a year younger. I loved her because she had freckles. I used to believe… freckles were…a sign of something. I wasn't sure what. But I love you more than her."

"I love you!" She found his rhythm, adapted to it, trying to take him all inside her. She wanted to see where they joined, and she imagined there was no longer any distinction between them, that their bodies had merged and were sealed together.

"I cheated in mathematics class, I could never do trigonometry. God… Catherine."

His voice receded, stopped, and the air seemed to grow solid around her, holding her in a rosy suspension. Light was gathering about them, frictive light from a strange heatless burning, and she heard herself crying out, calling his name, saying sweet things, childish things, telling him how wonderful he was, words like the words in a dream, important for their music, their sonority, rather than for any sense they made. She felt again the building of a dark wave in her belly. This time she flowed with it and let it carry her far.

Six

"LOVE'S STUPID," JOHN SAID TO her one day months later as they were sitting in the chamber of the heart, watching the complex eddying of golden light and whorls of shadow on the surface of the organ. "I feel like a damn sophomore. I keep finding myself thinking that I should do something noble. Feed the hungry, cure a disease." He made a noise of disgust. "It's as if I just woke up to the fact that the world has problems, and because I'm so happily in love, I want everyone else to be happy. But stuck…"

"Sometimes I feel like that myself," she said, startled by this outburst. "Maybe it's stupid, but it's not wrong. And neither is being happy."

"Stuck in here," he went on, "there's no chance of doing anything for ourselves, let alone saving the world. As for being happy, that's not going to last…not in here, anyway."

"It's lasted six months," she said. "And if it won't last here, why should it last anywhere?"

He drew up his knees, rubbed the spot on his ankle where it had been fractured. "What's the matter with you? When I got here, all you could talk about was how much you wanted to escape. You said you'd do anything to get out. It sounds now that you don't care one way or the other."

She watched him rubbing the ankle, knowing what was coming. "I'd like very much to escape. Now that you're here, it's more acceptable to me. I can't deny that. That doesn't mean I wouldn't leave if I had the chance. But at least I can think about staying here without despairing."

"Well, *I* can't! I…" He lowered his head, suddenly drained of animation, still rubbing his ankle. "I'm sorry, Catherine. My leg's hurting again, and I'm in a foul mood." He cut his eyes toward her. "Have you got that stuff with you?"

"Yes."

She made no move to get it for him.

"I realize I'm taking too much," he said. "It helps pass the time."

She bristled at that and wanted to ask if she was the reason for his boredom; but she repressed her anger, knowing that she was partly to blame for his dependency on the brianine, that during his convalescence she had responded to his demands for the drug as a lover and not as a nurse.

An impatient look crossed his face. "Can I have it?"

Reluctantly she opened her pack, removed a flask of water and some pellets of brianine wrapped in cloth, and handed them over. He fumbled at the cloth, hurrying to unscrew the cap of the flask, and then—as he was about to swallow two of the pellets—he noticed her watching him. His face tightened with anger, and he appeared ready to snap at her. But his expression softened, and he downed the pellets, held out two more. "Take some with me," he said. "I know I have to stop. And I will. But let's just relax today, let's pretend we don't have any troubles… all right?"

That was a ploy he had adopted recently, making her his accomplice in addiction and thus avoiding guilt; she knew she should refuse to join him, but at the moment she didn't have the strength for an argument. She took the pellets, washed them down with a swallow of water and lay back against the chamber wall. He settled beside her, leaning on one elbow, smiling, his eyes muddled-looking from the drug.

"You do have to stop, you know," she said.

His smile flickered, then steadied, as if his batteries were running low. "I suppose."

"If we're going to escape," she said, "you'll need a clear head."

He perked up at this. "That's a change."

"I haven't been thinking about escape for a long time. It didn't seem possible…it didn't even seem very important, anymore. I guess I'd given up on the idea. I mean just before you arrived, I'd been thinking about it again, but it wasn't serious…only frustration."

"And now?"

"It's become important again."

"Because of me, because I keep nagging about it?"

"Because of both of us. I'm not sure escape's possible, but I was wrong to stop trying."

He rolled onto his back, shielding his eyes with his forearm as if the heart's glow were too bright.

"John?" The name sounded thick and sluggish, and she could feel the drug taking her, making her drifty and slow.

"This place," he said. "This goddamn place."

"I thought,"—she was beginning to have difficulty in ordering her words—"I thought you were excited by it. You used to talk…"

"Oh, I am excited!" He laughed dully. "It's a storehouse of marvels. Fantastic! Overwhelming! It's too overwhelming. The feeling here…" He turned to her. "Don't you feel it?"

"I'm not sure what you mean."

"How could you stand living here for all these years? Are you that much stronger than me, or are you just insensitive?"

"I'm…"

"God!"

He turned away, stared at the heart wall, his face tattooed with a convoluted flow of light and shadow, then flaring gold.

"You're so at ease here. Look at that." He pointed to the heart. "It's not a heart, it's a bloody act of magic. Every time I come here I get the feeling it's going to display a pattern that'll make me disappear. Or crush me. Or something. And you just sit there looking at it with a thoughtful expression as if you're planning to put in curtains or repaint the damned thing."

"We don't have to come here anymore."

"I can't stay away," he said, and held up a pellet of brianine. "It's like this stuff."

They didn't speak for several minutes…perhaps a bit less, perhaps a little more. Time had become meaningless, and Catherine felt that she was floating away, her flesh suffused with a rosy warmth like the warmth of lovemaking. Flashes of dream imagery passed through her mind: a clown's monstrous face; an unfamiliar room with tilted walls and three-legged blue chairs; a painting whose paint was melting, dripping. The flashes lapsed into thoughts of John. He was becoming weaker every day, she realized. Losing his resilience, growing nervous and moody. She had tried to convince herself that sooner or later he would become adjusted to life inside Griaule, but she was beginning to accept the fact that he was not going to be able to survive here. She didn't understand why, whether it was due—as he had said—to the dragon's oppressiveness or to some inherent weakness. Or a combination of both. But she could no longer deny it, and the only option left was for them to effect an escape. It was easy to consider escape with the drug in her veins, feeling aloof and calm, possessed of a dreamlike overview; but she knew that once it wore off she would be at a loss as to how to proceed.

To avoid thinking, she let the heart's patterns dominate her attention. They seemed abnormally complex, and as she watched she began to have the impression of something new at work, some interior mechanism that she had never noticed before, and to become aware that the sense of imminence that pervaded the chamber was stronger than ever before; but she was so muzzy-headed that she could not concentrate upon these things. Her eyelids drooped, and she fell into her recurring dream of the sleeping dragon, focusing on the smooth scaleless skin of its chest, a patch of whiteness that came to surround her, to draw her into a world of whiteness with the serene constancy of its rhythmic rise and fall, as unvarying and predictable as the ticking of a perfect clock.

OVER THE NEXT six months Catherine devised numerous plans for escape, but discarded them all as unworkable until at last she thought of one that—although far from foolproof—seemed in its simplicity to offer the least risk of failure. Though without brianine the plan would have failed, the process of settling upon this particular plan would have gone faster had drugs not been available; unable to resist the combined pull of the drug and John's need for companionship in his addiction, she herself had become an addict, and much of her time was spent lying at the heart with John, stupified, too enervated even to make love. Her feelings toward John had changed; it could not have been otherwise, for he was not the man he had been. He had lost weight and muscle tone, grown vague and brooding, and she was concerned for the health of his body and soul. In some ways she felt closer than ever to him, her maternal instincts having been engaged by his dissolution; yet she couldn't help resenting the fact that he had failed her, that instead of offering relief, he had turned out to be a burden and a weakening influence; and as a result whenever some distance arose between them, she exerted herself to close it only if it was practical to do so. This was not often the case, because John had deteriorated to the point that closeness of any sort was a chore. However, Catherine clung to the hope that if they could escape, they would be able to make a new beginning.

The drug owned her. She carried a supply of pellets wherever she went, gradually increasing her dosages, and not only did it affect her health, her energy, it had a profound effect upon her mind. Her powers of concentration were diminished, her sleep became fitful, and she began to experience hallucinations. She heard voices, strange noises, and on one occasion she was certain that she had spotted old Amos Mauldry among a group of Feelys milling about at the bottom of the colony chamber. Her mental erosion caused her to mistrust the information of her senses and to dismiss as delusion the intimations of some climactic event that came to her in dreams and from the patterns of light and shadow on the heart; and recognizing that certain of her symptoms—hearkening to inaudible signals and the like—were similar to the behavior of the Feelys, she feared that she was becoming one of them. Yet this fear was not so pronounced as once it might have been. She sought now to be tolerant of them, to overlook their role in her imprisonment, perceiving them as unwitting agents of Griaule, and she could not be satisfied in hating either them or the dragon; Griaule and the subtle manifestations of his will were something too vast and incomprehensible to be a target for hatred, and she transferred all her wrath to Brianne, the woman who had betrayed her. The Feelys seemed to notice this evolution in her attitude, and they became more familiar, attaching themselves to her wherever she went, asking questions, touching her, and while this made it difficult to achieve privacy, in the end it was their increased affection that inspired her plan.

One day, accompanied by a group of giggling, chattering Feelys, she walked up toward the skull, to the channel that led to the cavity containing the ghostvine. She ducked into the channel, half-tempted to explore the cavity again; but she decided against this course and on crawling out of the channel, she discovered that the Feelys had vanished. Suddenly weak, as if their presence had been an actual physical support, she sank to her knees and stared along the narrow passage of pale red flesh that wound away into a golden murk like a burrow leading to a shining treasure. She felt a welling up of petulant anger at the Feelys for having deserted her. Of course she should have expected it. They shunned this area like…She sat up, struck by a realization attendant to that thought. How far, she wondered, had the Feelys retreated? Could they have gone beyond the side passage that opened into the throat? She came to her feet and crept along the passage until she reached the curve. She peeked out around it, and seeing no one, continued on, holding her breath until her chest began to ache. She heard voices, peered around the next curve, and caught sight of eight Feelys gathered by the entrance to the side passage, their silken rags agleam, their swords reflecting glints of the inconstant light. She went back around the curve, rested against the wall; she had trouble thinking, in shaping thought into a coherent stream, and out of reflex she fumbled in her pack for some brianine. Just touching one of the pellets acted to calm her, and once she had swallowed it she breathed easier. She fixed her eyes on the blurred shape of a vein buried beneath the glistening ceiling of the passage, letting the fluctuations of light mesmerize her. She felt she was blurring, becoming golden and liquid and slow, and in that feeling she found a core of confidence and hope.

There's a way, she told herself; *my God, maybe there really is a way.*

BY THE TIME she had fleshed out her plan three days later, her chief fear was that John wouldn't be able to function well enough to take part in it. He looked awful, his cheeks sunken, his color poor, and the first time she tried to tell him about the plan, he fell asleep. To counteract the brianine she began cutting his dosage, mixing it with the stimulant she had derived from the lichen growing on the dragon's lung, and after a few days, though his color and general appearance did not improve, he became more alert and energized. She knew the improvement was purely chemical, that the stimulant was a danger in his weakened state; but there was no alternative, and this at least offered him a chance at life. If he were to remain there, given the physical erosion caused by the drug, she did not believe he would last another six months.

It wasn't much of a plan, nothing subtle, nothing complex, and if she'd had her wits about her, she thought, she would have come up with it long before; but she doubted she would have had the courage to try it alone, and if there was trouble, then two people would stand a much better chance than one. John was elated by the prospect. After she had told him the particulars he paced up and down in their bedroom, his eyes bright, hectic spots of red dappling his cheeks, stopping now and again to question her or to make distracted comments.

"The Feelys," he said. "We...uh...we won't hurt them?"

"I told you...not unless it's necessary."

"That's good, that's good." He crossed the room to the curtains drawn across the entrance. "Of course it's not my field, but..."

"John?"

He peered out at the colony through the gap in the curtains, the skin on his forehead washing from gold to dark. "Uh-huh."

"What's not your field?"

After a long pause he said, "It's not...nothing."

"You were talking about the Feelys."

"They're very interesting," he said distractedly. He swayed, then moved sluggishly toward her, collapsed on the pile of furs where she was sitting. He turned his face to her, looked at her with a morose expression. "It'll be better," he said. "Once we're out of here, I'll...I know I haven't been... strong. I haven't been..."

"It's all right," she said, stroking his hair.

"No, it's not, it's not." Agitated, he struggled to sit up, but she restrained him, telling him not to be upset, and soon he lay still. "How can you love me?" he asked after a long silence.

"I don't have any choice in the matter." She bent to him, pushing back her hair so it wouldn't hang in his face, kissed his cheek, his eyes.

He started to say something, then laughed weakly, and she asked him what he found amusing.

"I was thinking about free will," he said. "How improbable a concept that's become. Here. Where it's so obviously not an option."

She settled down beside him, weary of trying to boost his spirits. She remembered how he'd been after his arrival: eager, alive, and full of curiosity despite his injuries. Now his moments of greatest vitality—like this one—were spent in sardonic rejection of happy possibility. She was tired of arguing with him, of making the point that everything in life could be reduced by negative logic to a sort of pitiful reflex, if that was the way you wanted to see it. His voice grew stronger, this prompted—she knew—by a rush of the stimulant within his system.

"It's Griaule," he said. "Everything here belongs to him, even to the most fleeting of hopes and wishes. What we feel, what we think. When I was a student and first heard about Griaule, about his method of dominion, the omnipotent functioning of his will, I thought it was foolishness pure and simple. But I was an optimist, then. And optimists are only fools without experience. Of course I didn't think of myself as an optimist. I saw myself as a realist. I had a romantic notion that I was alone, responsible for my actions, and I perceived that as being a noble beauty, a refinement of the tragic…that state of utter and forlorn independence. I thought how cozy and unrealistic it was for people to depend on gods and demons to define their roles in life. I didn't know how terrible it would be to realize that nothing you thought or did had any individual importance, that everything—love, hate, your petty likes and dislikes—was part of some unfathomable scheme. I couldn't comprehend how worthless that knowledge would make you feel."

He went on in this vein for some time, his words weighing on her, filling her with despair, pushing hope aside. Then, as if this monologue had aroused some bitter sexuality, he began to make love to her. She felt removed from the act, imprisoned within walls erected by his dour sentences; but she responded with desperate enthusiasm, her own arousal funded by a desolate prurience. She watched his spread-fingered hands knead and cup her breasts, actions that seemed to her as devoid of emotional value as those of a starfish gripping a rock; and yet because of this desolation, because she wanted to deny it and also because of the voyeuristic thrill she derived from watching herself being taken, used, her body reacted with unusual fervor. The sweaty film between them was like a silken cloth, and their movements seemed more accomplished and supple than ever before; each jolt of pleasure brought her to new and dizzying heights. But afterward she felt devastated and defeated, not loved, and lying there with him, listening to the muted gabble of the Feelys from without, bathed in their rich stench, she knew she had come to the nadir of her life, that she had finally united with the Feelys in their enactment of a perturbed and animalistic rhythm.

Over the next ten days she set the plan into motion. She took to dispensing little sweet cakes to the Feelys who guarded her on her daily walks with John, ending up each time at the channel that led to the ghostvine. And she also began to spread the rumor that at long last her study of the dragon was about to yield its promised revelation. On the day of the escape, prior to going forth, she stood at the bottom of the chamber, surrounded by hundreds of Feelys, more hanging on ropes just above her, and called out to them in ringing tones, "Today I will have word for you! Griaule's word! Bring together the hunters and those who gather food, and have them wait here for me! I will return soon, very soon, and speak to you of what is to come!"

The Feelys jostled and pawed one another, chattering, tittering, hopping up and down, and some of those hanging from the ropes were so overcome with excitement that they lost their grip and fell, landing atop their fellows, creating squirming heaps of Feelys who squalled and yelped and then started fumbling with the buttons of each other's clothing. Catherine waved at them, and with John at her side, set out toward the cavity, six Feelys with swords at their rear.

John was terribly nervous and all during the walk he kept casting backward glances at the Feelys, asking questions that only served to unnerve Catherine. "Are you sure they'll eat them?" he said. "Maybe they won't be hungry."

"They always eat them while we're in the channel," she said. "You know that."

"I know," he said. "But I'm just...I don't want anything to go wrong." He walked another half a dozen paces. "Are you sure you put enough in the cakes?"

"I'm sure." She watched him out of the corner of her eye. The muscles in his jaw bunched, nerves twitched in his cheek. A light sweat had broken on his forehead, and his pallor was extreme. She took his arm. "How do you feel?"

"Fine," he said, "I'm fine."

"It's going to work, so don't worry…please."

"I'm fine," he repeated, his voice dead, eyes fixed straight ahead.

The Feelys came to a halt just around the curve from the channel, and Catherine, smiling at them, handed them each a cake; then she and John went forward and crawled into the channel. There they sat in the darkness without speaking, their hips touching. At last John whispered, "How much longer?"

"Let's give it a few more minutes…just to be safe."

He shuddered, and she asked again how he felt.

"A little shaky," he said. "But I'm all right."

She put her hand on his arm; his muscles jumped at the touch. "Calm down," she said, and he nodded. But there was no slackening of his tension.

The seconds passed with the slowness of sap welling from cut bark, and despite her certainty that all would go as planned, Catherine's anxiety increased. Little shiny squiggles, velvety darknesses blacker than the air, wormed in front of her eyes. She imagined that she heard whispers out in the passage. She tried to think of something else, but the concerns she erected to occupy her mind materialized and vanished with a superficial and formal precision that did nothing to ease her, seeming mere transparencies shunted across the vision of a fearful prospect ahead. Finally she gave John a nudge and they crept from the channel, made their way cautiously along the passage. When they reached the curve beyond which the Feelys were waiting, she paused, listened. Not a sound. She looked out. Six bodies lay by the entrance to the side passage; even at that distance she could spot the half-eaten cakes that had fallen from their hands. Still wary, they approached the Feelys, and as they came near, Catherine thought that there was something unnatural about their stillness. She knelt beside a young male, caught a whiff of loosened bowel, saw the rapt character of death stamped on his features and realized that in measuring out the dosages of brianine in each cake, she had not taken the Feelys' slightness of build into account. She had killed them.

"Come on!" said John. He had picked up two swords; they were so short, they looked toylike in his hands. He handed over one of the swords and helped her to stand. "Let's go...there might be more of them!"

He wetted his lips, glanced from side to side. With his sunken cheeks and hollowed eyes, his face had the appearance of a skull, and for a moment, dumbstruck by the realization that she had killed, by the understanding that for all her disparagement of them, the Feelys were human, Catherine failed to recognize him. She stared at them—like ugly dolls in the ruins of their gaud—and felt again that same chill emptiness that had possessed her when she had killed Key Willen. John caught her arm, pushed her toward the side passage; it was covered by a loose flap, and though she had become used to seeing the dragon's flesh everywhere, she now shrank from touching it. John pulled back the flap, urged her into the passage, and then they were crawling through a golden gloom, following a twisting downward course.

In places the passage was only a few inches wider than her hips, and they were forced to worm their way along. She imagined that she could feel the immense weight of the dragon pressing in upon her, pictured some muscle twitching in reflex, the passage constricting and crushing them. The closed space made her breathing sound loud, and for awhile John's breathing sounded even louder, hoarse and labored. But then she could no longer hear it, and she discovered that he had fallen behind. She called out to him, and he said, "Keep going!"

She rolled onto her back in order to see him. He was gasping, his face twisted as if in pain. "What's wrong?" she cried, trying to turn completely, constrained from doing so by the narrowness of the passage.

He gave her a shove. "I'll be all right. Don't stop!"

"John!" She stretched out a hand to him, and he wedged his shoulder against her legs, pushing her along.

"Damn it...just keep going!" He continued to push and exhort her, and realizing that she could do nothing, she turned and crawled at an even faster pace, seeing his harrowed face in her mind's eye.

She couldn't tell how many minutes it took to reach the end of the passage; it was a timeless time, one long unfractionated moment of straining, squirming, pulling at the slick walls, her effort fueled by her concern;

but when she scrambled out into the dragon's throat, her heart racing, for an instant she forgot about John, about everything except the sight before her. From where she stood the throat sloped upward and widened into the mouth, and through that great opening came a golden light, not the heavy mineral brilliance of Griaule's blood, but a fresh clear light, penetrating the tangled shapes of the thickets in beams made crystalline by dust and moisture—the light of day. The tip of a huge fang hooking upward, stained gold with the morning sun, and the vault of the dragon's mouth above, with its vines and epiphytes. Stunned, gaping, she dropped her sword and went a couple of paces toward the light. It was so clean, so pure, its allure like a call. Remembering John, she turned back to the passage. He was pushing himself erect with his sword, his face flushed, panting.

"Look!" she said, hurrying to him, pointing at the light. "God, just look at that!" She steadied him, began steering him toward the mouth.

"We made it," he said. "I didn't believe we would."

His hand tightened on her arm in what she assumed was a sign of affection; but then his grip tightened cruelly, and he lurched backward.

"John!" She fought to hold onto him, saw that his eyes had rolled up into his head.

He sprawled onto his back, and she went down on her knees beside him, hands fluttering above his chest, saying, "John? John?" What felt like a shiver passed through his body, a faint guttering noise issued from his throat, and she knew, oh, she knew very well the meaning of that tremor, that signal passage of breath. She drew back, confused, staring at his face, certain that she had gotten things wrong, that in a second or two his eyelids would open. But they did not. "John?" she said, astonished by how calm she felt, by the measured tone of her voice, as if she were making a simple inquiry. She wanted to break through the shell of calmness, to let out what she was really feeling, but it was as if some strangely lucid twin had gained control over her muscles and will. Her face was cold, and she got to her feet, thinking that the coldness must be radiating from John's body and that distance would be a cure. The sight of him lying there frightened her, and she turned her back on him, folded her arms across her chest. She blinked against the daylight. It hurt her eyes, and the loops and interlacings of foliage standing out in silhouette also hurt her with their messy complexity, their disorder. She couldn't decide what to do. Get away, she told herself. Get out. She took a hesitant step toward the mouth, but that direction didn't make sense. No direction made sense, anymore.

Something moved in the bushes, but she paid it no mind. Her calm was beginning to crack, and a powerful gravity seemed to be pulling her back toward the body. She tried to resist it. More movement. Leaves were rustling, branches being pushed aside. Lots of little movements. She wiped at her eyes. There were no tears in them, but something was hampering her vision, something opaque and thin, a tattered film. The shreds of her calm, she thought, and laughed…more a hiccup than a laugh. She managed to focus on the bushes and saw ten, twenty, no, more, maybe two or three dozen diminutive figures, pale mongrel children in glittering rags standing at the verge of the thicket. She hiccuped again, and this time it felt nothing like a laugh. A sob, or maybe nausea. The Feelys shifted nearer, edging toward her. The bastards had been waiting for them. She and John had never had a chance of escaping.

Catherine retreated to the body, reached down, groping for John's sword. She picked it up, pointed it at them. "Stay away from me," she said. "Just stay away, and I won't hurt you."

They came closer, shuffling, their shoulders hunched, their attitudes fearful, but advancing steadily all the same.

"Stay away!" she shouted. "I swear I'll kill you!" She swung the sword, making a windy arc through the air. "I swear!"

The Feelys gave no sign of having heard, continuing their advance, and Catherine, sobbing now, shrieked for them to keep back, swinging the sword again and again. They encircled her, standing just beyond range. "You don't believe me?" she said. "You don't believe I'll kill you? I don't have any reason not to." All her grief and fury broke through, and with a scream she lunged at the Feelys, stabbing one in the stomach, slicing a line of blood across the satin and gilt chest of another. The two she had wounded fell, shrilling their agony, and the rest swarmed toward her. She split the skull of another, split it as easily as she might have a melon, saw gore and splintered bone fly from the terrible wound, the dead male's face nearly halved, more blood leaking from around his eyes as he toppled, and then the rest of them were on her, pulling her down, pummeling her, giving little fey cries. She had no chance against them, but she kept on fighting, knowing that when she stopped, when she surrendered, she would have to start feeling, and that she wanted badly to avoid. Their vapid faces hovered above her, seeming uniformly puzzled, as if unable to understand her behavior, and the mildness of their reactions infuriated her. Death should have brightened them, made them—like her—hot with rage. Screaming again, her thoughts reddening, pumped with adrenaline, she struggled to her knees, trying to shake off the Feelys who clung to her arms. Snapping her teeth at fingers, faces, arms. Then something struck the back of her head, and she sagged, her vision whirling, darkness closing in until all she could see was a tunnel of shadow with someone's watery eyes at the far end. The eyes grew wider, merged into a single eye that was itself a shadow with leathery wings and a forked tongue and a belly full of fire that swooped down, open-mouthed, to swallow her up and fly her home.

Seven

THE DRUG MODERATED CATHERINE'S GRIEF...OR
perhaps it was more than the drug. John's decline had begun so soon after
they had met, it seemed she had become accustomed to sadness in relation to him, and thus his death had not overwhelmed her, but rather had
manifested as an ache in her chest and a heaviness in her limbs, like small
stones she was forced to carry about. To rid herself of that ache, that heaviness, she increased her use of the drug, eating the pellets as if they were
candy, gradually withdrawing from life. She had no use for life any longer.
She knew she was going to die within the dragon, knew it with the same
clarity and certainty that accompanied all Griaule's sendings—death was
to be her punishment for seeking to avoid his will, for denying his right to
define and delimit her.

After the escape attempt, the Feelys had treated her with suspicion and
hostility; recently they had been absorbed by some internal matter, agitated
in the extreme, and they had taken to ignoring her. Without their minimal
companionship, without John, the patterns flowing across the surface of the
heart were the only thing that took Catherine out of herself, and she spent
hours at a time watching them, lying there half-conscious, registering their
changes through slitted eyes. As her addiction worsened, as she lost weight
and muscle tone, she became even more expert in interpreting the patterns,
and staring up at the vast curve of the heart, like the curve of a golden bell,
she came to realize that Mauldry had been right, that the dragon was a god,
a universe unto itself with its own laws and physical constants. A god that
she hated. She would try to beam her hatred at the heart, hoping to cause a
rupture, a seizure of some sort; but she knew that Griaule was impervious to
this, impervious to all human weapons, and that her hatred would have as
little effect upon him as an arrow loosed into an empty sky.

One day almost a year after John's death she waked abruptly from a dreamless sleep beside the heart, sitting bolt upright, feeling that a cold spike had been driven down the hollow of her spine. She rubbed sleep from her eyes, trying to shake off the lethargy of the drug, sensing danger at hand. Then she glanced up at the heart and was struck motionless. The patterns of shadow and golden radiance were changing more rapidly than ever before, and their complexity, too, was far greater than she had ever seen; yet they were as clear to her as her own script: pulsings of darkness and golden eddies flowing, unscrolling across the dimpled surface of the organ. It was a simple message, and for a few seconds she refused to accept the knowledge it conveyed, not wanting to believe that this was the culmination of her destiny, that her youth had been wasted in so trivial a matter; but recalling all the clues, the dreams of the sleeping dragon, the repetitious vision of the rise and fall of its chest, Mauldry's story of the first Feely, the exodus of animals and insects and birds, the muffled thud from deep within the dragon after which everything had remained calm for a thousand years…she knew it must be true.

As it had done a thousand years before, and as it would do again a thousand years in the future, the heart was going to beat.

She was infuriated, and she wanted to reject the fact that all her trials and griefs had been sacrifices made for the sole purpose of saving the Feelys. Her task, she realized, would be to clear them out of the chamber where they lived before it was flooded with the liquids that fueled the dragon's fires; and after the chamber had been emptied, she was to lead them back so they could go on with the work of keeping Griaule pest-free. The cause of their recent agitation, she thought, must have been due to their apprehension of the event, the result of one of Griaule's sendings; but because of their temerity they would tend to dismiss his warning, being more frightened of the outside world than of any peril within the dragon. They would need guidance to survive, and as once he had chosen Mauldry to assist her, now Griaule had chosen her to guide the Feelys.

She staggered up, as befuddled as a bird trapped between glass walls, making little rushes this way and that; then anger overcame confusion, and she beat with her fists on the heart wall, bawling her hatred of the dragon, her anguish at the ruin he had made of her life. Finally, breathless, she collapsed, her own heart pounding erratically, trying to think what to do. She wouldn't tell them, she decided; she would just let them die when the chamber flooded, and this way have her revenge. But an instant later she reversed her decision, knowing that the Feelys' deaths would merely be an inconvenience to Griaule, that he would simply gather a new group of idiots to serve him. And besides, she thought, she had already killed too many Feelys. There was no choice, she realized; over the span of almost eleven years she had been maneuvered by the dragon's will to this place and moment where, by virtue of her shaped history and conscience, she had only one course of action.

Full of muddle-headed good intentions, she made her way back to the colony, her guards trailing behind, and when she had reached the chamber, she stood with her back to the channel that led toward the throat, uncertain of how to proceed. Several hundred Feelys were milling about the bottom of the chamber, and others were clinging to ropes, hanging together in front of one or another of the cubicles, looking in that immense space like clusters of glittering, many-colored fruit; the constant motion and complexity of the colony added to Catherine's hesitancy and bewilderment, and when she tried to call out to the Feelys, to gain their attention, she managed only a feeble, scratchy noise. But she gathered her strength and called out again and again, until at last they were all assembled before her, silent and staring, hemming her in against the entrance to the channel, next to some chests that contained the torches and swords and other items used by the hunters. The Feelys gaped at her, plucking at their gaudy rags; their silence seemed to have a slow vibration. Catherine started to speak, but faltered; she took a deep breath, let it out explosively and made a second try.

"We have to leave," she said, hearing the shakiness of her voice. "We have to go outside. Not for long. Just for a little while…a few hours. The chamber, it's going…" She broke off, realizing that they weren't following her, "The thing Griaule has meant me to learn," she went on in a louder voice, "at last I know it. I know why I was brought to you. I know the purpose for which I have studied all these years. Griaule's heart is going to beat, and when it does the chamber will fill with liquid. If you remain here, you'll all drown."

The front ranks shifted, and some of the Feelys exchanged glances, but otherwise they displayed no reaction.

Catherine shook her fists in frustration. "You'll die if you don't listen to me! You have to leave! When the heart contracts, the chamber will be flooded...don't you understand?" She pointed up to the mist-hung ceiling of the chamber. "Look! The birds...the birds have gone! They know what's coming! And so do you! Don't you feel the danger? I know you do!"

They edged back, some of them turning away, entering into whispered exchanges with their fellows.

Catherine grabbed the nearest of them, a young female dressed in ruby silks. "Listen to me!" she shouted.

"Liar, Cat'rine, liar," said one of the males, jerking the female away from her. "We not goin' be mo' fools."

"I'm not lying! I'm not!" She went from one to another, putting her hands on their shoulders, meeting their eyes in an attempt to impress them with her sincerity. "The heart is going to beat! Once...just once. You won't have to stay outside long. Not long at all."

They were all walking away, all beginning to involve themselves in their own affairs, and Catherine, desperate, hurried after them, pulling them back, saying, "Listen to me! Please!" Explaining what was to happen, and receiving cold stares in return. One of the males shoved her aside, baring his teeth in a hiss, his eyes blank and bright, and she retreated to the entrance of the channel, feeling rattled and disoriented, in need of another pellet. She couldn't collect her thoughts, and she looked around in every direction as if hoping to find some sight that would steady her; but nothing she saw was of any help. Then her gaze settled on the chests where the swords and torches were stored. She felt as if her head were being held in a vise and forced toward the chests, and the knowledge of what she must do was a coldness inside her head—the unmistakable touch of Griaule's thought. It was the only way. She saw that clearly. But the idea of doing something so extreme frightened her, and she hesitated, looking behind her to make sure that none of the Feelys were keeping track of her movements. She inched toward the chests, keeping her eyes lowered, trying to make it appear that she was moving aimlessly. In one of the chests were a number of tinderboxes resting beside some torches; she stooped, grabbed a torch and one of the tinderboxes, and went walking briskly up the slope. She paused by the lowest rank of cubicles, noticed that some of the Feelys had turned to watch her; when she lit the torch, alarm surfaced in their faces and they surged up the slope toward her. She held the torch up to the curtains that covered the entrance to the cubicle, and the Feelys fell back, muttering, some letting out piercing wails.

"Please!" Catherine cried, her knees rubbery from the tension, a chill knot in her breast. "I don't want to do this! But you have to leave!"

A few of the Feelys edged toward the channel, and encouraged by this, Catherine shouted, "Yes! That's it! If you'll just go outside, just for a little while, I won't have to do it!"

Several Feelys entered the channel, and the crowd around Catherine began to erode, whimpering, breaking into tears, trickles of five and six at a time breaking away and moving out of sight within the channel, until there were no more than thirty of them left within the chamber, forming a ragged semi-circle around her. She would have liked to believe that they would do as she had suggested without further coercion on her part, but she knew that they were all packed into the channel or the chamber beyond, waiting for her to put down the torch. She gestured at the Feelys surrounding her, and they, too, began easing toward the channel; when only a handful of them remained visible, she touched the torch to the curtains.

She was amazed by how quickly the fire spread, rushing like waves up the silk drapes, following the rickety outlines of the cubicles, appearing to dress them in a fancywork of reddish yellow flame, making crispy, chuckling noises. The fire seemed to have a will of its own, to be playfully seeking out all the intricate shapes of the colony and illuminating them, the separate flames chasing one another with merry abandon, sending little trains of fire along poles and stanchions, geysering up from corners, flinging out fiery fingers to touch tips across a gap.

She was so caught up in this display, her drugged mind finding in it an aesthetic, that she forgot all about the Feelys, and when a cold sharp pain penetrated her left side, she associated this not with them but thought it a side-effect of the drug, a sudden attack brought on by her abuse of it. Then, horribly weak, sinking to her knees, she saw one of them standing next to her, a male with a pale thatch of thinning hair wisping across his scalp, holding a sword tipped with red, and she knew that he had stabbed her. She had the giddy urge to speak to him, not out of anger, just to ask a question that she wasn't able to speak, for instead of being afraid of the weakness invading her limbs, she had a terrific curiosity about what would happen next, and she had the irrational thought that her executioner might have the answer, that in his role as the instrument of Griaule's will he might have some knowledge of absolutes. He spat something at her, an accusation or an insult made inaudible by the crackling of the flames, and fled down the slope and out of the chamber, leaving her alone. She rolled onto her back, gazing at the fire, and the pain seemed to roll inside her as if it were a separate thing. Some of the cubicles were collapsing, spraying sparks, twists of black smoke boiling up, smoldering pieces of blackened wood tumbling down to the chamber floor, the entire structure appearing to ripple through the heat haze, looking unreal, an absurd construction of flaming skeletal framework and billowing, burning silks, and growing dizzy, feeling that she was falling upward into that huge fiery space, Catherine passed out.

She must have been unconscious for only a matter of seconds, because nothing had changed when she opened her eyes, except that a section of the fabric covering the chamber floor had caught fire. The flames were roaring, the snaps of cracking timber as sharp as explosions, and her nostrils were choked with an acrid stink. With a tremendous effort that brought her once again to the edge of unconsciousness, she came to her feet, clutching the wound in her side, and stumbled toward the channel; at the entrance she fell and crawled into it, choking on the smoke that poured along the passageway. Her eyes teared from the smoke, and she wriggled on her stomach, pulling herself along with her hands. She nearly passed out a half dozen times before reaching the adjoining chamber, and then she staggered, crawled, stopping frequently to catch her breath, to let the pain of her wound subside, somehow negotiating a circuitous path among the pools of burning liquid and the pale red warty bumps that sprouted everywhere. Then into the throat. She wanted to surrender to the darkness there, to let go, but she kept going, not motivated by fear, but by some reflex of survival, simply obeying the impulse to continue for as long as it was possible. Her eyes blurred, and darkness frittered at the edges of her vision. But even so, she was able to make out the light of day, the menagerie of shapes erected by the interlocking branches of the thickets, and she thought that now she could stop, that this had been what she wanted—to see the light again, not to die bathed in the uncanny radiance of Griaule's blood.

She lay down, lowering herself cautiously among a bed of ferns, her back against the side of the throat, the same position—she remembered—in which she had fallen asleep that first night inside the dragon so many years before. She started to slip, to dwindle inside herself, but was alerted by a whispery rustling that grew louder and louder, and a moment later swarms of insects began to pour from the dragon's throat, passing overhead with a whirring rush and in such density that they cut off most of the light issuing from the mouth. Far above, like the shadows of spiders, apes were swinging on the vines that depended from the roof of the mouth, heading for the outer world, and Catherine could hear smaller animals scuttling through the brush. The sight of these flights made her feel accomplished, secure in what she had done, and she settled back, resting her head against Griaule's flesh, as peaceful as she could ever recall, almost eager to be done with life, with drugs and solitude and violence. She had a moment's worry about the Feelys, wondering where they were; but then she realized that they would probably do no differently than had their remote ancestor, that they would hide in the thickets until all was calm.

She let her eyes close. The pain of the wound had diminished to a distant throb that scarcely troubled her, and the throbbing made a rhythm that seemed to be bearing her up. Somebody was talking to her, saying her name, and she resisted the urge to open her eyes, not wanting to be called back. She must be hearing things, she thought. But the voice persisted, and at last she did open her eyes. She gave a weak laugh on seeing Amos Mauldry kneeling before her, wavering and vague as a ghost, and realized that she was seeing things, too.

"Catherine," he said. "Can you hear me?"

"No," she said, and laughed again, a laugh that sent her into a bout of gasping; she felt her weakness in a new and poignant way, and it frightened her.

"Catherine?"

She blinked, trying to make him disappear; but he appeared to solidify as if she were becoming more part of his world than that of life. "What is it, Mauldry?" she said, and coughed. "Have you come to guide me to heaven...is that it?"

His lips moved, and she had the idea that he was trying to reassure her of something; but she couldn't hear his words, no matter how hard she strained her ears. He was beginning to fade, becoming opaque, proving himself to be no more than a phantom; yet as she blacked out, experiencing a final moment of panic, Catherine could have sworn that she felt him take her hand.

SHE AWOKE IN a golden glow that dimmed and brightened, and found herself staring into a face; after a moment, a long moment, because the face was much different than she had imagined it during these past few years, she recognized that it was hers. She lay still, trying to accommodate to this state of affairs, wondering why she wasn't dead, puzzling over the face and uncertain why she wasn't afraid; she felt strong and alert and at peace. She sat up and discovered that she was naked, that she was sitting in a small chamber lit by veins of golden blood branching across the ceiling, its walls obscured by vines with glossy dark green leaves. The body—her body—was lying on its back, and one side of the shirt it wore was soaked with blood. Folded beside the body was a fresh shirt, trousers, and resting atop these was a pair of sandals.

She checked her side—there was no sign of a wound. Her emotions were a mix of relief and self-loathing. She understood that somehow she had been conveyed to this cavity, to the ghostvine, and her essences had been transferred to a likeness, and yet she had trouble accepting the fact, because she felt no different than she had before...except for the feelings of peace and strength, and the fact that she had no craving for the drug. She tried to deny what had happened, to deny that she was now a thing, the bizarre contrivance of a plant, and it seemed that her thoughts, familiar in their ordinary process, were proofs that she must be wrong in her assumption. However, the body was an even more powerful evidence to the contrary. She would have liked to take refuge in panic, but her over-all feeling of well-being prevented this. She began to grow cold, her skin pebbling, and reluctantly she dressed in the clothing folded beside the body. Something hard in the breast pocket of the shirt. She opened the pocket, took out a small leather sack; she loosed the tie of the sack and from it poured a fortune of cut gems into her hand: diamonds, emeralds, and sunstones. She put the sack back into the pocket, not knowing what to make of the stones, and sat looking at the body. It was much changed from its youth, leaner, less voluptuous, and in the repose of death, the face had lost its gloss and perfection, and was merely the face of an attractive woman…a disheartened woman. She thought she should feel something, that she should be oppressed by the sight, but she had no reaction to it; it might have been a skin she had shed, something of no more consequence than that.

She had no idea where to go, but realizing that she couldn't stay there forever, she stood and with a last glance at the body, she made her way down the narrow channel leading away from the cavity. When she emerged into the passage, she hesitated, unsure of which direction to choose, unsure, too, of which direction was open to her. At length, deciding not to tempt Griaule's judgment, she headed back toward the colony, thinking that she would take part in helping them rebuild; but before she had gone ten feet she heard Mauldry's voice calling her name.

He was standing by the entrance to the cavity, dressed as he had been that first night—in a satin frock coat, carrying his gold-knobbed cane—and as she approached him, a smile broke across his wrinkled face, and he nodded as if in approval of her resurrection. "Surprised to see me?" he asked.

"I…I don't know," she said, a little afraid of him. "Was that you…in the mouth?"

He favored her with a polite bow. "None other. After things settled down, I had some of the Feelys bear you to the cavity. Or rather I was the one who effected Griaule's will in the matter. Did you look in the pocket of your shirt?"

"Yes."

"Then you found the gems. Good, good."

She was at a loss for words at first. "I thought I saw you once before," she said finally. "A few years back."

"I'm sure you did. After my rebirth,"—he gestured toward the cavity—"I was no longer of any use to you. You were forging your own path and my presence would have hampered your process. So I hid among the Feelys, waiting for the time when you would need me." He squinted at her. "You look troubled."

"I don't understand any of this," she said. "How can I feel like my old self, when I'm obviously so different?"

"Are you?" he asked. "Isn't sameness or difference mostly a matter of feeling?" He took her arm, steered her along the passage away from the colony. "You'll adjust to it, Catherine. I have, and I had the same reaction as you when I first awoke." He spread his arms, inviting her to examine him. "Do I look different to you? Aren't I the same old fool as ever?"

"So it seems," she said drily. She walked a few paces in silence, then something occurred to her. "The Feelys…do they…"

"Rebirth is only for the chosen, the select. The Feelys receive another sort of reward, one not given me to understand."

"You call this a reward? To be subject to more of Griaule's whims? And what's next for me? Am I to discover when his bowels are due to move?"

He stopped walking, frowning at her.

"Next? Why, whatever pleases you, Catherine. I've been assuming that you'd want to leave, but you're free to do as you wish. Those gems I gave you will buy you any kind of life you desire."

"I can leave?"

"Most assuredly. You've accomplished your purpose here, and you're your own agent now. *Do* you want to leave?"

Catherine looked at him, unable to speak, and nodded.

"Well, then." He took her arm again. "Let's be off."

As they walked down to the chamber behind the throat and then into the throat itself, Catherine felt as one is supposed to feel at the moment of death, all the memories of her life within the dragon passing before her eyes with their attendant emotions—her flight, her labors and studies, John, the long hours spent beside the heart—and she thought that this was most appropriate, because she was not re-entering life but rather passing through into a kind of afterlife, a place beyond death that would be as unfamiliar and new a place as Griaule himself had once seemed. And she was astounded to realize that she was frightened of these new possibilities, that the thing she had wanted for so long could pose a menace and that it was the dragon who now offered the prospect of security. On several occasions she considered turning back, but each time she did, she rebuked herself for her timidity and continued on. However, on reaching the mouth and wending her way through the thickets, her fear grew more pronounced. The sunlight, that same light that not so many months before had been alluring, now hurt her eyes and made her want to draw back into the dim golden murk of Griaule's blood; and as they neared the lip, as she stepped into the shadow of a fang, she began to tremble with cold and stopped, hugging herself to keep warm.

Mauldry took up a position facing her, jogged her arm. "What is it?" he asked. "You seem frightened."

"I am," she said; she glanced up at him. "Maybe…"

"Don't be silly," he said. "You'll be fine once you're away from here. And,"—he cocked his eye toward the declining sun—"you should be pushing along. You don't want to be hanging about the mouth when it's dark. I doubt anything would harm you, but since you're no longer part of Griaule's plan…well, better safe than sorry." He gave her a push. "Get along with you, now."

"You're not coming with me?"

"Me?" Mauldry chuckled. "What would I do out there? I'm an old man, set in my ways. No, I'm far better off staying with the Feelys. I've become half a Feely myself after all these years. But you're young, you've got a whole world of life ahead of you." He nudged her forward. "Do what I say, girl. There's no use in your hanging about any longer."

She went a couple of steps toward the lip, paused, feeling sentimental about leaving the old man; though they had never been close, he had been like a father to her…and thinking this, remembering her real father, whom she had scarcely thought of these last years, with whom she'd had the same lack of closeness, that made her aware of all the things she had to look forward to, all the lost things she might now regain. She moved into the thickets with a firmer step, and behind her, old Mauldry called to her for a last time.

"That's my girl!" he sang out. "You just keep going, and you'll start to feel at rights soon enough! There's nothing to be afraid of...nothing you can avoid, in any case! Goodbye, goodbye!"

She glanced back, waved, saw him shaking his cane in a gesture of farewell, and laughed at his eccentric appearance: a funny little man in satin rags hopping up and down in that great shadow between the fangs. Out from beneath that shadow herself, the rich light warmed her, seeming to penetrate and dissolve all the coldness that had been lodged in her bones and thoughts.

"Goodbye!" cried Mauldry. "Goodbye! Don't be sad! You're not leaving anything important behind, and you're taking the best parts with you. Just walk fast and think about what you're going to tell everyone. They'll be amazed by all you've done! Flabbergasted! Tell them about Griaule! Tell them what he's like, tell them all you've seen and all you've learned. Tell them what a grand adventure you've had!"

Eight

RETURNING TO HANGTOWN WAS IN some ways a more unsettling experience than had been Catherine's flight into the dragon. She had expected the place to have changed, and while there had been minor changes, she had assumed that it would be as different from its old self as was she. But standing at the edge of the village, looking out at the gray weathered shacks ringing the fouled shallows of the lake, thin smokes issuing from tin chimneys, the cliff of the fronto-parietal plate casting its gloomy shadow, the chokecherry thickets, the hawthorns, the dark brown dirt of the streets, three elderly men sitting on cane chairs in front of one of the shacks, smoking their pipes and staring back at her with unabashed curiosity...superficially it was no different than it had been ten years before, and this seemed to imply that her years of imprisonment, her death and rebirth had been of small importance. She did not demand that they be important to anyone else, yet it galled her that the world had passed through those years of ordeal without significant scars, and it also imbued her with the irrational fear that if she were to enter the village, she might suffer some magical slippage back through time and re-inhabit her old life. At last, with a hesitant step, she walked over to the men and wished them a good morning.

"Mornin'," said a paunchy fellow with a mottled bald scalp and a fringe of gray beard, whom she recognized as Tim Weedlon. "What can I do for you, ma'am? Got some nice bits of scale inside."

"That place over there,"—she pointed to an abandoned shack down the street, its roof holed and missing the door—"where can I find the owner?"

The other man, Mardo Koren, thin as a mantis, his face seamed and blotched, said, "Can't nobody say for sure. Ol' Riall died...must be goin' on nine, ten years back."

"He's dead?" She felt weak inside, dazed.

"Yep," said Tim Weedlon, studying her face, his brow furrowed, his expression bewildered. "His daughter run away, killed a village man name of Willen and vanished into nowhere...or so ever'body figured. Then when Willen's brothers turned up missin', people thought ol' Riall musta done 'em. He didn't deny it. Acted like he didn't care whether he lived or died."

"What happened?"

"They had a trial, found Riall guilty." He leaned forward, squinting at her. "Catherine...is that you?"

She nodded, struggling for control. "What did they do with him?"

"How can it be you?" he said. "Where you been?"

"What happened to my father?"

"God, Catherine. You know what happens to them that's found guilty of murder. If it's any comfort, the truth come out finally."

"They took him in under the wing...they left him under the wing?" Her fists clenched, nails pricking hard into her palm. "Is that what they did?"

He lowered his eyes, picked at a fray on his trouserleg.

Her eyes filled, and she turned away, facing the mossy overhang of the fronto-parietal plate. "You said the truth came out."

"That's right. A girl confessed to having seen the whole thing. Said the Willens chased you into Griaule's mouth. She woulda come forward sooner, but ol' man Willen had her feared for her life. Said he'd kill her if she told. You probably remember her. Friend of yours, if I recall. Brianne."

She whirled around, repeated the name with venom.

"Wasn't she your friend?" Weedlon asked.

"What happened to her?"

"Why...nothing," said Weedlon. "She's married, got hitched to Zev Mallison. Got herself a batch of children. I 'spect she's home now if you wanna see her. You know the Mallison place, don'tcha?"

"Yes."

"You want to know more about it, you oughta drop by there and talk to Brianne."

"I guess...I will, I'll do that."

"Now tell us where you been, Catherine. Ten years! Musta been something important to keep you from home for so long."

Coldness was spreading through her, turning her to ice. "I was thinking, Tim…I was thinking I might like to do some scaling while I'm here. Just for old time's sake, you know." She could hear the shakiness in her voice and tried to smooth it out; she forced a smile. "I wonder if I could borrow some hooks."

"Hooks?" He scratched his head, still regarding her with confusion. "Sure, I suppose you can. But aren't you going to tell us where you've been? We thought you were dead."

"I will, I promise. Before I leave…I'll come back and tell you all about it. All right?"

"Well, all right." He heaved up from his chair. "But it's a cruel thing you're doing, Catherine."

"No crueler than what's been done to me," she said distractedly. "Not half so cruel."

"Pardon," said Tim. "How's that?"

"What?"

He gave her a searching look and said, "I was telling you it was a cruel thing, keeping an old man in suspense about where you've been. Why you're going to make the choicest bit of gossip we've had in years. And you came back with…"

"Oh! I'm sorry," she said, "I was thinking about something else."

THE MALLISON PLACE was among the larger shanties in Hangtown, half-a-dozen rooms, most of which had been added on over the years since Catherine had left; but its size was no evidence of wealth or status, only of a more expansive poverty. Next to the steps leading to a badly hung door was a litter of bones and mango skins and other garbage. Fruit flies hovered above a watermelon rind; a gray dog with its ribs showing slunk off around the corner, and there was a stink of fried onions and boiled greens. From inside came the squalling of a child. The shanty looked false to Catherine, an unassuming facade behind which lay a monstrous reality—the woman who had betrayed her, killed her father—and yet its drabness was sufficient to disarm her anger somewhat.

But as she mounted the steps there was a thud as of something heavy falling, and a woman shouted. The voice was harsh, deeper than Catherine remembered, but she knew it must belong to Brianne, and that restored her vengeful mood. She knocked on the door with one of Tim Weedlon's scaling hooks, and a second later it was flung open and she was confronted by an olive-skinned woman in torn gray skirts—almost the same color as the weathered boards, as if she were the quintessential product of the environment—and gray streaks in her dark brown hair. She looked Catherine up and down, her face hard with displeasure, and said, "What do you want?"

It was Brianne, but Brianne warped, melted, disfigured as a waxwork might be disfigured by heat. Her waist gone, features thickened, cheeks sagging into jowls. Shock washed away Catherine's anger, and shock, too, materialized in Brianne's face. "No," she said, giving the word an abstracted value, as if denying an inconsequential accusation; then she shouted it: "No!" She slammed the door, and Catherine pounded on it, crying, "Damn you! Brianne!"

The child screamed, but Brianne made no reply.

Enraged, Catherine swung the hook at the door; the point sank deep into the wood, and when she tried to pull it out, one of the boards came partially loose; she pried at it, managed to rip it away, the nails coming free with a shriek of tortured metal. Through the gap she saw Brianne cowering against the rear wall of a dilapidated room, her arms around a little boy in shorts. Using the hook as a lever, she pulled loose another board, reached in and undid the latch. Brianne pushed the child behind her and grabbed a broom as Catherine stepped inside.

"Get out of here!" she said, holding the broom like a spear.

The gray poverty of the shanty made Catherine feel huge in her anger, too bright for the place, like a sun shining in a cave, and although her attention was fixed on Brianne, the peripheral details of the room imprinted themselves on her: the wood stove upon which a covered pot was steaming; an overturned wooden chair with a hole in the seat; cobwebs spanning the corners, rat turds along the wall; a rickety table set with cracked dishes and dust thick as fur beneath it. These things didn't arouse her pity or mute her anger; instead, they seemed extensions of Brianne, new targets for hatred.

She moved closer, and Brianne jabbed the broom at her. "Go away," she said weakly. "Please...leave us alone!"

Catherine swung the hook, snagging the twine that bound the broom straws and knocking it from Brianne's hands. Brianne retreated to the corner where the wood stove stood, hauling the child along. She held up her hand to ward off another blow and said, "Don't hurt us."

"Why not? Because you've got children, because you've had an unhappy life?" Catherine spat at Brianne. "You killed my father!"

"I was afraid! Key's father..."

"I don't care," said Catherine coldly. "I don't care why you did it. I don't care how good your reasons were for betraying me in the first place."

"That's right! You never cared about anything!" Brianne clawed at her breast. "You killed my heart! You didn't care about Glynn, you just wanted him because he wasn't yours!"

It took Catherine a few seconds to dredge that name up from memory, to connect it with Brianne's old lover and recall that it was her callousness and self-absorption that had set the events of the past years in motion. But although this roused her guilt, it did not abolish her anger. She couldn't equate Brianne's crimes with her excesses. Still, she was confused about what to do, uncomfortable now with the very concept of justice, and she wondered if she should leave, just throw down the hook and leave vengeance to whatever ordering principle governed the fates in Hangtown. Then Brianne shifted her feet, made a noise in her throat, and Catherine felt rage boiling up inside her.

"Don't throw that up to me," she said with flat menace. "Nothing I've done to you merited what you did to me. You don't even know what you did!"

She raised the hook, and Brianne shrank back into the corner. The child twisted its head to look at Catherine, fixing her with brimming eyes, and she held back.

"Send the child away," she told Brianne. Brianne leaned down to the child. "Go to your father," she said.

"No, wait," said Catherine, fearing that the child might bring Zev Mallison.

"Must you kill us both?" said Brianne, her voice hoarse with emotion. Hearing this, the child once more began to cry.

"Stop it," Catherine said to him, and when he continued to cry, she shouted it.

Brianne muffled the child's wails in her skirts. "Go ahead!" she said, her face twisted with fear. "Just do it!" She broke down into sobs, ducked her head and waited for the blow. Catherine stepped close to Brianne, yanked her head back by the hair, exposing her throat, and set the point of the hook against the big vein there. Brianne's eyes rolled down, trying to see the hook; her breath came in gaspy shrieks, and the child, caught between the two women, squirmed and wailed. Catherine's hand was trembling, and that slight motion pricked Brianne's skin, drawing a bead of blood. She stiffened, her eyelids fluttered down, her mouth fell open—an expression, at least so it seemed to Catherine, of ecstatic expectation. Catherine studied the face, feeling as if her emotions were being purified, drawn into a fine wire; she had an almost aesthetic appreciation of the stillness gathering around her, the hard poise of Brianne's musculature, the sensitive pulse in the throat that transmitted its frail rhythm along the hook, and she restrained herself from pressing the point deeper, wanting to prolong Brianne's suffering.

But then the hook grew heavy in Catherine's hands, and she understood that the moment had passed, that her need for vengeance had lost the immediacy and thrust of passion. She imagined herself skewering Brianne, and then imagined dragging her out to confront a village tribunal, forcing her to confess her lies, having her sentenced to be tied up and left for whatever creatures foraged beneath Griaule's wing. But while it provided her a measure of satisfaction to picture Brianne dead or dying, she saw now that anticipation was the peak of vengeance, that carrying out the necessary actions would only harm her. It frustrated her that all these years and the deaths would have no resolution, and she thought that she must have changed more than she had assumed to put aside vengeance so easily; this caused her to wonder again about the nature of the change, to question whether she was truly herself or merely an arcane likeness. But then she realized that the change had been her resolution, and that vengeance was an artifact of her old life, nothing more, and that her new life, whatever its secret character, must find other concerns to fuel it apart from old griefs and unworthy passions. This struck her with the force of a revelation, and she let out a long sighing breath that seemed to carry away with it all the sad vibrations of the past, all the residues of hates and loves, and she could finally believe that she was no longer the dragon's prisoner. She felt new in her whole being, subject to new compulsions, as alive as tears, as strong as wheat, far too strong and alive for this pallid environment, and she could hardly recall now why she had come.

She looked at Brianne and her son, feeling only the ghost of hatred, seeing them not as objects of pity or wrath, but as unfamiliar, irrelevant, lives trapped in the prison of their own self-regard, and without a word she turned and walked to the steps, slamming the hook deep into the boards of the wall, a gesture of fierce resignation, the closing of a door opening onto anger and the opening of one that led to uncharted climes, and went down out of the village, leaving old Tim Weedlon's thirst for gossip unquenched, passing along Griaule's back, pushing through thickets and fording streams, and not noticing for quite some time that she had crossed onto another hill and left the dragon far behind. Three weeks later she came to Cabrecavela, a small town at the opposite end of the Carbonales Valley, and there, using the gems provided her by Mauldry, she bought a house and settled in and began to write about Griaule, creating not a personal memoir but a reference work containing an afterword dealing with certain metaphysical speculations, for she did not wish her adventures published, considering them banal by comparison to her primary subjects, the dragon's physiology and ecology. After the publication of her book, which she entitled *The Heart's Millennium,* she experienced a brief celebrity; but she shunned most of the opportunities for travel and lecture and lionization that came her way, and satisfied her desire to impart the knowledge she had gained by teaching in the local school and speaking privately with those scientists from Port Chantay who came to interview her. Some of these visitors had been colleagues of John Colmacos, yet she never mentioned their relationship, believing that her memories of the man needed no modification; but perhaps this was a less than honest self-appraisal, perhaps she had not come to terms with that portion of her past, for in the spring five years after she had returned to the world she married one of these scientists, a man named Brian Ocoi, who in his calm demeanor and modest easiness of speech appeared cast from the same mold as Colmacos.

From that point on little is known of her other than the fact that she bore two sons and confined her writing to a journal that has gone unpublished. However, it is said of her—as is said of all those who perform similar acts of faith in the shadows of other dragons yet unearthed from beneath their hills of ordinary-seeming earth and grass, believing that their bond serves through gentle constancy to enhance and not further delimit the boundaries of this prison world—from that day forward she lived happily ever after. Except for the dying at the end. And the heartbreak in between.

THE FATHER OF STONES

For Jack, Jeanne, and Jody Dann

One

HOW THE FATHER OF STONES came into the possession of the gemcutter William Lemos continues to be a subject for debate among the citizens of Port Chantay. That Lemos purchased the stone from the importer Henry Sichi is not in question, nor is it in doubt that Sichi had traded several bolts of raw silk for the stone to a tailor in Teocinte, and although the tailor has not admitted it, witnesses have clearly established that he took the stone by force from his niece, who had seen it glinting amid a clump of ferns growing beneath the lip of the dragon Griaule. But how the stone came to be in that spot at that exact moment, therein lies the cause of the debate. Some hold that the stone is a natural artifact of Griaule, a slow production of his flesh, perhaps a kind of tumor, and that it served to embody his wishes, to move Lemos—who lived beyond the natural range of his domination—to do the dragon's bidding in the affair of the priest Mardo Zemaille and the Temple of the Dragon. Others will say that, yes, Griaule is indeed a marvel, a creature the size of a mountain, immobilized millennia before in a magical duel, who controls the population of the Carbonales Valley through the subtle exercise of his will and is capable of manipulating the most delicate and discreet of effects, the most complex of events; but to think that his tumors or kidney stones have the aspect of fabulous gems…well, that is stretching things a bit. Lemos, they claim, is merely attempting to use the fact of Griaule's mastery to justify his crime, and doubtless The Father of Stones is a relic of the dragon's hoard, probably dropped beneath the lip by one of the pitiful half-wits who inhabit his innards. Of course that's how it got there, their opponents will say; do you believe Griaule incapable of such a simple machination as that of directing one of his minions to leave a stone in a certain place at a certain time? And as for the origin of the stone, here we have a vast, mysterious, and nearly immortal intelligence, one whose body supports forests and villages and parasites large enough to destroy a city—given all that, is the possibility that he might have fabricated The Father of Stones in some dark tuck of his interior really so far removed?

These arguments aside, the facts are as follows. One misty night in February some years ago, a young boy burst into the headquarters of the constabulary in Port Chantay, bursting with the news that Mardo Zemaille, the priest of the Temple of the Dragon, had been murdered, and that his assassin, William Lemos, was awaiting the pleasure of the constabulary at the temple gates. When the constables arrived at the temple, which was located a few hundred yards from the landward end of Ayler Point, they found Lemos, a pale sandy-haired man of forty-three with a pleasant yet unremarkable face and gray eyes and a distracted professorial air, pacing back and forth in front of the temple; after placing him in restraints, the constables proceeded onto the grounds, which were uncharacteristically deserted. In a corner building of the compound they discovered Zemaille lying crumpled beside an altar of black marble, his skull fractured, the fatal blow having been struck with a fist-sized gem of an inferior milky water, one side left rough, affording an excellent grip for someone wishing to hurl it, and the other side cut into a pattern of sharply edged facets. They also discovered Mirielle, Lemos' daughter, stretched naked on the altar, drugged into a state of torpor. Port Chantay, while a fairly large city, was not so large that the constabulary had been unaware of the conflict between Lemos and Zemaille. Lemos' wife Patricia, drowned in the waters off Ayler Point three years before (she had, it was rumored, been visiting her lover, a wealthy gentleman with a home at the seaward end of the point), had willed her portion of the gem-cutting business to Mirielle, and Mirielle, who had been deeply involved with the dragon cult and with Zemaille himself, had donated the half-share to the temple. Zemaille was accustomed to using rare gems in certain of his rituals, and he soon began to drain the resources of the shop; the imminent failure of the gemcutter's business, along with his daughter's rejection, her wantonness and sluttish obeisance to the priest, had driven him to the depths of despair and thence, it seemed, to murder. And so, with a confession in hand, one backed by clear motive and a wealth of physical evidence, the constables felt confident that justice would be swift and sure. But they had not reckoned on the nature of Lemos' defense. Nor, it appeared from his initial reaction, had Lemos' attorney, Adam Korrogly.

"You must be mad," he told Lemos after the gemcutter had related his version of the events. "Or else you're damned clever."

"It's the truth," Lemos said glumly. He was slumped in a chair in a windowless interrogation room lit by a glass bowl depended from the ceiling that held clumps of luminous moss; he gazed at his hands, which were spread upon a wooden table, as if unable to accept that they had betrayed him.

Korrogly, a tall, thin, intense man with receding black hair and features that looked to have been whittled into sharpness out of smooth white wood, walked to the door and, facing it, said, "I see where you're trying to lead me."

"I'm not trying to lead you anywhere," Lemos said. "I don't care what you think, it's the truth."

"You should care very much what I think," said Korrogly, turning to him. "In the first place, I don't have to accept your case; in the second, my performance will be greatly abetted if I believe you."

Lemos lifted his head and engaged Korrogly's eyes with a look of such abject hopelessness that for an instant the attorney imagined it had struck him with a physical force. "Proceed as you will," Lemos said. "The quality of your performance matters little to me."

Korrogly walked to the table and leaned forward, resting his hands so that the splayed tips of his fingers were nearly touching Lemos' fingers. Lemos did not move his hands away, did not appear to notice the closeness of Korrogly's hands, and this indicated that he was truly overborne by all that had happened, and not putting on an act. Either that, Korrogly thought, or the man's got the nervous system of a snail.

"You're asking me to attempt a defense that's never been used before," he said. "Now that I think of it, I'm amazed no one's ever tried it. Griaule's influence—over the Carbonales Valley, anyway—is not in doubt. But to claim you were enacting his will, that some essence embodied in the gem inspired you to serve as his agent, to use that as a defense in a criminal case...I don't know."

Lemos appeared not to have heard: after a moment he said, "Mirielle... is she all right?"

Irritated, Korrogly said, "Yes, yes, she's fine. Were you listening to what I just said?"

Lemos stared at him uncomprehendingly.

"Your story," Korrogly said, "appears to demand a defense that has never been used. Never. Do you know what will attend that?"

"No," said Lemos, and lowered his eyes.

"Judges are not delighted by the prospect of setting precedent, and whoever presides over your trial is going to be particularly loath to establish this sort of precedent. Because if it is established, God knows how many villains will seek to use it to avoid punishment."

Lemos was silent for a few seconds and then said, "I don't understand. What do you wish me to say?"

Studying his face, Korrogly had a feeling of uneasiness: Lemos' despair seemed too uniform, too all-encompassing. He had acted for a number of clients who had been in the grip of terrible despair, but even the most despondent of these had on occasion suddenly realized their plight and exhibited fright or desperation or some variant emotion. He had the idea that Lemos was an intelligent man, one capable of such a subtle deceit as this might be.

"It's not necessary that you say anything," he told Lemos. "I simply want you to understand the course you've set me. If I were to plead for mercy from the court, ask them to recognize the passions involved, to take into account the unscrupulous nature of the deceased, I'm confident that your sentence would be light. Zemaille was not well loved, and there are many who consider what you've done an act of conscience."

"Not I," said Lemos in such an agonized tone that Korrogly was persuaded for the moment to complete belief.

"However," he went on, "should I pursue the defense that your story suggests, you may wind up facing a much harsher sentence, perhaps even the ultimate. That you choose to defend in this manner might imply to the judge that the crime was premeditated. Thus he would allow no mediating circumstance in his instructions to the jury. He would dismiss all possibility of it being a crime of passion."

Lemos gave a dispirited laugh.

"That amuses you?" Korrogly asked.

"I find it simplistic that passion and premeditation are deemed to be mutually exclusive."

Korrogly moved away from the table, folded his arms, and regarded the luminous globe overhead. "Of course that's not always the case. Not all crimes of passion are considered acts of the moment. There is leeway left for obsession, for irresistible compulsion. But what I'm telling you is that the judge in his desire to avoid setting precedent might block these avenues of mercy in his instructions to the jury."

Once again Lemos appeared to have slipped into a reverie.

"Have you decided?" Korrogly insisted. "I can't decide for you, I can only recommend."

"You seem to be recommending that I lie," said Lemos.

"How do you arrive at that?"

"You tell me the truth is a risk, that the secure course is best."

"I'm merely counseling you as to the potential pitfalls."

"There's a fine line, is there not, between recommendation and counsel?"

"Between guilt and innocence also," said Korrogly, thinking he might get a rise out of Lemos with this; but the gemcutter only stared at the table, brushed back his sandy forelock from his eyes.

"Very well." Korrogly picked up his case from the floor. "I'll assume you want me to go forward with the case as you've presented it."

"Mirielle," said Lemos. "Will you ask her to come and visit me?"

"I will."

"Today…will you ask her today?"

"I plan to see her this afternoon, and I'll ask her. But according to the constables, she may not respond favorably to anything I ask on your behalf. She is apparently quite bereft."

Lemos muttered something, and when Korrogly asked him to repeat it, he said, "Nothing."

"Is there anything else I can do for you?"

Lemos shook his head.

"I'll be back tomorrow," said Korrogly; he started to tell Lemos to be of good cheer, but partly in recognition of the profundity of Lemos' despair, partly due to his continuing sense of uneasiness, he thought better of it.

THE GEMCUTTER'S SHOP was in the Almintra quarter of Port Chantay, a section of the city bordering the ocean, touched yet not over-whelmed by decay and poverty. Dozens of shops were situated on the bottom floors of old peeling frame houses with witchy-looking peaked roofs and gables, and between them, Korrogly could see the houses of the wealthy ranging Ayler Point: airy mansions with wide verandahs and gilt roofs nestled among stands of thistle palms. The sea beyond the point was a smooth jade-colored expanse broken by creamy surf, seeming to carry out the theme of elegance stated by the mansions; on the other hand, the breakers that heaped foam upon the beaches of the Almintra quarter were fouled with seaweed and driftwood and offal. It must, he thought, be dis-maying to the residents of the quarter, which not so long ago had been considered exclusive, to have this view of success and beauty, and then to turn back to their own lives and watch the rats scurrying in piles of veg-etable litter, the ghost crabs scuttling in the sandy streets, the beggars, the increasing dilapidation of their homes. He wondered if this could have played a part in the murder; he could discern no opportunity for profit in the crime, but there was so much still hidden, and he did not want to blind himself to the existence of such a motive. He did not believe Lemos, yet he could not fully discredit the gemcutter's story. That was the story's virtue: its elusiveness, the way it played upon the superstitious nature of the citizenry, how it employed the vast subtlety of Griaule to spread confusion through the mind of whomever sought to judge it. The jury was going to have one hell of a time. And, he thought, so was he. He could not deny the challenge presented him; a case of this sort came along but rarely, and its materials, so aptly suited to the game of the law, to the lawyerly sleights-of-hand that had turned the law into a game, afforded him the opportunity of making a quick reputation. His inability to discredit Lemos' story might be a product of his hope that the gemcutter was telling the truth, that precedent was indeed involved, for he was beginning to realize that he needed something spectacular, something unique and unsettling, to reawaken his old hopes and enthusiasms, to restore his sense of self-worth. For the nine years since his graduation from law school, he had devoted himself to his practice, achieving a small success, all that could be expected of someone who was the son of poor farmers; he had watched less skilled lawyers achieve greater success, and he had come to understand what he should have understood from the beginning: that the Law was subordinate to the unwritten laws of social status and blood relation. He was at the age of thirty-three an idealist whose ideals were foundering, yet whose fascination with the game remained undimmed, and this had left him open to a dangerous cynicism—dangerous in that it had produced in him a volatile mixture of old virtues and new half-understood compulsions. Lately the bubblings up of that mixture had tended to make him erratic, prone to wild swings of mood and sudden abandonments of hope and principle. He was, he thought, in much the same condition as the Almintra quarter: a working class neighborhood funded by solid values that had once looked forward to an upwardly mobile future, but that now aspired to be a slum.

The gemcutter's apartment was on the second floor of one of the frame houses, located directly above his shop, and it was there that Korrogly interviewed the daughter, Mirielle. She was a slim young woman in her early twenties with long black hair and hazel eyes and a heart-shaped face whose prettiness had been hardened by the stamp of dissipation; she wore a black dress with a lace collar, but her pose was hardly in keeping with the demureness of her garment or with her apparent grief. Her cheeks were puffy from weeping, her eyes reddened, and yet she lay asprawl on a sofa, smoking a crooked green cigar, her legs propped on the back and the arm, affording Korrogly a glimpse of the shadowy division between her thighs: it appeared that grief had offered her the chance to experience a new form of dissolution, and she had seized upon it wholeheartedly.

We're proud of our little treasure, are we not, he thought, we like to give it lots of ventilation.

But Mirielle Lemos, for all her dissipation, was an extremely attractive woman, and despite his sarcasm, Korrogly—a lonely man—felt drawn to her.

The air in the apartment was thick with stale cooking odors, and the living room was a typical bachelor's disarray of soiled dishes and tumbled piles of clothing and scattered books, all strewn across furniture that had seen better days: the sprung sofa, a couple of easy chairs shiny with dirt and grease, a threadbare brown carpet with a faded blue pattern, a small scarred table that bore several framed sketches, one depicting a woman who greatly resembled Mirielle and was holding a baby in her arms—thin winter sunlight cast a glaze of reflection over the glass, imbuing the sketch with a mystical vagueness. On the wall were several paintings, and the largest of these was a representation of Griaule half-buried beneath centuries of grass and trees, only a portion of a wing and his entire massive head, as high as a hill itself, left visible; this painting, Korrogly noticed, was signed W. Lemos. He pushed aside some dirty clothing and perched on the edge of an easy chair facing Mirielle.

"So you're my father's lawyer," she said after exhaling a stream of gray smoke. "You don't look competent."

"Be assured that I am," said Korrogly, who had been prepared for her hostility. "If you were hoping for some white-haired old man with ink on his fingers and crumpled legal notes peeping from his waistcoat pockets, I'm…"

"No," she said, "I was hoping for someone exactly like you. Somebody with a minimum of experience and skill."

"I take it, then, that you're anticipating a hard judgment for your father. That you're embittered by his act."

"Embittered?" She laughed. "I despised him before he killed Mardo. Now I hate him."

"And yet he saved your life."

"Is that what he told you?" Another laugh. "That's scarcely the case."

"You were drugged," he said. "Lying naked on an altar. A knife was found on Zemaille's body."

"I've spent other nights lying on that altar in exactly the same state," she said, "and never once have I experienced other than pleasure." Her sultry, smirking tone made clear the nature of that pleasure. "As for the knife, Mardo always went armed. He was in constant danger from fools like my father."

"What do you remember of the murder?"

"I remember hearing my father's voice. I thought I was dreaming. Then I heard a crack, a splintering sound. I looked up and saw Mardo fall with blood all over his face." She tensed, looked up to the ceiling, apparently made uncomfortable by the memory; but then, as though also inflamed by it, she ran a hand along her belly and thigh. Korrogly averted his eyes, feeling an accumulation of heat in his own belly.

"Your father claims there were nine witnesses, nine hooded figures, all of whom fled the chamber. None of them have come forward. Do you know why this might be?"

"Why should they come forward? To experience more persecution from people who have no idea of what Mardo was attempting?"

'And what was that?"

She exhaled another stream of smoke and said nothing.

"You'll be asked this question in court."

"I will not betray our secrets," she said. "I don't care what happens to me."

"Neither does your father…or so he says. He's very depressed, and he wants to see you."

She made a noise of contempt. "I'll see him on the gallows."

"You know," Korrogly said, "despite what your father has done, he really does believe he was acting to save you."

"You don't know what he believes," she said, sitting up, fixing him with a dead stare, her voice full of venom. "You don't understand him at all. He pretends to be a humble craftsman, an artisan, a good honest soul. But in his heart he considers himself a superior being. Life, he used to say, had thrown obstacle after obstacle into his path, keeping him from achieving his proper station. He feels he's been penalized with bad luck for his intelligence. He's a schemer, a plotter. And his bad luck stems from the fact that he's not so intelligent as he thinks. He bungles everything."

The first part of what she had said was in such accord with Korrogly's impression of Lemos that he was taken aback; hearing his feelings issue from Mirielle's mouth acted both to reinforce his impression and—because she was so obviously her father's antagonist—to invalidate it.

"That may be," he said, covering his confusion by shuffling through papers, "but I doubt it."

"Oh, you'll find out," she said. "If there's one thing you'll end up knowing about my father, it's his capacity for deceit." She settled back on the sofa, her skirt riding up onto her thigh. "He's been wanting to kill Mardo ever since I got involved with him." A smile hitched up the corners of her mouth. "He was jealous."

"Jealous?" said Korrogly.

"Yes…as a lover is jealous. He delights in touching me."

Korrogly did not reject the notion of incestuous desire out of hand, but after going through the mental file he had begun on Lemos, he refused to believe Mirielle's accusation; she had been so committed to Zemaille and his way of life that he could not, he realized, believe anything she told him. She was ruined, abandoned to the point of dissolution; the stink pervading the apartment, he thought, was scarcely distinguishable from the reek of her own spoilage.

"Why do you despise your father?" he asked.

"His pomposity," she said, "and his stodginess. His stale conception of what happiness should be, his inability to embrace life, his dull presence, his…"

"All that sounds quite adolescent," he said. "Like the reaction of a stubborn child who's been denied her favorite treat."

She shrugged. "Perhaps. He rejected my suitors, he prevented me from becoming an actress…and I could have been a good one. Everybody said so. But how I am, how I was, doesn't have any bearing on the truth of what I've said. And it's not relevant to what my father did."

"Relevant…possibly not. But it speaks to the fact that you're not in the least interested in helping him."

"I've made no secret of that."

"No, you haven't. But the history of your emotions will be helpful in pointing up that you're a vindictive bitch and that your idea of the truth is whatever will hurt your father. It has no relation to what really happened."

He had been trying to make her angry, wanting to get an idea of her boiling point, knowledge that would come in handy during the trial; but her smile only broadened, she crossed her legs and traced a florid shape in the air with the tip of her cigar. She was very cool, he thought, very cool. But in court that would work against her; it would cast Lemos in a more benign light, show him to be the patient, caring parent in contrast to her vengeful ingrate. Of course that would be more significant to a defense based on compulsion, on wrong-headed passion; but Korrogly believed he could color his actual defense with this other and so win the jury's sympathy.

"Well," he said, coming to his feet. "I may have some more questions later, but I don't see any use in continuing this now."

"You think you've got me, don't you?"

"Got you? I don't know what you mean."

"You think you've got me figured out."

"As a matter of fact, I do."

"And how you would portray me in court?"

"I'm sure you must have an idea."

"Oh, but I'd like to hear it."

"All right. If necessary I'll paint a picture of a spoiled, indulgent creature who has no real feelings for anyone. Even her grief for her lover seems to be no more than a kind of adornment, an accessory to be worn with a black dress. And in her degeneracy, a condition prompted by drugs and the black arts, by the depraved rituals of the dragon cult, the only emotions she is capable of mustering are those she thinks will serve her ends. Greed, perhaps. And vengefulness."

She let out a lazy chuckle.

"That strikes you as inaccurate?"

"Not at all, lawyer. What amuses me is that knowing this, you think you can use it to your advantage." She turned on her side, supporting her head with one hand, her skirt twisting beneath her, exposing even more pale firm flesh. "I'll look forward to our next meeting. Perhaps by then your understanding of the situation will have grown more complex, and you'll have more...more interesting questions to ask."

"May I ask one further question now?"

"Yes, of course." She rolled onto her back, cutting her eyes toward him.

"This display of yours, the dress up to your waist and all that, is it intended to arouse me?"

She nodded. "Mmm-hmm. Is it working?"

"Why?" he said. "What possible benefit do you think that'll gain you? Do you think I'll defend your father with less enthusiasm?"

"I don't know...will you?"

"Not at all."

"Then it'll be for nothing," she said. "But that's all right, too."

He couldn't tear his eyes away from her legs.

"Really, it's all right," she said. "I need a lover now. And I like you. You're funny, but I like you anyway."

He stared at her, his anger alternating with desire. Knowing that he could have her alarmed him. He could go to her now, this moment, and it would affect nothing, it would have no resonance with the trial, it would merely be an indulgence. Yet he understood that it was this increasing openness to indulgence that signaled his impending moral shipwreck. To reject her would not be an act of prudishness, but one of salvation.

"It'll be good with us," she said. "I have a feeling for these things."

His eye followed the line of her thigh to the white seashell curve of her hip; her fingers were long, slender, and he imagined how they might touch him.

"I have to be going," he said.

"Yes, I think you'd better." Her voice was charged with gleeful spite. "That was a near thing, wasn't it? You might have actually enjoyed yourself."

Two

DURING THE NEXT WEEK KORROGLY interviewed many
witnessess, among them Henry Sichi, who reported that when Lemos purchased the gemstone, he had been so entranced by it, so absorbed, that
Sichi had found it necessary to give him a nudge in order to alert him sufficiently to complete the deal. He spoke to various members of Lemos' guild,
all of whom were willing to testify to the mildness and honesty of his character; they described him as a man obsessed with his work, obsessed to the
point of absentmindness, drawing a vastly different picture of the man than
had Mirielle. Korrogly had known quite a few men who had presented an
exemplary public face and a wholly contradictory one in private; yet there
was no doubt that the guildsmen's testimony would outweigh Mirielle's…
in fact, whatever Mirielle said in evidence would, no matter how hostile,
benefit Lemos' case because of its vile context. He sought out experts on
Griaule's history and talked to people who'd had personal experience of
Griaule's influence. The only witness whose testimony ran contrary to the
defense was that of an old man, a drunkard who was in the habit of sleeping it off in the dunes south of Ayler Point and on several occasions had
seen Lemos hurling stones at a sign post, hurling them over and over again
as if practicing for the fatal toss; the old man's alcoholism would diminish
the impact of the testimony, but it was nevertheless of consequence.

When Korrogly related it to Lemos, the gemcutter said, "I often walk
out past the point of an afternoon, and sometimes I throw stones to relax.
It was my only talent as a child, and I suppose I seek refuge in it when the
world becomes too much to bear."

Like every other bit of evidence, this too, Korrogly saw, was open to
interpretation; it was conceivable, for instance, that Griaule's choice of
Lemos as an agent had been in part made because of this aptitude for

throwing stones, that he had been moved by the dragon to practice in preparation for the violent act. He looked across the table at his client. Jail, it appeared, was turning Lemos gray. His skin, the tenor of his emotions, everything about him was going gray, and Korrogly felt infected by that grayness, felt that the gray was the color of the case, of all its indistinct structures and indefinite truths, and that it was spreading through him and wearing him away. He asked again if he could do anything for Lemos, and again Lemos' answer was that he wished to see Mirielle.

On a Sunday in late March, Korrogly interviewed an elderly and wealthy woman who had until shortly before the murder been an active member of the Temple of the Dragon. The woman was known only as Kirin, and her past was a shadow; she seemed not to have existed prior to her emergence within the strictures of the temple, and since leaving it, she had lived a secretive life, known to the public only through the letters that she occasionally wrote to the newspaper attacking the cult. He was met at the door by a thick-waisted drab, apparently the woman's servant, who led him in a room that seemed to have been less decorated than to have sprung from a green and leafy enchantment. It was roofed by a faceted skylight, divided by carved wooden screens, all twined with vines and epiphytes; plants of every variety choked the avenues among the screens, their foliage so luxuriant that sprays of leaves hid the pots in which they were rooted. The sun illuminated a profusion of greens—pale pomona, nile, emerald, viridian, and chartreuse; intricate shadows dappled the hardwood floors. The fronds of sword ferns twitched in the breeze like the feelers of enormous insects.

After wandering through this jungly environment for nearly half an hour, growing more and more impatient, Korrogly was hailed by a fluting female voice, which asked him to call out so that she might find him among the leaves. Moments later, a tall white-haired woman in a floor-length gown of gray watered silk came up beside him; her face was the color of old ivory, deeply wrinkled and stamped with what struck Korrogly as a stern and suspicious character, and her hands moved ceaselessly, plucking at the nearby leaves as if they were the telling beads of some meditative religion. Despite her age, she radiated energy, and Korrogly thought that if he were to close his eyes, he would have the impression that he was in the presence of a vital young woman. She directed him to a bench in a corner of the room and sat next to him, gazing out into the lushness of her sanctum, continuing to pluck and pick at stem and leaf.

"I distrust lawyers, Mister Korrogly," she said. "You should know that from the outset."

"So do I, Ma'am," he said, hoping to elicit a laugh, some softening of her attitude, but she only pursed her lips.

"Had you represented any other client, I would not have agreed to see you. But the man who has rid the world of Mardo Zemaille deserves any help I can give...though I'm not at all certain how I can help."

"I was hoping you might provide me with some background on Zemaille, particularly as regards his relationship with Mirielle Lemos."

"Ah," she said. "That."

"Mirielle herself has not been forthcoming, and the other members of the cult have gone to ground."

"They're afraid."

"Of what?"

She gave an amused hiss. "Of everything, Mister Korrogly. Mardo has addicted them to fear. And of course now that he's gone, now that he's abandoned them to the fear he instilled in them, they've fled. The temple will never thrive again." She tore a strip of green off a frond. "That was Mardo's one truth, that in the proper environment, fear can be a form of sustenance. It's a truth that underlies many religions. Mirielle understands it as well."

"Tell me about her."

The old woman fingered a spray of bamboo leaves. "She's not a bad girl...or at least she didn't used to be. It was Mardo who corrupted her. He corrupted everyone, he broke them and then poured his black juice into their cracks. When I first met her, that was five years ago, I took her for a typical convert. She was an agitated, moody girl when she came to the temple. All dance and no standstill, as the saying goes. I assumed Mardo would have her—he had all the pretty ones and that then he would let her fall from grace, become an ordinary devotee. But I underestimated Mirielle. She had something, some quality, that fascinated Mardo. I originally thought that he might have met his match sexually, for I knew from some of the other members that she was"—she seemed to be searching for the right word—"rapacious. And perhaps that did have something to do with it. But of greater relevance, I believe, was that she was driven in much the same way as he. And thus she is equally untrustworthy."

"How do you mean 'driven'?"

The old woman looked down at the floor. "It's difficult to explain Mardo to anyone who never knew him, and it's entirely unnecessary to explain him to anyone who did. When you examine what he said closely, it was all doctrinal persiflage, mumbo jumbo, a welter of half-baked ideas stirred together with high-flown empty language. But despite that, you always had the idea that he knew something, or that he was onto something, some course that would carry him to great achievement. I'm not speaking of charisma…not that Mardo was short in that department. What I'm trying to get to is something more substantial. There was about him an air that he was being moved by forces within him that not even he fully comprehended."

"And you're saying Mirielle had this air as well."

"Yes, yes, she was driven by something. Again, I don't know if she understood its nature. But she was driven much like Mardo. He recognized this in her, and that's why he trusted her so."

"And yet it appears that he was going to kill her."

She sighed. "The reason I left the temple…no, let me tell you first the reasons I joined it. I fancied myself a seeker, but even at the height of my self-deception, I realized that I was merely bored. Bored and old…too old to find better entertainment. The temple was for me a violent dark romance whose characters were constantly changing, and I was completely taken with it. And there was always the sense that Griaule was near. That chill scaly presence…that awful cold power." She gave a dramatic shudder. "At any rate, two years ago I began to have a sense that things were getting serious, that the great work Mardo had talked of for so long was finally getting under way. It frightened me. And being frightened awakened me to the deceits and evils of the temple."

"Do you know what it was…the great work?"

She hesitated. "No."

He studied her, thinking that she was holding back something. "I have no one else to turn to in this," he said. "The cult members have gone to ground."

"They may have gone to ground, but some of them are watching even now. If I revealed secrets, they would kill me."

"I could subpoena you."

"You could," she said, "but I would say no more than I have. And there is also the fact that I would not make a very reliable witness. The prosecutor would ask questions about my past, and those I would not answer."

"I assume the great work had something to do with Griaule."

She shrugged. "Everything did."

"Can't you even give me a clue? Something?"

"I'll tell you this much. You have to understand the nature of the cult. They did not so much worship Griaule as they elevated their fear of him to the status of worship. Mardo saw himself in a peculiar relationship to Griaule; he felt he was the spiritual descendant of that first wizard who long ago did battle with the dragon...a sort of ritual adversary, both celebrant and enemy. That kind of duality appealed to Mardo; he considered it the height of subtlety."

Korrogly continued to press her, but she would say no more and finally he gave it up. "Did Mirielle know about the work?"

"I doubt it. Mardo's trust of her extended to the material world, but this was something else, something magical. Something serious. And that troubled me. I didn't want things to be serious, I began to be afraid. People vanished, conversations became whispered, the darkness inside the temple seemed to be spreading everywhere. Finally I couldn't bear it. I started to notice things. Perhaps I'd always noticed them, but had preferred not to see them. At any rate, I realized then how dangerous a thing had been my boredom, how low I had let it drag me. I understood that for all his drive and intensity, Mardo Zemaille was an evil man...evil in the blackest of definitions. He sought to master wizardly arts that have died away for lack of adherents corrupt enough to dig in the nightsoil where the roots of such power are buried."

"What things did you notice?"

"Rituals of torture...sacrifices."

"Human sacrifice?"

"Perhaps...I can't be sure. But I believe at the least that Mardo was capable of it."

"Then you think that he was going to sacrifice Mirielle."

"It's hard to credit. He doted on her. But, yes, it's possible that he would feel he had to sacrifice the thing he most cared about in order to complete the great work. She may not have known it, but I think he may have had that in mind."

Korrogly watched leaf shadows trembling on the sunlit floor; he felt tired, out of his element. What, he thought, am I doing here, talking to an old lady about evil, trying to prove that a dragon has committed murder, what am I doing?

"You mentioned trust between the two of them."

"Yes, Mardo made it plain to everyone that in the event anything happened to him, she was to lead the temple. There was something…"

"What?" Korrogly asked.

"I was going to say I always suspected that there was a secret history between them, and that was another reason for Mardo's trust. It was something I felt was true…but it was only a feeling. Nothing admissible, nothing you could use. Anyway, I suppose he drew up documents that would grant her some kind of legal succession. He was a stickler for that sort of detail." She tilted her head to the side as if trying to make out some indefinite quality in his face. "You look surprised. I've never known a lawyer whose expressions were so readable."

Failure, he thought, even my face is failing me now.

"I had no idea the bond between them had been ratified in any way," he said.

"Perhaps it hasn't. I can't be sure. But if I'm correct and it has, you'll have no end of trouble unearthing the documents. Mardo would have never gone to a lawyer. If they exist they're probably hidden in the temple somewhere."

"I see."

"What are you thinking?"

He made a noise of baffled amusement. "I thought this would be such a simple case, but everywhere I turn I come upon some new complexity."

"It *is* a simple case," she said, her wrinkled face tightening with a grim expression. "Take my word, no matter how villainous a creature you believe William Lemos to be, his act has made him an innocent."

THE FATHER OF STONES

ONE NIGHT SHORTLY before the opening of the trial, Korrogly visited the constabulary headquarters to have another look at the murder weapon—The Father of Stones, as Lemos had named it. Standing alone by a table in the evidence room, looking down at the stone, which rested at the center of a nest of tissue paper within a tin box, he was as confounded by it as he had been by every other element of the case. At one moment it seemed to enclose profane fractions of encysted light, its surface clouded and occult, a milky bulge with the reek of a thousand-year-old egg trapped inside; the next, it would appear lovely, subtle, embodying the delicate essence of some numinous philosophy. And at its heart was a dark flaw that resembled a man with upflung arms. Like Griaule himself, it was a thing of infinite shadings, of a thousand possible interpretations, and Korrogly could easily believe that its point of origin was a cavity in the dragon's body. He was, however, still unable to believe Lemos' story; it, too, was flawed, and this flaw would be enough to lead the gemcutter to the gallows. There was just no good reason, at least none he, Korrogly, could discern, why Griaule would have wanted Lemos to kill Zemaille. Not even Lemos could come up with a good reason; he simply continued to insist that it was so, and mere insistence would not save him. Yet it was that same flaw, the lack of patness to the story, that kept forcing Korrogly to relent in his judgment, to be tempted to belief. What a case, he thought; when he was back in law school he'd dreamt of having a case like this, and now he had it, and all it was doing was making him weary, making him wonder if he had wasted his life, if every question, even the most fundamental, was as elusive as this one, and he just hadn't noticed before.

He picked up The Father of Stones and juggled it; it was unusually heavy. Like dragon scale, like ancient thought.

Damn, he thought, damn this whole business, I should give it up and start a religion, there must be sufficient fools out there for some of them to consider me wise and wonderful.

"Thinking about murdering someone?" said a dry voice behind him. "Your client, perhaps?"

It was the prosecutor, Ian Mervale, a reedy, aristocratic-looking man in a stylishly cut black suit; his dark hair, combed back from a noble forehead, was salted with gray, and the vagueness of his eyes, which were watery blue, set in sleepy folds, belied a quick and aggressive mentality.

"I'm more likely to go after you," said Korrogly wryly.

"Me?" Mervale affected shocked dismay. "I'm by far the least of your worries. If not your client, I'd consider an attack upon our venerable Judge Wymer. It appears he's not at all sympathetic to your defense tactics."

"I can't blame him for that," Korrogly muttered.

Mervale studied him a moment, then shook his head and chuckled. "It's always the same every time I run up against you. I know you're being honest, you're not trying to underplay your hand; but even though I know it, as soon as the trial begins I become positively convinced that you're being duplicitous, that you've got some devastating trick up your sleeve."

"You don't trust yourself," Korrogly said. "How can you trust anyone else?"

"I suppose you're right. My greatest strength is my greatest weakness." He started to turn toward the door, hesitated and then said, "Care for a drink?" Korrogly juggled The Father of Stones one last time; it seemed to have grown heavier yet. "I suppose a drink might help," he said.

The Blind Lady, a pub in Chancrey's Lane, was as usual crowded with law clerks and young solicitors, whose body heat fogged the mirrors on the walls, whose errant darts lodged in white plaster or blackened beam, and whose uproarious babble made quiet conversation impossible. Korrogly and Mervale worked their way through the press, holding their glasses high to avoid spillage, and at last found an unoccupied table at the rear of the pub. As they seated themselves, a group of clerks standing nearby began to sing a bawdy song. Mervale winced, then lifted his glass in a toast to Korrogly.

The singers moved off toward the front of the pub; Mervale leaned back, regarding Korrogly with fond condescension, an attitude more of social habit than one relating to their adversary positions. Mervale was the son of a moneyed shipbuilder, and there was always an edge of class struggle to their conversations, an edge they blunted by pretending to have a fund of mutual respect.

"So what do you think?" Mervale asked. "Is Lemos lying...demented? What?"

"Demented, no. Lying..." Korrogly sipped his rum. "Every time I think I have the answer to that, I see another side to things. I wouldn't want to hazard a guess at this stage. What do you think?"

"Of course he's lying! The man had every motive in the world to kill Zemaille. His daughter, his business. My God! He could have done nothing else but kill him. But I have to admit his story's ingenious. Brilliant."

"Is it? I might have gotten him off with a couple of years if he'd pled some version of diminished capacity."

"Yes, but that's what makes it so brilliant, the fact that everyone knows that's so. They'll say to themselves, God, the man must be innocent or else he wouldn't stick to such a far-fetched tale."

"I'd hardly call it far-fetched."

"Oh, very well! Let's call it inspired then, shall we?"

Growing annoyed, Korrogly thought, you pompous piece of shit, I'm going to beat you this time.

He smiled. "As you wish."

"Ah," said Mervale, "I sense that a trial lawyer has suddenly taken possession of your body."

Korrogly drank. "I'm not in the mood tonight, Mervale. What are you after that you think I'm willing to give away?"

Displeasure registered on Mervale's face.

"What's wrong?" Korrogly asked. "Am I spoiling your fun?"

"I don't know what's got into you," said Mervale. "Maybe you've been working too hard."

"These little ritual fishing expeditions are beginning to bore me, that's all. They always come to the same thing. Nothing. They're just your way of reminding me of my station. You drag me in here and butter me up with the old school smile and talk about parties to which I haven't been invited. I expect you believe this gives you a psychological advantage, but I think the false sense of superiority it lends you actually weakens your delivery. And you need all the strength you can muster. You're simply not that proficient a prosecutor."

Mervale got stiffly to his feet, cast a scornful look down at Korrogly. "You're a joke, you know that?" he said. "A tiresome drudge without a life, with only the law for a bed partner." He tossed some coins onto the table. "Buy yourself a couple of drinks. Perhaps drunk you'll be able to entertain yourself."

Korrogly watched him move through the crowd, accepting the good wishes of the law clerks who closed around him. Now why, he thought, why did I bother doing that?

He waited until Mervale was out of sight before leaving, and then, instead of going directly home, he walked west along Biscaya Boulevard, heading nowhere in particular, moving aimlessly through the accumulating mist, his thoughts in a despondent muddle; the dank salt air seemed redolent of his own heaviness, of the damp dark moil inside his head. Only peripherally did he notice that he had entered the Almintra quarter, and it was not until he found himself standing in front of the gemcutter's shop that he suspected he had tried to hide from himself the fact that he had intended to come this way. Or perhaps, he thought, I was moved to come here by some vast and ineluctable agency whose essence spoke to me from The Father of Stones. Though that thought had been formed in derision, it caused the hairs on the back of his neck to prickle, and he wondered, what if Lemos' story is true, could I also be vulnerable to Griaule's directives? The silence of the dead street unnerved him; the peaks of the rooftops looked like black simple mountains rising from plateaus of mist, and the few streetlamps left unbroken shone through the haze like evil phosphorescent flowers, and the shop windows were obsidian, reflective, hiding their secrets. It was still fairly early, but all the good artisans and shopkeepers were abed...all except the occupant of the apartment above Lemos' shop. Her light still burned. He gazed up at it, thinking now that Mervale's insulting and accurate depiction of his life might have motivated him to visit Mirielle, thereby to disprove it. He decided to leave, to return home, but remained standing in front of the shop, held in place, it seemed, by the glow of the lamp and the sodden crush of the surf from the darkness beyond. A dog began to bark nearby; from somewhere farther away came the call of voices singing, violins and horns, a melancholy tune that he felt was sounding the configuration of his own loneliness.

This is folly, he said to himself, she'll probably kick you down the stairs, she was only playing with you the last time, and why the hell would you want it anyway…just to be away from your thoughts for awhile, no matter how temporary the cure?

That's right, that's exactly right.

"Hell!" he said to the dark, to the whole unlistening world. "Hell, why not?"

The woman who opened the door, though physically the same woman who had sprawled brazenly on the sofa during their first meeting, was in all other ways quite different. Distracted; twitchy; pale to the point of seeming bloodless, her black hair loose and in disarray; clad in a white robe of some heavy coarse cloth. The dissolute hardness had emptied from her face, and she seemed to have thrown off a handful of years, to be a troubled young girl. She stared for a second as if failing to recognize him and then said, "Oh…you."

He was about to apologize for having come so late, to beat a retreat, put off by her manner; but before he could frame the words, she stepped back from the door and invited him in.

"I'm glad you're here," she said, following him into the living room, which had undergone a cleaning. "I haven't been able to sleep."

She dropped onto the sofa, fumbled about on the end table, picked up a cigar, then set it down; she looked up at him expectantly.

"Well, have a seat."

He did as instructed, taking his perch again on the easy chair. "I was hoping you wouldn't mind answering a few more questions."

"Questions…you want…oh, all right. Questions," She gave a fey laugh and picked nervously at the fringe on the arm of the sofa. "Ask away."

"I've heard," he said, "that Mardo had in mind for you to take over the leadership of the temple in case of his death. Is that correct?"

She nodded, kept nodding, too forcefully for mere affirmation, as if trying to clear some painful entanglement from her head.

"Yes, indeed," she said. "That's what he had in mind."

"Were there papers drawn up to this effect?"

"No…yes, maybe…I don't know. He talked about doing it, but I never saw them." She rocked back and forth on the edge of the sofa, her hands plucking at ridges of its old embroidered pattern. "It doesn't matter now."

"Why…why doesn't it matter?"

"There is no temple."

"What do you mean?"

"There is no temple! Simple as that. No more adherents, no more ceremonies. Just empty buildings."

"What happened?"

"I don't want to talk about it."

"But…"

She jumped to her feet, paced toward the back of the room; then she spun about to face him, brushing hair back from her cheek. "I don't want to talk about it! I don't want to talk at all…not about…not about anything important." She put a hand to her brow as if testing for a fever. "I'm sorry, I'm sorry."

"What's the matter?" he asked.

"Oh, nothing," she said. "My life's a shambles, my lover's dead, and my father goes on trial for his murder tomorrow morning. Everything's fine."

"I don't know why your father's plight should disturb you. I thought you hated him."

"He's still my father. I have feelings that hate won't dissolve. Reflex feelings, you understand. But they have their pull." She came back to the sofa and sat down; once again she began picking at the embroidered pattern. "Look, I can't help you. I don't know anything that can help you with the trial. Not a thing. If I did I think I'd tell you…that's how I feel now, anyway. But there's nothing, nothing at all."

He sensed that the crack in her callous veneer ran deeper than she cared to admit, and, too, he thought that her anxiety might be due to the fact that she did know something helpful and was holding it back; but he decided not to push the matter.

"Very well," he said. "What would you like to talk about?"

She glanced around the room, as if searching for something that would support a conversation.

He noticed that her eye lingered on the framed sketch of the woman and baby. "Is that your mother?" he asked, pointing to it.

That appeared to unsettle her.

"Yes," she murmured, looking quickly away from the sketch.

"She's very much like you. Her name was Patricia, wasn't it?"

Mirielle nodded.

"It's a terrible thing," he said, "for a woman so lovely to be taken before her time. How did she drown?"

"Don't you know how to talk without interrogating people?" she asked angrily.

"I'm sorry," he said, wondering at the vehemence of her reaction. "I just…"

"My mother's dead," she said. "Let that be enough for you."

"I was only making conversation. You choose the subject, all right?"

"All right," she said after a moment. "Let's talk about you."

"There's not much to tell."

"There never is with people, but that's all right. I won't be bored, I promise."

He began, reluctantly at first, to talk about his life, his childhood, the tiny farm in the hills above the city, with its banana grove, its corral and three cows—Rose, Alvina, and Esmeralda—and as he spoke, that old innocent life seemed to be resurrected, to be breathing just beyond the apartment walls. He told her how he used to sit on a hilltop and look down at the city and dream of owning one of the fine houses.

"And now you do," she said.

"No, I don't. There's a law against it. The fine houses belong to those with status, with history on their side. There are laws against people like me, laws that keep us in our place."

"Of course," she said. "I know that."

He told her about his first interest in the law, how it had seemed in its logical construction and order to be a lever with which one could move any obstruction, but how he had discovered that there were so many levers and obstructions, when you moved one, another would drop down to crush you, and the trick was to keep in constant motion, to be moving things constantly and dancing out of the way.

"Did you always want to be a lawyer?"

He laughed. "No, my first ambition was to be the man who slew the dragon Griaule, to claim the reward offered in Teocinte, to buy my mother silver bowls and my father a new guitar."

Her expression, happy a moment before, had gone slack and distraught; he asked if she was all right.

"Don't even say his name," she said. "You don't know, you don't know…"

"What don't I know?"

"Griaule…God! I used to feel him in the temple. Perhaps you think that's just my imagination, but I swear it's true. We all concentrated on him, we sang to him, we believed in him, we conjured him in our thoughts, and soon we could feel him. Cold and vast. Inhuman. This great scaly chill that owned a world."

Korrogly was struck by the similarity of phrasing with which the old woman Kirin and now Mirielle had referred to their apprehension of Griaule, and thought to make mention of it, but Mirielle continued speaking, and he let the matter drop.

"I can still feel his touch in my mind. Heavy and steeped in blackness. Each one of his thoughts a century in forming, a tonnage of hatred, of sheer enmity. He'd brush against me, and I'd be cold for hours. That's why…"

"What?"

"Nothing." She was trembling violently, hugging herself.

He crossed to the sofa, sat beside her, and, after hesitating for a few seconds, draped an arm about her shoulder. Her hair had the smell of fresh oranges. "What is it?" he asked.

"I can feel him still, I'll always feel him." She glanced up at Korrogly and then blurted out, "Come to bed with me. I know you don't like me, but it's warmth I want, not affection. Please, I won't…"

"I do like you," he said.

"No, you can't, you…no."

"I do," he said, believing it as he spoke. "Tonight I like you, tonight you're someone it's possible to care about."

"You don't understand, you can't see how he's changed me."

"Griaule, you mean?"

"Please," she said, her arms going around his waist. "No more questions…not now. Please, just keep me warm."

Three

AS KORROGLY BEGAN HIS OPENING statement, half his mind was back in the gemcutter's apartment with Mirielle, still embraced by her white arms, nourished by the rosy points of her breasts and her long supple legs, finding that beneath her veneer of depravity there existed a woman of virtue and sweetness, replaying in memory the joys of mastery and submission. None of this posed a distraction, but acted rather to inspire him, to urge him on to a more impassioned appeal than that he had originally contrived. Strolling alongside the jury box, stuffed with twelve pasty-faced models of good citizenship culled from an assortment of less worthy souls, he felt like a sea captain striding the deck of his ship, and the courtroom, it struck him, was essentially a cross between church and vessel, the ship of state sailing toward the coast of justice, with white walls for sails and boxy divisions of black wood holding a cargo of witnesses and jurors and the curious, and lording over all, the judge's bench, an immense teak block carved into the semblance of dragon scales, where sat the oracular figurehead of this magical ship: the Honorable Ernest Wymer, white-haired and florid, an alcoholic old beast with a cruel mouth and tufted brows and a shiny red beak, hunched in the folds of his black-winged gown, ready to pounce upon any lawyerly mouse that should happen to stray into his field of vision. Korrogly was not afraid of Wymer; he, not the judge, was in command this day. He knew the jury's mind, knew that they wanted to believe Griaule was the guilty party, that this suited the mystical yearning of their hearts, and with all his wiles, he set about consolidating that yearning into intent. There was urgency in his voice, yet it was neither too strident nor too subdued, perfect, a blend of power and fluency; he felt that this harmony of intent and skill stemmed from his night with Mirielle. He was not in love with her, or perhaps he was...but love was not the salient matter. What most inspired him was to have found something unspoiled in her, in himself, and whether that was love or merely a place left untouched by the world, it was sufficient to renew his old enthusiasms.

"We are all aware," he said toward the conclusion of his statement, "that Griaule's power exists. The question remains, is he capable of reaching out from the Carbonales to touch us here in Port Chantay. That is a question we should not need ask. Look there." He pointed to the judge's bench and its carved scales. "And there." He pointed to crude representations of the dragon carved twining the lintel posts at the back of the hall. "His image is everywhere in Port Chantay, and this is emblematic of his propinquity, of the tendrils of his will that have infiltrated our lives. Perhaps he cannot move us with the facility that he does those who dwell in Teocinte, but we are not so far beyond the range of his thoughts that he does not know us. He knows us well. He sees us, he holds us in his mind, and if he requires something of us, do you really believe he is incapable of affecting our lives in a more pronounced fashion? Griaule is, if anything, capable. He is an immortal, unfathomable creature who is as pervasive in our lives as the idea of God. And as with God, we do not have the wisdom to establish the limits of his capacities." Korrogly paused, letting his gaze fall on each of their rapt faces in turn, seeing therein a measure of anxiety, understanding how to play upon it; the slants of winter sunlight made them all look wan and sickly, like terminal patients hopeful of a cure. "Griaule is here, ladies and gentlemen of the jury. He is watching this proceeding. Perhaps he is even involved in it. Search inside yourselves. Can you feel secure that his eye is not upon you? And this"—he picked up The Father of Stones from the prosecution table—"can you be sure that this is not his eye? The prosecution will tell you that it is only a stone, but I tell you that it is much more." He held it up to their faces as he passed along the jury box and was pleased to see them shrink from it. "This is Griaule's instrument, the embodiment of his will, the vehicle by which his will has been effected here in Port Chantay, miles and miles beyond the range of his usual sphere of influence. If you doubt this, if you doubt that he could have formed it and injected it with the complex values of his wish and need, then I urge you to touch it. It brims with his cold vigor. And just as you now perceive it, so it is perceiving you."

THE FATHER OF STONES

The prosecution's case was elementary. A constable testified to the authenticity of Lemos' confession; several witnesses were called to testify to the fact that they had seen him working at cutting The Father of Stones; the old drunkard related his story of Lemos throwing stones on the beach; others claimed to have seen him breaking into the temple. Korrogly limited his cross-examination to establishing the point that none of the witnesses had known the gemcutter's mind. No more was needed. The defense would rise or fall on its own merits.

Late in the day, Mirielle was called to the stand. Her testimony, while not as embittered as Korrogly had assumed it would be, was nonetheless of great benefit to Lemos; it was obvious that she was of two minds about her father, that she despised him, and that this attitude warred with the guilt that arose from testifying against him—that she should be in the least guilty implied that Lemos must have been a good parent, that her spite was doubtless a product of Zemaille's corrupting influence. It was also evident that she was not being entirely forthcoming. She denied knowledge of Zemaille's great work, and there was—Korrogly was certain—something else that she was keeping from the light. In his cross-examination he touched upon it, establishing the area of vagueness, one having to do with her reasons for entering the temple.

"I'm not quite clear on this," he said to her. "Surely you didn't enter into such a dark society on a whim?"

"It was years ago," she said. "Perhaps it was a whim, perhaps I simply wanted to escape my father."

"Yes," he said, "your father, who simply wanted to spare you the violent excesses of the temple. Truly, that was overly severe of him."

Mervale leaped to his feet. "If the defense wishes to frame his lectoral remarks in a question, I suggest he do it."

"I agree," said Judge Wymer, with a cautionary nod to Korrogly.

"Your pardon." Korrogly inclined his head in a respectful bow. "The temple," he went on musingly, "what attracted you to it? Was it Zemaille?"

"I don't know...yes, I think so."

"A physical attraction?"

"It was more complex than that."

"How so?"

Her face worked, she worried her lower lip. "I don't know how to answer that."

"Why not? It's a simple question."

"Nothing is simple!" she said, her voice growing shrill. "You couldn't possibly understand!"

Korrogly wondered if she might be restraining herself from speaking of her father's alleged abuse—he was not afraid of the topic, yet he did not want to break her down into tears and that seemed a likelihood. He would not have minded rage; but he did not wish to make her in any way an object of sympathy. He could, he knew, always recall her.

Questioning her, even though her adversary, he felt that a strange connection had been forged between them, as if they were partners in a plot, and it was difficult to maintain a professional distance; she looked beautiful in her lacy black dress, and standing beside the witness box, inhaling her scent of heat and oranges, he began to believe that his feelings for her did run deep, that something powerful had been dredged up from beneath the years of disappointment and failure.

The close of Mirielle's testimony was also the close of the prosecution's case, and Judge Wymer called for a recess until the morning. Lemos, as he had throughout the proceeding, sat without displaying any emotion—a gray statement of despair—and nothing Korrogly could say had a cheering effect upon him. He had been given a haircut in jail, his sandy forelock trimmed away, his ears left totally exposed, and this, along with his loss of weight and increased pallor, made him look as if he had been the victim of a prolonged and dehumanizing abuse.

"It's going well," Korrogly told him as they sat at the defense table afterward. "Before today I wasn't sure how the jury would react to our tactics, I was concerned that we didn't have sufficient detail. But now I don't know if we'll need it. They want to believe you."

Lemos grunted, traced an imperfection in the wood of the table with his forefinger.

"Still, it would help a great deal if we could present a reason that would explain why Griaule wanted Zemaille dead," Korrogly went on.

"Mirielle," Lemos said, "she didn't seem to be as distant from me today as before. I wonder, could you ask her again to visit me?"

Korrogly felt a rippling of guilt. "Yes, I'll ask her tonight."

"Tonight?" Lemos looked askance at him.

"Yes," said Korrogly, hurrying to cover the slip, "I'll make a special trip to see her. I want you to see her, I'm in favor of anything that'll wake you up. You're on trial for your life, man!"

"I know that."

"You don't much act like you do. I'll ask Mirielle to see you, but my advice is to forget about her for the time being, concentrate on the trial. Once you're free, then you can repair the relationship."

Lemos blinked, gazed out the window at the reddening western sky. "All right," he said listlessly.

Frustrated, Korrogly began packing up his papers.

"I know," Lemos said.

"What?" Korrogly asked, preoccupied.

"I know about you and Mirielle. I've always been able to tell who she was bedding. She looks at them differently."

"Don't be ridiculous! I…"

"I know!" said Lemos, suddenly energized, turning a bright stare on him. "I'm not a fool!"

Korrogly, taken aback, began to wonder if Mirielle's veiled accusations of parental lust might have had substance, "Even if I were…"

"I don't want you to see her like that!" Lemos gripped the edge of the table. "I want you to stop!"

"We'll talk more after you've calmed down."

"I won't have it! Ever since she's been old enough, men like you have taken advantage of her. This time…"

Korrogly slammed his case shut. "Now listen to me! Do you want to die? Because if you do, alienating your lawyer's a fine first step. I promise you, if you don't stop this right now, I'll start treating your case with the same lack of concern you've shown toward it. You don't seem to care very much about living…or maybe that's just an act. If it is an act, I caution you to be temperate with me."

Lemos sank back into his chair, looking defeated, and Korrogly felt he had at last penetrated the man's mask. The gemcutter did care about his fate; his pose of unconcern was a fake, his entire story a lie. Which made

Korrogly an accomplice. He could back out of the case, he thought, claiming to have stumbled upon new information; but given Judge Wymer's hostility toward the defense, it might be that charges would be brought against him in any event. And he could not be sure of the matter; there was nothing sure in this case. He had become so confused by the conflicting flows of evidence that he was unable to trust his own judgments. Lemos' perverse desire for his daughter—if that, too, was not a fraud—might have enlivened him sufficiently to react to his peril.

After the guard had led Lemos back to his cell, Korrogly walked slowly through the twilight across town toward the Almintra quarter, ignoring the bustle of the evening traffic; his mind was in a turmoil, the greater part of his agitation caused not by the snarls of the case, but by the fact that he had threatened to turn against a client. It was the final tattering of his ideals, the ultimate violation of his contract with the law. How could he have done it, he thought. Was it Mirielle, her influence? No, he could not blame her—blame attached only to himself. The sole course open to him was to defend the gemcutter from this point forward to the best of his abilities, his guilt or innocence notwithstanding. And he would have to break it off with Mirielle; he could not in good faith continue to upset Lemos. It had been a long time since he had felt so at ease with a woman. But he would do it nevertheless, he told himself; he would not allow this case to become a drain down which the last of his conscience flowed.

When he reached the gemcutter's apartment, however, his resolve went glimmering. Mirielle was even more ardent than she had been the previous night; it was not until much later that Korrogly thought of Lemos again, and then it was only in passing, produced by a flicker of remorse. Mirielle was lying on her side, one leg flung across his hip, still joined to him; her breasts were small and white, glowing in the misted light from the streetlamps with the milky purity of The Father of Stones; beneath the skin, faint blue veins forked upward to vanish in the hollow of her throat. He traced their path with his tongue, making her breath come fast; he cupped her buttocks with his hands, holding her against him while his hips moved with sinuous insistence. Her nails pricked his back, the rhythm of her own movements quickened, and then she let out the last best part of her feeling in a hoarse cry.

"God!" she said. "God, you feel so good!" And without thinking of what he was saying, he told her that he loved her.

A shadow seemed to cross her face, "Don't say that."

"What's wrong?"

"Just don't say it."

"I'm afraid it's true," he said. "I don't have much choice."

"You don't know me, you don't know the things I've done."

"With Zemaille?"

"I had sex with other people, with whomever Mardo wanted me to. I did things..." She closed her eyes. "It wasn't so much what I did, it's that I stood by while Mardo..." She broke off, buried her face in the join of his neck and shoulder. "God, I don't want to tell you any of this."

"It doesn't matter, anyway."

"It does," she said. "You can't go through what I have and come out a whole person. You may think you love me, but..."

"How do you feel about me?"

"Don't expect me to say I love you."

"I'm not expecting anything more than the truth."

"Oh!" She laughed. "Is that all? If I knew the truth, things would be much easier."

"I don't understand what you mean."

"Look." She took his face in both hands. "Don't make me say anything. It's good between us, it helps. Sometimes I want to say things to you, but I'm not ready. I hope I will be someday, but if you force me to say anything now...I'm perverse that way. I'll just try to deny it to myself. That's what I've been taught to do with things that make me happy."

"That says enough."

"Does it? I hope so."

He kissed her mouth, touched her breasts, feeling the nipples stiffen between his spread fingers.

"There's something I'd like you to do for me, though. I want you to visit your father."

She turned away from him. "I can't."

"Because he...he abused you?"

"What do you think?"

LUCIUS SHEPARD

"I think there's some evidence you were abused by him."

"Abused," she said, enunciating the word precisely as if judging its flavor; then, after a moment, she added, "I can't talk about it, I've never been able to talk about it. I just can't bring myself to...to say what happened."

"Well?" he said. "Will you see him?"

"It wouldn't do any good, it wouldn't make him any happier. And that's what you're after, isn't it."

"That's one way of putting it."

"A visit would just upset him, believe me."

"I suppose I'll have to," he said. "I can't force you. I just wish I could get him more involved."

"You still think he's innocent, don't you?"

"I'm not sure...perhaps. I don't think you're sure, either."

She looked as if she were going to respond, but her mouth thinned and she remained silent for a long moment. Finally she said, "I'm sure."

He started to say something, and she put a finger to his lips.

"Don't talk about it anymore, please."

He lay on his back, watching frail shadows of the mist coiling across the white ceiling, thinking about Lemos; he could accept nothing, believe nothing. That the gemcutter had molested his daughter seemed both apparent and unlikely, as was the case with his guilt and innocence. He did not doubt that Mirielle believed her father had abused her; but while he loved her, he was not assured of her stability, and thus her beliefs were in question. And in question also were her motives in being with him. He found it difficult to accept that she was anything but sincere in her responses; her reluctance to voice a commitment seemed clear evidence of the inner turmoil he was causing her. Still, he could not wholly reject the notion that she was using him... though for what reason he had no idea. He was walking across quicksand, in shadows, with inarticulate voices calling to him from every direction.

"You're worrying about something," she said. "Don't...it'll be all right."

"Between us?"

"Is that what you're worrying about?"

"Among other things."

"I can't promise you that you'll like what will happen," she said. "But I will try with you."

He started to ask her why she was going to try, what she had found that would make her want something with him; but he reminded himself of her caution against pushing her.

"You're still worrying," she said.

"I can't stop."

"Yes, you can." Her hand slid down across his chest, his belly, kindling a slow warmth. "That much I can promise."

AGAINST KORROGLY'S OBJECTIONS, the case for the prosecution was reopened the following morning and Mirielle recalled to the stand. Mervale offered into evidence a sheaf of legal documents, which proved to have been signed by Mardo Zemaille and witnessed by Mirielle, and constituted a last will and testament, deeding the temple and its grounds to Mirielle on the event of the priest's death. Mervale had unearthed the papers from the city archives and produced ample evidence to substantiate that the signatures were authentic and that the papers were legal.

"How much would you say the properties mentioned in the will are worth?" Mervale asked Mirielle, who was wearing a high-collared dress of blue velvet.

"I have no idea."

"Would it be inaccurate to say that they're worth quite a large sum of money? A sizeable fortune?"

"The witness has already answered the question," said Korrogly.

"Indeed she has," said Judge Wymer, with a stern look at Mervale, who shrugged, stepped to the prosecution table, and offered into evidence the tax assessor's report on the properties.

"Did your father know of this will?" Mervale asked after the exhibits had been marked.

Mirielle murmured, "Yes."

Korrogly glanced at Lemos, who appeared not to be listening.

"And how did he come to know about them?"

"I told him."

"On what occasion?"

"He came to the temple." She drew in breath sharply, let it out slowly, as if ordering herself. "He wanted me to leave the cult, he said that once Mardo tired of me he would drop me and then the family would be without a penny. The shop would be gone...everything." She drew in another breath. "He made me angry. I told him about the will, I said that Mardo had taken care of me far better than he had. And he said that he'd have me declared incompetent. He said he'd get a lawyer and take everything Mardo left me."

"Do you know if he ever did see a lawyer?"

"Yes, he did.

"And was that lawyer's name Artis Colari?"

"Yes."

Mervale picked up more papers from his table. "Mister Colari is currently trying another case and cannot attend this proceeding. However, I have here a deposition wherein he states that he was approached by the defendant two weeks before the murder with the intent of having his daughter declared mentally incompetent for reasons of instability caused by her abuse of drugs." He smiled at Korrogly. "Your witness."

Korrogly requested a consultation with his client, and once they were sequestered he asked Lemos, "Did you know about the will?"

A nod. "But that wasn't why I went to see Colari. I didn't care about the money, I didn't want anything that Zemaille had touched. I was afraid for Mirielle. I wanted her out of that place, and I thought the only way I could manage that was to have her declared incompetent."

The uncharacteristic passion with which he had spoken startled Korrogly: it was the first sign of vitality that Lemos had displayed since his arrest.

"Why didn't you tell me this before?"

"I didn't think of it."

"It seems an odd thing to have forgotten."

"It wasn't so much that I forgot...Look." Lemos sat up straight, absentmindedly putting his hand to his brow. "I realize I've given you a hard time, but I...it's been...I can't explain what it's been like for me. I didn't think you believed my story. I'm still not sure you do. And that's just added to the despair I've been feeling. I'm sorry, I know I should have been more cooperative."

Despite his prison haircut and coverall, his unhealthy complexion, Lemos seemed the picture of eager contrition, boyish in his renewed vigor, and Korrogly did not know whether to be pleased or disgusted. Incredible, he thought, more than incredible, the man was impossible to believe, except that somehow his very implausibility seemed believable. As for Mirielle, how could she have hidden this from him? What did that signal as to their relationship? Was her hatred for her father such a powerful taint that it could abrogate all other rules? Had he misjudged her in every way?

"It doesn't look good, does it?" Lemos said.

Korrogly resisted the temptation to laugh. "We still have our witnesses, and I'm not going to let Mirielle's testimony go unchallenged."

"What are you going to do?"

"Try to overcome the effects of your despondency," said Korrogly. "Come on."

Once back in the courtroom, Korrogly took a turn around the witness box, studying Mirielle, who appeared nervous, picking at the seams of her dress, and at last he said, "Why do you hate your father?"

She looked surprised.

"It's not a difficult question," Korrogly said. "It's obvious to everyone here that you want him found guilty."

"Objection!" Mervale shrilled.

Judge Wymer said, "Limit yourself to proper questions, Mister Korrogly."

Korrogly nodded. "Why do you hate your father?"

"Because…" Mirielle stared at him, pleading with her eyes. "Because…"

"Is it because you consider him a restrictive parent?"

"Yes."

"Because he tried to separate you and your lover?"

"Yes."

"Because you feel he is contemptible in the stodginess and staleness of his life?"

"Yes."

"And can we assume you have other reasons yet for hating him?"

"Yes!" she cried. "Yes! What are you doing?"

"I'm establishing that you hate your father, Miss Lemos. That you hate him with sufficient passion to attempt to turn this trial into a melodrama so as to guarantee his conviction. That you've hidden evidence from the court so that it could be produced at a particularly theatrical moment. Perhaps you've had help in this from the theatrical Mister Mervale…"

"Objection!"

"Mister Korrogly!" said Judge Wymer.

"…but whatever the case, you most certainly have been duplicitous in your testimony…"

"Mister Korrogly!"

"Duplicitous in your intent, in your every action before this court!"

"Mister Korrogly! If you don't stop this immediately…"

"I apologize, Your Honor."

"You're on thin ice, Mister Korrogly. I won't permit another such outburst."

"I can assure you, Your Honor, it won't happen again." He walked over to the jury box, leaned against it, hoping to ally himself thereby with the jurors, to make it seem that he was asking their questions. "Miss Lemos, you knew of the will prior to this morning…correct?"

"Yes."

"Did you make mention of it to the prosecutor?"

"Yes."

"When did you mention it to him?"

"Yesterday afternoon."

"Why not before? Surely you must have recognized its importance."

"I…it slipped my mind, I guess."

"It slipped your mind," said Korrogly, injecting heavy sarcasm into his tone. "You guess." He turned to the jury, shook his head ruefully. "Is there anything else you have forgotten to mention?"

"Objection!"

"Overruled. The witness will answer."

"I…no."

"I hope not for your sake," Korrogly said. "Did your father ever tell you that the reason he wanted to declare you incompetent was to remove you from the temple, to prevent you from being destroyed by Zemaille?"

"Oh, he said that, but..."

"Just answer the question Yes or No."

"Yes."

"This will," said Korrogly, "you knew its contents...I mean you were versed in its contents, you knew its exact particulars."

"Yes, of course."

"Now the conversation during which you told your father about the will, it was, I take it, rather heated, was it not?"

"Yes."

"And so in the midst of a heated conversation, a violent argument, if you will, you had the presence of mind to inform your father of the contents of a most complicated document. I assume you filled him in on every detail."

"Well, no, not everything."

"Oh!" Korrogly arched an eyebrow. "What exactly did you tell him?"

"I...I can't recall. Not exactly."

"Now let me get this straight, Miss Lemos. You remember telling him about the will, but you can't recall if you informed him of its contents. It is possible then that you merely blurted out something to the effect that Mardo had seen to your future?"

"No, I..."

"Or did you say..."

"He knew what it meant!" she shouted, standing up in the box. "He knew!" She stared with fierce loathing at Lemos. "He killed him for the money! But he'll never..."

"Sit down, Miss Lemos!" said Judge Wymer. "Now!" Once she had obeyed, he warned her in no uncertain terms to restrain her behavior.

"So," Korrogly went on, "in the midst of an argument you blurted out some incoherent..."

"Objection!"

"Sustained."

"You blurted out something, you can't recall exactly what, about the will. Is that a fair statement?"

"You're twisting my words!"

"On the contrary, Miss Lemos, I'm simply repeating what you've said. It appears that the only persons who were absolutely clear as to the contents of the will were you and Mardo Zemaille."

"No, that's…"

"That wasn't a question, Miss Lemos. Merely the preamble to one. Since you are likely to benefit greatly from your father's conviction, since that will in effect prevented him from initiating a competency hearing, doesn't that color your testimony the color of greed?"

"I never wanted anything except Mardo."

"I believe everyone within earshot will second your characterization of Mardo Zemaille as a thing."

"No need to object, Mister Mervale," said Judge Wymer; then, to Korrogly: "I've given you a great deal of leeway. That leeway is now at end. Do you understand me?"

"Yes, Your Honor." Korrogly crossed to the defense table, picked up some of his notes, and leafing through them, walked to the witness box and stood facing Mirielle; her face was tight with anger. "Did you believe in Mardo Zemaille, Miss Lemos?"

"I don't know what you mean."

"I mean did you believe in what he said, in his public statements, in his theological doctrines? In his work?"

"Yes."

"What was his work? His great work?"

"I don't know…nobody except Mardo knew."

"Yet you believed in it?"

"I believed that Mardo was inspired."

"Inspired…I see. Then you accepted his precepts as being the code by which you lived."

"Yes."

"Then it would be illuminating to examine some of those precepts, might it not?"

"I don't know."

"Oh, I think it would." Korrogly turned a page. "Ah, here we are." He read from his notes. "'Do what thou wilt, that is all the law.' Did you believe that?"

"I...yes, I did."

"Hmmm. And this, did you believe this? 'If blood is needed for the great work, blood will be provided.'"

"I don't...I never knew what he meant by that."

"Really? But you accepted it, did you not, as part of his inspired doctrine?"

"I suppose."

"And this? 'No crime, no sin, no breach of the rules of what is considered ordinary human conduct, shall be considered such so long as it serves the great work.'"

She nodded. "Yes."

"And I assume that included under the label of sin would be the sin of lying?"

Her stare was hard and bright.

"Do you understand the question?"

"Yes."

"Well?"

"Yes, I suppose. But..."

"And included under the label of crime would be the crime of perjury?"

"Yes, but I no longer hold to those beliefs."

"Don't you? You've been heard recently to characterize Mardo Zemaille as a paragon."

Her mouth thinned. "Things have changed."

Korrogly knew he was invading dangerous territory, that she might make specific reference to the changes he had brought to her life; but he thought he could make his point and clear out before damage was done.

"I submit that things have not changed, Miss Lemos. I submit that the great work, whatever its nature, will go on under your aegis. I submit that all the miscreant rules attaching to that work still hold, and that you would tell any lie, commit any..."

"You bastard!" she cried. "I'll..."

The courtroom was filled with babble, Mervale was objecting, Wymer pounding his gavel.

"And commit any crime," Korrogly went on, "in order to assure its continuance. I submit that the great work is your sole concern, and the truth is the farthest thing from your mind."

"You can't do this!" she shrilled. "You can't come to my..."

Judge Wymer's bellow drowned her out.

"No further questions," said Korrogly, watching with mixed emotions as the bailiffs led her, still shouting, from the courtroom.

Shortly after beginning the examination of the first witness for the defense, the historian and biologist Catherine Ocoi, a striking blond woman in her late thirties, Korrogly was summoned to the bench for a whispered conversation with Judge Wymer. The judge leaned over the bench, pointing at the various displays that Catherine had brought with her, indicating with particular emphasis the huge painting of the mountainous dragon set beside the defense table.

"I warned you not to turn this into a circus," he said.

"I scarcely think that displaying Griaule's image..."

"Your opening statement was a masterpiece of intimidation," said Wymer. "I didn't censure you for it, but from now on I will not allow you to intimidate the jury. I want that painting removed."

Korrogly started to object, but then saw virtue in having it done; that it was deemed important enough to be removed only gave added weight to his thesis.

"As you wish," he said.

"Be careful, Mister Korrogly," Wymer said. "Be very careful."

As the painting was carried out, the jury's eyes followed it, and once the painting was out of sight, they expressed a visible degree of relief. That relief, Korrogly thought, might be more valuable than the oppressive presence of the painting; he would be able to play them, to remind them of Griaule, to let them swing between relief and anxiety, and so exercise all the more control.

He led Catherine Ocoi through her testimony, the story of how she had been manipulated by Griaule to live inside the dragon for ten years, the sole purpose being for her to oversee a single event of Griaule's internal economy; then he let her testify as to the marvels to be found within the dragon, the drugs she had distilled from his various secretions, the strange and in some instances miraculous parasites and plants that flourished there. She had no knowledge of The Father of Stones, but the wonders to which she was able to testify left little doubt in the jury's mind that the stone could have been produced by Griaule. Her exhibits—every one of them taken from the interior of the dragon—included a glass case filled with spiders in whose webs could be seen all manner of fantastic imagery; cuttings of a most unusual plant that was capable of creating replicas of the animals who fell asleep in its coils; and most pertinently, nodes of an amber material, very like a mineral form, which she claimed was produced by the petrification of Griaule's stomach acid.

"I have no doubt," she said, "that Griaule could have produced this." She held up The Father of Stones. "And touching it now, I know it is of Griaule. I had ten years to become intimately familiar with the feeling that attaches to his every element, and this stone is his."

There was little Mervale could do to weaken her testimony: Catherine Ocoi's reputation was above reproach, her story and discoveries celebrated throughout the region. However, with the witnesses that followed, philosophers and priests, all of whom presented opinions concerning on Griaule's capacity for manipulation, Mervale was not so gentle; he railed and ranted, accusing the witnesses of wild speculation and Korrogly of debasing the legal process.

"This does seem to be degenerating into something of a metaphysical debate," said Wymer after calling the attorneys for consultation at the bench.

"Metaphysical?" said Korrogly. "Perhaps, but no more so than the debate that underlies any fundamental point of law. Our laws are founded upon a moral code which comes down to us through the tenets of religious faith. Is that not metaphysics? Metaphysics are rendered into law based upon a consensus moral view, the view nourished by religion and commonly held in our society as to what is right and appropriate as regards the limitations that should be placed upon men in their behavior. What I'm establishing first and foremost is that there is a consensus regarding the fact of Griaule's influence. I could go out into the street and not find a single person who doesn't believe to some degree or another in Griaule. That kind of unanimity can't even be found as relates to a belief in God."

"This is ridiculous!" said Mervale.

"Secondly," Korrogly continued, "I'm establishing through expert testimony the consensus regarding the extent of Griaule's influence, the range and limitations of his will. This is simple foundation. Essential to any decision regarding the validity not only of my client's claim to innocence, but also to the validity of the precedent. If you disallow it, you disallow the plea. And since you have already allowed the plea, you'll have to allow foundation to support it."

Wymer appeared to be absorbing all this; he glanced inquiringly at Mervale, who sighed.

"All right," he said, "I'm willing in the interests of brevity to stipulate that Griaule's influence exists, that it is…"

"I'm afraid the interests of brevity are not altogether congruent with those of my client," said Korrogly. "In order for precedent to be established, I wish to lay a proper foundation. I intend to make the jury aware of the history of Griaule and his various acts of influence. I think it's absolutely essential they have a complete understanding of his subtlety in order to arrive at an equitable judgment."

Wymer heaved a sigh. "Mister Mervale?"

Mervale's mouth opened and closed; then he threw up his hands and stalked back to the prosecution table.

"Carry on, Mister Korrogly," said Wymer. "But let's try to keep the floorshow to a minimum, shall we? I doubt that anything you produce here is going to outweigh the evidence of the will, and there's no point in wasting time."

It came to be late in the day, but Korrogly did not ask for a recess; he wanted Lemos to tell his story, to give the jury a night to let it sink in, before exposing him to cross-examination. He conducted Lemos through some background testimony, allowing him to get a feel for the witness stand and the jury and then asked him to tell in his own words what had happened after he had bought The Father of Stones from Henry Sichi.

Lemos wet his lips, gazed down at the rail of the witness box, sighed, and then, meeting the jury's eyes as he had been coached, said, "I remember

THE FATHER OF STONES

I was in a great hurry to get home with the stone. I didn't know why at the time, I just knew I wanted to examine it more closely. When I reached the shop, I went to my workbench and sat with it awhile. The part you see now was gripped by what appeared to be claws of corroded-looking orange material, whose color came away on my fingers; it was flaky, soft, rather like old wood or some other organic matter. As for the stone itself, I couldn't tear my eyes away from it. Its clouded surface seemed so lovely, so mysterious. I became certain that an even greater beauty was trapped within it, beauty I knew I could unlock. Usually I will not cut a stone until I have lived with it for weeks, sometimes months. But I was in a kind of trance, invested with a strange confidence that I knew this stone, that I had known it always, that its internal structures were as familiar as the patterns of my thoughts. I cleaned off the orange material, then clamped the stone in a vise, put on my goggles and began to cut it.

"With each blow of my chisel, light seemed to fracture within the stone, to spray forth in beams that penetrated my eyes, and these beams acted to strike sprays of images from my brain, as if it too were a gemstone in process of being cut. The first image was of Griaule, not as he is now, but vital, spitting fire toward a tiny man in a wizard's robes, a lean, swarthy man with a blade of a nose. There followed another image that depicted both dragon and man immobilized as a result of that battle. Then other images came, too rapidly for me to catalogue. My mind was alive with light, and the ringing in my ears was the music of light, and I knew with every fiber of my being that I was cutting one of the great gems. I would call it The Father of Stones, I thought, because it would be the archetype of mineral beauty. But when at last I set down my chisel and considered what I'd done, I was more than a little disappointed. The stone was flashy, full of glint and sparkle, but had no depth and subtlety of color. Indeed, it appeared to have a hollow center. Except for its weight, it might have been an intricate piece of blown glass.

"I was distressed that I'd wasted money on the thing. I couldn't imagine what I'd been thinking—I should have realized it was worthless, I told myself. The shop was already in danger of going under, and I'd had no business in making the purchase under any circumstance. Finally I decided to present the stone to Zemaille. He'd been harrassing me to come up with something unusual for one of his rituals, and perhaps, I thought, he would allow the superficial brilliance of the stone to blind him to its worthlessness. And I also hoped I might get the chance to see Mirielle. I wrapped the stone in a velvet cloth and hurried toward the temple, but when I reached it I found the gates locked. I knocked again and again, but no one responded. I've never considered myself an intemperate man; however, being locked out after having walked all that way, it seemed a terrible affront. I paced up and down in front of the gates, stopping now and again to shout, my anger building into a towering frustration. Finally, unable to contain my rage, I set about climbing the temple walls, using the creepers that grew upon them for handholds. I pushed my way through the garden—if such noxious growths as flourish there can be called such—becoming even more angry, and when I heard chanting coming from a building that stood at a corner of the compound, I rushed toward it, so angry now that I intended to fling the stone at Zemaille's feet, to cast a scornful look at Mirielle, and then storm out, leaving them to their perversions. But once inside the building, my anger was muted by the barbarity of the scene that met my eyes. The chamber into which I'd entered was pentagonal in shape, enclosed by screens of carved ebony. The floor was carpeted in black moss and declined into a pit where lay an altar of black stone worked with representations of Griaule. It was flanked by torches held in wrought-iron stands of grotesque design. Zemaille, robed in black and silver, was standing beside the altar—a swarthy hook-nosed man with his arms lifted in supplication, chanting in company with nine hooded figures who were ranged about the altar. Moments later, a door at the rear of the chamber opened, and Mirielle was led forth, naked except for a necklace of polished dragon scale. She was in an obvious state of intoxication, her head lolling, her eyes showing as crescents of white.

"I was so appalled at seeing my daughter in this pitiful condition that I was stunned, unable to act. It was as if the sight had ratified all the hopelessness of my life, and I think for awhile I believed that this was proper, that I deserved such a fate. I watched as Mirielle was stretched out on the altar, her head tossing about, incapable—it appeared—of knowing what was happening to her. The chanting grew louder, and Zemaille, lifting his arms higher, cried, 'Father! Soon you will be free!' Then he lapsed into a tongue with which I was unfamiliar.

THE FATHER OF STONES

"It was at this point that I sensed Griaule's presence. There was no great physical symptom or striking effect…except perhaps an intensification of the distance I felt from what I was seeing. I was absolutely unemotional, and that seems to me most peculiar, because I have never been unemotional where Mirielle is concerned. But I was nonetheless certain of his presence, and as I stood there overlooking the altar, I knew exactly what was going on and why it had to be stopped. This knowledge was nothing so simple as an awareness of my daughter's peril, it was the knowledge of something old and violent and mystic. I can still feel the shape it made in my brain, though the particulars have fled me.

"I stepped forward and called to Zemaille. He turned his head. It was strange…never before had he displayed any reaction to me other than disdain, but there was tremendous fear in his face then, as if he knew that Griaule and not me was his adversary. I swear before God it was not in my mind to kill him before that moment, but as I moved toward him I knew not only that I must kill him, but that I must act that very second. I'd forgotten the stone in my hand, but then, without thinking, without even making a conscious decision to act, I hurled it at him. It was an uncanny throw. I could not have been less than fifty feet away, and the stone struck with a terrible crack dead center of his forehead. He dropped without a cry."

Lemos lowered his head for a second, his grip tightening on the rail of the witness box. "I had expected that the nine gathered around the altar would attack me, but instead they ran out into the night. Perhaps they, too, sensed Griaule's hand in all this. I was horrified by what I'd done. As I've stated, the knowledge of what was intended by the act had fled, had flown from my brain, evaporated like a mist. I knew only that I had killed a man…a despicable man, but a man nonetheless. I went over to Zemaille, hoping that he might still be alive. The Father of Stones was lying beside him. Something about it had changed, I realized, and on picking it up I saw that the center was no longer hollow. At the heart of the stone was the flaw that you can see there now, a flaw in the shape of a man with uplifted arms." He leaned back and sighed. "The rest you know."

Mervale's cross-examination was thorough, incisive, yet if it had not been for the will, Korrogly thought after the day's proceedings had been concluded, he would have had an excellent chance to win an acquittal; the weight of the material evidence would not have impressed the jury any more than his witnesses and Lemos' account. But as things stood, the fact that Lemos could not put forward any reason why Griaule had wanted Zemaille dead, that seemed to Korrogly to tip the balance in favor of the prosecution. He stayed late at the courthouse, running over the details of the case in his mind, and finally, just after eleven o'clock, more frustrated than he had yet been, he packed up his papers and set out for the Almintra quarter, hoping that he could mend his fences with Mirielle; perhaps he could convince her of his good intentions, help her to understand that his responsibilities had demanded he treat her roughly.

By the time he reached the quarter, the streets were deserted and mist had sealed in the dilapidated houses from the beach, from the sky and the rest of the world, turning the streetlamps into fuzzy white blooms; the surf sounded sluggish, like slaps being delivered by an enormous hand, and the dampness of the air caused Korrogly to turn up his collar and hurry along, his footsteps scraping on the drifted sand. He caught a glimpse of his reflection in a shop window, a pale anxious man, clasping his coat shut with one hand, his brow furrowed, rushing through a glossy black medium…the medium of Griaule, he imagined it, the medium of guilt and innocence, of every human question. He walked faster, wanting to subsume his doubts in Mirielle's warmth. Up ahead, he made out an indistinct figure standing wreathed in mist. Just standing, but there was something ominous about its stillness. Idiot, he said to himself, and kept going. But as the figure grew more solid, his nervousness increased; it was wearing a cloak or a robe of some kind. He peered through the mist. A hooded robe. He stopped by an alley mouth, remembering Lemos' story and the nine hooded witnesses. Once again he told himself that he was being foolish, but he was unable to shake the feeling that the figure—no more than forty or fifty feet away— was waiting for him. He held his briefcase to his chest, took a few tentative steps forward. The figure remained motionless.

There was no point, Korrogly thought, in taking chances. He backed toward the alley mouth, keeping his eyes on the figure, then bolted down the alley; he stopped at the end of it, on the margin of the beach, and, hidden behind a pile of rotted boards, gazed back toward the street. A moment later, the figure appeared at the alley mouth and began walking down it.

Icy cold flowed down Korrogly's spine, his testicles shriveled, his legs felt trembly and weak. Clutching his case, he ran through the darkness, slipping in the soft sand, stumbling, nearly falling across an overturned dory. He could see nothing, he might have been sprinting in the glossy darkness he had glimpsed within the shop window. Things came blooming suddenly out of the mist, visible in the faint glow from the windows of the houses—dead fish bones, a bucket, driftwood—and the erratic rhythm of the surf had the glutinous sound of huge laboring lungs.

He ran for several minutes, stopping for fractions of seconds to cast about for sign of pursuit, spinning about, jumping at every noise, peering into the misted blackness; at last he ran straight into what felt like a sticky thick spiderweb and fell tangled in its mesh. Panicked, he let out a strangled cry, tearing at the mesh, and it was only after he had freed himself that he discovered the web had been a fishing net hung on a wooden rack to dry. He began running again, making for the street, visible as a spectral white glow between houses. When he reached it, he found that he was less than a block from the gemcutter's shop. He sprinted toward it, fetching up against the door, gasping, bracing against it with one hand, catching his breath. Then a terrible shock, and pain lanced through his hand, drawing forth a scream; he saw to his horror that it had been pierced by a long-bladed dagger, whose handle—entwined with the image of a coiled dragon—was still quivering. Blood trickled from the wound, flowing down his wrist and forearm. Making little shrieks, he managed to pull the blade free; the accompanying surge of pain almost caused him to lose consciousness, but he managed to keep his feet, staring at the neat incision in his palm, at the blood welling forth. Then he glanced wildly along the misted street—there was no one in sight. He pounded on the door with his good hand and called to Mirielle. No answer. He pounded again, kept it up. What could be taking her so long? At last steps sounded on the stairs, and Mirielle called, "Who is it? Who's there?"

"It's me," he said, staring at his hand; the sight of the blood made him nauseated and dizzy. The wound throbbed, and he squeezed his wrist, trying to stifle the pain.

"Go away!"

"Help me!" he said. "Please, help me!"

The door swung inward.

He turned to Mirielle, suddenly weak and fading, holding up the injured hand as if it were something she could explain to him. Her face was a mask of shock; her lips were moving, but he could hear no sound. Then, without knowing how he had gotten there, he was lying on the sand, looking at her foot. He had never seen a foot from that particular angle, and he gazed at it from the perspective of a dazed aesthetic. Then the foot was replaced by a bare knee. Milky white. The same clouded color as that of The Father of Stones. Against that white backdrop he seemed to see the various witnesses, the evidence, all the confounding materials of the case, arrayed before him like the scenes that reportedly came to the eyes of a dying man, as if it were the case and not the details of his own life that were of most significance to him. Just as he passed out he believed that he was about to understand something important.

Four

BECAUSE OF HIS INJURY, KORROGLY was granted a day off from the trial, and since the following two days would be given over to a religious festival, he had nearly seventy-two hours in which to come up with some tactic or evidence that would save Lemos' life. He was not sure how to proceed, nor was he sure that he wanted to proceed. He had not been the only victim of the previous night; Kirin, the old woman he had interviewed prior to the trial, was missing, and a bloody dagger identical to the one that had pierced his hand had been found on her stoop. Apparently the members of the cult were seeking to assure Lemos' conviction by silencing everyone who could possibly help him.

He spent the first day going over his notes and was distressed to see how many avenues of investigation he had neglected; he had been so caught up with Mirielle, with all the complexities of the case, complexities that had led nowhere, he had failed to do much of what he normally would consider basic pretrial work. For example, apart from digging up character witnesses, he had done nothing by way of researching Lemos' background; he should, he realized, have checked into the gemcutter's marriage, the drowning of his wife, Mirielle's childhood, her friends...there were so many routine things that he should have done and had not, he could spend most of the next two days in merely listing them. He had intended to interview Kirin a second time, certain that the old woman had known more than she was saying; but his infatuation with Mirielle had caused him to forget that intent, and now the old woman was gone, her secrets with her.

After a day, a night and another day, he realized that he did not have sufficient time left to carry out further investigations, that he had been derelict in his duty to the court and to Lemos, and that—barring a miracle—his client was doomed. Oh, he could file an appeal. Then there would be time to investigate everything. But with precedent having been denied by a respected judge, he would have to present overwhelming proof of innocence in order to win an appeal, and given the nature of the case, such proof would likely not be forthcoming. Realizing this, he closed his notebooks, pushed aside his papers and sat brooding, gazing out the window of his study at Ayler Point and the twilit ocean. If he were to lean forward and crane his neck, he would be able to see the black pagoda roofs of the dragon cult standing up among palms and sea grape on the beach a few hundred yards beyond the point; but he had no desire to do so, to do anything that would remind him further of his failure. Lemos might well be guilty of the crime, but the fact remained that he had deserved a better defense than Korrogly had provided; even if he was a villain, he was not a great villain, certainly not as great a one as Mardo Zemaille had been.

It was a relatively clear night that fell over Port Chantay; the mists typical of the season failed to materialize, stars flickered between the pale masses of cloud that drove across the winded sky, and the lights of the houses picked out the toiling darkness along Ayler Point. White combers piled in toward the beach; then, as the tide receded, they were swept sideways to break on the end of the point. Korrogly watched them, feeling there was something instructive in the process, that he was learning something by watching; but if a lesson were being taught, he did not recognize it. He began to grow restless, and he thought with frustration and longing of Mirielle. At length he decided to go to *The Blind Lady* and have a drink…or maybe several drinks; but before he could set out for the tavern there came a knock at his door and a woman's voice called to him. Thinking it was Mirielle, he hurried to the door and flung it open; but the woman who faced him was much older than the gemcutter's daughter, her head cowled in a dark shawl, the lumpiness of her body evident beneath a loose jacket and skirt. He backed away a step, reminded by her shawl of the cowled figure who had attacked him.

"I've something for you," the woman said in a voice with a thick northern accent; she held out an envelope. "From Kirin."

He recognized her then for Kirin's servant, the drab who had admitted him to the old woman's house some weeks before. Heavy-breasted and thick-waisted, with features so stuporous that they looked masklike.

She pushed the envelope at him. "Kirin said I was to give this to you if anything happened to her."

Korrogly opened the envelope; inside were two ornate keys and an unsigned note.

> Mr. Korrogly,
>
> If you are reading this, you will know that I am dead. Perhaps you will not know by whose hand, though if you don't, then you're not the astute individual I reckon you to be.
>
> The keys open the outer gate of the temple and the door to Mardo's private apartment in the main building. If you wish to learn the nature of the great work, go with Janice to the temple as soon as you have received this. She will be helpful to you. You dare not wait longer, for it's possible that others will know what I know. Do not involve the police; there are cult members among them. The cult has become afraid of the temple, afraid of what has happened there, and most of them have no wish to come near the place. However, the fanatics will be anxious to protect Mardo's secrets.
>
> Once in Mardo's apartment, if you search carefully, I know you will find what you need to save your client.
>
> Be thorough, but be swift.

Korrogly folded the note and looked at Janice, who, in turn, regarded him with bovine stolidity; he could not for the life of him think how she would be helpful.

"Do you have a weapon?" she asked.

Ruefully, he showed her his bandaged hand.

"When we reach the temple," she said, "I'll take the lead. But keep close behind me."

He was about to ask how this would be an advantage, when she pulled a long knife from her jacket; the sight of it made him reconsider his options. This might be a trick, a trap set by the members of the cult.

"Why are you helping me?" he asked.

She looked perplexed. "Kirin asked it of me."

"You'd put yourself in danger simply because she asked?"

She continued staring at him for a long moment; at last she said, "I've no love for dragons." She tugged at her blouse, pulling the hem up from the waistband of her skirt, then turned away from him, exposing her naked back; the smooth pale skin below her shoulderblades had been branded by an iron in the shape of a coiled dragon; the flesh surrounding it was puckered and discolored.

"Zemaille did this to you?" asked Korrogly.

"And more."

Korrogly remained unconvinced; the more fanatical of the cult members might have adopted such mutilations as a fashion.

"Are you coming?" Janice asked, and when he hesitated, she said, "You're afraid of me, aren't you?"

"I'm wary of you," he said.

"I don't care if you come or not, but make up your mind quickly. If we are to go the temple, we need to make use of the cover of darkness."

She glanced about the room, then crossed to a table on which stood a decanter of brandy and glasses. She poured a glass and handed it to him.

"Courage," she said.

Shamed by this, he drank the brandy down; he poured a second and sipped it, considering the situation. He questioned Janice concerning her mistress, and though her answers were circumspect, he derived from them the sense of an old brave woman who had done her best to thwart the evil ambitions of Zemaille. That, too, shamed him. What kind of lawyer was he, he thought, to refuse to risk himself for his client? Perhaps it was the effects of the brandy, perhaps a product of the self-loathing he felt concerning his failure to provide Lemos with an adequate defense, but for whatever reason he soon began to feel brave and resolute, to perceive that unless he did his utmost now in Lemos' defense, he would never be able to practice his profession again.

"All right," he said finally, taking his cloak from its peg. "I'm ready."

He had expected Janice to be pleased, to approve of his decision, but she only grunted and said, "Let's just hope you haven't waited too long."

THE FATHER OF STONES

THE ROAD THAT led to the temple was paved with enormous slabs of gray stone and continued along the coast for several miles, then turned inland toward the Carbonares Valley, where Griaule held sway; it was said that the location had been chosen because it stood in the dragon's imaginary line of sight, so that his eye would be always fixed upon the cult. At the spot where the road passed the temple it widened considerably as if its builders had wanted to offer travelers the option of giving the place a wide berth. That option now greatly appealed to Korrogly. Standing before the gate, looking at the immense brass lock in the shape of a dragon, at the high black walls twined with vines that bore orchidaceous blooms the color of raw beef, the pagoda roofs that loomed like strange terraced mountains, he was inclined to discard any pretense he had of being a moral man and a committed officer of the court, and to hurry back to the security of his apartment. Not even the clarity of the night could diminish the temple's forbidding aspect, and each concatenation of the surf, driven in onto the shore by a blustery wind, made him jump. If he had been alone, he would have had no compunction about fleeing. Only Janice's dull regard, in which he saw a reflection of Lemos' despondent stare, kept him there; he felt outfaced by her, and though he told himself that her courage was born of ignorance and thus not courage at all, he was unable to persuade himself that this was relevant to his own lack of fortitude.

With an unsteady hand, he unlocked the gate; it swung inward with surprising ease, as if either the place or its controlling agency were eager to receive him. Following Janice, who went with her knife at the ready, he moved along a path winding among shrubs hung with overripe berries and low spreading trees with blackish green leaves; the foliage was so dense that he was unable to see anything of the buildings other than the rooftops. The wind did not penetrate there, and the stillness was such that every rustle he made in brushing against the bushes seemed inordinately loud; he fancied he could hear his heartbeat. Moonlight lacquered the leaves and applied lattices of shadow to the flagstones. He felt he was choking, moving deeper into an inimical hothouse atmosphere that clotted his lungs; he realized this was merely a symptom of fear, but knowing that did nothing to alleviate the symptom. He fastened his eyes on Janice's broad back and tried to clear his mind; but as they drew near the building where

Zemaille's apartment was situated, he had the notion that someone was watching…not just an ordinary someone. Someone cold, vast, and powerful. He recalled how Kirin and Mirielle had described their apprehension of Griaule, and the thought that the dragon's eye might be turned his way panicked him. His fists clenched, his jaw tightened, he had difficulty in swallowing. The shadows appeared to be acquiring volume and substance, and he imagined that terrible creatures were materializing within their black demarcations, preparing to leap out and tear at him.

Once inside the door, which opened onto a corridor lit by eerie mosaic patterns of bioluminescent moss, like veins of a radiant blue-green mineral wending through the teakwood walls, his fear increased. He was certain now that he could feel Griaule; with every step his impression of the dragon grew more discrete. There was an aura of timelessness, or rather that time itself was not so large and elemental as the dragon, that it was something on which Griaule had gained a perspective, something he could control. And the walls, the veins of moss…he had the sense that those patterns reflected the patterns of the dragon's thoughts. It was, he thought, as if he were inside Griaule, passing along some internal channel, and thinking this, he realized that it might be true, that the building, its function aligned with Griaule for so long, might well have become attuned with the dragon, might have in effect become the analogue of his body, subject to his full control. That idea produced in him an intense claustrophobia, and he had to bite back a cry. This was ridiculous, he told himself, absolutely ridiculous, he was letting his imagination run away with him. And yet he could not escape the feeling of enclosure, of being trapped beneath tons of cold flesh and bones the size of ships' keels.

When at last Janice pointed out the door to Zemaille's apartment, it was with tremendous relief that Korrogly inserted the key, eager to be out of the corridor, hoping that the apartment would provide a less oppressive environment; but although well-lit by globes of moss, the room that greeted his eye added more fuel to the fires of his imagination. Beyond an alcove was a bedchamber of a most grotesque design, the walls covered in a rich paper of crimson with a magenta stripe, and coiling around the entire room was a relief depicting a tail and a swollen reptile body, all worked in brass, every scale cunningly wrought, resolving into a huge dragon's head with an open fanged mouth that protruded some nine feet out from the far wall, wherein lay a bed like a plush red tongue. The eyes of the dragon were lidded, with opalescent crescents showing beneath, and its claws extended from the foot of the bed; above the head, suspended from the ceiling, was a section of polished scale some four feet wide and five feet long, angled slightly downward so that whoever entered would see—as Korrogly did now—their dark reflection. He stood frozen, his eyes darting between the scale and the dragon, certain that through some mystic apparatus he was being perceived by Griaule, and he might have stood there for a good long time if Janice had not said, "Hurry! This is no place to linger!"

There was little furniture in the room—a bureau, a small chest, two chairs. Korrogly made a hasty search of the chest and bureau, finding only robes and linens. Then he turned to Janice and said, "What am I looking for?"

"Papers, I think," she said. "Kirin told me once that Mardo kept records. But I'm not sure."

Korrogly began feeling along the walls, searching for a hidden panel, while Janice stood watch at the door. Where, he thought, where would Zemaille have hidden his valuables? Then it struck him. Where else? He stared at the bed within the dragon's mouth. The idea that Mirielle had once slept there repelled him, and he was no less repelled by the prospect of exploring the dark recess behind the bed; but it appeared he had no choice. He knelt on the bed, his trouserleg catching on one of the fangs, stalling his heart for an instant, and then he crawled back into the darkness, tossing aside pillows. The recess extended for about six feet and was walled with a smooth material that felt like stone; he ran his hands along it, hunting for a crack, a bulge, some sign of concealment. At last his fingers encountered a slight depression...no, five depressions, each about the size of his fingertips. He pressed against them, but achieved nothing; he tapped on the stone and it resounded hollowly.

"Have you found it?" Janice called.

"There's something here, but I can't get it open."

In a moment she came crawling up beside him, bringing with her a faint sweetish smell that seemed familiar. He showed her the depressions, and she began to push at them.

"Maybe it's a sequence," he said. "Maybe you have to push them one at a time in some order."

"I felt something," she said. "A tremor. Here...put your weight against the wall."

He set his shoulder to the wall, heaved and felt the stone shift; the next second the stone gave way and he went sprawling forward. Terrified, he pushed up into a sitting position and found himself in a small round chamber whose pale walls, veined like marble, gave off a ruddy glow. At the rear of the chamber was a lacquered black box. He started to reach for it, but as he picked it up the veins in the stone began to writhe and to thicken, melting up from the surface of the chamber, becoming adders with puffy sacs beneath their throats, and behind the wall, as if trapped in a reddish gel, there appeared the image of Mardo Zemaille, a dark hook-nosed man robed in black and silver, his hands arranged into tortuous mudras from which spat infant lightnings.

Korrogly screamed and pounded on the wall; he looked behind him and saw that the serpents were twining around one another, some beginning to slither toward him. Zemaille was intoning words in some guttural tongue, staring with demonic intent, and the detonations of light emerging from the fingertips were forming into balls of pale fire that spat and crackled and arrowed away in all directions. Korrogly pried at the wall, his breath coming in shrieks, expecting the adders to strike at any second, to be scorched by the balls of fire. A searing pain in his ankle, and he saw that one of the adders had sunk its fangs deep. His screams grew frantic, he lashed out his foot, shaking the adder loose, but another struck at his calf, and another. The pain was almost unendurable. He could feel the venom coursing through his veins like black ice. Half-a-dozen of the serpents were clinging to his legs, and his blood was flowing in rivulets from the wounds. He began to shiver, his right leg spasmed in a convulsion. His heart was huge, swelling larger yet, bloating with poison; it felt like a fist clenched about a thorn inside his chest. One of the fireballs struck his arm and clung there, eating into his arm, charring cloth and flesh. Zemaille's voice echoed, the voice of doom, as meaningless and potent as the voice of a gong. Then the wall swung outward, and he scrambled from the chamber, falling, coming to his knees, making a clumsy dive toward the bed, only to be caught up by Janice.

"Easy," she said. "Easy, it's only one of Mardo's illusions."

"Illusion?" Korrogly, his heart racing, turned back to the chamber; it was empty of all but the ruddy light. The pain, he realized, had receded. There were no wounds, no blood.

Janice picked up the box from where he had let it fall, held it to her ear and shook it. "Sounds like something solid. Not papers. Maybe this isn't it."

"There's nothing else there," said Korrogly, snatching the box from her, desperate to be away from there. "Come on!"

He crawled to the edge of the bed, started for the door, then glanced back to see if Janice was following. She was swinging her legs off the side of the bed, and he was about to tell her to hurry when movement above the bed drew his eye. In the polished scale that overhung the bed he saw his own reflection...that and more. Deeper within the scale another figure was materializing, that of a man lying on his back, wearing the robes of a wizard. At first Korrogly thought it must be Zemaille, for the man was very like him: hook-nosed and swarthy. But then he realized that the figure was shrunken and old, incredibly old, and the eyes, half-lidded, showed no sign of white or iris or pupil, but were black and wound through by thready structures of blue-green fire. The image faded after a second, but was so striking in aspect that Korrogly continued staring at the scale, feeling that more might be forthcoming, that it had been part of a sending. Janice pulled at him, making him aware once again of their danger, and together they went sprinting along the corridor toward the door.

The wind had grown stronger, the tops of the bushes were seething and the boughs of the trees lifting as if in sluggish acclaim. After the silence within the building, the roil of wind and surf was an assault, disorienting Korrogly, and he let Janice, who seemed untroubled by all that happened, lead him toward the gate. They had gone halfway through the toiling thickets, when she came to a sudden stop and stood with her head tilted to the side.

"Someone's coming," she said.

"I don't hear anything," he said. But she hauled at him, dragging him back the way they had come, and he trusted in her direction.

"There's a rear gate," she said. "It opens out onto the bluff. If we get separated, go west along the beach and hide in the dunes."

Korrogly hustled after her, clutching the lacquered box to his chest, glancing back once to try and make out their pursuers; he could have sworn he saw dark hooded figures as he went around a bend. It took them less than a minute to reach the gate, another few seconds for Janice to unlatch it, and then they were slogging through the soft sand atop the bluff, heading away from Ayler Point; the moonstruck waves below were flowing sideways, obeying the drag of the outgoing tide. Korrogly was relieved to have left the temple behind, and he was more confused than afraid; he thought that Janice might have been mistaken about hearing someone, that he had not really seen the hooded figures. He ran easily, feeling amazingly sound. It was as if something about the temple had occluded his faculties, diminished his strength. He soon began to out-pace Janice, and when he slowed to let her catch up, she gestured for him to keep going; her face was drawn tight with fear, and seeing this, he redoubled his efforts. Just as he came to the slope that led down from the bluff onto the beach, a path of white sand winding through tall grasses, he heard an agonized cry behind him, and turning, he had a glimpse of Janice, her shawl blown by the wind into a pennant, her dark hair loose, teetering on the edge of the bluff, clutching at her breast, at the handle of a dagger that sprouted bloody between her hands. Her eyes rolled up, she toppled over the edge and was gone.

It had happened so suddenly that Korrogly stopped running, scarcely able to believe what he had seen, but after a split-second, hearing a shout above the wind, he set out in a mad dash along the path. Three-quarters of the way down, he lost his footing and went tumbling head over heels the rest of the way. At the bottom of the slope, he groped for the box, found it, and bright with fear, made for the dunes which rose pale as salt above the narrow strip of mucky sand. By the time he had reached the top of the dunes, he was nearly out of breath, and he stood gasping, looking out over a rumpled moonlit terrain of grasses and hillocks, the folds between them holding bays of shadow. He set out running again, stumbling, dropping to his knees in a depression, tripping over exposed roots, and finally, his stamina exhausted, he dove into a cleft beneath a little rise and covered himself as best he could with sand and loose grass.

For awhile he heard nothing except the wind and the muffled crunch of the surf. Clouds began to pass across the moon, their edges catching silver fire, and he stared at them, praying that they would close and draw a curtain of darkness across the land. After about ten minutes he heard a shout, and it was followed a moment later by another shout. He could not make out any words, but the outcries had, he thought, the quality of angry desperation. He tucked his head down and made promises to God, swearing to uphold every sacred tenet, to do good works, if only he would be permitted to survive the night.

At long last the shouts ceased, but Korrogly remained where he was, afraid even to lift his head. He gazed at the clouds; the wind had lessened, and they were coasting past the moon like huge ragged blue galleons, like continents, like anything he wanted to make of their indefinite shapes. A dragon, for instance. An immense cloudy bulk with a vicious head and one globed, glaring silver eye, coiled throughout the heavens, the edges of its scales glinting like stars on its blue-dark hide, spying him out, watching over him, or else merely watching him, merely keeping track of its frightened pawn. He watched it take wing and fly in soaring arcs, diving and looping, making a pattern that drew him in, that trapped him like a devil within a pentagram and, eventually, hypnotized him into a dream-ridden sleep.

Dawn came gray and drizzly, with clouds that resembled heaps of dirty soap suds massing on the horizon. Korrogly's head ached as if he had been drinking all night; he was sore, filthy...even his eyes felt soiled. He peered about and saw only the hillocks, the flattened grasses, the heaving slate-colored ocean, gulls scything down the sky and keening. He rested his head against the sand, gathering himself for the walk back to town, and then remembered the box. It was unlocked. Zemaille, he supposed, had thought that his illusion would dissuade any intruders. He opened it cautiously on the chance that there were more tricks inside. It contained a leather-bound diary. He leafed through the pages, stopping occasionally to read a section; after going over a third of it, he knew that he could win an acquittal, yet he felt no triumph, no satisfaction, nothing. Perhaps, he thought, it was because he still was not sure that he believed in Lemos. Perhaps it was because he knew he should have unearthed the motive sooner; Kirin had given him a clue to it, one he had neglected in his confusion. Perhaps the deaths of Kirin and Janice were muting his reaction. Perhaps…he laughed, a sour little noise that the wind blew away. There was no use in trying to understand anything now. He needed a bath, a sleep, food. Then maybe things would make sense. But he doubted it.

Five

THE FOLLOWING MORNING, AGAINST MERVALE'S objection, Korrogly recalled Mirielle to the stand. She had on a brown dress with a modest neckline—a schoolteacher's dress—and her hair was done up primly like that of a young spinster. She had, it appeared, passed beyond mourning, and he wondered why she had not worn black; it might signal, he thought, some indecision on her part, some change of heart as related to her father. But whether or not that was so was unimportant. Looking at her, he had no emotional reaction; she seemed familiar yet distant, like someone he had known briefly years before. He knew that he could break down that distance and dredge up his feelings for her, but he was not moved to do so, for while he knew they were still strong, he was not sure whether they would manifest as love or hate. She had used him, had confused him with her sexuality, had undermined his concentration, and nearly succeeded in killing her father, who was very likely innocent. She had told him that she could have been a good actress, and she had been unsurpassable in her counterfeit of love, so perfect in the role that he believed she had won a piece of his heart for all time. But she was a perjurer and probably worse, and he was duty-bound to make her true colors known to the court, no matter what the cost.

"Good morning, Miss Lemos," he said.

She gave him a quizzical look and returned the greeting.

"Did you sleep well last night?" he asked.

"Oh, dear," said Mervale. "Is the counsel for the defense next going to inquire about the lady's breakfast, or perhaps her dreams?"

Judge Wymer stared glumly at Korrogly.

"I was simply trying to make the witness feel comfortable," Korrogly said. "I'm concerned for her welfare. She's had a terrible weight on her conscience."

"Mister Korrogly," said the judge in tone of warning.

Korrogly waved his hand as if both to accede to the caution and dismiss its importance. He rested both hands on the witness box, leaning toward Mirielle, and said, "What is the great work?"

"The witness has already answered that question," said Mervale, and at the same time, Mirielle said, "I don't know what more I can tell you, I…"

"The truth would be refreshing," said Korrogly. "You see, I know for a fact you haven't been candid with this court."

"If the counselor has facts to present," said Mervale, "I suggest that he present them and stop badgering the witness."

"I will," said Korrogly, addressing the bench. "In due course. But it's important to my presentation that I show exactly to what extent and to what end the facts have been covered up."

Wymer heaved a forlorn sigh. "Proceed."

"I ask you again," said Korrogly to Mirielle, "what is the great work? And I warn you, be truthful, for you will not escape prosecution for any lie you may tell from this point on."

Doubt surfaced in Mirielle's face, but she only said, "I've told you all I know."

Korrogly took a turn around the witness box and stopped facing the jury. "What was the purpose of the ceremony in progress on the night that Zemaille was killed?"

"I don't know."

"Was it part of the great work?"

"No…I mean I don't think so."

"For someone who was Zemaille's intimate you appear to know very little about him."

"Mardo was a secretive man."

"Was he, now? Did he ever discuss his parents with you?"

"Yes."

"So he was not secretive concerning his origins?"

"No."

"Did he ever discuss his grandparents?"

"I'm not sure. I believe he may have mentioned them once or twice."

"Other relatives…did he ever discuss them?"

"I can't remember."

"Did he ever make mention of a remote ancestor, a man who—like himself—was involved in the occult?"

Her face tightened. "No."

"You seem quite certain of that, yet a moment ago you claimed that you couldn't recall if he had ever talked about other relatives."

"I would have remembered something like that."

"Indeed, I believe you would." Korrogly crossed to the defense table. "Does the name Archiochus strike a chord in your memory?"

Mirielle sat motionless, her eyes widened slightly.

"Should I repeat the question?"

"No, I heard it...I was trying to think."

"And have you finished thinking?"

"Yes, I've heard the name."

"And who might this Archiochus be?"

"A wizard, I believe."

"A wizard of some accomplishment, was he not? One who lived some time ago...thousands of years?"

"I think so." Mirielle seemed to be mulling something over. "Yes, I remember now. Mardo considered him his spiritual father. He wasn't an actual relation...at least I don't think he was."

"And that is the extent of your knowledge concerning him?"

"It's all I can remember."

"Odd," said Korrogly, toying with the lid of his briefcase. "Let's return to the ceremony on the night Zemaille was killed. Did this have anything to do with Archiochus?"

"It may have."

"But you're not sure?"

"No."

"Your father has testified that Zemaille cried out to his father at one point, saying, 'Soon you will be free!' Might he not have been referring at that moment to his spiritual father?"

"Yes." Mirielle sat up straight, adopting an earnest expression as if she wanted to be helpful. "Now that you mention it, it's possible he was trying to contact Archiochus. Mardo believed in the spirit world. He would often hold seances."

"Then you're suggesting that the ceremony in question was something on the order of a seance?"

"It could have been."

"To contact the soul of Archiochus?"

"It's possible."

"Are you certain, Miss Lemos, that you know nothing more about this Archiochus? For instance, did he have anything to do with Griaule?"

"I…maybe."

"Maybe," said Korrogly bemusedly. "Maybe. I believe he had quite a bit to do with Griaule. As a matter of fact, was it not the wizard Archiochus, the man with whom Zemaille felt a spiritual—if not an actual—kinship, who thousands of years ago did battle with the dragon Griaule?"

Babble erupted from the onlookers, and Wymer gaveled them to silence.

Korrogly said to Mirielle, "Well?"

"Yes," she said, "I believe it was he. I'd forgotten."

"Of course," said Korrogly. "Your flawed memory again." He engaged the jury's eyes and smiled. "According to legend, just as Griaule lies dormant, so that same fate struck the wizard who stilled him…have you ever heard that?"

"Yes."

"Had Mardo?"

"I believe so."

"So then Mardo believed that this powerful wizard was yet alive? Moribund, but alive?"

"Yes."

"Let's talk about the work for a moment. Not the great work, just the ordinary run-of-the-mill work. Is it true that you took part in sexual rituals with Zemaille in that same room where he died?"

The vein in her temple pulsed.

"Yes."

"And these rituals involved intercourse with Zemaille?"

"Yes!"

"And others?"

Mervale stood at the prosecution table. "Your Honor, I see no point in this line."

"Nor do I," said Wymer.

"But there is a point," said Korrogly, "one I will shortly make plain."

"Very well," said Wymer impatiently. "But be succinct. The witness will answer."

"What was the question?" Mirielle asked.

"Did you participate in sex with others aside from Zemaille for ritual purposes?" said Korrogly.

"Yes."

"Why? What use did this wantonness serve?"

"Objection."

"I'll rephrase." Korrogly leaned against the defense table. "Did sex have a specific function in these rituals?"

"I suppose...yes."

"And what was it?"

"I'm not sure."

Korrogly opened his briefcase, using the lid to hide the diary inside it from Mirielle's eyes; he opened the little book. "Was it to prepare the flesh?"

Mirielle stiffened.

"Shall I repeat the question?"

"No, I..."

"What does that mean, Miss Lemos...'to prepare the flesh'?"

She shook her head. "Mardo knew...I was never clear on it."

"Did you practice any sort of birth control prior to these rituals? Did you for instance drink some infusion of roots and herbs, or in other way attempt to prevent yourself from becoming pregnant?"

"Yes."

"Yet on the night Zemaille died, you used no birth control."

Mirielle came to her feet. "How do you..." She bit her lip and sat back down.

"I believe that night was considered by Zemaille to be the anniversary of the battle between Griaule and Archiochus, was it not?"

"I don't know."

"I will introduce evidence," said Korrogly addressing the bench, "to show that this was indeed Zemaille's opinion." He turned again to Mirielle. "Was it your intent on that night to become pregnant?"

She sat mute.

"Answer the question, Miss Lemos," said Judge Wymer.

"Yes," she whispered.

"Why of all the nights did you hope to become pregnant on that one? Was it because you were hoping for a specific sort of child?"

She stared hatefully at him.

Korrogly let the lid of the briefcase fall, let her see the diary. "The name of the child whom you were to bear, was it to be Archiochus?"

Her jaw dropped, her eyes were fixed on the leather book.

"Was it not Zemaille's intent, the long focus of his great work, to achieve by some foul magic the liberation and repair of Archiochus' soul? And for that purpose did he not need flesh that was so soiled and degraded, it would offer a natural habitat for the black mind of that evil and moribund man? Your soiled flesh, Miss Lemos. Was it not your function to provide the vile womb that would allow the soul of this loathsome wizard to be reborn in innocent flesh? And would he not, once he had come to manhood and regained his full powers, with Zemaille's aid, seek once again to destroy the dragon Griaule?"

Instead of answering, Mirielle let out a scream of such pure agony and despair that the courtroom was thrown into a stunned silence. She lowered her head, resting it on the rail of the witness box; at last she sat up straight, her face transformed into a mask of hatred.

"Yes!" she said, "Yes! And if hadn't been for him"—she flung out a hand, pointing to Lemos—"we would have killed the damned lizard! You would have thanked us...all of you! You would have praised Mardo as a liberator! You would have built statues, memorials. You..."

Judge Wymer cautioned her to silence, but she continued to rant; every muscle in her face was leaping, her eyes were distended, her hands gripping the rail.

"Mardo!" she cried, turning her face to the ceiling as if seeing through it into the kingdom of the dead. "Mardo, hear me!"

At length, unable to silence her, Wymer had her taken in restraints to an interrogation room, returned Lemos to his cell, and ordered a recess. After the courtroom had been cleared, Korrogly sat at the defense table, fingering the diary, staring gloomily into the middle distance; his thoughts seemed to arc out and upward like flares, bright for a moment, but then falling into darkness.

"Well," said Mervale, coming to sit on the edge of the table, "I suppose I should offer my congratulations."

"It's not over yet."

"Oh, yes it is! They'll never convict now, and you know it."

Korrogly nodded.

"You don't seem very happy about it."

"I'm just tired."

"It'll sink in soon," Mervale said. "This is a tremendous victory for you. You've made your fortune."

"Hmm."

Mervale got to his feet and extended a hand. "No hard feelings," he said. "I realize you were overwrought the other night. I'm willing to let bygones be bygones if you are."

Korrogly took his hand and was surprised to see actual respect in Mervale's face—his surprise stemmed from the fact that he felt no respect for himself; he could not stop thinking of Mirielle, wanting her, even though he realized that everything between them had been a sham. And, too, he was dissatisfied. The case struck him as a jigsaw puzzle whose pieces fit neatly together, but whose picture made no sense.

"Want a drink?" Mervale asked.

"No," said Korrogly.

"Come on, man. Maybe there was some truth in what you said the other night, but I'm won over. You won't find me patronizing you any-more. Let me buy you a drink."

"No," said Korrogly; then he looked up at Mervale with a grin. "You can buy me several."

Six

KORROGLY'S DISSATISFACTION DID NOT WANE
with time; he remained uncertain of Lemos' innocence, and everything
that happened as a result of the gemcutter's acquittal caused his dissatisfaction to grow more extreme.

Mirielle was declared incompetent, and the temple and its grounds
were ceded to Lemos, who promptly sold them for an enormous sum;
the buildings were razed and a hotel was planned for the site. Lemos
also sold The Father of Stones at a large profit back to Henry Sichi, for
it was now considered a relic of Griaule and thus of inestimable worth,
and Sichi wanted it for an exhibit in the museum he had built to house
such items. Lemos had invested the majority of his new wealth in indigo
mills and silver mines, and had purchased a mansion out on Ayler Point;
there, with the court's permission, he and a staff of nurses took charge
of nursing Mirielle back to health. They were rarely seen in public, but
word had it that she was doing splendidly, and that father and daughter
had reconciled.

Whenever he had a spare hour, his practice having grown large and
profitable following the trial, Korrogly would use the time to do the pretrial work that he neglected and continued to investigate all the circumstances surrounding Zemaille's death. In this he made no headway until
almost a year and a half later, when he interviewed an ex-member of the
dragon cult on the beach below the bluff where the temple had once stood.
The man, a slight balding fellow whose innocuous appearance belied his
dissolute past, was nervous, and Korrogly had been forced to pay him well
in order to elicit his candor. He was of little help for the most part, and it
was only toward the end of the interview that he provided information that
substantiated Korrogly's doubts.

"We all thought it strange that Mirielle took up with Mardo," he said, "considering what happened to her mother."

"What are you talking about?" Korrogly asked.

"Her mother," said the man. "Patricia. She came to the temple one night, the night she died as a matter of fact."

"What?"

"You didn't know?"

"No, I've heard nothing about it."

"Well, I don't suppose it's public knowledge. She only came the once, and that same night she drowned."

"What happened?"

"Who can say? Word was that Mardo had her into his bed. Probably drugged her. Maybe she fought him. Mardo wouldn't have liked that."

"Are you saying he killed her?"

"Somebody did."

"Why didn't any of you come forward with this?"

"We were afraid."

"Of what?"

"Griaule."

"That's ludicrous."

"Is it, now? You're the man who got Lemos off, you must understand what Griaule's capable of."

"But what you're saying, it throws a different light on things. Perhaps Lemos and Mirielle plotted this whole affair to get revenge, perhaps…"

"Even if they did," said the man, "it was still Griaule's idea."

Following this interview, Korrogly checked the tides on the night of Patricia Lemos' death and discovered that they had been sweeping out from the temple bluff toward Ayler Point, that had her body entered the water in the early morning, she might well—as had been the case—have washed ashore on Ayler Point. That, however, was the extent of his enlightenment. Despite exploring every avenue, he could come up with no evidence to implicate Lemos or his daughter in a plot against Zemaille. The matter continued to prey on him, to cause him bad dreams and sleepless nights; having been used, he had an overwhelming compulsion to understand the nature of that usage, to put into perspective all that happened, so that he could know the character of his fate. He did not know whether he wanted more to believe that he had been manipulated by Griaule or by Lemos and his daughter. Some nights he thought he would prefer to cling to the notion of free will, to think that he had been the victim of human wiles, not those of some creature as inexplicable as God; other nights he hoped that he had won the case fairly and freed an innocent man. The only thing he was certain of was that he wanted clarity.

Finally, having no other course of action open, he went to the source, to Lemos' mansion on Ayler Point, and asked to see the gemcutter. A maid advised him that the master was not in, but that if he would wait, she would find out if the mistress was at home. After a brief absence she returned and ushered him onto a sunny verandah that overlooked the sea and provided a breathtaking view of the Almintra quarter. The strong sunlight applied a crust of diamantine glitter to the surface of the water, spreading it wider whenever the wind riffled the tops of the wavelets, and the gabled houses on the shore looked charming, quaint, their squalor hidden by distance. Mirielle, clad in a beige silk robe, was reclining on a lounge; on a small table close to her hand lay a long pipe and a number of dark pellets that Korrogly suspected to be opium. There was a clouded look to her eyes, and though she was still lovely, the marks of dissipation had eroded the fine edge of her good looks; a black curl was plastered to her sweaty cheek, and there was an unhealthy shine to her skin.

"It's wonderful to see you," she said lazily, indicating that he should take a chair beside her.

"Is it?" he said, feeling the rise of old longings, old bitternesses. God, he thought, I still love her, despite everything, she could commit any excess, any vileness, and I would love her.

"Of course." She let out a fey laugh. "I doubt you'll believe me, but I was quite fond of you."

"Fond!" He made the word into an epithet.

"I told you I couldn't love you."

"You told me you'd try."

She shrugged; her hand twitched toward the pipe. "Things didn't work out."

"Oh, I don't know about that." He gestured at the luxurious surround. "Things have worked out quite well for you."

"And for you," she said. "I've heard you've become a great success. All the ladies want you for their…" A giggle. "Their solicitor."

A large wave broke on the shore beneath the verandah, spreading a lace of foam halfway up the beach; the sound appeared to make Mirielle sleepy; her lids fluttered down, and she gave a long sigh that caused her robe to slip partway off one pale, poppling breast.

"I tried to be honest with you," she said. "And I was. As honest as I knew how to be."

"Then why didn't you tell me about your mother and Zemaille?"

Her eyes blinked open. "What?"

"You heard me." She sat up, pulling her robe closed, and regarded him with a mixture of confusion and displeasure.

"Why have you come here?"

"For answers. I need answers."

"Answers!" She laughed again. "You're more a fool than I thought."

Stung by that, he said, "Maybe I'm a fool, but I'm no whore."

"A lawyer who thinks he's not a whore! Will wonders never cease!"

"Tell me," he demanded. "Nothing can happen to you now, your father can't be tried again. It was you, wasn't it? This was all a scheme, a plot to kill Zemaille and avenge your mother. I don't know how you pulled it off, but…"

"I don't know what you're talking about."

"Mirielle," he said. "I need to know. I won't hurt you, I promise. I could never hurt you. It almost killed me to have to do what I did to you in court."

She met his eyes for a long moment. "It was easy," she said at last. "You were easy. That's why we picked you…because you were so lonely, so naive. We just kept you spinning. With love, with fear, with misdirection. And finally with drugs. Before I—or rather Janice—took you to the temple, I slipped a drug into your drink. It made you highly suggestible."

"That's what made me hallucinate?"

She looked perplexed.

"The hidey hole behind the bed. The snakes, the…"

"No, that was Mardo's illusion. It was real enough. The drug only made you believe what I wanted you to—that we were in danger, being pursued. All that."

"What about the scale?"

"The scale?"

"Yes, the image of the dead wizard in the scale above Zemaille's bed. Archiochus, I guess it was."

Her brow wrinkled. "You were so frightened, you must have been seeing things."

She got to her feet, swayed, righted herself by catching hold of the verandah railing. He thought he saw a softening in her face, the trace of a longing equal to his own, and he also thought he saw her madness, her instability. She would have had to be insane to do what she had, to be in love and not in love at the same time, to inhabit those roles fully, to lie and deceive with such compulsive thoroughness.

"If we'd presented our evidence in a straightforward way," she said, "Daddy still might have been convicted. We needed to orchestrate the trial, to manipulate the jury. So we chose you to be the conductor. And you were wonderful! You believed everything we handed you." She turned, let her robe drop to expose her perfect back and said in a northern accent, "I've no great love for dragons."

It was Janice's voice.

He gazed at her, uncomprehending. "But she fell," he said. "I saw it."

"A net," she said. "Rigged just below the bluff." This she said in a fluting voice, the voice of the old woman, Kirin.

"My God!" he said.

"A little make-up can do miracles," she said. "And I've always been good at doing voices. We planned for years and years."

"I still don't understand. There were so many variables. How could you control them all? The nine witnesses, for example. How could you know they would run?"

She gave him a pitying look.

"Oh," he said. "Right. There were no witnesses, were there?"

"Only Mardo and I. And of course Daddy didn't throw the stone. We couldn't take a chance on him missing. We overpowered Mardo, and then he smashed in his skull with it. Then I took drugs to make it look as if I'd been laid out on the altar. The cult had already disbanded, you see. They were all afraid of the great work. It was already in process of breaking up when I joined. That was the heart of the plan. Isolating Mardo. I spent hours encouraging him in the great work; I knew the others would abandon him if they thought he actually might complete it. They were more afraid of Griaule than of him."

"Then that part of it was the truth?"

She nodded. "Mardo was obsessed with killing Griaule. He was mad!"

"What about the knife, the hooded figure?"

She bowed. "I didn't intend to injure your hand, merely to frighten you. I was so worried because I'd hurt you. I had to run around to the rear of the shop and climb the back stairs in order to make you think I'd been in the apartment, and I almost decided to forget about the plan, just to run to you and take care of you. I'm sorry."

"You're sorry! God!"

"You haven't got anything to complain about! Your life's better than it's ever been. And like you said, Mardo's death was no great loss to anyone. He was evil."

"I don't even know what that word means anymore."

Looking back, he could see now the clues he should have seen long before, the similarities in nervous gesture between her and Kirin, her overwrought reaction when he had tried to talk about her mother, all the little inconsistencies, the too-pat connections. What an idiot he had been!

"Poor Adam." She walked over to him, stroked his hair. "You expect the world to be so simple, and it is…just not in the way you want it to be."

Her smell of heated oranges aroused him, and he pulled her onto his lap, both angry and lustful. With half his mind he tried to reject her, because to want her would ratify all the duplicity in which he had played a part and further weaken his fraying moral fiber; but the stronger half needed her, and he kissed her mouth, tasting the smoky sweetness of the opium. His lips moved along the curve of her neck to the slopes of her breasts. She responded sluggishly at first, then with abandon, whispering, "I've missed you so much, I love you, I really do," and it seemed she was as she once had been, open and giving and soft. It startled him to see this, to realize that the vulnerability underlying her dissipation was no act, for he had come to doubt everything about her. He kissed her mouth again, and he might have taken her then and there, but a man's voice interrupted them, saying, "I wish you'd be more discreet, darling."

Korrogly jumped up, dumping Mirielle onto the floor.

Lemos was standing in the doorway, a smile touching the corners of his lips. He looked prosperous, content, a far cry from the gray failure whom Korrogly had defended. His clothes were expensive, rings adorned his hands, and there was about him such an air of health and well-being, it seemed an obscenity, like the ruddy complexion of a sated vampire. Mirielle scrambled up and went to him; he draped an arm about her shoulders.

"I'm surprised to find you here, Mister Korrogly," said Lemos. "But I don't suppose I should be. My daughter is alluring, is she not?"

"I told him, Daddy," Mirielle said in a sugary, babyish voice. "About Mardo."

"Did you now?"

To his horror, Korrogly saw that Lemos was fondling his daughter's breast beneath the beige silk; she arched her back to meet the pressure of his hand, but he thought he detected tension in her expression.

Lemos, apparently registering Korrogly's revulsion, said, "But you didn't tell him everything, did you?"

"Not about Mama. He thinks…"

"I can imagine what he thinks."

Lemos' smile was unwavering, but behind it, in those gray eyes, was something cold and implacable that made Korrogly afraid.

"You look disturbed," Lemos said. "Surely a man of your experience can imagine how love might spring up between a man and his daughter. It's frowned upon, true. But society's condemnation of such a relationship need not diminish it. In our case, it only made us desperate."

The final pieces were beginning to fall into place for Korrogly. "It wasn't Zemaille who killed your wife, was it?"

Lemos smiled.

"It was you…you killed her!"

"You'd play hell proving it. But let's say for the sake of argument that you're right. Let's say that in order to…to enjoy one another fully, Mirielle and I needed privacy, something that Patricia prevented us from having. What better villain to use as our foil than Mardo Zemaille? The temple was at that time always open to the curious. It would have been easy for someone, someone like myself, to convince Patricia that it might be fun to pay the place a visit one night."

"You killed her…and you were going to blame it on Zemaille?"

"Her death was ruled an accident," Lemos said with a shrug. "So there was no need to blame anyone."

"And then you saw your opportunity with Zemaille."

"Mardo was a weak man with power. Such men are easy to maneuver. It took some time, but the result was inevitable."

Lemos' hand slid lower to caress Mirielle's belly. Despite her acquiescence, Korrogly sensed that she was less lover than slave, that her enjoyment was due to coercion, to confusion; a slack, sick look had come to her face, one that had not been evident when he had been touching her.

"I don't believe I've ever properly expressed my gratitude to you," Lemos continued. "Without you, I might still be back in Almintra. I'm forever in your debt."

Korrogly just stared at them, uncertain of what to do.

"Perhaps you're wondering why I'm being so open," Lemos said. "It's really no mystery. You're a dogged man, Mister Korrogly. I have a lot of respect for you. Once you got the scent, and I've been aware that you've had the scent for some time, I knew you'd keep at it until you learned all there was to learn. I knew we'd play this scene sooner or later. I could have had you killed, but as I've said, I'm grateful to you, and I prefer to let you live. It's unlikely you can harm me in any event. But you can consider this a warning. I'm watching you. If you ever get it in mind to try and harm me, it'll be one of your last thoughts. And if you should doubt that, then I want you to think back to what you've heard today, to realize what I'm capable of, what I was able to do when I had no power, and to imagine what I might do now that I am powerful. Do you understand?"

Korrogly said, "Yes, I do."

"Well." Lemos disengaged from Mirielle, who tottered back to her lounge. "Then there's nothing else to do except to bid you good day. Perhaps you'll visit us again. For dinner, perhaps. Of course you're always welcome to visit Mirielle. She does like you, she really does, and I've learned not to be jealous. I would hate to deny her whatever joy she might find with you. I'm afraid the things I've asked her to do have damaged her, and maybe you can help her overcome all that." He put his hand on Korrogly's back and began steering him through the house and toward the front door. "Pleasure's a rare commodity. I don't begrudge any man his share. That's something that being wealthy has given me to understand about life. Yet another reason to be grateful to you. So"—he opened the front door— "when I say to you that what's mine is yours, I mean it in the most profound and intimate sense. Do take advantage of our hospitality. Anytime."

And with that, he waved and shut the door, leaving Korrogly blinking in the bright sunlight, feeling as if he had been marooned on a stone island in an uncharted sea.

TOWARD TWILIGHT, AFTER walking and thinking for the remainder of the afternoon, Korrogly ended up in Henry Sichi's museum, standing in front of the glass case in which The Father of Stones was displayed. Lemos had been right—there was nothing he could do to achieve justice, and he would have to accept the fact that he had been used by someone who if anything was more monstrous than Griaule. His best course, he decided, would be to leave Port Chantay and to leave soon, for while Lemos might have meant all he had said, he might well change his mind and begin to consider Korrogly a threat. But the danger he was in, that was not the thing that rankled him; he was still enough of a moral soul—a fool, Lemos would say—to want a judgment upon Lemos, and that there would be none left him full of gloom and self-destructive impulse, regarding the shattered fragments of his wished-for orderly universe.

He gazed down at The Father of Stones. It sat winking in its nest of blue velvet, a clouded lump of mystery giving back prismatic refractions of the light, the peculiar man-shaped darkness at its heart appearing to shift and writhe as if it truly were the soul of an imprisoned wizard. Korrogly focused on that darkness, and suddenly it was all around him, like a little pocket of night into which he had fallen, and he was looking at a man lying on the ground, an old, old man with sunken cheeks and a hooked nose and dressed in wizard's robes, with black eyes threaded by veins of blue-green fire. The vision lasted only a few seconds, but before it faded, he became aware of the propinquity of that same cold, powerful mind that he had sensed back in the temple, and when he found himself once again standing in front of the glass case, looking down at The Father of Stones, he felt not afraid, not shocked, but delighted. It had been Griaule after all, he realized; the vision could mean only that Zemaille had been a serious threat, one that Griaule had been forced to eliminate. And he, Korrogly, had actually seen the moribund wizard that night in the temple; it had been no hallucination. The dragon had even then been trying to illuminate him. He laughed and slapped his thigh. Oh, Lemos had worked his plan, but as the ex-member of the cult had said, it had still been Griaule's idea, he had inspired Lemos to act...and he had done it through the agency of this shard of milky stone.

Korrogly's delight stemmed not from his realization that in a way Lemos had been innocent—innocence was not a word he could apply to the gemcutter—but from a new comprehension of the intricate subtlety with which Griaule had acted; it spoke to him, it commanded him, it instructed him in a kind of law that he had neglected throughout his entire life. The law of self-determination. It was the only kind, he saw, that could produce justice. If he wanted justice, he would have to effect it, not the system, not the courts, and that was something he was well-equipped to do. He was amazed that he had not come to this conclusion before, but then he supposed that until this moment he had been too confused, too involved with the complexities of the case, to think of taking direct action. And perhaps he had not been ready to act, perhaps his motivation had been insufficient.

Well, he was motivated now.

Mirielle.

It might be that she was unsalvageable, that she had gone too far into perversity ever to emerge from it; but for a moment in his arms she had again been the woman he had loved. It had not been fraudulent. The least he could do was to deliver her from the man who had dominated her and seduced her into iniquity. That he would be also serving justice only made the act sweeter.

He strolled out of the museum and stood on the steps gazing over the shadowed lavender water toward Ayler Point. He knew exactly how he would proceed. Lemos himself had given him the key to successful action in his words concerning Zemaille.

"Mardo was a weak man with power," he had said. "Such men are easy to maneuver."

And of course Lemos was no different.

He was rife with weakness. His investments, Mirielle, his crimes, his false sense of control. That last, that was his greatest weakness. He was enamored of his own power, he believed his judgments to be infallible and he would never believe that Korrogly could be other than as he perceived him; he would think that the lawyer would either do nothing or seek redress through the courts; he would not suspect that Korrogly might move against him in the way that he had moved against Zemaille. Zemaille had probably thought the same of him.

Korrogly smiled, understanding how marvelously complex was this chain of consecutive illuminations, of one man after another being induced to take decisive action. He stepped briskly down the steps and out onto Biscaya Boulevard, heading for *The Blind Lady* and a glass of beer, for a bout of peaceful contemplation, of deciding his future and Lemos' fate. By the time he had walked a block he had already come up with the beginnings of a plan.

But then he was brought up short by a disturbing thought.

What if he was obeying Griaule's will in all this, what if The Father of Stones had had an effect upon him? What if instead of taking his destiny in hand, he was merely obeying Griaule's wishes, serving as an element in some dire scheme? What if he was by dismissing ordinary means and moral tactics taking a chance on becoming a monster like Lemos, one who would in the end be cut down by yet another of Griaule's pawns? There was no way of telling. His sudden determination to act might be laid to a long inner process of deliberation, it might be the result of years of failed idealism; the resolution of the Lemos case could have been the weight that caused the final caving-in of his unsound moral structure.

He stood for a long moment considering these things, knowing that he might never come to the end of considering them, but searching for some rationalization that would allow him to put aside such concerns, to cease his analysis and questioning of events, and he found that this had become for him a matter of choice; it was as if the decision to act had freed him from an old snare, from the hampering spell of his ideals, and introduced him into a new and—though less moral—much more effective magic. What did he care who was in control, who was pulling the strings? Sooner or later a man had to stop thinking and start being, to leave off fretting over the vicissitudes and intricacies of life, and begin to live. There was no certainty, no secure path, no absolutely moral one. You did the best you could for yourself and those you cared about, and hoped that this would be a sufficiently broad spectrum of concern to keep your soul in healthy condition. If not…well, there was no use in fretting over the prospect. Why trouble yourself with guilt in a world in which everyone was guilty?

He set off walking again, walking with a firm step and a smile for everyone who passed him by, bowing politely to an old woman sweeping off her stoop, stopping once to pat a young boy on the head, all the while giving thought to his campaign against Lemos, picturing the gemcutter in various states of ruinous defeat, imagining Mirielle in his arms, letting his mind roam freely through the realms of possibility, posing himself in judge's robes, dispensing the dispassionate rule of the law, fair yet inflexible, full of imponderable wisdoms, and he saw himself as well on the sunny verandah of a mansion on Ayler Point, on a white yacht, in a glittering ballroom, in every manner of luxurious environment, with loyal friends and beautiful lovers and enemies whose secrets he had mastered. Life, which for so long had seemed distant, a treasure beyond his grasp, now seemed to embrace him, to close around him and make him dizzy with its rich scents and sights. What did it matter, he said to himself, who ran the world, it tasted no less sweet, it gave no less pleasure. He laughed out loud, he winked at a pretty girl, he plotted violence and duplicity, all things that brought him joy.

One way or another, the dragon was loose in Port Chantay.

LIAR'S
HOUSE

IN THE ETERNAL INSTANT BEFORE the Beginning, before the Word was pronounced in fire, long before the tiny dust of history came to settle from the flames, something whose actions no verb can truly describe seemed to enfold possibility, to surround it in the manner of a cloud or an idea, and everything fashioned from the genesis fire came to express in some way the structure of that fundamental duality. It has been said that of all living creatures, this duality was best perceived in dragons, for they had flown fully formed from out the mouth of the Uncreate, the first of creation's kings, and gone soaring through a conflagration that, eons hence, would coalesce into worlds and stars and all the dream of matter. Thus the relation of their souls to their flesh accurately reflected the constitution of the Creator, enveloping and controlling their material bodies from without rather than, as with the souls of men, coming to be lodged within. And of all their kind, none incarnated this principle more poignantly, more spectacularly, than did the dragon Griaule.

How Griaule came to be paralyzed by a wizard's magical contrivance is a story without witness, but it has been documented that in this deathlike condition he lived on for millennia, continuing to grow, until he measured more than a mile in length, lying athwart and nearly spanning the westernmost section of the Carbonales Valley. Over the years he came to resemble a high hill covered in grass and shrubs and stunted trees, with here and there a portion of scale showing through, and the colossal head entirely emergent, unclothed by vegetation, engaging everything that passed before him with huge, slit-pupiled golden eyes, exerting a malefic influence over the events that flowed around him, twisting them into shapes that conformed to the cruel designs his discarnate intellect delighted in the weaving of, and profited his vengeful will. During his latter days, a considerable city, Teocinte, sprawled away from Griaule's flank over the adjoining hill, but centuries before, when few were willing to approach the dragon, Teocinte was scarcely more than an outsized village enclosed by dense growths of palms and bananas, hemmed in between the eminence of Griaule and a pine-forested hill. Scruffy and unlovely; flyblown; its irregularly laid-out dirt streets lined by hovels with rusting tin roofs; it was lent the status of a town by a scattering of unstable frame structures housing taverns, shops, and a single inn, and was populated by several thousand men and women who, in the main, embodied a debased extreme of the human condition. Murderers and thieves and outlaws of various stamp. Almost to a one, they believed that proximity to the dragon imbued them with a certain potency (as perhaps it did) and refused to concern themselves with the commonly held notion that they had been drawn to Teocinte because their depravity resonated with the dragon's depraved nature, thus making them especially vulnerable to his manipulations. What does it matter whose purpose we serve, they might have asked, so long as it satisfies our own?

By all accounts, the most fearsome of Teocinte's citizens and, at forty-two, its eldest, was Hota Kotieb, a brooding stump of a man with graying, unkempt hair, his cheeks and jaw scarred by knife cuts. His hands were huge, capable of englobing a cantaloupe and squeezing it to a pulp, and his powerful arms and oxlike shoulders had been developed through years of unloading ships at the docks in Port Chantay. Deep-socketed eyes provided the only vital accent in what otherwise seemed the sort of brutish face sometimes produced by the erosion of great stones. Unlike his fellows, who would make lengthy forays out into the world to perpetrate their crimes, then returned to restore themselves by steeping in the dragon's aura, Hota never strayed from the valley. Eleven summers previously, after his wife had been run over in the street by a coach belonging to the harbormaster in Port Chantay, he had forsworn the unreliable processes of justice and forced his way into the man's home. When the harbormaster ordered him ejected, Hota stabbed him, his two sons and several retainers, himself receiving numerous wounds during the skirmish. On realizing that he would be hung were he to remain in the town, he looted the house and fled, killing three policemen who sought to stop him outside the door. Casting aside a lifetime of unobtrusive action and docile labor, he had murdered ten men in the space of less than an hour.

Though he had never attended school and was ignorant of many things, Hota was by no means dull-witted, and when he meditated on these events, his red victory and the grim chaos that preceded it, he was able to place his actions in a rational context. He felt little remorse over the murders of the harbormaster and his sons. They were oppressors and had received an oppressor's due. As for the rest, he regretted their deaths and believed that some would have been spared had he not been enraged to the point of derangement; yet he refused to use derangement as a sop to his conscience and recognized that the potential for extreme violence had always been his. He had not wished his wife to die, but neither had he loved her. Thirteen years of marriage had doused the spark that once leaped between them. Their union had decayed into indifference and sham. They were like two plow horses harnessed together, endlessly tilling a field barren of children and every other promise, yet led to continue their dreary progress by the litany of empty promises they spoke to one another. It seemed her death had less inspired than legitimized a violent release, and that he had been longing to kill someone for quite some time, motivated in this by feelings of impotence bred over years of abject poverty. Now this tendency had made itself known, he supposed it would rise all the more easily to the surface. For this reason, though he was lonely, he kept no one close.

The money and gems he had stolen from the harbormaster enabled Hota to live as comfortably as the rough consolations of Teocinte permitted. He occupied a third-floor room at the rear of Dragonwood House, a weathered, boxlike building with a tin roof and a tavern downstairs and a newer, less ruinous single-story wing attached, where prostitutes were housed. Its ashen gray facade was dressed with a garishly painted sign that depicted a dragon soaring through a fiery heaven. The inn was situated near the edge of town and serviced the steady stream of visitors that came to look at Griaule, offering views of the dragon's side from its front windows. Its owner, Benno Grustark, claimed that the boards employed in its construction were manufactured from trees that had grown atop Griaule's back, but his patrons, knowing that few dared to set foot upon the dragon, let alone cut timber, referred to the inn as Liar's House.

Having no need to work, Hota passed many of his days at woodcarving, a hobby of his childhood that still pleased him, though he displayed no talent for the work. Since there was little in the town to attract his eye, he took to carving likenesses of Griaule. Dozens of such pieces were crowded together on his shelves, atop the bureau and chairs, and scattered across the floor of his room. On occasion he would give one to a child or to a prostitute who shared his bed, but this made no appreciable dent in the clutter. To avoid further clutter, he began working on a grander scale, walking out into the hills, felling trees, chiseling dragons from the trunks, and leaving the completed figures to the depredations of the rain and the insects. He set no great store by the work, caring only that it distracted him, but was nonetheless pleased that the woods were becoming littered with his sculptures, crude figures weathering into objects that—like their model—appeared to be natural formations that bore a striking resemblance to dragons.

In the early spring, eleven years after his arrival in Teocinte, Hota hired a carter to haul the trunk of a white oak to the crest of a hill from which he had a profile view of Griaule with the valley spreading beyond, an undulant reach of palms and palmettos, figs and aguacates, threaded by red dirt paths. There he set about his most ambitious project. Previously he had carved the dragon as he might have appeared during more vital days—flying, crouched, or rampant; now he intended to create a sculpture that would depict Griaule as he was: the oddly delicate, birdlike head, jaws half open, tongue and fangs embroidered with lichen, vines depending in loops and snarls from the roof of the mouth; the bluish green folds and struts of the sagittal crest, that same color edging the golden scales; his sinuous body, the haunches, flanks, and back mapped by a forest whose dark green conformation was so similar to the shapes of the hills that lifted higher behind him, it caused Hota to wonder if they, too, might not conceal gigantic dragons. He spent a week in laying out the design and then several days more gathering the details of Griaule's shape in his mind and letting that knowledge flow into his hands.

Toward noon one morning, as Hota was busy carving, he noticed something flying in loops above Griaule's snout, difficult to make out against the strong sun, as tiny in relation to the dragon as a swallow fluttering about a bull's nose. To his astonishment, for Hota had thought Griaule to be the sole survivor of his species, he realized it was another dragon. Thirty to forty feet long, by his estimate. With bronze scales. Enthralled, he watched the creature swoop and soar, maintaining a predictable circuit, as if she (because of her daintiness by contrast to Griaule, Hota thought of the second dragon as she) were tracing the same character over and over, enacting a ritual of some kind. Her wings seemed to ripple rather than to beat against the air, and her long neck glided through its attitudes with the suppleness of a reed borne on a stream, and her tail lashed about with what struck him as a lascivious ferocity. She might be, he surmised, attempting to communicate with Griaule. Or perhaps *he* was communicating with her; perhaps the patterns of her flight gave visual form to the eddies of his thoughts. At length she broke off her circling and settled onto Griaule's broad back, passing out of sight behind his sagittal crest.

Dropping his chisel, Hota hurried down the hill, following a track that merged with one of the red dirt paths crisscrossing the valley, and approached Griaule from the side, heading for the bulge of his foreleg. As the dragon came to loom above him, he felt a surge of terror. The tightly nested scales of the jaw; the gray teeth with their traceries of lichen, like the broken wall of a fortress city; the bulge of an orbital ridge: seen close to hand, the monumental aspect of these things dismayed him, and when he moved into the dragon's shadow, something colder and thicker than air seemed to glove him, as if he were moving in invisible mud. But fascination overbore his fright. The prospect of observing a dragon who was capable of motion excited him. There was nothing of the academic or the artistic in his interest. He simply wanted to see it.

He scrambled up the slope afforded by the brush-covered foreleg, then ascended to the dragon's thicketed shoulder, catching at shrubs to pull himself higher. His breath labored, sweat poured off him. On several occasions he nearly fell. When at last he stood atop Griaule's back, clinging for support to a pine branch, looking down at the valley hundreds of feet below, Teocinte showing as an ugly grayish patch amid the greenery, he understood the foolishness of what he had done. He felt unarmored against the arrows of fate, as if he had violated a taboo and been stripped of all his immunities. And adding to his anxiety was the fact that nearby was a dragon who, upon sensing him, would seek to tear him to pieces... unless she had flown away while he was climbing, and he doubted this to be the case. Fear mounted in him once again, but he did not place so much value on his life as once he had—indeed, he often wondered why he had bothered to save himself from the hangman's rope that night in Port Chantay—and his desire to see her remained strong. Planting his feet with care, easing branches aside, he pressed on into the brush and headed for the spot where he supposed the second dragon had landed.

The heat of the day came full and Hota continued to sweat profusely. The needle sprays of stunted pine and the yellowed round leaves of the shrubs that dominated the thicket limited his view to a few yards ahead and stuck to his damp neck and cheeks and arms. After wandering blindly about for a quarter of an hour, he began to speculate that the second dragon had made no landing at all, but merely swooped down behind the sagittal crest and then leveled off and flew away over the hills. He found a bare patch of ground and sat, deliberating whether or not to give up the search. Scutterings issued from the brush and this alarmed him. Rumor had it that many of the animals living in and on Griaule were poisonous. Deciding that he had been foolish enough for one day, Hota stood and headed back the way he had come. After half an hour, when he had not reached the edge of the thicket, he realized with annoyance that he must have gotten turned around and was walking along the spine. He stood on tiptoes, caught sight of the dragon's crest, and, thus oriented, started off parallel to it. Another half hour passed and his annoyance blossomed into panic. Someone—doubtless Griaule himself—was playing a trick on him. Clouding his thoughts, causing him to go in circles. Again he sighted the sagittal crest and beat his way through the brush; but the ground beneath his feet did not slope away as it should have done and when he checked the crest once more, he saw that he had made no progress whatsoever.

After two hours, Hota's panic lapsed into resignation. This, then, was the fate to which his violence had led him. Trapped in a magical circumstance that he could not hope to fathom, he would wander Griaule's back until he grew too weak to walk and died of thirst and exposure. He would, he thought, have preferred to be hung. Yet he could not deny that he was deserving of worse and there was no defiance in him. He kicked broken branches aside, cleaning a spot where he could sit and wait for death; but upon reflection, he kept on walking, deciding it would be best to wear himself out and so hasten the inevitable. He hurried through the thicket, no longer trying to hide his presence, for he assumed that the second dragon had been an illusion, bait in the trap Griaule had set. He swatted boughs aside and shouldered through entangled places, forcing himself whenever possible into a lumbering trot. As he went, he began to feel exhilarated and it occurred to him that this might be because he finally had something meaningful to do. All his years of drinking and inept woodcarving, and all the years prior, the numbing labor, silent evenings staring glumly at his wife, and shabby, juiceless days...It was right they should end here and now. They had profited no one, least of all himself.

The longer he contemplated the prospect of dying, the more eager to have done with life he became. What did he have to look forward to? A few uneventful years followed by the loss of his physical powers? Assaults by younger, stronger men who would rob him and leave him destitute? And that would not be the worst of it. Exhilaration turned to something approaching glee and he increased his pace. Twigs stabbed at him, abrading his skin, but he ignored the pain. He remembered another occasion on which he had felt a similar measure of...what? Enthusiasm? Vitality?

Delirium.

That was the word, he thought.

It was a feeling very like the one he had experienced at the harbormaster's house in Port Chantay.

Sobered by an awareness of this possible connection, he slowed to a walk, mulling it over, wondering if what he felt, then and now, might be an indication of mental infirmity or some physical ailment. He was still considering this notion when he slapped aside a pine bough and stepped into a clearing where stood a slender woman with bronze skin, long black hair falling to the small of her back, and wearing not a stitch of clothing.

The woman was so startling a sight, Hota's initial reaction was one of disbelief. He imagined her to be part of his delirium...or perhaps a further trick of Griaule's. She was half-turned away, a hand to her cheek, as if she had been struck by a remembrance. A pattern of dark irregular lines covered her body. Like, he thought, a sketch of reptilian scales. He first believed the lines to be a tattoo, but then noticed them growing fainter every second, and he recalled that the scales of the female dragon had been the exact shade of bronze as the woman's skin. On hearing his choked outcry, she glanced back at him over her shoulder, displaying no indication of fear such as might be expected of a naked woman alone on being surprised by a man of his threatening appearance. She remained motionless, calmly regarding, and Hota, unable to accept what he was tempted to believe— that here stood the dragon he had sought, transformed somehow—was torn between the desire to flee and the need to know more about her. In a matter of seconds, the lines on her skin faded utterly and, as if this signaled the completion of a process that had restrained her, she turned to face him and said in a dry, dusty voice, "Hota."

The sound of his name on her lips, freighted with a touch of menace, or so he heard it, spurred him to flight. Unwilling to look away from her, he took a backward step, tried to run, but stumbled, and went sprawling onto his belly. He scrambled to one knee and found her standing above him.

"Are you afraid?" she asked, tipping her head to the side.

Her eyes were dark, the irises large, leaving room for scarcely any white and her face, with its sharp cheekbones and full lips and delicate nose, was too perfect, lifeless, as might be an uninspired artist's rendering. She repeated her question and, like her face, her voice was empty of human temper. The question seemed pragmatic, as if she were unfamiliar with fear and was hoping to identify its symptoms. Though she looked to be a mature woman, not a girl, her breasts and hips and belly betrayed no marks of age or usage.

Hota sank back into a sitting position, dumbstruck.

"There's no reason to fear. We have a road to travel, you and I." A cloud passed across the sun; the woman glanced up sharply, scanning the sky, and then said, "I'll need some clothing."

Somewhat reassured, Hota edged away from her and got to his feet. He gave thought again to running, but remembered getting lost among the thickets and decided that running would probably do him no good.

"Did you hear?" she asked, and again her words conveyed no sense of impatience or anger. "I need clothing."

Hota framed a question of his own, but was too daunted to speak.

"Your name is Hota, isn't it?" the woman asked.

"Yes." He licked his lips, tried to dredge up the courage to ask his question, failed, and succeeded only in making a confused noise.

"Magali," said the woman, and touched the slope of a breast. "My name is Magali."

He could detect nothing of her mood. It was as if she were hidden inside a beautiful shell, her true self muffled. She waited for him to speak and finally, when he kept silent she said, "You know me. Is that what's troubling you?"

"I've never seen you before," Hota said.

"But you know who I am. You saw me fly. You saw me while I was yet changing."

This, though it was the answer to his unasked question, only confounded him further and, in response, he merely shook his head.

"How can you not believe it?" she said. "You saw what you saw. But you have nothing to fear from me. I'm a woman now. My flesh is as yours." She reached out and took his hand. Her palm was warm. "Do you understand?"

"No...I..." He shook his head vigorously. "No."

"You will in time." She released his hand. "Now can you bring me some clothing?"

"There are no shops that sell women's clothes in Teocinte."

"Borrow some...or bring me some of your own. I'll make do."

By agreeing to do her bidding, Hota thought he would be able to make his escape. "All right. I'll go now," he said.

"You'll come back. Don't think you won't."

"Of course I will."

She laughed at this—it was, he thought, the first purely human thing she had done. "That's not what is in your mind."

"How can you know what's in my mind?"

"It's written on your face," she said. "You can't wait to be gone. Once out of sight, you'll run. That's what you're thinking, anyway. But you'll tell yourself that if you don't return, I'll come after you. And it's true— I would. But you have deeper reasons for returning."

"How can that be?" he asked. "We have no history together, nothing that would furnish a depth of reason."

She moved away a few paces, turning toward the sun, and a pattern of leaf shadow fell across her hip, reminding him of the pattern that had faded from her skin. She arranged her hair so that it trailed across her breasts, dressing herself in the black skeins.

"You'll come back because there's no other direction for you," she said. "Your life until this moment has been empty and you hope I'll offer fulfillment of a kind. You'll come back because you want to. Because the road you and I must travel, we have already set foot upon it."

WHEN HOTA AND Magali, clad in an unflattering ankle-length dress he had borrowed from a prostitute, arrived at Liar's House that evening, Benno Grustark, portly and short-legged, his round, dark-complected face set in grouchy lines and framed by oily black ringlets, hurried out of his office and admonished Hota that if the woman were to spend the night, he would have to pay extra. After getting a closer look at Magali, however, and after she turned her flat stare upon him, his delivery sputtered. When they passed up the stairs, leaving Benno looking up from the dusty lobby, silent, not offering, as was his habit, further admonitions, Hota suspected that the innkeeper was unaccustomed to having so beautiful a woman frequent his establishment.

On ushering her into his room, Hota apologized for its sorry condition, but Magali paid no attention to the disarray and walked over to the wall beside his bed and began to inspect the weathered gray boards, running her forefinger along the black complexities of their grain, appearing to admire them as though they were made of the finest marble. Still daunted to a degree, Hota busied himself by straightening the room, picking up wooden dragons and stowing them into drawers, dusting his rude furniture with a shirt. Glancing up from these chores, he saw that Magali had taken a seat on the bed and was picking at the folds of her skirt.

"I'd like a green dress," she said. "Dark green. Do you have a seamstress in the town?"

Hota wadded up the dust-covered shirt and tossed it onto a chair. "I think so...Yes."

She nodded solemnly as if he had imparted a great wisdom and then swung her legs up and lay back on the bed. "I want to sleep for a while. Perhaps we can have something to eat afterward."

"The tavern downstairs...they have food. It's not so good."

She closed her eyes, let out a sigh, and after a minute or two Hota assumed that she had drifted off; but then, with a sudden violent twisting of her body, she turned onto her side and said, her words partially muffled by the pillow, "Just so long as there's meat."

THEIR FIRST DAYS together passed uncomfortably for Hota. Magali left the room only to visit the bathroom down the hall and spent much of both day and night asleep, as if, he thought, she were acclimating to her new form. When awake she would peer at the boards or sit on the bed silently. Their infrequent conversations were functional, pertaining to things she needed, and if he was not off running errands for her, he sat in the chair and waited for her to wake. The town's seamstress delivered two dark green dresses and Magali, without thought for modesty, would change from one to the other in full view of Hota and he would feel stirrings of desire. How could he not? He was not used to this sort of display. His wife had gone to bed each night swaddled in layers of clothing, and even the prostitutes with whom he slept would merely hike up their skirts. With its high, small breasts and sleek flanks and long, graceful legs, Magali's body was a sculptor's dream of unmarred sensuality. But desire would not catch in him. He was still afraid, his mind too full of questions to permit the increase of lust, and he never ventured near her, sleeping on the floor or in a chair. What, he wondered, was the road they were to travel? Was she truly a dragon recast as a woman, or was this all the result of a trick, a conspiracy of event and moment? And, most urgently, why had any of this happened? How could it be happening?

Sitting beside her day after day, week after week, Hota grew discontented with his surroundings and thought this might be because Magali's presence pointed up their shabbiness. He became assiduous in his cleaning, brought in flowers, new cushions for his chairs, and purchased prints to hang on the walls, brightening the long gray space. The footsteps and voices that sounded from the hallway irritated him and to mute them he hung blankets across the door. He dispersed the room's stale odor with sachets he bought in the market. None of these improvements registered with Magali. For no reason he could fathom, she seemed interested only in the boards. Then one night while she slept, as he was pacing about, he noticed that the grain of the planking looked sharper than before, considerably sharper than could be expected as a result of his daily dusting. Curious, he examined them in the light of an oil lamp and found that the patterns of the grain were, indeed, more pronounced, forming intricacies of dark lines in which it was possible to see almost anything. This was his initial impression, but as he continued to peer at them, certain shapes came to dominate. He saw narrow wings replete with struts and vanes, sinuous scaled bodies, fanged reptilian heads. A multiplicity of dragons. Every plank bore such images, all cunningly devised. And it seemed more were emerging all the time, as if they had been buried beneath gray snow that was now thawing. Holding the lamp above his head, he studied them and began to think he was not looking at many dragons, but at countless depictions of one. There were similarities in the architecture of the scales and the birdlike profile, the...

"What do you see?"

Given a start, Hota yipped and spun about to face Magali, who had padded up behind him. Her dress was unbuttoned to her navel, exposing the swell of her breasts, and though her hair was tousled from sleep, her usual neutral stare was not in evidence. She looked animated, excited, and this acted to suppress the anxiety her nearness inspired in him. She repeated her question and he said, "Dragons...or maybe one dragon. I'm not sure. Is that what you see?"

She ignored the question. "Anything else?"

"No. Is there more?"

"There's no end of things that can be seen."

She stepped up beside him and ran a hand along one of the boards, as if caressing it, then pointed at one of the images. "Here. Do you see the way this fang juts out at an angle? What does it remind you of?"

Uncomprehending, he gazed at the board for the better part of a minute and then he saw it. "Griaule! Is it Griaule?"

"All this"—she made a sweeping gesture, her voice quavering as with strong emotion—"it's his life. Ingrained within the trees that sprouted from his back. The entire inn is a record. All his days are written here."

So, Hota thought, Benno had not lied. It was difficult to believe. In Hota's experience, Benno had never exhibited an ounce of physical bravery, and the idea that he would chop down trees on Griaule's back was laughable. It was equally unlikely that he could have found anyone to do the cutting for him. Those few who claimed to have set foot upon the dragon spoke of climbing onto the tail—none had trespassed to the degree that Hota himself had. And yet he remembered the way Benno had gaped at Magali. Might that have been a recognition of sorts, evidence that Benno, being more familiar than most with dragons, had sensed her hidden nature?

"Whatever else there is to see..." Hota said. "Will I see it?"

"Who knows?" She returned to the bed and as she settled upon it, smoothing out her skirt beneath her, she said, "You've seen what's necessary."

"Why's it necessary for me to see this much and no more? What's the point?"

She reclined upon the bed, braced on an elbow. "So you'll understand the extent of Griaule's dominion. So you'll accept it."

This rankled him, but he was not sufficiently confident with her to express anger. "Why is that important? I already know he shapes our lives to some extent."

"Knowing a thing is far from accepting it."

"What are you talking about?"

She put an arm across her eyes and said nothing.

"Are you saying I need to make an acknowledgment of some sort? Why? Explain it to me."

She would say no more on the subject and, shortly thereafter, she asked him to bring food from the tavern. Hota did not care to be treated like a child, given answers that suggested there were things he was better off not knowing—that was how he interpreted her responses—and as he waited for Magali's food to be prepared, standing by the kitchen door, gazing through smoke and steam at the hubbub generated by two matronly cooks and several grimy children, he thought angrily about her. How could he doubt she was who she claimed to be? For all her good looks, the woman behaved like a lizard. Torpid the day long. Rising only to piss and stare at the boards. And the way she ate! She brought to mind geckos back in Port Chantay, clinging to the walls for hours, motionless, before finally flicking out their tongues to snag a mosquito, lifting their…

One of the serving boys, carrying a plate of rice and shredded pork into the tavern, brushed against Hota's hip. Hota snapped at him, then felt badly for having frightened the boy. What was he doing here? he asked himself. Cohabiting with a woman who had some mysterious plan for him. Languishing in a room where pictures of dragons manifested upon the walls. He should have done with her. With Teocinte. The next time she asked for food, he should take his bag of gems and cash, and head inland. Make for Caliche or cross the country altogether to Point Horizon. But could he leave? That was the question. Would he wander the valley, confused, unable to find his way out, always winding up back in Teocinte? The answer to this question, he decided, was probably yes. He was still caught in the snare Griaule had set for him the day he met Magali. If he were ever able to escape it, he supposed it would be because the dragon was done with him.

Despite his annoyance, that conversation marked a turning in their relationship. Though she remained less than talkative over the next month, now and then, in addition to asking him for things, she would inquire as to how he felt or, standing at a window, would offer comments on the weather, the unsightliness of the town, or laugh at, say, the misery of a carter whose wheels had gotten stuck in the mud. It appeared she was developing a personality. Mean-spirited, for the most part. Minimal. But a personality nonetheless. She continued her habit of disrobing in front of him and he noticed changes in her body: a faint crease demarking the lower reach of her abdomen; a hint of crow's-feet; the slightest sag to her breasts. Changes that would have been imperceptible to anyone else, but that to someone who had observed her for seven weeks, whose only occupation had been that observance, they stood out like mountains on a plain. He wondered if these marks and slackenings signaled the ultimate stage of her transformation, and he found himself, against the weight of logic, thinking of her as a woman more often than not. As a consequence, his desire burned hotter, despite an apprehension that such feelings were touched with the perverse.

During the eighth week of her stay at Liar's House, Magali became more active, sleeping less, enjoining Hota in conversations that, though brief, served to grow the relationship. One night, rather than sending him for food, she suggested that they eat in the tavern. Her suggestion did not sit easily with Hota. Under the best of circumstances, he preferred solitude. Further, he worried that Magali might not react well on being exposed to a crowd. But when they entered the tavern, a low-ceilinged room with the same gray weathered planking, furnished with long benches and tables, lit by lanterns of fanciful design, each consisting of frosted panes held in place by ironwork dragons, they found only five patrons in the place: two prostitutes and their clients dining together, and a burly blond man with a pink complexion and a pudgy, thick-lipped face who was drinking beer from a clay mug. They stationed themselves well away from the others, close to the wall, and ordered wine and venison. Magali sat without saying a word, taking in the scene, and Hota watched her with more than his usual fixity. The din and angry shouts from the kitchen, the laughter of the prostitutes, all the sounds of the tavern receded from him. It seemed a heartbeat was buried in the orange glow of the lamps, contriving a pulsing backdrop for the woman opposite him, whose bronze skin was in itself a radiant value. He gazed at her thoughtlessly, or else it was a single formless thought that uncoiled through his mind, imposing what seemed an almost ritual attentiveness.

When the food arrived, Magali picked up her venison steak and nibbled a bite, chewed, threw back her head and swallowed. She repeated this process over and over. Hota shoveled down his meal without tasting it, his attention unwavering. Like the icon of some faded gaiety, an old man with wisps of white hair fraying up from his mottled scalp, wearing a ratty purple cloak, entered the tavern and played a whistling music on bamboo pipes; he stopped at the other tables, begging for a coin, but veered away from Hota after receiving a hostile look.

Hota understood that something was wrong. The ordinary grind of his thoughts had been suppressed, damped down, but he had no will to contend against the agent of suppression, whatever it was, seduced by Magali's face and figure. He derived a proprietary pleasure from watching the convulsive working of her throat and the fastidious movements of her fingers and teeth. Like an old man watching a very young girl. Greedy for life, not sex. Lusting after some forbidden essence. Although he perceived this ugliness in himself and wanted to reject it, he found he could not and tracked her every gesture and change in expression. She gave no sign that she noticed the intensity or the character of his vigilance, but the fact that she never once engaged his eyes told him she knew he was looking and that all her actions were part of a show. The inside of his head felt warm, as if his brain, too, were pulsing with soft orange light.

More customers drifted into the tavern. The conversation and laughter outvoiced the kitchen noises, but it seemed quiet where Hota and Magali sat, their isolation unimpaired. Then two bulky men in work-stained clothes came to join the blond man at his table. They drank swiftly, draining their mugs in a few gulps, and began casting glances at Magali, who was now devouring her second steak. They leaned their heads together and whispered and then laughed uproariously. Typically, Hota would have ignored their derision, but anger mounted in him like a liquid heated in a glass tube. He heaved up from the bench and went over to the men's table and glared down at them. The newcomers appeared to know him, at least by reputation, for one, adopting an air of appeasement, muttered his name, and the other fitted his gaze to the tabletop. But either the blond man was only recently arrived in Teocinte or else he was immune to fear. He sneered at Hota and asked, "What do you want?"

One of the others made silent speech with his eyes to the blond man, as if encouraging him to be wary, but the man said, "Why are you afraid of this lump of shit? Let's hear what's on his mind."

Through the lens of anger, Hota saw him not as a man, but as a creature you might find clinging to the pitch-coated piling of a dock, an unlovely thing with loathsome urges and appetites, and a pink, rubbery face that was a caricature of the human.

"Can't you talk, then? Very well. I'll talk." Smirking, the blond man settled back against the wall, resting a foot on the bench. "Do you know who I am?"

Hota held his tongue.

"No? It doesn't matter. The thing that most matters is who you are. You're a man who needs no introduction. Useless. Dull. A clod. You might as well carry a sign with those words on it. You announce yourself everywhere you go."

Hota felt as if his skin were a crust that was restraining some molten substance beneath.

"I suppose it would be easiest for you to think of me as your opposite number," the blond man continued. "I employ men such as you. I turn them to my purposes. I might be persuaded to employ you...if you're as strong as you look. Are you?"

A smile came unbidden to Hota's face.

The blond man chuckled. "Well, strength's not everything, my friend. I've bested many men who were stronger than me. Do you know how?" He tapped the side of his head. "Because I'm strong up here. I could take things from you and you wouldn't be able to stop me. Your woman, for instance. Beautiful! I gave some thought to taking her off your hands. But I've concluded that she'll feel more at home with you." He gave a bemused sniff. "For your sake, I hope she fucks less like a pig than she eats."

As Hota reached for the blond man's leg, the closer of his two companions threw a punch at Hota's forehead. The punch did no damage and Hota struck him in the mouth with an elbow, breaking his teeth and knocking him beneath the adjoining table. He seized the blond man's ankle, yanked him out into the center of the tavern, holding his leg high so he could not get to his feet. The third man came at him, a lack of conviction apparent in the hesitancy of his attack. Hota kicked him in the groin and, taking a one-handed grip on the blond man's throat, lifted him so that his feet dangled several inches above the floor. He clawed at Hota, pried at his fingers.

His face empurpled. A froth fumed between his lips. He fumbled out a dagger and tried to stab Hota, but Hota knocked the dagger to the floor, caught his knife hand and squeezed, at the same time relaxing his grip on his throat. The blond man sank to his knees, screaming as the bones in his hand were snapped and ground together.

"Hota!"

Magali was standing by the door that led to the street. She appeared, despite the urgency of her shout, unruffled. Hota let go of the blond man, who rolled onto his side, cradling his bloody, mangled hand and cursing at Hota. Several other men had drawn near, their physical attitudes suggesting that they might be ready to fight. Hota faced them down, squaring his shoulders, and, instead of cautioning them, he roared.

The noise that issued from him was more than the sum of a troubled life, of anger, of social impotence—it seemed to spring from a vaster source, to be the roar of the turning world, a sound that all creation made in its spin toward oblivion, exultant and defiant even in dismay, and that went unheard until, as now, it found a host suitable to give it tongue.

Quailed, the men backed toward the kitchen. Recognizing that they no longer posed a threat, his anger emptied in that roar, Hota went to Magali's side. Her face was unreadable, but he felt from her a radiation of contentment. She took his arm and they stepped out into the town.

BY NIGHT, TEOCINTE had an even more derelict aspect than by day. The crooked little shacks, firelight flickering through cracks in the doors and from behind squares of cloth hung over windows; winded and quiet except for the occasional scream and burst of laughter; a naked infant, untended, splashing in a puddle formed by that afternoon's rain; the silhouette of Griaule's tree-lined back outlined in stars against a purple sky: it had the atmosphere of a tribal place, of people huddled together in frail shelters against the terrors of the dark, dwelling in the very shadow of those terrors. Hota felt estranged, from the town and from himself, troubled by the presence in his thoughts that had spurred him to such violence. But Magali's presence, her scent, the brush of her hip, the pressure of her breast against his arm, kept him from brooding. They idled along the down slope of the street that fronted Liar's House, moving toward the dragon's head, and as they walked she said, "We should be flying now."

"Flying," he said. "What do you mean?"

"It's the most wonderful thing, flying together…that's all."

He suspected that she was dissembling and knew she did not like being pressed; but he had the itch to press her. She rarely spoke about her life prior to their meeting and, though he was not convinced that she was who she claimed to be, he wanted to believe her. It surprised him that he wanted this. Until that instant he had been uncertain as to what he wanted, but he was clear about it now. He wanted her to be a fabulous creature, for himself to be part of her fabulous design, and, sensing that she might be receptive to him, he asked if she could tell him how it was to fly.

She was silent for such a length of time, he thought she would refuse to answer, but after five or six paces she said, "One day you'll know how it feels."

Puzzled, he said, "I don't understand."

"You can't…not yet."

That comment sparked new questions, but he chose to pursue the original one. "You must be able to say something about it."

They walked a while longer and then she said, "Each flight is like the first flight, the flight made at the instant of creation. You're in the dark, maybe you're drowsy. Almost not there. And then you wake to some need, some urgency. Your wings crack as you rise up. Like thunder. And then you're into the light, the wind… The wind is everything. All your strength and the rush of the wind, the sound of your wings, the light, it's one power, one voice."

As she spoke he seemed to understand her, but when she fell silent the echoes of the words lost energy and died, transformed into generalities. He tried to explore them, to recapture some sense of the feeling her voice had communicated, but failed.

The town ended in a palm hammock, and at the far edge of the hammock, resting among tall grasses, was a squarish boulder nearly twice the height of a man, like a giant's petrified tooth. They climbed atop it and sat gazing at Griaule's head, a hundred yards distant. The sagittal crest was visible in partial silhouette against the sky, but the bulk of the head was a mound of shadow.

"You keep telling me I can't understand things," he said. "It's frustrating. I want to understand something and I don't understand any of it. How is it you can be here with me like this…as a woman?"

She lifted her head and closed her eyes as she might if the sun were shining and she wanted to indulge in its warmth, and she told him of the souls of dragons. How, unlike the souls of men, they enclosed the material form rather than being shrouded within it.

"Our souls are not prisoners of the flesh, but its wardens," she said. "We control our shapes in ways you cannot."

"You can be anything you choose? Is that what you mean?"

"Only a dragon or a woman…I think. I'm not sure."

He pondered this. "Why can't Griaule change himself into a man?"

"What would be the point? Who would be more inviolate—a paralyzed dragon or a paralyzed man? As a dragon, Griaule lives on. As a man, he would long since have been eaten by lesser beasts. In any case, the change is painful. It's something done only out of great necessity."

"You didn't appear to be in pain…when I found you."

"It had ebbed by the time you reached me."

There were too many questions flocking Hota's thoughts for him to single any one out; but, before long, one soared higher than the rest: What great necessity had caused her to change? He was about to ask it of her when she said, "Soon you'll understand all of this. Flying. How the soul can grow larger than the flesh. How it is that I have come to you and why. Be patient."

Moonglow fanned up above the hills to the west and in that faint light she looked calm, emotionless. Yet as he considered her, it struck him that a new element was embodied in her face. Serenity…or perhaps it was an absence he perceived, some small increment of anxiety erased.

"Griaule," she said in a half-whisper.

"What of him?" he asked, perplexed by her worshipful tone. She only shook her head in response.

Something scurried through the grass behind the boulder. A dull gleam emerged from the shadow of Griaule's head, the tip of a fang holding the light. The wind picked up, bringing the still palms alive, swaying their fronds, breeding a sigh that seemed to voice a hushed anticipation. Magali folded her arms across her breasts.

"I'm ready now," she said.

HOTA ASSUMED THAT by those last words, she meant she was ready to return to Liar's House, for after saying them, she hopped down from the boulder and led him back toward the town; but once they closed the door of his room behind them, it became clear she had intended something more. She undressed quickly and stood before him in a silent yet unmistakable invitation, her skin agleam in the unsteady lamplight. Skeins of hair fell across her breasts, like black tributaries on the map of a voluptuous bronze country. Her eyes were cored with orange reflection. She looked to be a magical feminine treasure whose own light devalued that of the lamp. All his flimsy moral proscriptions against intimacy melted away. He took a step toward her and let her bring him down onto the bed.

During the first thirty-one years of his life, Hota had made love to but one woman: his wife. Since then, he had made love to many more and thought himself reasonably knowledgeable as to their ways. Magali's ways, however, enlarged his views on the subject. For the most part she lay quiescent, her eyes half-closed, as if her mind were elsewhere and she were merely allowing herself to be penetrated; but every so often, abruptly, she would begin to thrash and heave, pushing and clawing at him, breath shrieking out of her, throwing herself about with such apparent desperation, he was nearly unseated. Initially, he took this behavior for rejection and flung himself off her; but she pulled him back down between her legs and, once he had entered her, she lay quiet again. This alternation of corpselike stillness and frenzied motion distressed him and he was unable to lose himself in the act, half-listening to the sounds of more commercial passions emanating from adjoining rooms. When he had finished and was lying beside her, sweaty and breathing hard, she demanded that he repeat the performance. And so it went, the second encounter like the first, equally as awkward and emotionally unsatisfying. In her frenzied phase, she seemed even less a complicitor in pleasure than she did when she was still. She took to snapping at his arm, his shoulder, making cawing noises deep in her throat. But their third encounter, one into which Hota had to be vigorously coerced, was different. She drew up her knees and met his thrusts with sinuous abandon and kept her arms locked about his neck, her eyes upon his face, until at long last she offered up a shivery cry and clamped her knees to his sides, refusing to let him move.

After he withdrew, pleased, feeling that they had managed actual intimacy, he tried to be tender with her, but she shrank from his touch and would not speak. More confused than ever, he decided that her behavior must be due to a lack of familiarity with her body, and he counseled himself to remain patient. They had come this far and whatever road lay ahead, there would be time to smooth over these problems. Fatigued, his eyes went to the lamp-lit ceiling. It looked as if all the dragons imprinted in the grain were quivering, shifting agitatedly, as if preparing to take flight. He watched them, imagining that if he watched long enough he would see one fly, the tiny black sketch of a dragon flap up off the boards and make a circuit of the room. Eventually he slept.

The following morning, gray and drizzly, with a touch of chill, he woke to find Magali at the window, which stood half-open. She had on her green dress and was looking out onto the street. He sat up, groggy, rubbing his eyes. The bedsprings squeaked loudly, but she gave no sign of having heard.

"Magali?" he said.

She ignored him. The rain quickened, drumming on the tin roof. Feeling the bite of the cold, Hota swung his legs onto the floor, grabbed his shirt from among the rumpled bedclothes, and began to pull it over his head.

"Is something wrong?" he asked.

Without turning, she said glumly, "You've given me a child."

He paused, the shirt tangled about his neck, and started to ask how she could know such a thing, then remembered that she had knowledge inaccessible to him.

"A son," she said dully. "I'm going to have a son."

The idea of fathering children no longer figured into Hota's plans and his immediate reaction was uneasiness over having to shoulder such a responsibility. He tugged the shirt down to cover his belly. "You don't seem happy. Is it you don't want a child?"

"It isn't what I want that's of moment." She paused and then said, "The birth will be painful."

Her attitude, so contrary to what he would have expected, provoked an odd reaction in him—he wondered how it would feel to be a father. "It might not be so bad," he said. "I've known women to have easy childbirths. At the end we'll have our son and perhaps that'll give..."

"He's not *your* son," she said. "You fathered him, but he will be Griaule's son."

The rain came harder yet and, amplified by the tin, filled the room with a kind of roaring, a din that made it difficult for Hota to think, to hear his own voice. "That's impossible."

Magali turned from the window. "Haven't you heard a thing I've told you?"

"What have you told me that would explain this?"

She stared at him without expression. "Griaule is the eldest of all who live. Over the centuries, his soul has expanded with the growth of his body. How far it extends, I can't say. Far beyond the valley, though. I know that much. I was flying above the sea when he drew me to him." She dropped heavily into the chair beside the window and rested her hands on her knees. "His soul encloses him like a bubble. For all I know that bubble has grown to enclose the entire world. But I'm certain you live inside its reach. You've lived inside it your whole life. And now he's drawn you to him as well. It's possible he caused the events that drove you from Port Chantay. That would be in keeping with what I understand of his character. With the deviousness and complexity of his mind."

Hota felt the need to offer a denial, but could find no logical framework to support one.

"Don't you see?" she went on. "Griaule desired to father a son. Since he couldn't participate in the act of conception, he contrived a means by which he could father the child of his will. And for this purpose he sought out a man who embodied certain of his own qualities. Someone with a stolid temperament. With great strength and endurance. And great anger. A human equivalent of his nature who fit the shape of his design. Then he chose me to endure the birth."

Rain slanted in through the window. Hota crossed the room and closed it. As he returned to the bed, he said, "You must have known this all along? Why didn't you tell me?"

She clicked her tongue in annoyance. "I didn't know all of it. I still don't know it all. And it's as I've said—these things that have happened to us, they weren't my wish. Even if they were, I'm not like you. My thoughts are not like yours. My motives are not yours. You asked why I wasn't happy? I'm never happy. My emotions...You couldn't grasp them."

"You should have told me," he said sullenly.

"It would have only upset you. There's nothing you could have done."

"Nevertheless, you lied to me. I don't deserve to be kept in the dark about what's going on."

"I haven't lied!" she said. "Have I withheld things from you? Yes. I did what I was compelled to do. But all the things I know, the things I don't know, they may or may not be good for you. And that's what you truly want to know, isn't it? What's going to happen to you? In the end all your questions will be answered and you'll be pleased with that. That's what I think. But I can't be certain. That's the problem, you see? Any answer I can give you is essentially a lie, except for 'I don't know.'"

Her response had the same disorienting effect as the rain—he believed her, but it was like believing in nothing, knowing nothing. He sat with his head down, dull and listless, looking at his fingers, wiggling them for a distraction. "You and me...What about you and me?"

"We'll travel the road together and learn what fate has in store. That's all I can tell you."

"I don't believe you."

"What don't you believe?"

"About your feelings," he said. "I know you were happy last night. For a time, at least."

She leaned toward him and spoke slowly, with exaggerated emphasis, as if to a child. "I lived in the side of a cliff. A sea cave. I was alone, yet I wanted for nothing. I was content with the world I knew." She resettled in her chair. "Last night, that was…strange. Now it's done. We're past that turn of the road."

She appeared to lose interest in the conversation, her eyes traveling across the boards. In the rainy light, her beauty was subdued, diminished. "Are you happy?" she asked after a minute.

"Maybe I was, a little. I'm never happy much." He spotted his pants lying on the floor and stepped into them. "Why would Griaule do this? For what reason does he want a son?"

"I've no idea. Perhaps it's just a game he's playing. You can't know Griaule's intent. Some of his schemes play out over thousands of years. He's unique, as unlike me as I am unlike you. No one can understand what he intends."

Of a sudden the rain let up and a weak sun broke through the overcast; the wind gusted and a distorted shadow of the window, pale panes and darker divisions, canted out of true, trembled on the floor.

"I need food," Magali said.

THOUGH HOTA HELD out hope that their night together would be the beginning of intimacy, he soon recognized it to have been their peak. Thereafter the relationship settled back into one of functional disengagement. He brought her food, whatever she needed, and kept watch over her with devotional intensity. Their conversations grew less frequent, less far-ranging, as her belly swelled…and it swelled much more rapidly than would a typical pregnancy. Four weeks and she had the shape of a woman in late-term. She stayed in bed most of the day. Never again did they visit the tavern or walk out together in the town. Hota sat in a chair, brooding, or stood at the window and did the same. He became familiar with the window much in the way he had become familiar with Magali, noting all its detail: patches of greenish mold on the sill; a splintery centerpiece; areas of wood especially stained and swollen by dampness; rotted inches eaten away by infestation. Its gray dilapidation was, he thought, emblematic not only of the room, but of his life, which was itself a gray, dilapidated region, a space that contained and limited his spirit, stunting its growth.

LUCIUS SHEPARD

He recognized, too, that his position in the town had changed. Whereas formerly he had been someone whom people avoided, few had spoken against him, but now, when they passed him in the streets, no one offered a greeting or a salute: instead, men and women would stand closer together, whisper and dart wicked glances in his direction. The reasons for this change remained unclear until one afternoon, as he entered the inn, Benno Grustark accosted him at the door and demanded twice the usual rent.

"I'm losing business, having you here," Benno told him. "You need to compensate me."

Hota pointed out that his was the only place in town where visitors could stay and thus he doubted Benno's claim.

"When people hear about you, some will sleep outside rather than rent my rooms," Benno said.

"When they hear about me?" Hota said, bewildered. "What do they hear?"

Benno, who was that day dressed in his customary brown moleskin trousers and a red tunic that clung to his ample belly, a costume that lent him an inappropriately jolly look, shifted his feet and cut his eyes to the side as if fearing he would be overheard. "Your woman…people say she's a witch."

Hota grunted a laugh.

"It's not a joke for me," Benno said. "What do you expect them to think? She's about to give birth and yet she's only been with you a few months!"

"She was pregnant before I brought her here."

"Oh, I see! And where was she before that? Did you keep her in your pocket? Did you make her pregnant at a distance?"

"It's not my child," Hota said, and realized that this, unlike his previous statement, was only partially a lie.

An expression of incredulity on his face, Benno said, "I saw her when she came. She wasn't showing at all. And I've seen her since, in the hallway, no more than a month ago. She wasn't showing then, either."

"All pregnant women show differently. You know that."

Benno started to raise a further point, but Hota cut him off. "Since you're so observant, I have to assume you're the one who's been spreading rumors about her."

Benno popped his eyes and waggled his hands at chest-level in thespian display of denial. "Plenty of people have seen her. Other guests. Some of my girls. Her condition's hardly a secret."

Hota dug coins from his pocket and pressed them into Benno's hand. "Here," he said. "Now leave us alone."

With a plodding tread, he started up the stairs.

Benno followed to the first step and called out, "As soon as she's able to travel, I want the both of you gone! Do you hear me? Not one day longer than necessary!"

"It'll be our pleasure." Hota paused midway up the stairs and gazed down at him. "But take this to heart. Until that day, you would do well to suppress the rumors about her, rather than foster them." Then a thought struck him. "What possessed you to cut the boards of the inn from Griaule's back?"

Benno's defensive manner was swept away by a confounded look, one similar—Hota thought—to the looks he often wore these days. "I just did it," Benno said. "I wanted to."

"Is that another one of your lies?" Hota asked. "Or don't you know?"

OVER THE COURSE of the next two weeks, Magali became increasingly irritable, not asking things of Hota so much as giving orders and expressing her displeasure when he was slow to obey. She otherwise maintained a brittle silence. Thrown back onto his own resources, Hota fretted about the child and speculated that it might be some mutant thing, awful in aspect and nature. Burdened with such a monster, where could he take her that people would tolerate them? It was not in him to abandon her. Whether that was a function of his character or of Griaule's, he could not have said and was a question he did not seek to answer. He had accepted that this, for the time being, was his station in life. That being the case, he tried to steel himself against doubt and depression, but doubt and depression circled him like vultures above a wounded dog, and the rain, incessant now, drummed and drummed on the tin roof, echoing in his dreams and filling his waking hours with its muted roar. Out the window, he watched the street turn into a quagmire, people sending up splashes with every step, thatched roofs melting into brownish green decay, drenched pariah dogs curled in misery beneath eaves and stairs. The smell of mildew rose from the wood, from clothing. The world was drowning in gray rain and Hota felt he was drowning in the rain of his existence.

Then came a morning when the rain all but stopped and Magali's spirits lifted. She seemed calm, not irritable in the least, and she offered apology for her moodiness, then discussed with him what she would require after the child was born. He asked if she thought the birth would be soon.

"Soon enough," she said. "But that's not your worry. Just bring me food. Meat. And make sure no one disturbs me. The rest I'll take care of."

She needed an herb, she told him, that grew on the far side of the dragon's tail. It was most efficacious when picked at the height of the rains and she asked him to go that day and gather all he could find. She described the plant and urged him to hurry—she wanted to begin taking it as quickly as possible. Then she brushed her lips against his cheek, the closest she had ever come to giving him a kiss, and tried to send him on his way. But this diffident affection, so out of character for her, provoked Hota to ask what she felt for him.

She gave an impatient snort. "I told you—my emotions aren't like yours."

"I'm not an idiot. You could try to explain."

She sat on the edge of the bed, gazed at him consideringly. "What do you feel for me?"

"Devoted, I suppose," he said after a pause. "But my devotion changes. I remain dutiful, but there are times when I resent you...I fear you. Other times, when I desire you."

She appeared to be studying the floor, the boards figured by dragons, blackly emerging from the grain of the wood. "Love and desire," she said at last, imbuing the words with a wistful emphasis. "For me..." She shook her head in frustration. "I don't know."

"Try!" he insisted.

"This is so important to you?"

"It is."

She firmed her lips. "Inevitability and freedom. That's what I feel. For you, for the situation we're in..." She spread her hands, a gesture of helplessness. "That's as near as I can get."

At a loss, Hota asked her to explain further.

"None of this was our idea, yet it was inevitable," she said. "Its inevitability was thrust upon us by Griaule. But that's irrelevant. We have a road to travel and must make the best of it. And so we…we've formed an attachment."

"And freedom? What of that?"

"To find your way to freedom in what is inevitable, within the bonds of your fate…that, for me, is love. Only when you accept a limitation can you escape it."

Hota nodded as if he understood her, and to a degree he did; but he was unable to apply what he understood to the things he felt or the things he wanted her to feel.

Perhaps she read this in his face, for she said then, "Often I feel other emotions. Strains…whispers of them. I think they're akin to those you feel. They trouble me, but I've come to accept them." She beckoned him to come stand beside her and then took his hand. "We'll always be bound together. When you accept that, then you'll find your freedom." She lay back and turned onto her side. "Now, please. Bring me the herb. This is the day it should be picked."

There was no shortcut to the spot where the herb grew, unless you were to climb over Griaule's back. Hota was loath to run that course again and so he went up into the hills behind the town and walked through pine forest along the ridges for an hour until he reached a pass choked by a grassy mound that wound between hills: the dragon's tail. Once across the tail, he walked for half an hour more through scrub palmetto before he came to an undulant stretch of meadow close to the dragon's hind leg, where weeds bearing blue florets sprouted among tall grasses. He worked doggedly, plucking the weeds, cramming them into his sack and tamping them down. When the sack was two-thirds full, he sat beneath a palmetto whose fronds still dripped with rain, facing the massive green slope of the dragon, and unwrapped his lunch of bread and cheese and beer.

The trappings of his life seemed to arrange themselves in orderly ranks as he ate, and he realized that for the first time he had a significant purpose. Aside from momentary impulses, he had never truly wanted anything before Magali appeared atop Griaule's back. Nor, until the day of his wife's death, had he ever acted of his own volition. He had done everything by rote, copying the lives of his father and his uncles, compelled by the circumstance of birth to obey the laws of his class. Of course, it was conceivable… No, it was certain that he had always been the subject of manipulation, that what he had done in Port Chantay and since was not of his own choosing, and he was merely a minor figure in Griaule's design. It was immaterial, he supposed, whether the manipulative force were the arcane directives of a dragon or the compulsions of a society. The main distinction, as he saw it, was that his purpose now—that of surrogate father, caretaker, protector of a woman once a dragon—was a duty for which he had been singled out, for which he was best suited of all available candidates, and that bred in him an emotion he had felt so rarely, he scarcely knew it well enough to name: Pride. It pervaded him now, alleviating both his anxieties and his aversion toward being used in such a bizarre fashion.

An armada of clouds with dark bellies and silvered edges swept up from the south, grazing the sharp crests of the distant hills and thundering, as if their hulls were being ruptured. White lightnings pranced and stabbed. The rain began to pelt down in scatters, big drops that hit like cold shrapnel, and Hota, leaving the remnants of his food for the ants, returned to his task, tearing up fistfuls of weeds and stuffing them into the sack. Soon the thunder was all around, deafening, one peal rolling into the next. Then he heard a low rumble that came from somewhere closer than the sky, an immense, grating voice that seemed to articulate a gloating satiety, a brute pleasure, and lasted far too long to be an ordinary peal. Hota dropped the sack and stared at Griaule, expecting the hill to shake off its cloak of soil and trees, and walk. Expecting also that the head would lift and pin him with a golden eye. Rain matted his hair, poured down his face, and still he stood there, waiting to hear that voice again. When he did not, he became uncertain he had heard it the first time, and yet it resounded in memory, guttural and profound, a voice such as might have risen from the earth, from the throat of a demon pleased by the taste of a freshly digested mortal soul. If he *had* heard it, if it had been Griaule's voice, Griaule who never spoke, Hota could think of only one thing that would have summoned so unique a response. The child. He set about stuffing the sack with renewed vigor, ripping up weeds, unmindful of the rain, and when the sack was full, its girth that of a wagon wheel, he shouldered it and headed back into the hills and along the ridge toward Teocinte.

By the time he began descending through the pine forest, angling for the center of town, Hota was shivering, his clothes soaked through, but his thoughts were of Magali's well-being and not his own. She might have needed the herb in preparation for the birth and suffered greatly for lack of it. The idea that he had failed her plagued him more than the cold. He increased his pace, hustling down the slope with a choppy, sideways step, the sack bumping and rolling against his back. On reaching the lower slope, where the pines thinned out into stands of banana trees and shrubs, he heard voices and caught a glimpse of several men sprinting up the hill. He was too worried about Magali to make a presumption concerning the reason for their haste. Forcing his way through the last of the brush, he burst out onto a dirt street, repositioned the sack, which had slipped from his shoulder. Then he glanced to his left, toward Liar's House.

What he saw rooted him to the spot. Off along the bumpy, muddy street, many-puddled, strafed by slashing rain and lined with shanties that in their crookedness and decrepitude looked like desiccated wooden skulls with tin hats, lay the wreckage of the inn. There appeared to have been an explosion inside the place, the walls and roof blown outward...though not blown far. Just far enough so as to form, of shattered gray boards, crushed furniture, ripped mattresses, and scraps of tin, the semblance of an enormous nest...though one corner post with a shard of flooring attached had been left standing, distracting from the effect. Resting at the center of the ruin, her head high and her body curled about a grayish white egg twice the size of Hota's sack, was a dragon with bronze scales. Perhaps forty feet in length, tip to tail. Twists of black smoke fumed from the boards around her and were dispersed by the rain. Smoke also rose from the wreckage of a shack opposite the hotel. She had breathed fire, Hota told himself. He felt a twinge of regret that he had not been present to see it.

No one else was about and Hota could feel the emptiness of the town. Everyone had fled. All the thieves and murderers. Except for him. The men whom he had passed on the outskirts must have been stragglers. His sack grew heavy. He lowered it to the ground, with no thought of running in his mind, and drank in the scene with the greediness of a connoisseur of desolation, savoring every detail, every variation in tint, every fractured angle. Liar's House had been constructed from exactly the right amount of timber to make a nest, enough to provide protection, yet not so much as to interfere with Magali's field of vision as she lay beside the egg. Griaule's design at work, Hota imagined. The boards had fallen perfectly. Those that had been part of the interior rooms had collapsed outward and thus created a wall around the inner nest; those that had been part of the exterior had fallen inward, creating a field of debris that would be hard for anyone to cross.

Hota was still marveling over the rectitude and precision of Griaule's plan, when Magali's neck flexed, her head turned toward him, and she gave a cry that, though absent the chthonic power of the grumbling he had earlier heard, nonetheless owned power sufficient to terrify him. It started as a guttural cawing and narrowed to a violent whistling scream that seemed to skewer his brain with an icy wire. He wanted to run now, but the sight held him. How beautiful and strange she looked at the heart of her ruinous nest, with her child in his glossy shell, smoke rising about them like black incense burnt to celebrate an idol. Her sagittal crest was a darker bronze, a corroded color—some of her scales shaded toward this same hue at the edges. The shape of her head was different from Griaule's. Not bird-like…serpentine. Her eyes, also dark, set in deep orbits, were flecked with many-colored brightnesses; her folded wings were of an obsidian blackness, the struts wickedly sharp. All in all, like a relic treasure of the orient in her armored gaud. She screamed again and he thought he understood the urgency her voice conveyed.

The herb.

She needed the herb.

He hoisted the sack onto his shoulder. Got his feet moving. Shuffled toward her, resolute yet weak with fear, his scrotum cold and tightened. He paused at the point where the front steps of the hotel had stood, now smashed to kindling, and imagined the change, the floor giving way beneath her suddenly acquired weight, the walls sundered by lashings of her tail and blows from her head. Even with the heavy odor of the rain and smoke, he could smell her scent of bitter ozone. He opened the sack, preparing to dump the contents on the ground, and she screamed a third time, a blast that nearly deafened him.

Closer.

She wanted him closer.

He knew she could extend her neck and snap him up at this distance—there was no reason for him to be more afraid and yet he was. He reshouldered the sack and picked his way across the outer wreckage, scrambling over broken-backed couches, rain-heavied folds of carpet, barricades of splintered wood, and a litter of items belonging to guests: undergarments, shoes, spectacles, books, tin boxes, satchels, hip flasks, a trove of human accessories, all crushed and rent. As he crawled over the last of these obstacles, he saw a taloned foot ahead. The talons gleaming black, the neat scales into which they merged no larger than his hand. And the boards beneath him—those that had fallen so they formed a circular wall about the inner nest—they were alive with the images of dragons. Tiny perfect dragons flowing up from the grain of the wood, changing moment to moment, clearer than they had previously been and counterfeiting movement by their flow, as if they were pictographs emanating from Griaule's mind and he was telling a story in that language to his son, the story of a single dragon and how he flew and hunted and ruled. Like, Hota thought, a nursery decoration. Magical in character, yet serving a function similar to that of the fish he had painted on the ceiling of his own back room in Port Chantay when his wife had informed him she was pregnant. He had painted them over after learning it was a lie told to prevent him from straying.

Standing beneath the arch of Magali's scaled chest and throat, Hota found he could not look up at her. He dumped the weeds from the sack and remained with his head down, appalled by the chuffing engine of her breath, the terrible dimension of her vitality. He shut his eyes and waited to be bitten, chewed, and swallowed. Then a nudge that knocked him sideways. He fetched up against the wall of the nest and fell onto his back. She peered at him with one opaline eye, the great sleek wedge of her head hanging six feet above the ground, snorting gently through ridged nostrils. Her belly rumbled and her head swung in a short arc to face him and he was enveloped in steamy breath. The implausibility of it all bore in upon him. That his seed had been transformed into the stuff of dragons; that he was father to an egg; that the beautiful woman to whom he had made love now loomed above him, dressed in fangs and scales, an icon of fear. His eyes went to the egg, glistening grayly with the rain. Lying just beyond it was a sight that harrowed him. The lower portion of a leg, footless, the calf shredded bloodily. Tatters of brown moleskin adhering to the flesh. Benno. It seemed he had paid for his dutiful trespass by becoming Magali's first postpartum meal.

Magali's neck twisted, her head flipping up into the cloudy sky, and she vented a third scream. Once again, Hota understood her needs.

Bring me food, she was saying.

Meat.

HOW THE DAYS passed for them thereafter was very like the passage of all their days. Hota sat, usually on the steps of a shanty across the way, and watched over Magali. Intermittently, she would scream and he would walk to the livery where a number of horses were stabled, left behind by the panic-stricken citizens of Teocinte. He would lead one into the street (he could never manage to get them closer to the inn) and cut its throat; then he would butcher the animal and carry it to her in bloody sections. From time to time he spotted townspeople skulking on the outskirts, returned to reclaim personal possessions or perhaps to gauge when they might expect to reclaim their homes. They cursed at him and threw stones, but fled whenever he attempted to approach. He himself considered fleeing, but he seemed constrained by a mental regulation that enforced inaction and was as steady in its influence as the rain. He assumed that Griaule was its source, but that was of no real consequence. Everywhere you went, everything you did, some regulation turned you to its use. His thoughts ran in tedious circuits. He wondered if Magali had known she would change back into her original form. He believed she had, and he further believed that everything she had said to him was both lie and truth. She had wanted the herb, but she had also sent him to collect it in order to keep him away from the inn, to prevent him from being injured or killed during her transformation. That was the way of life. His life, at any rate. Even the truest of things eventually resolved into their lie. Every shining surface was tarred with blackness. Every light went dark. He speculated absently on what he would do after she left, as he knew she must, and devised infant plans for travel, for work. A job, he decided, might be in order. He had been idle far too long. But he realized this to be a lie he was telling himself—he doubted he would survive her and, though this might also have been a deception, he did not think he cared to survive her.

His habits became desultory. He fell to drinking, rummaging through the wreckage of the tavern for unbroken bottles and then downing them in a sitting. He slept wherever he was when sleep found him. Out in the street; in a shanty; amid the ruins of Liar's House. Not even the hatching of his golden-scaled child could spark his interest. The cracking of the shell started him from a drunken stupor, but he derived no joy from the event. He stared dumbly at the little monster mewling and stumbling at its mother's side, asking its first demanding questions, learning to feed on fresh horsemeat. At one point he attempted to name it, an exercise in self-derision inspired by his mock-paternity. The names that he conjured were insults, the type of names given to goblins in fairy tales. Tadwallow. Gruntswipe. Stinkpizzle. When he brought the food, Magali would nudge him with her snout, gestures he took for shows of affection; but he understood that her real concerns lay elsewhere. They always had.

That time was, in essence, an endless gray day striped with sodden nights, a solitude of almost unvarying despondency. Weeks of drinking, slaughtering horses, staring at the sleeping dragon and their reptilian issue. On rare occasions he would rouse himself to a clinical detachment and give thought to the nature of the child. Dragons, so the tradition held, bore litters, and that Magali had borne a single child caused him to suspect that embedded in the little dragon's flesh was a human heart or a human soul or some important human quality that would enable it to cross more easily between shapes and sensibilities than had its mother. And then he would look to Griaule, the mighty green hill with its protruding, lowered head, and to Magali in her nest, and he would have a sense of the mystery of their triangular liaison, the complex skein that had been woven and its imponderable potentials, and then he would briefly regain a perspective from which he was able to perceive the dual nature of her beauty, that of the woman and that of the sleek, sculptural beast with lacquered scales, monster and temptress in one.

The rainy season drew toward its close and often he woke to bright sunlight, but his thoughts remained gray and his routine stayed essentially the same. The child had grown half as big as an ox, ever beating its wings in an effort to fly. It required more food. After killing all the horses, Hota found it necessary to go into the hills and hunt wild boar, jumping from branches onto their backs, stabbing them or, failing that, breaking their necks. He felt debased by the brutality of these death struggles. The animal stench; the squeals; the hot blood gushing onto his hands—these things turned something inside him and he began to see himself as a primitive, an apelike creature inhabiting a ruin and pretending to be a man. At night he stumbled through the town carrying an open bottle, singing in an off-key baritone, howling at the night and serenading the tin-hatted wooden skulls, addressing himself by name, offering himself advice or just generally chatting himself up. He refused to believe this was a sign of deterioration. He knew what he was about. It was an indulgence, a means of passing the hours, nothing more. And yet it might be, he thought, the prelude to deterioration. He was not, however, prepared to give up the practice. The sound of his voice distracted him from thinking and frightened off the townspeople, whose incursions had become more frequent, though none would come near Liar's House. Day and night they shouted threats from the hills, where many had taken refuge, and he would respond by singing to them and telling them what he had recently learned—that a man's goals and preoccupations, perhaps his every thought, were the manufacture of a higher power. Whatever they threatened had been promised him since birth.

His dreams acquired a fanciful quality that went contrary to the grain of his waking life, and he came to have a recurring dream that seemed the crystallization of all the rest. He imagined himself running across fields, through woods, tireless and unafraid, in a state of exaltation, running for the joy of it, and when he approached the crest of a hill overlooking a steep drop, instead of halting, he ran faster and faster, leaping from the crest and being borne aloft on a sweep of wind, flying in the zones of the sun, and then seeing Magali, joining her in flight, swooping and curving, together weaving an endless pattern above a mighty green hill, the one from which he had leapt, and the child, too, was flying, albeit lower and less elegantly, testing itself against the air. It must be Griaule's dream, he thought. Though liberating, there was about it the cold touch of a sending. He recalled what Magali had said—that one day he would know how it felt to fly—and he wondered if the recurring dream was a reminder of that promise, or else the keeping of it. Set against all he had endured, it did not weigh out as a suitable reward. But suitable or not, he enjoyed the dream and sleep became the sole thing in his routine to which he looked forward.

One morning he woke lying in the street down from the inn. His joints stiff, eyelids crusted and stuck together, a fetid taste in his mouth. The brightness of the day pained him. Heat was beginning to cook from the abandoned town, a reek compounded of rotting flesh and vegetable spoilage. His vision blurry, he looked toward the inn. Magali, crouched in her nest, emitted a scream. In reflex, Hota took a step toward the hills, thinking that she was demanding food. Then she screamed a second time. He stopped and rubbed his eyes and tried to focus on her. Clinging atop her back, between her wings, its diminutive talons hooked into her crest, was the child. Before Hota could put reason to work and understand what he was seeing, Magali unfurled her obsidian wings—each longer than her body—and beat them once, producing a violent cracking sound and a buffet of wind that knocked Hota off-balance and caused him to fall. She leaped to the edge of the nest and, using her grip on the shattered boards as a boost, vaulted into the air, paper debris from the street whirling up in her wake. Within seconds she was soaring high above and Hota, stupefied by the abruptness of her departure, felt as empty and abandoned as the town.

Magali disappeared behind Griaule's back and Hota regained his feet. He stood a while with his hands at his sides, unable to summon a thought; then he walked over to the inn and clambered across the rubble to the inner nest. What he expected to find, he could not have said. Some token, perhaps. An accidental gift. A scale that had worked loose; a scrap from a green dress. But there were only wastes and bloody bones. The images on the boards had receded into the grain. No dragons were visible upon their surfaces, agitated or otherwise. The silence oppressed him. Irrational though it was, he missed Magali's rumblings, her newborn's trebly growls. Fool, he thought, and struck himself on the chest. To be mooning over a monstrosity, a twisted union that had been arranged by a still greater monstrosity. He picked up a fragment of board and slung it toward the looming green hill, as if his strength, inflamed by anger, could drive it like a missile through scale and flesh and guts to pierce the enormous heart. The plank splashed down into a puddle and he felt even more the fool. He crawled up out of the nest and went into the street and sat beneath the remaining corner post of the inn. If he stayed much longer, he thought, people would drift back into town and there would be trouble. It would be best to leave now. Forgo searching for his money, his gems, and walk away. He would find work somewhere. The notion tugged at him, but it refused to take hold. He clasped his hands, hung his head, and waited for another impulse to strike.

And then, as suddenly as she had departed, Magali returned, swooping low above Liar's House, the rush of her passage shattering the silence. She arrowed off over the hills behind the town, but returned again, swooping lower yet. Restored by the sight, Hota sprang to his feet. Watching her dive and loop, he soon recognized that she was repeating a pattern, that her flight was a signal, a ritual thing like the pattern she had flown above Griaule so many months ago. An acknowledgment. Or a farewell. Each time after passing above the street, a streaking of bronze scales, a shadowing of wings, she loosed a scream as she ascended. The guttural quality of her voice was inaudible at that distance, and her call had the sound of an eerie whistling music, three plaintive notes that might have been excerpted from a longer song whose melody played out closer to the sun. For an hour and more she flew above him. Like a scarf drawn through the sky. Entranced, he began to understand the meaning of the design her flight wove in the air. It was a knot, eloquent in its graceful twists, a sketch of the circumstance that had bound them. They had met, entwined into a minor theme that served the purpose of a larger music, one whose structure neither could discern, and now they would part. But only for a while. They would always be bound by that knot. All its loops led inward toward Liar's House. He understood what she had told him on the day he went to gather the herb. He understood the congruence of inevitability and love, fate and desire, and, having accepted this, he was able to take joy in her freedom, to be confident that a like freedom would soon be his.

Even after she had gone, flown beyond the hills, he watched the sky, hoping she would reappear. Yet there was no bitterness or regret in his heart. Though he did not know how it would happen, he believed she would always return to him. They would never be as he might have hoped them to be, but the connection between them was unbreakable. He would go inland, toward Point Horizon, and somewhere he would find a suitable home, a sinecure, and he would await the day of her return. No, he would do more than wait. For the first time in memory, he felt the sap of ambition rising in him. He would soar in his own way. He would not allow himself to settle for mere survival and drudgery.

His mind afire with half-formed plans, with possibility of every sort, Hota turned from the inn, preparing to take a first step along his new road, and saw a group of men approaching along the street. Several dozen men. Filthy and bearded from their exile in the hills. Clad in rags and carrying clubs and knives. A second group, equally proportioned, was approaching from the opposite end of the street. He ducked around the corner of the inn, onto a side street, only to be confronted by a third group. And a fourth group moved toward him from the other end of that street.

They had him boxed.

Hota was frightened, yet fear was not preeminent in him. He still brimmed with confidence, with the certainty that the best of life lay ahead, and refused to surrender to panic. The third group, he judged, was the smallest of the four. He drew his boar-killing knife and ran directly at them, hoping to unnerve them with this tactic. The center of the group, toward which he aimed, fell back a step, and, seeing this, Hota let out a hoarse cry and ran harder, slashing the air with his knife. Seconds later, he was among them. Their bearded, hollow-cheeked faces aghast, they clutched at him, tried to stab him, but his momentum was so great, he burst through their ranks without injury, and ran past the last shanties into the palms and bananas and palmettos that fringed the outskirts. Jubilant in the exercise of strength, he zigzagged through the trees, knocking fronds aside, stumbling now and again over a depression or a bump, yet keeping a good pace, liking the feel of his sweat, his exertions.

His muscles felt tireless, as in his recurring dream, and he wondered if the dream had foreshadowed this moment and he would climb the green hill of Griaule's back—he was, he realized, heading in that very direction— and leap from it and fly. But though strong, Hota was not fleet. Soon he heard men running beside and ahead of him. Heard their shouts. And as he passed a large banana tree with tattered yellow fronds, someone lying hidden in the grass reached out a hand and snagged his ankle, sending him sprawling. His knife flew from his hand. He scrambled to his knees, searching for it. Spotted it in the grass a dozen feet away. Before he could retrieve it, someone jumped onto his back, driving him face first into the ground. And before he could deal with whoever it was, other men piled onto him, pressing the air from his lungs, beating him with fists and sticks. A blow to his temple stunned him. They smelled like beasts, grunted like beasts, like the spirits of the boars he had killed come for their vengeance.

There seemed no dividing line between consciousness and uncon-sciousness, or perhaps Hota never completely blacked out and, instead, sank only a few inches beneath the surface of the waking world, and was, as with someone partially submerged in a stream, still able to hear muted voices and to glimpse distorted shapes. It seemed he was borne aloft, jostled and otherwise roughly handled, but he did not fully return to his senses until he stood beneath the remnant corner post of Liar's House, something tight about his neck, surrounded by a crowd of men and women and chil-dren, all of whom were shouting at once, cursing, screaming for his blood. He wanted to pluck the tight thing away from his neck and discovered his hands were lashed behind his back. Dazedly, he glanced up and saw that a rope had been slung over the wedge of flooring still attached to the corner post, and that one end of the rope was about his neck. Terrified now, he surged forward, trying to break free, but whoever held the rope pulled it tight, constricting his throat and forcing him to stand quietly. He breathed shallowly, staring at the faces ranged about him. He recognized none of them, yet they were all familiar. It was as if he were looking at cats or dogs or horses, incapable of registering the distinctions among them that they themselves noticed. A woman, her thin face contorted with anger, spat at him. The rest appeared to think this a brilliant idea and those closest to him all began spitting. Their saliva coated his face. It disturbed him to think that he would die with their slime dripping from him. He lifted a shoulder, rubbed some of it off his cheek. Then the blond man whom he had beaten in the tavern stepped forth from the crowd. Hota recognized him not by his pink complexion or pudgy features, but by his mangled right hand, which he held up to Hota's eyes, letting him see the damage he had caused. The man waved the crowd to silence and said to Hota, "Speak now, if ever you wish to speak again."

Still groggy, Hota said, "None of this is my doing."

Shouts and derisive laughter.

Once more, the man waved them to silence. "Who then should we blame?"

"Griaule," Hota said, and was forced to shout the rest of his statement over the renewed laughter of the crowd. "How could I have brought a dragon here? I'm only a man!"

"Are you?" The blond man caught the front of Hota's shirt with his good hand and brought his face close. "We've been wondering about that."

"Of course I am! I was manipulated! Used! Griaule used me!"

The blond man seemed to give the idea due consideration. "It's possible," he said at length. "In fact, I imagine it's probable."

The crowd at his back muttered unhappily.

"The thing is…" said the blond man, and smiled. "We can't hang Griaule, can we? You'll just have to stand in for him."

Hooting and howling their laughter, the crowd shook their fists in the air. Some snatched at Hota, others clawed and slapped at his head. The blond man moved them back. "You've killed our horses, you've stolen from us. You're responsible for that bitch tearing Benno Grustark to pieces. Any of these crimes would merit hanging."

"What could I have done!" Hota cried.

"You could have talked to us. Helped us. Brought us food." The blond man waved his damaged hand toward the hills. "Do you know how many of us died for want of food and shelter?"

"I *didn't* know! If you'd told me, if you hadn't threatened me…But I wasn't thinking about you! I couldn't! I had no choice!"

"Lack of choice. A common failing. But not, I think, a legal remedy." The blond man moved the crowd farther back, warning that Hota might kick them as he was being hauled up. He turned to Hota and asked blithely, "Anything else?"

A hundred things occurred to Hota. Pleas and arguments, statements, things about his life, things he had learned that he thought might be worth announcing. But he could muster the will to speak none of them. The rope made his neck itch. His balls were tightened and cold. His knees trembled. His eyes went out along the street, past the drying mud and the crooked shanties and their rust-patched roofs, and he felt a shape inside his head that seemed to have some correspondence with the green mountainous shape that lay beyond, as if Griaule were telling him a secret or offering an assurance or having a laugh at his expense. Impossible to guess which. A desire swelled in him, a great ache for life that grew and grew until he thought he might be able to burst his bonds and escape this old fate he had avoided for so long.

"Hang him," said the blond man. "But not too high. I want to watch his face."

As Hota was yanked off his feet, the crowd's roar ascended with him, and blended into another roar that issued from within his skull. The roar of his life, of his constricted blood. It was if he had been made buoyant by the sound. His face was forced downward by the rope and his vision reddened. He saw the upturned faces of the crowd, their gaping black mouths and widened eyes, and he also saw his legs spasming. He had kicked off a shoe. The inside of his head grew hot, but slowly, as if death's flame were burning low. Fighting for breath, he flexed the roped muscles of his neck and found that he could breathe. The heat lessened.

They had set the knot in the noose incorrectly.

Air was coming through.

Barely...but enough to sustain him.

That became a problem, then. To breathe, to hold out against fate, or to relax his muscles and let go. Soon the decision would be made for him, but he wanted it to be his.

A terrible new pressure cinched the rope tighter.

Two children had shinnied up his lower legs and were humping themselves up and down. Trying to break his neck, he realized. The little shits were giggling. He squeezed his eyes shut, focusing all his energy and will on maintaining breath.

Fiery pains jolted along his spine. White lights exploded behind his lids. One such flash swelled into a blinding radiance that opened before him, vast and shimmering and deep, a country all its own. He felt a shifting inside him, a strange powerful movement that bloomed outward…and then he could see himself! Not just his legs, but his entire bulky figure. The children jiggling up and down, and the crowd; the exhausted town leached of every color but the redness of his dying sight.

Then he lost interest in this phenomenon and in the world, borne outward on that curious expansion. He recalled Magali and he thought that this—here and now—must be the fulfillment of her promise, the beginning of fulfillment, and that his soul was growing large, coming to enclose the material in the way of a dragon's soul…

And then a violent crack, like that of a severing lightning stroke or an immense displacement, and a thought came to mind that stilled his fears, or else it was the last of him and there was no fear left…the thought that it was all a dream, his dream, how he had run and felt joy, how he had leaped—sprawled, really, but that was close enough—and been borne aloft and now he was soaring, and the crack he had heard was the crack of his wings as they caught the air, and the roaring was the rush of first flight, and the light was the high holy sun, and soon he would see Magali and they would fly together along the pattern of their curving fate, with the child flying below them, above the green hill of their religion, and this was his reward, this transformation, this was the fulfillment of every promise, or else it was the lie of it.

THE TABORIN SCALE

Chapter One

IF A MAN CAN BE measured by the size of his obsessions, George
Taborin might have been said to be a very small man, smaller even than
the quarter-men rumored to inhabit the forests of Tasmania. He was a
numismatist by trade, by avocation a lover of rare and ancient coins, and he
spent his days cataloguing, cleaning, and in contemplation of such coins,
picturing as he did the societies whose lifeblood they had emblematized.
Rubbing the face of Ptolemy, for instance, on a silver drachma found in
Alexandria, struck at the approximate time of the invasion of Cyprus by
Demetrios Poliokortes (probably in Salamis, the last city to fall to the
Besieger), would conjure not merely the historical context of the Roman
empire and Ptolemaic Egypt, but brought visions so vivid that he imag-
ined he felt the weight of an armored breastplate on his chest or caught

the scent of naphtha from an arrow dipped in Greek fire smoldering in its victim's flesh. It was as if the ball of his thumb stirred the energies of the coin, releasing some essence of the moments through which it had passed, and it had been thus ever since his sixth birthday when his uncle gave him a Phoenician copper as a present.

From this you might suppose George, in his fortieth year, to have been a fastidious, obsessive little man given to woolgathering, with spectacles and a potbelly and few close friends, his minimal life partitioned into orderly sections like the trays whereon he displayed the best of his collection. You would have been correct in this assessment save for one thing: George Taborin was not little. He stood a hand's breadth over six feet, more if you measured from the peak of his coarse black hair, which tended to arrange itself into spiky growths when left unwashed, causing it to be said that if George ran into you while walking with his head down (as was his habit), you would be fortunate to survive the encounter without a puncture or two. Thanks to his parents, a farm couple who had viewed him less as a beloved addition to the family than as child labor, he was powerfully built; his sedentary occupation had eroded his strengths and softened his mid-section, but not so much that he was often challenged—he had earned a schoolyard reputation for toughness and durability in a fight and that reputation clung to him yet. He had a slightly undershot chin, a straight nose whose only notable quality was that it was too big for his face, and a mouth through which he was prone to breathe due to a persistent sinus condition (for all that, his was a face that missed being handsome by an ounce here, a centimeter there, and might have passed muster had there been more self-confidence underlying it). These features conspired with his bulk to lend him a doltish aspect, like a gangling idiot boy thickened into a man. When gazing into a mirror, something he did as infrequently as possible, he would have the notion that his soul had not thickened commensurately and was rattling around inside its house, a poor fit for the flesh it animated, stunted and too small by half.

Pursuant to his family's wishes (the thought being that if George didn't marry young he would never find a woman), at the age of fifteen he wed Rosemary LeMaster, a chubby, sullen, unprepossessing girl who, over the course of a quarter-century, had matured into a flirtatious, Raphael-esque matron. They had not been blessed with children and, because George deeply desired a family, as did Rosemary (so she claimed, though he suspected her of taking steps to ensure her infertility), they still shared the marriage bed once a week, regular as clockwork; but now that George's business (Taborin Coins & Antiquities) had prospered, providing them the wherewithal to hire servants, Rosemary, freed from domestic duties, wasted no time in making up for the period of youthful experimentation she'd never had, aligning herself with a clutch of upper-middle-class wives in Port Chantay who called their group the Whitestone Rangers (named for the district in which many of them lived) and considered themselves prettier, more sophisticated and fashionable than they in fact were. She veered into a social orbit of parties and trivial causes (the placing of planter boxes along the harbor, for one) that served as opportunities to meet the men with whom she and her sisters would share dalliances and affairs. Although troubled by his wife's infidelities (he had no proof positive, yet he was aware of the Rangers' liberal attitude toward the matrimonial bond), George did not complain. He and Rosemary led essentially separate lives and this latest separation had not created any disruption in the routines of the marriage. Then, too, he had no grounds for complaint since he was regularly unfaithful to Rosemary.

In the spring of each year, George would travel to Teocinte and pass the next three weeks sporting in the brothels of Morningshade, a district that never received the morning sun, tucked so close beneath the dragon Griaule's[1] monstrous shadow, his ribcage bulged out over a portion of the area like a green-and-gold sky.[2] Apart from its brothels, Morningshade was known for its junk shops and stalls where you could find antiquities and relics of Griaule (mostly fakes) among the dragon-shaped pipes and pendants, his image adorning a variety of merchandise including plates, pennants, toys (wooden swords were a big seller), tablecloths, teaspoons,

---

1 The mile-long dragon, paralyzed by a wizard's spell, in whose lee Teocinte had grown.

2 Portions of this sky, scales shed by the dragon, would occasionally fall on the rooftops below, crushing the houses beneath, causing the plots of land upon which they had stood to appreciate in value because they would be unlikely to experience another such disaster.

mugs, and maps purporting to divulge the location of his hoard[3]. George would spend his afternoons combing through these shops, searching for old coins. One evening in May, after such an expedition, he took himself to Ali's Eternal Reward (the crudely-lettered word "Hellish" had been added and marked for insertion between Ali's and Eternal), a brothel on the sunnier edge of Morningshade, there to examine his day's treasures over a pint of bitters.

The common room of the tavern, lit by kerosene lamps and almost empty at that early hour, was shaped like a capital I and smelled of fried onions, stale beer, and several decades of grease. Pitch-covered beams quartered the ceiling, beneath which lay benches and boards, and whitewashed walls gone a splotchy gray from kitchen smoke and innumerable grimy touches, and a counter behind which a corpulent barman wearing a fez (not Ali, who was a purely fictive personage) stood lordly and watchful, punctuating the quiet with the occasional *thwack* of a flyswatter. Three young women in loosely belted dressing gowns sat at the center of the room, talking softly. Carts rattled by outside, and a vendor shrilled the virtues of her coconut sweets. To George, sitting at a window in a rear corner of the I, the conversations of passersby came as bursts of unintelligible words peppered with curses.

While inspecting the contents of a glass jar containing coins and buttons and tin badges that he had purchased as a lot, he unearthed a dark leathern chip stiff with age and grime, shaped like a thumbnail, though three times the size and much thicker. He opened his cleaning kit and dabbed at the chip with a cotton ball dipped in solvent, after some exercise clearing a speck of bluish green at the center. His interest enlisted, he put on the spectacles he used for close work, bent to the chip and rubbed at it vigorously with the cotton ball, widening the speck. The blue-green color held a gem-like luster. He fitted a jeweler's loupe to his spectacles and held the chip to his eye.

"What you got there?"

---

3 As the tale was told, over the centuries people came from the ends of the earth to lay offerings before him, and these offering had been transported by a succession of creatures and men controlled by the dragon to a hiding place known only to him (its location having been subsequently erased from the minds of his minions). The treasure was said by some to be fabulous beyond belief, and by others to be a complete fabrication.

A prostitute clad in a robe of peach silk, a thin brunette in her early twenties with curly hair, a dusky complexion, and a face that, though pretty, was too sharp-featured for his tastes, slid onto the bench beside him and held out a hand. "Can I see?"

Startled not only by her, but by the fact that the tavern had, without his notice, filled with a noisy crowd, he dropped the chip into her hand, an action he instantly regretted, worried that she might abscond with it.

"I haven't seen one of these since I was a bare-ass kid," the woman said, pushing her hair back from her eyes. "My granny wore one like this around her neck. She promised she'd leave it to me, but they buried the old hag with it."

"You know what it is, then?"

"A dragon scale...not off a monster like Griaule. The babies have this blue color when they're born, or so I hear.[4] I suppose it could be Griaule's from when he was little. There ain't been any baby dragons around these parts for centuries. The scale my granny wore was passed down from her great-great-great."

George reached for the scale, but the woman closed her hand.

"I'll give you a ride for it." She opened her robe, exposing her breasts, and shimmied her shoulders.

"Let me have it," said George, snapping his fingers.

"Don't act so stern!" She jiggled the scale in her palm, as if assessing its weight, and then passed it to him. "Tell you what. I'll give you liberties for a week. When you go back to Port Chantay, you'll have more than a guided tour of Griaule to remember, I promise."

"How can you tell I'm from Port Chantay?"

With a disdainful sniff, she said, "I have a gift."

Her breasts were fuller than he had thought, quite shapely, with large cinnamon areolae. Ever a pragmatic sort when it came to business affairs, he reckoned the scale to be a curiosity piece, not worth that much to the run of his customers; but he pressed his seller's advantage.

---

4 This was true only as so far as dragons native to the region went. Dragons bred in other climes displayed a variety of coloration, ranging from ivory-scaled snow dragons of the Antarctic to the reddish-gold hue of those dragons that once inhabited the wastes north of Lake Baikal, a shade that deepened to a rich bronze at maturity.

"I'm here two more weeks," he said. "Put yourself at my disposal for that time and the scale is yours."

"At your disposal? You'll have to speak plainer than that. I ain't letting you tie me up, if that's how you're bent."

"I'm staying at the Weathers. I'd want you there with me."

"The Weathers," she said, and made an appreciative face. "What else would you want?"

George spelled out his needs in clinical detail; the woman nodded and said, "Done."

She extended a hand and, as if imitating George, snapped her fingers. "Give it here."

"When the two weeks are up. One of us will have to trust the other to fulfill their end of the bargain. I'd prefer it be you."

Chapter Two

WITH THE DEATH OF THE dragon Griaule, the city council of
Teocinte were forced to confront a question they had failed to anticipate:
When dealing with a creature whose heart beat once every thousand years,
how does one determine whether he is actually dead? Since the sole percep-
tible sign of death was the closing of his eyes, it was suggested that he had
merely lapsed into a coma induced by the countless gallons of poisoned
paint slapped onto his side during the creation of Meric Cattanay's mural.[5]
The parasites that lived on and inside him had not fled the body and there
was no evidence of corruption (nor would there be for many years if the
rate of decay were as glacially slow as the rest of his metabolic processes).
Indeed, it had been ventured that since Griaule was a magical being, the
possibility existed that his corpse would prove to be uncorrupting.

Decades before, when the council accepted Cattanay's plan, they had
acted in confidence and contracted with various entrepreneurs for the disposal of Griaule's corpse, selling it piecemeal in advance of his death, thus
adding millions to the town coffers; but the current council regretted their
predecessors' decision and refused to honor the contracts.[6] Due to their

---

5   The process by which Griaule purportedly had been killed took more than thirty
years to complete and was achieved by the utilization of arsenic- and lead-based
paints in a mural painted on his side. The manufacture of these paints had destroyed
the lush forests of the Carbonales (a steady supply of timber was necessary to heat the
vats in which the paint was distilled) and placed such a stress on the economy that a
number of wars had been fought with neighboring city-states in order to replenish
Teocinte's exchequer.

6   Cele Van Alstyne of Port Chantay, who had secured the rights to Griaule's
heart, estimated to weigh nine million pounds, was desperate to revive her failing
pharmaceutical company and initiated legal action. She was joined in this by a
group of speculators who had bought the approximately one hundred and sixty
million pounds of bones (except for the skull, sold to the King of neighboring
Temalagua) and planned to export them to foreign countries for use as sexual

uncertainty about his mortal condition, they still feared Griaule. If he were alive, they could only imagine his reaction to an attempted dissection. Then there was the matter of aesthetics. Thanks to the discovery of mineral springs south of town and, in no small part, to Griaule himself, Teocinte had become a tourist destination. Turning a portion of the town into an abattoir, with several hundred thousand tons of dragon meat and guts and bones lying about, would be an inappropriate advertisement for fun and relaxation. The council was hesitant to act, yet the citizenry of Teocinte, who for generations had lived under Griaule's ineffable dominion, clamored for an official judgment. It was a touchy situation, one that demanded a delicate resolution, and therefore the council tried—as do all accomplished politicians—to make doing next to nothing seem like a compromise. They tore down the scaffolding Cattanay had erected in order to create his mural, scoured the moss from the teeth, cut away the vegetation from his body, leaving in place only the thickets surrounding the ruin of Hangtown on his back (now uninhabited except for a caretaker), which they designated a historical site. They constructed rope walkways leading to every quarter of the dragon and offered tours, inducing tourists to go where most of the townspeople feared to tread. This, they thought, would promote the idea that they believed Griaule to be dead, yet would provide no evidentiary proof and put off a final determination. If Griaule were still alive and a few tourists died as a result of this experiment in the social dynamic, well, so be it. They further built several luxury hotels, among them the Seven Weathers, on the slopes of Haver's Roost, each offering excellent views of the dragon. And so, on the day after he found the scale, George stood at a window in his suite at the Weathers, sipping coffee and having a morning cigar, gazing at Griaule: an enormous green-and-gold lizard looming like a hill with an evil head over the smoking slum in his shadow, his tail winding off between lesser hills, light glinting from the tip of a fang and coursing along the ribbing of the sagittal crest rising from his neck, the mural on its side glazed with

---

remedies, charms, souvenirs, etc.; and by a second consortium who had bought the skin, all two hundred and twenty million pounds of it (not counting the mural, destined to be housed in the Cattanay Museum). Lawyers for the council fought a delaying action, claiming that since the dragon's death could not be proven absolutely, the lawsuits were invalid.

sun, making it indecipherable at that angle. The huge paint vats that had occupied the flat portion of his skull had been dismantled so as not to distract from the dramatic view.

The woman, Sylvia,[7] stirred in the bedroom and George sat down at a writing desk and took up cleaning the scale once again, thinking he might as well make it nice for her. The dirt on the scale was peculiarly resistant and he had managed to clear only a small central patch, about a quarter of its surface, when Sylvia entered, toweling her hair, wearing only sandals and a pair of beige lounging trousers. She dropped heavily into the armchair beside the desk and sighed. He acknowledged her with a nod and bent to his task. She made an impatient noise, which he ignored; she flung her legs over the arm of the chair, the towel slipping down onto her thighs, and said blithely, "Well, you don't fuck like a shopkeeper, I'll say that much for you."

Amused, he said, "I assume that's intended as an endearment."

"A what-ment?"

"Praise of a kind."

She shrugged. "If that's how you want to take it."

"So…" He scraped at a fleck of stubborn grime with a fingernail. "How do shopkeepers fuck?"

"With most of them, it's like they're embarrassed to be between my legs. They want to get it over quick and be gone. They turn their backs when they button their trousers. And they don't want me saying nothing while they're riding." She shook out her wet hair. "Not that they don't want me making noises. They like that well enough."

"Then that raises the question: How do I fuck?"

"Like a desperate man."

"Desperate?" He kept on rubbing at the scale. "Surely not."

"Maybe desperate's not the right word." She lazily scratched her hip. "It's like you truly needed what I had to offer, and not just my tra-la-la. I could tell you wanted me to be myself and not some Sylvia."

---

7 She had adopted this *nom d'amour* after George expressed dissatisfaction with the first name she gave, Ursula, and a selection process that winnowed the choices down to three: Otile, Amaryllis, and Sylvia. He had settled on the latter because it reminded him of a grocer's wife he had admired in Port Chantay, a woman from the extreme south of the country, a region "Sylvia" also claimed as home.

"I expect I did." He was making good progress—the blue portion of the scale had come to resemble an aerial view of a river bordered by banks of mud and black earth. "From now on I'll call you Ursula."

"That's not my proper name, either."

"What is it, then?"

"You don't want to hear—it's horrible." She stretched like a cat on its back in the sun; her face, turned to the window, blurred with brightness. "Truth be told, I don't mind being Sylvia. Suits me, don't you think?"

"Mmm-hmm."

She lapsed into silence, watching him work, attentive to the occasional squeak his cloth made on the scale, and then she said, "Do you fancy me? I mean, the way I'm talking with you now?"

He cocked an eye toward her.

"I'm curious is all," she said.

"I have to admit you're growing on me."

"I was thinking I might try being myself more often. Always having to be someone else is an awful pressure." She scrambled to her knees in the chair, the towel falling away completely, and leaned over the desk, peering at the scale. "Oh, that blue's lovely! How long you reckon 'til it's done?"

"I'll give it a polish once it's clean. A week or so."

She bent closer, her breasts grazing the desktop, holding her hair back from her eyes, fixed on the streak of blue dividing the scale. How different she seemed from the brittle businesswoman he had met at Ali's! She had tried to sustain that pose, but she let it drop more and more frequently, revealing the country girl beneath. He suspected he knew the basics of her story—a farm family with too many children; sold to a brothel keeper; earning her way by the time she was twelve—and thought knowing the specifics might uncover a deeper compatibility. But that, he reminded himself, was what she would want him to think in hopes of getting a bigger tip. Such was the beauty of whores: No matter how devious, how subtle their pretense, you always knew where you stood with them. He studied her face, prettied by concentration, and absently stroked the scale with his thumb.

A sound came to him, barely audible, part hiss, part ripping noise, as of some fundamental tissue, something huge and far away, cleaved by a cosmic sword (or else it was something near at hand, a rotten piece of cloth parting from the simple strain of being worn, giving way under a sudden stress). This sound was accompanied by a vision unlike any he had heretofore known: It was as if the objects that composed the room, the heavy mahogany furniture, the cream-colored wallpaper with its pattern of sailing vessels, the entire surround, were in fact a sea of color and form, and this sea was now rapidly withdrawing, rolling back, much as the ocean withdraws from shore prior to a tidal wave. As it receded, it revealed neither the floors and walls of adjoining rooms nor the white buildings of Teocinte, but a sun-drenched plain with tall lion-colored grasses and stands of palmetto, bordered on all sides by hills forested with pines. They were marooned in the midst of that landscape, smelling its vegetable scents, hearing the chirr and buzz of insects, touched by the soft intricacy of its breezes…and then it was gone, trees and plain and hills so quickly erased, they might have been a painted cloth whisked away, and the room was restored to view. George was left gaping at a portmanteau against the far wall. Sylvia, arms crossed so as to shield her breasts, squatted in the easy chair, her eyes shifting from one point to another.

"What did you do?" she asked in a shaky voice. She repeated the question accusingly, shrilly, as if growing certain of his complicity in the event.

"I didn't do anything." George looked down at the scale.

"You rubbed it! I saw you!" She wrested the scale from him and rubbed it furiously; when nothing came of her efforts she handed it back and said, "You try."

It had not escaped George that there might be a correspondence between the apparition of the plain and the visions that arose when he rubbed his thumb across the face of a coin; but none of those visions had supplied the sensory detail of this last and no one else had ever seen them. He experienced some trepidation at the thought of trying it again and dropped the scale into his shirt pocket.

"Finish dressing," he said. "Let's go down to breakfast."

A flash of anger ruled her face. He folded his penknife and packed up his cleaning kit and pocketed them as well.

"Won't you give it one more rub?" she asked.

He ignored her.

Wrapping the towel around her upper body, she gave him a scornful look and flounced into the bedroom.

George sipped his coffee and discovered it was tepid. Through the thin fabric of his shirt, the scale felt unnaturally cold against his chest and he set it on the desk. It might be more valuable than he had presumed. He nudged it with the tip of a finger—the room remained stable.

Sylvia re-entered, still wearing the towel and still angry, though she tried to mask her anger behind a cajoling air. "Please! Give it one little rub." She kissed the nape of his neck. "For me?"

"It frightened you the first time. Why are you so eager to repeat the experience?"

"I wasn't frightened! I was startled. You're the one who was frightened! You should have seen your face."

"That begs the question: Why so eager?"

"When Griaule makes himself known, you'd do well to pay heed or misfortune will follow."

He leaned back, amused. "So you believe this nonsense about Griaule being a god."

"It ain't nonsense. You'd know it for true if you lived here." Hands on hips, she proceeded to deliver what was obviously a quoted passage: "He was once mortal, long-lived yet born to die, but Griaule has increased not only in size, but in scope. Demiurge may be too great a word to describe an overgrown lizard, yet surely he is akin to such a being. His flesh has become one with the earth. He knows its every tremor and convulsion. His thoughts roam the plenum, his mind is a cloud that encompasses our world. His blood is the marrow of time. Centuries flow through him, leaving behind a residue that he incorporates into his being. Is it any wonder he controls our lives and knows our fates?"[8]

"That sounds grand, but it proves nothing. What's it from?"

"A book someone left at Ali's."

8 The excerpt is from the preface to Richard Rossacher's *Griaule Incarnate*. Rossacher, a young medical doctor, while studying Griaule's blood derived from it a potent narcotic that succeeded in addicting a goodly portion of the population of the Temalaguan littoral. After experiencing an epiphany of sorts, he became evangelic as regarded the dragon and spent his last years writing and proselytising about Griaule's divinity.

"You don't recall its name?"

"Not so I could say."

"And yet you memorized the passage."

"Sometimes there's not much to do except sit around. I get bored and I read. Sometimes I write things."

"What kind of things?"

"Little stories about the other girls, like. All sorts of things." She caressed his cheek "Try again! Please!"

With a show of patience tried that was only partly a show, expecting that nothing (or next to nothing) would occur, he picked up the scale and ran his thumb along the lustrous blue streak, pressing down hard. This time the ripping sound was louder and the transition from hotel room to sun-drenched plain instantaneous. He fell thuddingly among the tall grasses, the chair beneath him having vanished, and lay grasping the scale, squinting up at the diamond glare of the sun and a sky empty of clouds, like a sheet of blue enamel. Sylvia made a frightened noise and clutched his shoulder as he scrambled to his knees. She said something that—his mind dominated by an evolving sense of dismay—he failed to register. The smells that had earlier seemed generic, a vague effluvia of grass and dirt, now were particularized and pungent, and the sun's heat was no longer a gentle warmth, but an ox-roasting presence. A droplet of sweat trickled down his side from his armpit. Insects whirred past their heads and a hawk circled high above. This was no vision, he told himself. The scale had transported them somewhere, perhaps to another section of the valley. In the distance stood a ring of rolling, forested hills enclosing the lumpish shapes of lesser, nearby hills—his coach had traversed similar hills as it ascended from the coastal plain toward Teocinte, though those had been denuded of vegetation. Panic inspired him to rub at the scale, hoping to be transported back to the room; but his actions proved fruitless.

Sylvia sank to the ground and lowered her head, and this display of helplessness served to stiffen George's spine, engaging his protective instincts. He scanned the valley for signs of life.

"We should find shelter," he said dazedly. "And water."

She made an indefinite noise and half-turned her head away.

"Perhaps there's water there." He pointed to the far-off hills. "And a village."

"I doubt we'll find a village."

"Why not?"

"Don't you recognize where we are?" She waved dejectedly at the closest hill, which lay behind them on the right. "There's Haver's Roost, where the Weathers stood. And the rise over yonder is where Griaule's head rested. The sunken area to the left, with all the shrimp plants and cabbage palms—that's where Morningshade used to lie. There's Yulin Grove. It's all there except the houses and the people."

She continued her cataloging of notable landmarks and he was forced to admit that she was correct. He would have expected her to be upset by this development, fearful and verging on hysteria; but she was outwardly calm (calmer than he), albeit dejected. He asked why she was so unruffled.

"We're accustomed to such doings around here," she replied. "It's Griaule's work. The scale...he must have shed it when he was young and it wound up in that jar. For some reason he set you to find it. So you could clean it and rub on it, I imagine."

In reflex he said, "That's ridiculous."

With a loose-armed gesture toward Haver's Roost, she said, "Teocinte is gone. How else do you think it happened?"

Aside from grass swaying, palmetto fronds lifting in the wind, birds scattering about the sky, the land was empty. Odd, he thought, that birds would act so carefree with a hawk in the vicinity. Shielding his eyes against the glare, he tried to spot the hawk, but it had vanished against the sun field. His uneasiness increased.

"We can't stay here," he said.

Sylvia arranged her towel into a makeshift blouse and appeared to be awaiting instruction.

A bug zinged past George's ear—he swatted at it half-heartedly. "Which way should we go?"

She tugged at a loose curl, a gesture that conveyed a listless air—it had become apparent that she had surrendered herself to Griaule or to some other implausible agency. George grabbed her by the wrist and pulled her to him.

"If this is where Teocinte stood, you know where we can find water," he said

Sullenly she said, "There should be a creek over that way somewhere." She pointed toward the depression in which Morningshade had once sprawled. "It was filthy last I saw it, but now, with nobody around, the water ought to be all right."

"Let's go," he said, and when she showed no sign of complying, he shoved her forward. She swung her fist, striking him in the forehead, an impact that caused her to cry out in pain and cradle her hand.

"Are you angry?" he asked. "Good."

"Don't go pushing me!" she said tearfully. "I won't have it!"

"If you're going to act like your spine's been sucked out, I'll push you whenever I choose," he said. "You can mope about and wait to die on your own time."

Chapter Three

BY THE TIME THEY HAD hiked a third of the distance to the creek, George's practical side had re-established dominance and he had developed a scheme for survival in case their situation, whatever it might be,[9] failed to reverse itself. But as he prepared for a solitary life with Sylvia (of whatever duration), planning a shelter that could be added to over the months and years, and devising ways in which they could usefully occupy their time, the hawk reappeared above, swelling to such a size as it dropped toward them that George could no longer believe it was a hawk or any familiar predator. He scooped up Sylvia by the waist, lifting her off the ground, and began to run, ignoring her shrieks, just as a dragon swooped low overhead, coming so near that they felt the wind of its passage. Its scales glinting bright green and gold, the dragon banked in a high turn and arrowed toward them again, and then, with a furious beating of its jointed wings, landed facing them in the tall grasses no more than fifty feet away. It dipped its snout and roared, a complicated noise like half-a-dozen lions roaring not quite in unison. George glimpsed a drop of orange brilliance hanging like a jewel in the darkness of its gullet and threw Sylvia to the ground, covering her with his body, expecting flames to wash over them. When no flames manifested, he lifted his head. The dragon maintained its distance, breath chuffing like an overstrained engine—it seemed to be waiting for them to act. Sylvia complained and George eased from atop her. When she saw the dragon she moaned and put her face down in the grass.

---

9 Though a rift in time or dimensionality would seem to be indicated, George subscribed to the theory espoused by Peri Haukkola, holder of the Carbajal Chair of Philosophy at the University of Helvetia. Haukkola believed that people under extreme stress could alter the physical universe even to the point of creating pocket realities, and George assumed that a reality formed by Sylvia's self-avowed identity crisis comprised the relatively empty landscape they currently inhabited.

Taking care to avoid sudden movements, George climbed to his feet. He was so afraid, so weak in the knees, he thought he might have to sit down, but he maintained a shaky half-crouch. The dragon's lowered head was almost on a level with his, but its back and crest rose much higher. He estimated it to be twenty-five feet long, perhaps a touch more, from the tip of the tail to its snout. The green-and-gold scales fit cunningly to its musculature, a tight overlay like the scales of a pangolin. It emitted a rumbling, its mouth opening to display fangs longer than his arms. A dry, gamey scent seemed to coil about him like a tendril, causing a fresh tightness in his throat. Yet for all its wicked design and innate enmity, there was something of the canine in the way it cocked its head and scrutinized them, like a puppy (one the size of a cottage) confounded by a curious pair of bugs.

"Sylvia." He reached down, groping for her, his fingers brushing her towel.

In response he received a weak, "No."

"If it wanted to kill us, it would have done so by now," he said without the least confidence.

Not taking his eyes from the dragon, he groped again, caught her wrist and yanked her up. She buried her face in his shoulder, refusing to look at the dragon. Putting an arm about her waist, he steered her back in the direction from which they had come, experiencing a new increment of dread with each step. They had gone no more than thirty feet when, with a percussive rattling of its wings, the dragon scuttled ahead of them, cutting them off. It settled on its haunches and gave forth with a grumbling noise and tossed its head to the side. Sylvia squeaked and George was too frightened to think. Again the dragon tossed its head and loosed a full-throated roar that bent the nearby grasses. Sylvia and George clung together, their eyes closed. The dragon lifted its snout to the sky and screamed—the trebly pitch and intensity of the cry seemed to express frustration. It tossed its head a third and a fourth time, all to the same side, gestures that struck George as exaggerated and deliberate. Taking a cue from them, he went a couple of halting steps in the direction they indicated, dragging Sylvia along. The dragon displayed neither approval nor disapproval, so George continued on this path, heading toward the rise where Griaule's massive head once had rested.

So began a faltering march, the two of them stumbling over broken ground, harried along by the dragon's rumbles, herded from the former site of Teocinte, past the rise and out onto a vast plain of yellowish green thickets and sugarloaf hills, crisscrossed by animal tracks. On occasion the dragon bulled ahead of them to divert their course, flattening wide swaths of vegetation. The heat grew almost unbearable and George's grip on reality frayed to the point that once, when they stopped to rest and the dragon urged them on with a roar, he sprang to his feet and shouted at the beast. After what must have been several hours of sweat and torment, they reached a spot where a stream widened into a clear pool some eighty or ninety feet across at the widest, flowing into other, smaller ponds and fringed by towering sabal palms, hedged by lesser trees and bushes, a cool green complexity amid the desert of thorny bushes and prickly weeds. There the dragon abandoned them, belching out a final cautionary (thus George characterized it) roar and soaring up into the sky until it once again appeared no bigger than a hawk and vanished into a cloud, leaving them exhausted and stunned, relieved yet despairing. They bathed in the largest pool and felt somewhat refreshed. As night fell, George picked shriveled oranges from a tree beside the pool and they made a meal of nuts and fruit. Shortly thereafter, too fatigued to talk, they fell asleep.

In the morning they had a discussion about returning to the spot to which they had been transported, but the sight of the dragon circling overhead ended that conversation and George began constructing a lean-to from bamboo and vines and palmetto fronds, while Sylvia set herself to catch fish, a task for which she claimed an aptitude. After watching her for half an hour, bent over and motionless in the pool, waiting for the fish to forget her presence and attempting to scoop them up when they swam between her legs, he held out little hope for a fish dinner; but to his amazement, when next he checked in on her he saw that she had caught two medium-sized perch.

That night, with enough of a breeze to keep off the mosquitoes, the two of them reclining on a bed of fronds and banana leaves inside the shelter, gazing at the lacquered reflection of a purple sky so thickly adorned with stars, it might have been a theatrical backdrop, a silk cloth embroidered with sequins…that night their predicament was reduced to a shadow in George's mind by these comforts and a full belly; but it became apparent

LUCIUS SHEPARD

that Sylvia did not feel so at ease with things, for when he tried to draw her into an embrace, she resisted him vigorously and said, "We're at death's door and that's all you can think about?"

"We're not at death's door," said George. "The dragon was rather solicitous of our welfare. He could have conveyed us to a far more inhospitable spot."

"Be that as it may, we're not exactly sitting pretty."

"Oh, I don't know. One of us is." George gave a broad wink, attempting to jolly her with this compliment.

Sylvia returned a withering look.

"We might as well make the best of things," said George.

She sniffed. "To my mind, making the best of it would include figuring a way out of this mess."

"We had a bargain," George said weakly.

"Back in Teocinte we had a bargain. Here all bets are off."

"I don't see it that way."

"Well, I do...and I'm in charge of the sweet shop. I don't have my medicines with me and I won't risk getting pregnant out here. When we return to Teocinte, I'll do right by you. Until then you'll have to take care of your own needs. And I'll thank you to not do so in my presence."

A pour of wind rustled the thatched roof of the shelter, carrying a spicy scent. Despite understanding that Sylvia's reaction was to be expected, George's feelings were hurt.

"This is your fault," he said glumly.

She sat up, her face pale and simplified by the starlight. "What?"

He sketched out Peri Haukkola's theory concerning the effects of stress on consensus reality.

"You say I'm ridiculous to blame this on Griaule," she said. "Then you put forward this Haukkerman as if..."

"Haukkola."

"...as if it were proof of something. As if because he wrote some stupid theory down, it must be true. And I'm the ridiculous one?" She gave a sarcastic laugh. "You saw the dragon, I assume?"

"Of course! That's just more evidence in support of Haukkola. You're obsessed with Griaule, so you incorporated one of his little friends into your fantasy."

Dumfounded, Sylvia stared at him. "The dragon *is* Griaule! Didn't you notice he's got the same coloring, the same head shape? True, he's not all nicked up and scarred, and he's quite a bit smaller. But it's him, all right."

"You can distinguish between lizards?" He chuckled.

"I've been looking at Griaule most of my life and I can distinguish him." She turned onto her side, showing him her back. "You and Haukkola! You're both idiots! If it helps you to blame me, fine. I'm going to sleep."

Chapter Four

THE WIND DIED SHORTLY BEFORE dawn and mosquitoes swarmed the interior of the shelter, waking Sylvia and George, driving them into the water for cover. The sun climbed higher and they sat beside the pool, miserable, baking in the heat. Having nothing better to do, George shored up the walls of the shelter and elevated the ceiling, making it less of a lean-to, and then went off foraging. To avoid the thickets, the thorn bushes and the gnats, he followed the meanders of the stream through stands of bamboo and clusters of palmettos with parched brownish fronds. Once he sighted the dragon circling above the plain and lay flat until it passed from view. From that point on, for the better part of an hour, his thoughts became a grim drone accompanying his exertions. At length he happened upon a patch of dirt and grass enclosed by dense brush, an oval of relative coolness and shade cast by a solitary mango tree with ripening fruit hanging from its boughs in chandelier-like clusters. He fashioned his shirt into a sling and had begun loading it with mangos when he saw two figures slipping through the brush. Alarmed by their furtive manner, he knotted the shirt to keep the mangos safe and turned to leave. Two men blocked his path. A scrawny, balding, pinch-faced fellow dressed in a skirt woven of vines and leaves, his tanned body speckled with inflamed mosquito bites, shook a fist at George and said, "Them's our mangos!" Grime deepened the lines on his face, adding a sinister emphasis to his scowl.

His companion was a plump young man with unkempt, shoulder-length hair and a brow as broad and unwritten on as a newly cut tombstone—his head was rather large and his features small and unremarkable, imbuing his face with a weak, unfinished quality. He wore the remnants of corduroy trousers and carried a stick stout enough to be used as a club, but hid it behind his leg and refused to meet George's stare, the very image of a reluctant warrior. George decided the men posed no threat, yet he kept an eye on the figures hiding in the brush.

"I've only taken a dozen or so," he said. "Surely there's enough for everyone."

The balding man adopted an expression that might have been an attempt at ferocity, but instead gave the impression that he suffered from a sour stomach. The plump man whispered to him and he made a disagreeable noise.

"We're camped a long way from here—I hate to return empty-handed," said George. "Let me pass. I won't bother you again."

The plump man looked to his friend and after brief consideration the balding man said, "We can spare a few, I reckon. I apologize for treating you rude, but we've had problems with our neighbors poaching our supplies."

"Neighbors? Is there a village nearby?"

"Naw, just people like us. And you. People what Griaule chased onto the plain. Maybe fifty or sixty of 'em. It's hard to say exactly because most keep to themselves and they're scattered all over. Might be more."

George hefted his mangos, slung them over his shoulder. "Griaule, you say? You're talking about that smallish dragon?"

"Same as chased you out here," said the man. "Quite different from the Griaule we're used to, he is. But you can see it's him if you looks close."

"How long have you been out here?" George asked.

"Three months, a piece more. At least that's how long me and the family's been here." He gestured at the plump man. "Edgar joined us a week or so later."

Edgar grinned at George and nodded.

"Is that your family?" George pointed to the figures in the brush. "Please assure them I mean no harm."

"I'm sure they know that, sir. It's obvious you're a gentleman." The balding man toed the dirt, as if embarrassed. "My daughter took a terrible fright, what with all Griaule's bellowing. She's never been right in the head. Now she ain't comfortable around people...except for Edgar here." Resentment, or something akin, seeped into his voice. "She fair dotes on him."

"How many people are with you, Mister?" asked Edgar, startling George, who had begun to think he was a mute.

"Just a friend and I."

He introduced himself and learned that the balding man was Peter Snelling, his wife was named Sandra and his daughter Peony. These formalities concluded, he asked what use they thought the dragon had for them.

"Might as well ask how much the moon weighs," said Edgar, and Snelling chimed in, "You'll get nowhere attempting to divine his purposes."

"You must have had some thoughts on the subject," said George.

"Don't reckon he wants to eat us," Snelling said. "He wouldn't go to all this trouble...yet he did eat that one fellow."

"Didn't really eat him." Edgar scratched a jowl. "Chewed on him and spit him out is all."

"That was because he tried to run off," said Snelling. "It were Griaule's way of telling the rest of us to stay put."

The idea that anyone could undergo this trial and not expend a great deal of energy in trying to comprehend it was alien to George. In his opinion, it did not speak highly of the two men's intellect. He asked how they had wound up in this desolate place to begin with. Had they, like him, been transported by a magical agency?

"You'd have to talk to Peony," Snelling said. "She were fooling around with something, but she wouldn't show me what it was. Then the walls of our house vanished and there we were, with nothing but nature around us. Peony let out a screech and flung the thing in her hand away. I suppose I should have searched for it." He hunched his shoulders and made a rueful face. "It was hard to swallow, you know, that she were the one responsible. But I'm sure now it was her doing."

"Even if you had found it, it wouldn't have done you much good," said George.

Edgar's eyes darted to the side and George followed his gaze. An immensely fat woman with gray tangles of hair framing a lumpish, sunburned face and wearing a tent-sized piece of canvas for a dress, rushed at him, swinging a tree branch. The branch struck him on the neck and shoulder. Twigs scratched his face; sprays of leaves impaired his vision—a confusing blow yet not that concussive. He staggered to the side, but did not fall. Snelling threw himself on him, riding him piggyback, and as husband and wife sought to wrestle him to the ground, Edgar poked him with his stick, more annoyance than threat, his moony face bobbing now and then into sight. George managed to shove the woman away and, when she came at him again, he planted a foot in the pit of her stomach, sending her waddling backwards across the clearing, her arms making circular motions as if attempting to fly out of danger. She made a cawing noise and toppled into a bush—her dress rode up around her hips, leaving the raddled flesh of her legs protruding from the leaves. Snelling clung to him, biting and clawing, until George grabbed him by the hair and punched him in the mouth. Edgar dropped his stick, retreated to the edge of the clearing, and stood wringing his hands, his expression shifting from pained to vacant, and finally lapsing into the feckless grin that George took to be the natural resolution of his features.

He wiped blood from his chin, where a twig had nicked him. Snelling lay on his side, breathing through his mouth, blood crimsoning his teeth. His wife struggled to sit up, teetered for a moment, flirting with the perpendicular before falling back again.

"Sandra!" Snelling's cry sounded forlorn, almost wistful, not like a shout of warning, or even one of sympathy.

"Are you mad?" George kicked dirt on him and scooped up his shirt, along with the mangos it held. "Risking your lives for a few mangos! Fucking idiots!"

A noise behind him—he spun about, ready to defend himself. Standing at the margin of the clearing was a gangly young girl in deplorable condition, twelve or thirteen years old. Ginger hair hung across her face in thick snarls and her faded blue rag of a dress did little to hide her immature breasts. In addition to a freckling of inflamed insect bites, the skin of her torso and legs was striped with welts, some of them fresh, evidence of harsh usage. Her lips trembled and she tottered forward. "Help me," she said in a frail voice. She stumbled and might have fallen had George not caught her. She was so slight, when he put an arm about her, he inadvertently lifted her off the ground.

Snelling collapsed onto his back, breath shuddering, but his wife, displaying renewed vigor, shrilled, "Take your hands off my daughter!"

Edgar, displaying unexpected ferocity, charged George with arms outstretched and fingers hooked, as if intending to scratch out his eyes. George stepped to the side and, using the mangos knotted in his shirt, clubbed him in the face. Edgar dropped like a stone, blood spurting from his nose, and began to sob. Between the sobs, George heard Peony speaking almost inaudibly, saying, "She's not my mother…she's not my mother."

"Liar!" Mrs. Snelling shrieked. "Ingrate!"

"She may be your daughter, but you most certainly are not her mother," George said. "No real mother would allow her child to endure such abuse."

"Bastard! If we were in Morningshade, I'd have you beaten."

"Lucky for me we're not in Morningshade. And lucky for you I'm less concerned with justice than I am with caring for your daughter's injuries." George's outrage crested. "My God! What sort of people are you to treat a child so? Wild animals would show more humanity! I'm taking her with me. If you attempt to interfere in any way, I'll finish what I've begun. I'll kill you all!"

To illustrate this message, George kicked Edgar in the thigh. He backed from the clearing and, once he could no longer see them, he picked up Peony and ran.

HE HAD GONE no more than twenty-five yards when a blast of sound assailed him, seeming to come from on high, followed by a windy rush. Glancing up, he glimpsed a pale swollen belly and a twitching serpentine tail passing overhead. Moments later, the bushes crunched under an enormous weight and a low grumbling signaled that Griaule had landed nearby and was crashing through the thickets. George flung himself down, burrowed under the dead fronds scattered beneath a palmetto tree, and gathered Peony to him, clamping a hand to her mouth to prevent an outcry. More crunching, dry twigs snapping like strings of firecrackers; then the great glutinous huff of the dragon breathing. Through a gap in the leaves George saw a thick scaly leg that terminated in a foot as broad as a sofa cushion, with a spike protruding from its heel and four yellowish talons, much discolored. Peony, who had been squirming about, went limp in his arms, and a cold sensation settled over his brain. Cold and seething, like the margins of a tide. He had the impression of an ego gone wormy with age and anger, a malefic, indulgent potency whose whims dwarfed his deepest desires, an entity to which he was intrinsically subservient. A message resolved from the coldness, clear as the reverberations of a gong, silencing every other mental voice, and he knew, as surely as he might know the worn portrait of an empress on a Roman sestercius, that his place was beside the pools, that he should never return to the mango tree. Such behavior would not be tolerated a second time. He shut his eyes, terror-struck by this brush with Griaule's mind (it had been too alien and powerful to write off as imagination born of fear), and he refused to open them again until he heard leathery wings battering the air and a scream issuing from above the plain.

AS THEY MADE their way toward home, he rejected all interior conversation concerning the possibility that the dragon had spoken to him (though he was certain it had), and he stuffed any material relating to the encounter into his mental attic and locked it away. Denial was the only rational course in the face of such power. To distract himself further, he poked around in the fume and bubble of his thoughts, hoping to learn what had provoked him to such a rage against the Snellings. Not since his schoolboy days had he lifted a hand in anger and, while he had acted in self-defense, the murderous character of the emotions that had attended his actions astonished him. He could not unearth any inciting event from his past that would have predisposed him to such a vicious reaction, yet he realized he had tapped into a reservoir of ferocity that must have been simmering inside him for years, waiting a proper outlet. His threats had not been empty bluster. He meant every word.

Chapter Five

PEONY WAS TOO WEAK TO manage a hike and George had to carry her much of the way. When he questioned her about the Snellings, she put her head down on his shoulder and slept, her heart beating against his chest, frail and rapid as a bird's. With every step, her vulnerability impressed itself on him and his commitment to her deepened. He stopped now and then, hiding in the thickets, waiting until certain no one was trailing them before moving on, and before they reached camp in early afternoon he had reversed the basic situation in his mind and thought about Peony in terms such as might befit a protective parent.

Sylvia was fishing, crouched half-naked in the pool, wearing only her rolled-up trousers. She pretended not to hear his approach. He called out to her and she turned on him a look of exasperation that changed to one of displeasure when she caught sight of Peony.

"Adding to your stable?" she said nastily. "One woman's not enough for a man of your dimensions?"

"Use your eyes," he replied. "She's hardly a woman."

He explained what had occurred and she had him carry Peony inside the shelter, then shooed him away, saying she would tend to the girl.

Five good-sized fish lay on flat stones by the edge of the pool, their glistening sides pulsing with last breaths. One had silvery tiger-stripes on its olive green back—George couldn't identify it. He sliced off their heads, gutted and filleted them, and wrapped their flesh in banana leaves. That done, he took a stroll into the thickets, located a banderilla tree growing beside a cluster of hibiscus bushes, and began removing the barbs from the tips of the twigs, placing them on banana leaves and carrying the leaves to the perimeter of the camp. He was loading his ninth leaf when Sylvia pushed through the bushes to his side and asked what he was doing.

"I'm going to rig some booby traps along the trails," he said. "They won't do serious damage, but we'll hear when someone trips them."

She said nothing, watching him work.

"Is Peony sleeping?" he asked.

She nodded and knelt beside him. "She's going to require a lot of care. I'll do what I can, but…I don't know."

"What's wrong?"

Sylvia shook her head.

"Tell me," George insisted.

"It's what happens to beautiful young girls when there's no one to care for them."

Recalling the way Peony had looked, it was difficult to think of her as beautiful. "What do you mean?"

"Men. As best I can tell, they've been at her since she was eight."

Sylvia's voice quavered with emotion and George suspected that her empathy for the girl might be due to a similarity of experience.

"Men did most of the damage," she said. "But her mother used her as well."

George had the impulse to suggest that being sexually abused by one's mother would have a momentous effect. A centipede crawled onto his ankle—he flicked it off. "Did she say whether the Snellings were her parents?"

"I asked, but she's not clear about it. She's hazy about most things. It's good you brought her here." She uprooted a weed. "I'm sorry for earlier… what I said about you."

"It's all right."

"I had no business saying it. You've treated me better than most." She paused. "She saw Griaule's scale in your kit. I let her keep it, if that suits you."

"That's up to you. It's yours, after all."

After a pause she said, "Could you sleep somewhere else for a while? Peony's grateful for what you did, but it would do her a world of good not to sleep at close quarters with a man."

George mulled this over. "I should build a larger shelter, anyway. We could be here for a while. There's a nice spot by one of the smaller ponds. If I put it there, that should give her enough privacy."

"Thank you."

"Once I finish with the booby traps, I'll get started."

She made as if to stand, but held in a crouch with one hand flat to the ground, and then settled back onto her knees. "One more thing. Can I have your shirt? I want to cut it up and make her a halter."

"There's no need to cut it up. It'll be too big for her, but it'll do the job."

"I thought I might make something for myself to wear, too. I know you like watching my titties, but they're an encumbrance for me."

He heard resentment in her tone, but her face remained neutral.

"You were using it as a carry-all," she said. "I don't figure you'll miss it so much."

He shrugged out of the shirt and handed it to her. "I'd give it a wash first."

She stood, holding the shirt in both hands. Again he thought she might speak and when she did not he lowered his head and went to twisting banderilla barbs from the twigs.

"Save me a fish," he said.

Chapter Six

WORN OUT BY HIS LABORS, by emotional tumult, George fell asleep in the partially completed new shelter shortly after dark. He was overtired and slept fitfully, now and again waking to a twinge of strained muscles, conscious of scudding dark clouds that obscured all but thin seams of stars, and of wind rattling the palm thatch, raising a susurrus from the surrounding thickets. During such an interlude a shadow slipped inside the shelter and lay next to him, her fingers spidering across his belly and his groin. He intended to tell her that he was too tired, too sore, but while he was still half-asleep, his senses pleasantly muddled, she took him in her mouth, her tongue doing clever things, finishing him quickly, and then she slipped from the shelter and was gone, leaving him with the impression that the wind and the darkness had conspired to produce a lover whose sensuality was the warm, breathing analogue of the rustling thatch and the sighing thickets. Waking late the next morning, he half-believed it had been a dream or a visitation of some sort until he saw Sylvia beside the pool and she flashed a smile that persuaded him the intimacy had neither been imagined nor supernatural in origin.

Peony stood by her on the bank, but on spotting George she stepped behind Sylvia as if anxious. He would not have recognized her in a different context, though the marks of abuse were more prominent now that her skin was clean. Her hair was pulled back from her face, exposing high cheekbones and huge cornflower blue eyes and a mouth too wide for her delicate jaw and pointed chin. It was a face of such otherworldly beauty, George's initial glimpse of it affected him like a slap and he felt a measure of alarm. Both Peony and Sylvia wore halters fashioned from his shirt and, while they did not much resemble one another, this made them seem like a mother and daughter—he doubted Sylvia was older than twenty-two or twenty-three, yet she possessed a maturity that lent her a maternal aspect when compared with Peony. George found appealing the notion that the three of them might constitute a family.

"I'm George," he said to Peony. "Do you remember me?"

Peony had been peering at him over Sylvia's shoulder, but now she looked away, showing him her left profile.

"How are you feeling?" he asked.

She kept her eyes averted. "I'm afraid."

"You needn't be afraid. The people who hurt you…"

"It's not them she's afraid of," Sylvia said. "It's Griaule."

"He wants to show me something," Peony said. "But I won't look."

George rubbed at an ache in his shoulder. "I don't understand."

"We'll be fine." Sylvia fixed him with a stare, as if daring him to object. "Peony will be safe here, won't she?"

"Oh, yes. Absolutely." He continued to rub his shoulder and asked Peony how she knew Griaule's mind.

"It's not so clear with the scale Sylvia gave me," Peony said. "Mine was better. But…"

George waited for her to go on. She fingered the ends of her hair and did not speak.

"What's not so clear?" he asked.

"It's like he's whispering to me, but there's no voice."

"You hear him talking? He talks to you?"

"He wants me to look at something awful," she said. "He wants us all to look."

"Do you ever hear him without touching the scale? After I took you from the Snellings, did you hear him then?"

She shot George a quizzical look. "Lots of people hear him when he's angry."

"Do you think the Snellings heard him?"

"I've got to get to my fishing. The later the hour, the harder they are to catch." Sylvia went to one knee and began rolling up a pants leg. "If you two could look after each other, maybe gather some fruit, that would be nice."

George frowned. "I was going to collect some saplings I can use for poles. You know, for the shelter."

"Is there a reason you can't take her with you?" Sylvia came to her feet and said under her breath, "I need time to myself." She nodded at Peony and grimaced, as if to imply the girl was a trial, and then, in a normal voice: "See if you can bring back some grapes. I'm told there used to be grapevines out here."

"Grapes!" Peony's giggle seemed edged with dementia.

"Yes," said Sylvia. "What about them?"

"You might as well eat eyes. That's what Edgar says."

"Edgar?"

"The man living with her parents," said George.

"They don't taste like eyes," Peony said. "But they're squishy like eyes."

"How does he know?" Sylvia asked her. "Is Edgar an eye-eater? Does he relish a nice eye on occasion? Does he dip 'em in melted butter and let 'em slide down his gullet?"

Peony appeared to struggle with the question; her expression lost its sharpness and her gaze wandered.

"I'll wager he's an eye-eater," Sylvia said. "Most men are."

THAT CONVERSATION, GEORGE discovered, was Peony at her most coherent. Much of the time she was unresponsive, even when asked a direct question, and she would hum or sing in her pale voice, fiddling with a leaf or a pebble, whatever fell to hand. Nevertheless he managed to piece together a vision of her life with Edgar and the Snellings. She declined to talk about Sandra—her face tightened each time George broached the subject—but said that Mr. Snelling had been in the habit of grabbing her whenever Sandra chose not to perform her wifely duty; he would turn Peony "bottoms up" and beat her for her lack of enthusiasm. Edgar had weaseled his way into her affections, pretending to be a friend, and cajoled her into using her mouth to soothe him after a hard day of eating mangos. His fondness for sexual practices associated with sailors on long voyages had alienated Peony, yet she spoke of him fondly in contrast to her remarks about the Snellings. Having learned all this, George reserved the majority of his loathing for Edgar. Younger and stronger than the Snellings, he might have assisted Peony, but chose instead to gratify his lust, helping transform her into this broken thing.

Thenceforth George cared for Peony from the time he woke until late afternoon, at which point Sylvia took charge. He dragged her along whenever he searched for edibles (feeding three people occupied most of their day and though they went about it with diligence, they lost weight and strength at a startling rate). As a consequence, he and Sylvia were rarely alone together. It was hardly the family life he had envisioned, yet it was not dissimilar to the life he and Rosemary had shared, albeit with greater responsibilities and less frequent sex. Sylvia had not visited him in the new shelter since the night after he had returned with Peony. He believed on that occasion she must have been grateful for his intercession on Peony's behalf, and he told himself that in order to obtain sexual favors on a regular basis he might have to save other young women from exigent circumstances. He was tempted to coerce her by saying that he needed this consolation, that the strain of days spent worrying and watching out for the dragon was taking its toll (it would not have been an outright lie—his waking hours were marked by depressive fugues). Then seventeen days after Peony had entered their lives, Sylvia visited him again, crawling into the shelter as he was falling asleep.

A three-quarter moon shone into the shelter, gilding their bed of banana leaves, and when Sylvia mounted him she became a silhouette limned in golden light, her hair tossing about like black flames, an impression supported by the thatch crackling in the wind. She was eager and enthusiastic as never before, and George, fancying this increase signaled more than mere animal intensity, responded with enthusiasm. Afterward, however, she broke the post-coital silence by saying, "I don't want you taking this personal. I had an itch I couldn't scratch, you understand."

"Why would I suppose otherwise?"

Moonlight erased the marks of strain on her face and she seemed a younger, less troubled version of herself. "Because I know how men get," she said.

George scoffed at this. "They're such primitive creatures, aren't they? Quick to arouse and to anger. Otherwise they're like backward children."

"About some things they are. Do you think I'm such a ninny, I can't tell your feelings are hurt? I'm sorry, but I don't want you to come away with the wrong idea."

"Let me assure you, I know exactly where we stand."

Another silence stretched between them, and then George said, "One thing is puzzling. You told me intercourse was out of the question because you didn't have your 'medicines.'"

"Peony says we won't be here long. If you get me in a family way, I'll fix it when we return to Teocinte."

"You believe her? You'd take the word of a child who'd stare into the sun all day if we allowed it?"

"I've had to accept greater improbabilities. I've accepted that you brought us to this place by rubbing a dragon's scale. People like Peony are often compensated for their impairment with a gift. But who..."

"Don't tell me you put any stock in that old business!"

"Who'd imagine a solid citizen like yourself would be so blessed?"

"Is that an insult in your view? Calling me a solid citizen?"

"I didn't mean it as such, but if that's how you choose to interpret it."

"I suppose 'solid citizen' must seem an insult to..." George bit back the last of his sentence.

"A whore? Is that the word you want?"

"We're trapped in this situation. It's pointless to fight."

"Pointless it may be, but I..."

"Stop it!" he said, wrapping his arms about her and drawing her close, so that they were pressed chest-to-chest. "We've greater troubles to deal with. And greater enemies."

"Let me go!"

She sought to wriggle free, but he held her tightly. She pulled away from him as far as his grip permitted, as if to gain a fresh perspective, and asked, "What do you want?"

"Just that we try to get along."

"This..." Although under restraint, she succeeded in conveying that she was speaking of their closeness. "This isn't getting along?"

"You know what I mean."

"We share the work, we each do our part in taking care of Peony. What else is there?"

"You could be pleasant."

"Ah! You want me to pretend."

"No! I want you to be like you were at the hotel. You remember. When you asked if I liked you when you weren't pretending to be someone else."

Amused, she said, "You don't believe I was pretending then?"

He tamped down his anger. "I don't care what you were doing, only that you do more of it. In spite of your faith in Peony's clairvoyance, it could be months or years before we find our way home. We could be stuck here the rest of our lives. We need to make a better effort at getting along or we'll drive each other mad."

"We don't have to get along. We're not married."

"Is that right? We bicker constantly, we have sex infrequently, and we're responsible for a child. That sounds like a marriage to me. Unlike a marriage, however, we can't escape its context by having a night out. Whatever you were doing, pretending, not pretending, it might be helpful if you started doing it again. Neither of us is a trusting person, but we have to trust one another. We have no idea what's going on and we may have to depend on each other more than we do now. We need to develop a bond. If we can't, we have no chance of surviving."

"Are you finished?"

"Yes, I suppose I am."

"Let me go."

With a frustrated noise, he pushed her away and she rolled up to her knees. Curls and flecks of banana leaf were stuck to the sweat on her hip and thigh—they might have been the remnants of script, as if their love-making had written a green sentence on her flesh that their argument had mostly erased. He expected her to bolt without further word, but once she regained her footing she stood with her head down, hair hanging in her face, her fingers intertwined at her waist.

"Are you all right?" he asked.

She wiped her nose.

"I didn't mean to upset you," he said. "I'm merely suggesting we'd be better off if we were honest with one another. If we make a sincere effort at establishing a relationship, a friendship, then who knows what may develop. If a spark is given sufficient tinder..."

"Don't you ever stop?" She clasped both hands to her head as though to prevent it from exploding. "You get an idea and you go on and fucking on about it! You don't care what anyone else is going through so long as you hear the sound of your voice." She sniffled, wiped her nose again, and squared her shoulders. "I'm sorry. I truly am."

With that, she hurried off into the darkness, leaving George to contemplate the error of his ways, to puzzle over her apology, and to listen to the wind intoning its ceaseless consonant-less sentence, like a mantra invoking an idiot god.

JUDGING BY THE way their conversation ended, George did not expect a happy result; but the upshot of the encounter was that Sylvia began coming to him every few nights, and they would make love and discuss practical considerations, most having to do with Peony. They were, he reflected, becoming if not a traditional family, then a functional one. He suspected that Sylvia's heart was not in the relationship, but her pretence pleased him, nourishing a longstanding fantasy and sustaining him against the two oppressive, unvarying presences that ruled over the plain: the heat and the dragon. At times he was unable to distinguish between them—the dragon patrolling overhead seemed emblematic of the terrible heat, and the heat seemed the enfeebling by-product of the dragon's mystery and menace. Without Sylvia's affections and his paternal regard for Peony, he might have succumbed to depression. The days played out with unrelenting sameness: too-bright mornings and oven-like noons giving way to skies with low gray clouds sliding past, their bellies dark with rain that never fell, and a damp closeness turning the air to soup—it was as if they were living in the humid mouth of a vast creature too large to apprehend, one of which they had only unpleasant and unreliable intimations. Of course the dragon was the most salient threat, the one for which there was neither explanation nor remedy. Though he had denigrated Edgar and Snelling for their lack of interest in the question, George soon realized that any attempted analysis relating to the dragon's purposes would be pure speculation. The most sensible explanation he came up with was that the dragon was using the plain as storehouse for its food supply, but this raised other questions, notably why would Griaule bother to choose its human treats by so indirect a procedure (assuming the others had been transported to the plain by touching or rubbing immature dragon scales). He inquired of Peony again, asking what she knew of Griaule's designs, but she spoke in generalities, repeating her original statement that he wanted them to witness something, adding to this that they were "the lucky ones." When he pressed her, she grew tearful and mumbled something about "fire."

GEORGE HAD NOT entirely accepted that the dragon of the moment was Griaule, or that, as this would imply, Griaule was still alive, and he found Peony's failure to resolve the question unbearably frustrating. He tried every means of coercion at his disposal, but nothing caused her to elaborate on the subject and he decided that the only thing to do was to table the matter. To occupy his mind, he began teaching Peony about the natural world, lessons she did not appear capable of absorbing. As they wandered the plain in their never-ending search for food, he would point out the various trees and bushes and repeat their names, and he explained processes like the sunrise and rain, often over-explaining them, a tactic that may have annoyed Sylvia but to which Peony raised no objection.

One day while they were exploring the thickets to the west of the stream, they happened upon a kumquat tree that had escaped the attention of the birds, its boughs laden with dusky orange fruit. George sat beneath it and fashioned a makeshift basket out of banana leaves, while Peony nibbled at the fruit, gnawing away the flesh from around the big brown pits. After she had consumed over a dozen kumquats he told her that if she didn't stop she might experience stomach trouble. She plucked another kumquat. He repeated his warning to no effect and finally snapped at her, forbidding her to eat more—she dropped the kumquat and refused to look at him. He patted her on the arm, feeling like a bully, and lectured her in detail on the consequences of eating too much fruit.

As the sun approached its zenith, George located a patch of shade large enough to shelter them and stretched out for a nap with Peony beside him. He emerged from an erotic dream to find that Peony had unbuttoned the remnants of his trousers and was fondling him. At first he thought it part of the dream, but then he pushed her away. She made a pleading sound and tried once more to fondle him—he shouted at her to quit and she covered her head with her hands, as if to shield herself from a blow.

"You mustn't do that," he said. "You don't have to do that anymore. No one will hurt you if you don't."

She met his eyes without the least sign of comprehension; a tear cut a track though a spot of grime on her cheek.

"It's all right," he said. "I'm not angry at you. I'm angry at the people who taught you this was how you should please them."

She gazed at him blankly, her face empty as a fresh-washed bowl embossed with an exotic pattern. She drew a wavy line in the dirt with a fingertip and looked at him again.

"Do you understand?" he said. "You never have to do this anymore. Not with anyone."

A worry line creased her brow. "I want to make people happy."

"Where this is concerned, touching people, allowing them to touch you…the important thing is to please yourself."

She made a clumsy pawing gesture and lowered her eyes; she saw the kumquat she had let fall and reached for it, then pulled back her hand.

"From now on," he said, "if you have the urge to make anyone happy that way, if anyone asks you to make them happy, you come to me and ask what to do. Or ask Sylvia. Will you do that?"

She nodded and reached for the kumquat. He started again to reproach her, but decided that she had enough to think about.

It was not until after he handed her off to Sylvia that he began to speculate about his hesitation in pushing Peony away, thinking his reflexes may have been slowed not by sleep as much as by perversity; and it was not until that evening that he began to wonder about that first night after he had rescued Peony, when Sylvia had come to him…if it had been Sylvia. Her touch seemed in memory less practiced, less confident, akin to Peony's in that regard. And surely Sylvia would have spoken to him—it was not like her to be so shy. The longer he thought about it, the greater his certitude that Peony had expressed gratitude the only way she knew. The idea repelled him yet he could not stop dwelling on it. As he went over the events of that night, a measure of prurience crept into his thoughts, repelling him further. He hewed to the notion that this was how the obsessive mind worked, seeking ever to betray itself, subverting every clean impulse by assigning it a base motive; yet as the days wore on he insisted upon punishing himself for his crimes. Even when occupied by the basics of survival, part of him was always focused upon Peony, upon what he had or hadn't done.

The matter should have been easy to resolve, but when Sylvia next visited him, George had feared that anything she said about that night would support his self-imposed verdict. Better, he decided, to maintain a modicum of doubt concerning his moral turpitude than to have none. He was unable to perform with Sylvia, excusing his failure by claiming to have stomach trouble, and as they lay listening to the wind flowing across the plain, watching clouds skimming a half-moon that set their edges on silvery fire, he allowed this intimacy to change his mind and blurted out what had happened between him and Peony the day before, and asked Sylvia if she had come to him the night following the rescue, because he feared now that it had not been her.

She was silent for a beat and then turned to face him. "Is that what's got you in a twist? Of course it was me!" She gave him a playful punch. "I'm insulted you didn't recognize me!"

Later he realized that if he had desired an honest response, he would have asked the question without preamble, not letting on that he suspected his visitor had been Peony, telling Sylvia that he'd had a dream and he wondered whether or nor it was real. He should never have afforded her the opportunity to weigh the situation, to determine that it would be best for her if she lied, thus giving his confidence a boost and assuring that he would remain capable of defending her. This scenario called for a complex understanding on her part, but he had long since discarded the idea that she was other than an intelligent, subtle woman. And so the conflict remained unresolved, continuing to erode his mental underpinnings, distracting him from more important considerations.

George could not separate himself from Peony during the day, but he minimized their physical contact and treated her with a rigid formality, permitting neither hugs nor holding hands. That the loss of a simple animal comfort appeared to have no effect on her should have offered him a degree of absolution, since it pointed out how damaged she was, how trivial an influence the actions of others had upon her inner turmoil; but instead it served to distress him further, seeming to add to his offense, and made him even more mindful of her well-being than he had been before. Every scraped knee and pricked finger was cause for worry; every complaining noise engaged his full concern. When he was unable to sleep (something that happened with increasing frequency), in order to safeguard her more thoroughly he would patrol the perimeter of the camp with a regularity that rivaled the dragon's, taking pains to avoid his own booby traps. One evening as he made his rounds, he heard a succession of cries coming from the thickets out past his shelter. They subsided as he approached and he could hear nothing except the wind. An oblate moon emerged from cloud cover to the south, silvering the fluttering tops of the bushes and showing his path. Soon he heard the voices again. Men's querulous voices. He crept toward the sound, peeking between leaves. Separated from the bank of one of the lesser pools by a thin fringe of vegetation, two men sat athwart an animal trail. Delicate rills of blood, black in the moonlight, trickled from wounds on their legs—they had fallen into one of his traps and were picking out banderilla barbs from their flesh. The smaller of the two, a sinewy man with a mane of dark hair half-hiding his face, wearing a pair of rotting trousers, cursed as he removed a barb, digging at his calf with the tip of a fishing knife. The other man was Edgar. He had received fewer injuries and was cautious with the barbs, yipping as he worked them free.

Anger flowed into George's mind, like a rider swinging with practiced ease onto his mount—it was as if he'd been preparing for this moment for weeks and, now it had arrived, he was more than ready to perform whatever duties were required. He stepped onto the trail, but before he could speak the sinewy man sprang to his feet, and made an awkward, hobbling lunge toward George and slashed with the knife, drawing a line of hot pain across his abdomen. A second stroke sliced his forearm. Panicking, George flung himself forward and grappled with the man, locking onto the wrist of his knife-hand. They swayed together like drunken dancers and careened through the bushes and out onto the bank. His opponent was strong, but George, much the larger of the two, had leverage on his side—he turned the man and secured a hold from behind and rode him down onto his knees at the brink of the pool. The knife went skittering along the bank and, as the man sought to retrieve it, George moved atop him, using his weight to flatten him out, and forced his head underwater. He surfaced and twisted his neck about, offering a view of his grizzled cheek, grimacing mouth, and a mad, glaring eye that glittered through a webbing of wet hair. His fetid odor enveloped them both. He grunted and gulped in air; then his head went under again and his struggles grew spastic, frantic, churning the water. He reached back with his left hand, trying to claw George's face, and George latched his fingers behind the man's neck and pushed down harder, his eyes fixed on the opposite side of the pool. He spotted Sylvia in a half-crouch at the verge of the bushes, but took no salient notice of her. Spasms passed through the man's flesh, lewd convulsions like those of a lover nearing completion. George kept pushing down on his neck, making sure. Finally he rolled off the body and lay panting beside it. The moonlight had brightened. His stomach throbbed. He sat up to inspect the wound: it appeared superficial. The cut on his forearm was more worrisome. If the man hadn't been impeded by injuries, George thought, then he might be the one who lay motionless. His hands shook. A placid current set the dead man's head to bobbing. George imagined fish nibbling at the eyes and thought to pull the body from the water, but wasn't moved to act. The smell of the man was on his skin, nauseatingly thick. Sylvia kneeled beside him, saying words he couldn't make sense of. The sight of her confused him on a fundamental level, disordered all his certainties. He wanted to look away, but her insistent stare held him. She spoke again, her tone fretful, and he said, "I'm all right."

She slapped him. "The other one's getting away!"

He cast about, but saw no one.

"Here!" She pressed the dead man's knife into his hand, its blade frilled with red. Resting on his palm, it had an incomprehensible value.

"It's only Edgar," he said.

"Edgar? The one who was holding Peony captive? And that..." She gestured at the body. "That was Snelling?"

"I don't know who he was." George set the knife down on the grass. "But Edgar's no threat. He's harmless on his own."

"But he wasn't on his own, was he? He must have talked his friend into having a little adventure. Told him there was a nice piece over this way and suggested they fetch her back. Do you call that harmless?" She left a pause and, when he kept silent, she said, "If you won't do something, I will."

She snatched at the knife, but George closed his hand on the hilt and creakily came to his feet, feeling light-headed and feverish, moved not by an urge to seek out Edgar, but by the desire to stop her talking.

Edgar was not difficult to track. After they had walked the trail for several minutes, George heard a voice nattering on at a conversational volume. Thirty feet farther along they reached a creosote bush—many of its leaves were stripped away and it threw a complicated shadow across the ground—Edgar sat at the center of this shadow, like an innocent young demon with a moony face summoned by a magical design. He picked at a spine in his heel, noticed them and grinned sheepishly, as if he had been caught at something naughty.

"I told you, didn't I?" he said, apparently addressing himself. "Leave 'em alone, I said."

George hunkered down in front of him. "Where are the Snellings?"

Edgar was thinner than before, his cheeks hollowed, his belly flab reduced. He nodded, as if listening to an invisible someone responding to his chiding. George yelled at him to gain his attention and repeated his inquiry.

"Peter's dead," Edgar said. "And Sandra's took ill. That's why me and Tony come. To see if you had medicine."

Sylvia made a disparaging noise.

"If that was your purpose," George said, "why did Tony try to kill me?"

Edgar puzzled over this. "I reckon because you surprised him. He didn't know you from Adam."

"You could have said something, couldn't you? You could have told him who I was."

He fingered his ratty hair. "I reckon you surprised me, too."

"Finish this," Sylvia said flatly.

"I want to ask him some more questions," said George.

"He's making things up as he goes along. It's obvious!"

George spoke to Edgar. "You wanted to see Peony, didn't you?"

"I'm always wanting to see Peony, but that weren't why we come."

"Did you tell Tony about her?"

Edgar's mouth worked, as if tasting some sourness. "I don't recall."

Sylvia threw up her hands. "Can't we have done with this?"

George stood and pulled her aside, out of Edgar's hearing. "Lying or not, he can't harm us. He's simple."

"You say he's simple, I say it's an act. But be that as it may, suppose another Tony happens along—do you think he won't tell him about Peony? He wants her back, can't you see that?"

"We survived Tony, we'll survive the next one."

"We barely survived! You may be willing to put yourself at risk for no good reason, but not me."

George glanced at Edgar—he was picking at his heel.

"This is the man you blamed for Peony's condition," said Sylvia. "I'm not wrong about that, am I?"

"I think we need to step back a moment," George said. "We don't always have to react straightaway."

"You great fucking idiot!" Sylvia looked as though she wanted to spit. "All this time out here, after everything we've been through, and you still don't know who you are...or where you are. You just killed a man in self-defense. Held him under the water until his lungs burst because he threatened us. Now you're reluctant to finish the job. I guess you'd rather pretend you're a moral sort. That you're too sensitive to be a killer. You need time to contemplate the idea, to fit it into your philosophy of life. Well, maybe that'll make you feel better, but feeling better won't change the fact that there's no place for morality here. If truth be told, there's no place for it in Morningshade, either. Nor anywhere, really."

"You're being ridiculous. I keep telling you Edgar's not a threat."

"Everyone's a threat! There's no law here except Griaule's. If he wasn't flying around all hours, frightening everybody, people would be braver, they'd explore their surroundings. And if that were the case, like as not Peony and I would be slaving away on our backs day and night, and you'd be dead. We're fortunate the people camped close to us were cowards."

She prodded his chest with a finger. "Sooner or later Edgar's bound to tell his story to someone more adept at killing than you. Someone who's not hampered by morality. Then we'll find out how moral you are."

Edgar started to mumble. The wind tailed off—George could hear the rush of the stream. The sound fatigued him and filled him with melancholy.

"You want him dead?" He offered her the knife. "I've shed enough blood this evening."

Her face closed down, armored by a blank expression. George expected her to back away from his challenge, but after a pause, as he was about to say, "What are you waiting for?", she seized the knife and went toward Edgar with a decisive step. At the last instant he turned his head, grinning at her, and she drove the knife into the side of his neck, giving a truncated cry as she struck. The force of the blow knocked Edgar onto his side, tearing the hilt from her grasp, and she fell back, as if shocked by the result. He made a mewling noise and pressed his fingers to the steel protruding from his neck; dark blood jumped between them, spattering his pale shoulder. He seemed to be straining at something, trying to preserve a critical balance, perhaps torn between the desire to yank out the blade and the thought that such an action would be the end of him. His legs kicked out, briefly causing it to appear that he was running in place. Then the straining aspect ebbed from his limbs and he lay staring at the base of the creosote bush. Off in the night, the dragon screamed.

Chapter Seven

FROM THEN ON, CERTAIN ILLUSIONS went by the board, the illusion that they were a family foremost among them. George and Sylvia stopped having sex, a decision that was mutual albeit unspoken, and there was an overall diminution of pleasantries; yet these things seemed to indicate a larger change, one whose most profound symptom was an atmosphere of dejection, if not outright defeat. It was as if the spark that gave them life had been dampened. Occasionally that spark sputtered and sparked, providing a bright moment, as on the night when Sylvia told a story she'd written and memorized, one of several she related, all set in Ali's Eternal Reward, concerning a girl of the brothel and her romance with a man who was the spitting image of the Sinistral from a deck of fortune-telling cards. Peony was entranced by the story and George offered extravagant praise that brought a smile to Sylvia's face; but that flare of good feeling quickly faded and they were as before—three damaged people with no palpable bond to shield them against the oppressions of heaven and the disappointments of the world.

Peony became severely agitated in the week that followed Edgar's death, and, though Sylvia swore Peony had been asleep, George assumed that it was due to her having witnessed Edgar's execution...or perhaps sensed it in some fashion. She would rock on her haunches, fists clenched, making noises like a tiny teakettle, and nothing would console her. After four days she ceased being agitated and instead sat fiddling with the dragon scale, sometimes lapsing into a state that resembled catatonia, drooling and listless and completely unresponsive. Memories and dreams of the man he had killed and of Edgar, the man in whose death he had been complicit, plagued George's nights. He wondered if Sylvia had trouble sleeping, curious as to how efficient her justifications were in protecting her against the depredations of conscience—he suspected they served her very well, indeed. His own sleep was fitful at best. He commonly woke well before sunrise, a circumstance that left him exhausted and slow-brained by day's end, and he would nod off while sitting or even standing. At dusk, ten days after the killings, following a brief lapse of this sort, he stood at the margin of the camp, looking blearily across the plain, and observed a yellowish red glow on the horizon beneath a line of slate clouds. Sunset was his first thought, but then he realized that he was not facing west and what he had taken for clouds were actually the peaks of the eastern hills. The glow issued from an area between the hills and his vantage point. For a minute he watched it brighten and spread, thinking it odd. He heard piping cries and saw four or five people running through the thickets, their heads visible over the tops of the bushes. The dragon wheeled above and he assumed they were fleeing him. Fools, though. The edges of the glow wavered and he thought he detected a smoky odor. He stared dumbly a moment before recognizing the source of the glow. The plain was burning and a brisk wind was driving a wall of flame toward them.

SHOUTING THE ALARM, he raced to the shelter and found Sylvia and Peony outside, frightened and clinging together, asking questions with their eyes. He flung out an arm toward the east and said, "The thickets are on fire, the wind's bringing it straight for us. We have to run!"

Light had almost faded from the sky when they began their westward flight, going at a steady pace, carrying nothing other than the rags on their back and a few meager possessions, like a family out of prehistory, united in fear. Soon they were racing in full night, yet before long the darkness was illuminated by the fire—they could see the spikes of separate flames and hear a dim roaring. George tried to keep close to the stream, but Griaule harried and herded them in a direction of his choosing. George had little doubt that he had set the plain afire in order to simplify that chore. Now and again the dragon would drop out of the sky, a creature of shadow with scales burnished by flame, and bellow at them, altering their course and adding his fierce noise to the din of the fire. On several occasions they made contact with other groups, but the people never materialized from the darkness sufficiently to identify or count their number. They shied away, as if their time on the plain had acclimated them to fear and suspicion. Hedgerows of fire closed around them. They stumbled and reeled through the thickets, their glistening faces dark with soot, darting this way and that to avoid sudden new channels of flame that threatened to hem them in. Peony fell and George picked her up; when Sylvia began to stagger and her pace faltered, he supported her with his free hand. There was so much smoke in the air, breathing was a chore, and this broke his concentration, causing him to feel fatigue. Griaule harrowed them onward, looming out of the night with his wings half-unfolded, seeming more terrible for being partially visible in the dark, here a reddened fang gleaming, here flame reflected in a golden eye, his roar outvoicing the roar of the flames, snapping, gusting flames that sucked oxygen from the air and heated it so that he felt his throat crack whenever he inhaled. He lost his bearings and suspected that Griaule was toying with them, that he would wear them out and let them to burn in a cul de sac; but he was too weary to come up with an escape plan, too wasted to care, and found himself hoping for a swift resolution, whatever form it might take.

The wind must have changed, because the temperature dropped and the light from the burning plain dimmed, occulted by a mixture of smoke and fog—still the dragon herded them along. They emerged from the thickets onto a grassy slope and, after no more than thirty yards, the slope grew steeper, rockier. Visibility was poor and George had to feel his way—it was as if they were ascending a crag whose lower reaches had the semblance of a crude stair, each step a couple of feet high. He couldn't hear the fire anymore and, though perplexed by this development, he was too enervated to worry. Soon what sounded like muted voices came to his ear. As his eyes adjusted to the darkness he realized that the steps of the stair were very wide and scattered about on them were small groups of people. He steered clear of these and found an unoccupied space where they could sit. The dragon rumbled below, but it was a ruminative sound, or so George chose to interpret it. He was done with running, unable to go another foot.

"Where are we?" Sylvia asked, pressing close for warmth—it had gotten cold and she and Peony sheltered under his arms.

"Don't you know?"

"I thought we were heading back toward Teocinte…where it used to stand. But there's no place like this near the city."

"We'll puzzle it out in the morning," he said. "Get some rest."

George made a manful effort to keep watch, but the gentle breathing of the women seduced him and he fell into a dreamless sleep, waking to discover that the sky had grayed and a dense fog sealed them in against tiers of stone, a kind of amphitheater, perhaps a natural formation.[10] The morning wind picked up, causing eddies and rifts in the fog, revealing sections of the plain—it disquieted him to see that the thickets showed yellowish green, not a trace of the previous night's fire, and there was no smell of burning. Every part of his body ached and he would have liked to shake out the kinks and have a look around, as people on the tiers beneath were doing (from what he could tell, there were less than fifty altogether, though he could not be certain, what with the fog); but he wanted to let Peony and Sylvia sleep as long as they could and contented himself with passive observation.

The people clustered on the steps, as sooty and ragged as George, kept an eye on the other groups around them, displaying no inclination to socialize, perhaps focused on the hope that their ordeal might be over, thus having no interest in anything apart from their own preoccupations. That hope, however, did not long persist, for an immense shape began to materialize from the fog directly in front of the amphitheater and, while he had no reason to despair (on the contrary, the vista that opened before him should by its familiarity have relieved his every concern), the sight of Griaule, not his lesser incarnation but the great paralyzed, recumbent beast

---

10 The amphitheater was not natural, but had been excavated from the side of a hill during Sylvia and George's absence from Teocinte (a term of years, and not of months, as they perceived it), its purpose being to provide seating for audiences who had come to witness a Sound and Light performance. Such a performance never occurred, though the lamps had been set in place and a stage built for the orchestra, and some have conjectured that the impulse to construct the amphitheater came not from the city fathers, as had been thought, but from a more subtle agency whose penchant for such ironies had been noted throughout the long history of Teocinte, and it was also thought that the seating had not been intended for tourists, but for precisely the audience that occupied it on the morning after George, Sylvia, and Peony had been forced to flee their encampment.

with his evil snout, his fangs festooned with vines and epiphytes, and scales embroidered with lichen and bird droppings, his greens and golds muted by an overcast, ghost-dressed in streamers of mist, the cavern of his mouth enclosing enough darkness to fill the naves of four or five cathedrals, the hill of his body looming above the tin roofs, the shanty districts and factory precincts of Morningshade from which now arose a clangor of bells... that sight had such a grim, iconic value, like a gigantic conceit enclosing the gates of some abyssal domain, George's strength failed him and the other witnesses appeared similarly afflicted. Their murmurous voices grew silent and they stopped milling about and stood frozen in a dozen separate tableaus. Waking, Peony screamed and buried her face in George's shoulder, and Sylvia drew in a breath sharply and pricked his arm with her fingernails. A chthonic rumbling was heard, so all-encompassing a sound it seemed to issue from the earth, the sky, from the core of all things, as if the basic stuff of matter had gained a voice and were offering complaint, and from Griaule's mouth, in a trickle at first, and then a tide darkening the grass, came the creatures that dwelled within his enormous bulk, slithering, crawling, creeping, flying, hopping, running on four legs and two (for among the snakes and spiders and skizzers and flakes[11] were a number of derelict men and women who, for whatever reason, had sought to shelter inside the dragon, in the hollows and caves and canyons formed by his organs and bones and cartilage). As they fled, dispersing across the plain, the witnesses made out a distant clamor composed of the affrighted cries of the citizens of Morningshade and various alarms being sounded. Griaule's eyes blinked open, wheels of gold flecked with mineral hues, each divided by a horizontal slit pupil, lending a vile animus to his face. In the depths of his throat bloomed an orange radiance that whitened and shone more fiercely until it resembled a star lodged in his gullet. Seeing this, between ten or fifteen of the witnesses broke from the tiers of the amphitheater and raced toward the town below. Among them was Peony. She shrugged off George's arm, eluded his lunging attempt to snatch her back, and scampered down the tiers.

---

11 Parasitic creatures peculiar to Griaule. Skizzers were relatively benign, but flakes, commonly camouflaging themselves as part of a scale, exuded a poison from their skin that led to the deaths of countless unwary scalehunters.

Somewhat reluctantly, Sylvia made to stand, and George said, "It'll be less of a risk if I go alone. Wait for us on the plain. We'll find you."

Relief and shame mixed in her face. "I don't think she knows where she used to live," she said. "Look for her at Griaule's temple. She thought it was pretty inside."

"Where else?"

She shook her head. "I don't know." And then, as he started off, she called, "The brothel! Maybe there! Because of my stories!"

They had been seated near the top tier and George had descended about two-thirds of its height when Griaule, with a coughing grunt that signaled a mighty effort, turned his head and twisted his body in the direction of Haver's Roost, his snout projecting out across the tin roofs—in the same motion, with a tremendous creaking and popping of calcified joints, noises that might have been created by tree trunks snapping, he pushed himself erect, moving with a ponderous, rickety deliberation bred by thousands of years of muscular disuse. It was an unreal sight, a mountainous transformation, the coming-to-life of a colossus. Griaule took a step forward and, with an earthshaking thump, planted a front foot among the shanties of Morningshade, crushing a considerable acreage and all that lived thereon, raising a dust cloud that boiled up around his foreleg, obscuring it. The soil and vegetation surrounding Hangtown, the village on the dragon's back, slid off his side and wings in huge clumps, and the shacks that constituted the village followed, disintegrating in midair; from his position, George could not tell where the debris landed. Griaule roared, a blast of raw noise that deafened him.[12] Pain drove him to his knees; he clasped both hands to his ears, squeezed his eyes shut, and when he looked again he saw a gush of flame (patterned with a shifting orange efflorescence that gave it an odd, lacy delicacy) spew from Griaule's mouth and lance across the valley to engulf the hotels on the slopes of Haver's Roost. Within seconds, every building on the Roost, even the government offices atop it, was burning. The dragon appeared to wobble for a instant, but maintained his stance and, lowering and turning his head slightly to the right,

---

12 The roar killed and injured several thousand people, most of them struck by flying glass from a myriad shattered windows. Nearly half the population suffered damage to their hearing to one degree or another.

breathed out a swath of fire to encompass a section of the outlying district of Cerro Bonito, among whose rolling hills the estates of wealthy foreigners were situated. Dollops of flame dropping from the dragon's lip and from the jet of its exhalation ignited conflagrations in other sections of the city. The smell of the burning held an acrid chemical undertone that stung George's nostrils.

An animal fear possessed him, but the mental contract he had made to protect Peony enabled him to ignore both fear and pain. It may have been a blessing that he could not hear, for by the time he came to the foot of the hill, the greater portion of the city was on fire (only those areas adjoining and beneath the dragon were left untouched) and streams of panic-stricken people rushed past in the opposite direction, some bleeding and burned, their mouths open in what he assumed to be screams, a sound that would have encouraged his own nascent panic. The streams increased to a flood when he reached the outskirts of Morningshade. He had to fight his way through streets thronged by crowds surging toward the plain. Directly ahead, seen through the dust and across rooftops striped with rust, Griaule's foreleg sprouted from the slum like a thewy green-and-gold tree thrust up from an orchard in hell; his dirty white belly sagged low above the finial atop a four-story temple devoted to his worship, more like a billow in a giant's dirty bed sheet than a piece of sky. An alley opened between storefronts on George's left. He wedged through the crowd and stepped into it in order to formulate a plan of action without being jostled; however, once away from the turbulence of the crowd, the situation seemed hopeless and he understood he had taken on a fool's errand. He made ready to plunge back into the crowd, intending to join them in flight, but at the far end of the alley he spotted a sign bearing the crude painting of a cornucopia—the business that it advertised, a pawnshop, was close to Ali's. He could spare a moment, he told himself, before surrendering to fear. Peony loved Sylvia's fantasies about the brothel and, if she had survived, she might well have taken refuge in a place Sylvia described as home to a loving sisterhood. He raced along the alley, forged a path toward Ali's through the sparser crowds on the side street, and burst through the door.

A SCRAWNY, STOOP-SHOULDERED, white-haired man drinking two-handed at the bar was the sole occupant of the common room. Boards and benches had been overturned; bottles and broken crockery littered the floor. George's hearing had returned to a degree—his ears rang, but he could detect the brighter range of sounds. He asked if the old man had seen Peony and the man did not turn from the bar to confront George and gave no other response. Drying blood from one ear made a track down his seamed cheek. Then the walls shimmied, the floorboards bounced, dust sifted down from the rafters and more bottles fell from a shelf behind the counter—Griaule shifting position once again. Two steps and their world was in chaos.

Upstairs, George hurried along a corridor, throwing open the doors, giving the rooms a cursory inspection, finding unmade beds and nightgowns draped over chairs, but no Peony. He was certain that he would be crushed or incinerated, and that certainty grew stronger with each second. In a room at the end of the hall whose window framed a view of the city, ruddy light flickered on creamy wallpaper with a pyramid pattern, and a pudgy, dark-haired woman in a pink flannel robe sat on the edge of the bed, watching Teocinte burn. Her eyes fell upon him and an expression of mirth spread like butter melting across her features. She patted the sheet beside her, inviting him to sit. He wanted to urge her to run, but something in her face, some central weakness, told him not to bother. A muscular balding man pushed past him into the room and, after a hostile glance at George, removed his trousers. The woman turned again to the window, plucking fretfully at the lapel of her robe. Abandoning them to whatever exercise they planned, George fled down the stairs and out into the street, almost overlooking the slight ginger-haired figure squatting on her haunches outside the door, rocking back and forth. Peony didn't complain when he caught her up—she appeared stunned and uncaring.

Whereas the behavior of the couple in Ali's had impressed George as being utterly final in its dissolution, the streets were an evolution of that finality, a Babel of dimly perceived sounds and voices, a bedlam of people who clawed and clutched and kicked. At one point somebody knocked him off-balance, sending him to a knee; he put out a hand to prevent a fall and braced against the bruised, misshapen face of a boy who had been trampled beneath the feet of the crowd. He yanked back his hand, repelled, yet this intimate contact with death firmed his resolve and he became single-minded in his pursuit of survival, using his size to full advantage, treating people like impediments, clubbing them with his fist, shoving them down and tossing them aside without a thought for their fate or the state of his soul, stained by one death and now, doubtless, by others. Aghast faces surfaced from the melee and he dispatched them one after the other. Dust and the smell of fear, of fury…all the toxins of dementia poisoned the air. Yet he felt immune to fear, unstoppable, invincible in his lack of emotion. Then, as he reached the outskirts of the city, where the dirt street gave out onto an upward slope, the crowd fanning out across it, a splintering crack ripped across the other noises, seeming to come both from inside him and from without. George looked back and saw that the dragon's leg had buckled, a shockingly white shard of bone protruding from the scales above the knee, blood oozing from the break, and he recognized that Cattanay's prediction had come to pass.[13] Griaule's gargantuan head swiveled to the left, a malefic golden eye canted downward, and though others must have thought the same, George had the idea that the dragon was staring directly at him, a white star shining deep within his throat. The leg buckled further, the dragon listed toward them, and George sprinted up the hill, running even more desperately than before, carrying Peony under an arm like a small rolled-up rug. The crowd's wailing became a shriek as they fled from beneath Griaule's fall.

Perhaps time slowed, subject to a new gravity now that Griaule was truly dying, or perhaps it was simply the chemistry of terror stretching seconds into wider fractions; but George ran for what felt like a long, long time. He heard an eerie hiss and a blast of heat at his back sent him veering out of control; he righted himself and kept going. Time slowed further and he could clearly make out his labored breathing above the ringing in his ears and the shouts of people around him; and then, the last thing he would ever hear: the dragon's final roar, a percussive sound that shot

---

13 Though he did not predict that Griaule would awaken, Cattanay told the city fathers that the poisons in the paint would seep into his system, weakening his internal structure, and, unable to support his weight, the dragon would eventually "cave in like an old barn."

lightning through his ears and resolved into a fizzing that banished every other sound, grew faint and fainter yet, then faded and faded, stranding him in the midst of a pure unmodulated silence. The earth convulsed, twitching like the skin on a cat's back, and he was flung through the air, somehow managing to hang onto Peony and shield her from harm. He did not black out, but lay facedown for ten or fifteen minutes, longer perhaps, moving an arm, a leg, not testing his mobility, just incidental movements, content to rest and be thoughtless. When he sat up he found that Peony was unconscious, but breathing steadily. Only then did he turn and gaze through the pall of dust and smoke toward Teocinte.

The better sections of town, Cerro Bonito, Haver's Roost, and Yulin's Grove, were still afire, releasing black smoke into the sky from half a thousand conflagrations; but the shanties of Morningshade had gone up as if made of paper and all that was left of them were smoldering piles of wreckage; indeed, the blaze had moved through the slum at such a pace that a handful of more substantial buildings in the district, those with their own water supply (Griaule's temple for instance), had survived relatively unscathed, the fire sweeping past them so rapidly that they had not been endangered for long—presumably their staffs and inhabitants had taken steps to protect them. Dwarfing the ruinous landscape, the immensity that was Griaule lay on his side, his back toward the hill where George and Peony were situated, his neck twisted so that his snout angled toward the sky like a scaly tower, a forked tongue lolling between his fangs. His ribcage had shattered and bones poked through the skin in five or six places. It was a sight of such scope and implausibility, George could not frame the whole picture in his mind and for years thereafter, until his actual memories were replaced by a popular rendering of the death of Griaule, he recalled it in fragments. The most memorable element of the scene for him was not Griaule, but the slope that led up from the outskirts of the city. Although the majority of the dead had been incinerated by the dragon's uncanny fire, reduced to piles of unidentifiable ash, his flame must have weakened toward the end, because several thousand carbonized corpses decorated the hill, replicas of their living selves save for the fact they were blackened and so fragile that the pressure of a finger upon them would cause them to collapse and lose their shape. They were dust held together by habit and little else, yet they looked solid, an intricate weaving together of human forms that might have been mistaken for a work accomplished by some apocalyptic artist.

Peony stirred; her fist opened—the scale slipped from her palm. George picked it up and was startled to feel that cold, crawly vitality he had become aware of in the thickets on the day he and Peony met. An image slipped into his mind, that of a gold coin, a Byzantine solidus, very rare, from the reign of the emperor Aleksii. Then an unfamiliar silver coin, yet Egyptian in aspect, came into his mind, and it was followed by another and another yet, and he saw gems of superb luster and clarity, golden cups of great antiquity beset with uncut stones, bejeweled daggers and mirrors with gold frames, a small mountain of such objects, a treasure like no other. He knew he should be about the business of survival (they were not safe yet), but he was tired and the gold was so alluring and that other world of death and smoke and flame seemed far away. And then he was exiting the cavern where the gold was kept, going by torchlight along a meandering tunnel, walking slowly and silently as in a dream, and once out in the light of day he could no longer see the entrance to the tunnel. It had vanished, hidden by ferns and vines and perhaps by some ancient magic, but he didn't concern himself with such trivia—he had the confidence, a serene sense of fate and his relation to it, that he would find his treasure again.

Chapter Eight

Excerpt from The
Last Days of Griaule
by Sylvia Monteverdi

THEY WERE AT HIM THE next day, all the hustlers, the thieves, and the entrepreneurs, inclusive of those who had legal rights to his body and those who did not. Their awe annihilated by greed, a force nearly equal to fear, they swarmed over the corpse, cutting, prying, digging up the hillside where the dragon had rested, searching for his hoard. In light of what had transpired, it was disgusting, but it was fascinating as well. I spent much of the next decade documenting the period in my books and stories about the town's rebirth and its newest industry, the sale and distribution of Griaule's relics, fraudulent and real. During that time I rarely left Teocinte, but almost eight years to the day after I had last seen George and Peony in the amphitheater, I was in Port Chantay on some protracted business with my publisher and, on a whim, I contacted George, inviting him and Peony for a glass of wine. He suggested we meet at Silk, a trendy waterfront café with wide glass windows, dainty tables and chairs, and no silk whatsoever apart from the woman whose name it bore.

I'd heard that they had both been deafened, that Peony suffered from amnesia and now lived with George as his ward, and that George, who had divorced, was quite wealthy—rumor had it that he had been the one to unearth Griaule's hoard. It was also rumored that he had an improper relationship with Peony, though on the face of things they appeared to be a typical father-and-daughter. He slurred his words a bit due to his deafness, but otherwise appeared fit; he sported a mustache and a goatee (his hair had gone gray) that, along with a tailored suit and the fastidiousness that attended his movements, lent him a cultivated air. Yet his physical changes were nothing compared to the mental. Gone was every trace of the city bumpkin I had known, the insecurity, earnestness, the paranoia. He possessed a coolness of manner that was informed, I thought, by an utter absence of emotionality, and this unnerved me. I would not have trusted myself to be able to control him as once I had.

Drastic as these changes were, Peony's were even more extreme. She had developed into a beautiful, poised young woman who was, in every respect, quite charming. George claimed that her amnesia had wiped out all memory of abuse and thus had assisted in her maturation. Her attempts at speech were difficult to understand, for she did not recall the sound of words, and she relied on sign language to communicate, with George serving as her interpreter. After an exchange of pleasantries, she apologized for having forgotten me and went to have coffee with a friend at an outside table, leaving George and me to talk.

"Monteverdi," he said. "I don't suppose that is your real name."

"Of course not! What would I be without an alias?"

I had meant this as a joke, but George did not smile—he nodded as if my statement had revealed some essential truth about me, and this caused me to think that perhaps it had.

"I'm sorry I didn't try to find you," I said. "After the fire and everything."

"It was chaos," said George. "You would have been wasting your time."

"That wasn't why I didn't look for you."

"Oh?"

"I was afraid you were falling in love with me."

He nodded thoughtfully. "I could have fallen in love with almost anyone in those days. You happened to be in the right place at the right time."

"And you were acting crazy. At least you were before Griaule herded us back to Teocinte. I didn't want to be around you."

George let four or five seconds elapse before smiling thinly and saying, "Well, you're safe from me now."

"I don't feel safe." I waited for a response, but none came. "You make me uneasy."

"Peony says I often have that effect on other people. In your case, I imagine it's exacerbated by guilt."

"Guilt? What would I have to be guilty about? I did nothing…"

"It's not important," he said. "Really. It's quite trivial."

"I want to know what you're accusing me of!"

"Not a thing. Forget I mentioned it." He reached a hand into a side pocket of his jacket as if to withdraw something, but let it hang there. "I've read the little book you wrote about us."

I was irritated, yet at the same time curious to know what he thought about my work. "And how did it strike you?"

"Accurate," he said. "As far as it went. I was as you initially described me. Desperate. Desperate to escape my old life. But I would never have admitted it then."

"What do you mean, '…as far as it went?'"

"You missed the best part of the story."

"I saw enough of Griaule's death, if that's what you're talking about. What's more, I've seen the city rebuilt, which you didn't see."

"The city's of no consequence. As for Griaule…" He chuckled. "We've always underestimated him. By hacking him apart and carrying the pieces to the far corners of the earth, we did exactly what he wanted. Now he rules in every quarter of the globe."

"I beg your pardon?"

"You once quoted me a passage from Rossacher. Do you remember? 'His thoughts roam the plenum, his mind is a cloud that encompasses our world.' Something of an overstatement, yet it's true enough. Do you find it so hard to accept now?"

"Are you telling me Griaule is alive? Bodiless…or alive in all his separate parts?"

He inclined his head and made a delicate gesture with his hand, as if to suggest that he had no interest in pursuing the matter.

I drained the dregs of my wine. "Don't you find it strange that we've reversed roles? I was once the believer and you the skeptic."

He took his hand from his pocket and held it out, his palm open to display a glass pendant in which was embedded a chip of lustrous blue-green, darkening to a dull azurine blue at the edges.

"Is that my scale?" I asked.

"Peony and I have no further use for it. I think Griaule intended it to be yours."

The glass enclosing the scale was cold and somewhat tingly to the touch. I remarked on this and George said, "It may be that I am mad, and that Peony is mad, and that we have not been guided in our lives ever since Griaule was disembodied. You can prove this one way or the other by shattering the glass and touching the scale. The sensation will be much stronger that way."

"Will it reveal the location of Griaule's hoard?" I asked half in jest.

"Too late for that," he said. "But he will have something for you, I'm sure. Since we met, everything in our lives has been part of Griaule's design."

I tucked the scale into my purse. "Perhaps you can explain, since you seem so certain in your knowledge, why he deemed it necessary to uproot so many people and drive us onto the plain. Was it simply to witness his death, or was it something more?"

"I have come to understand Griaule to an extent, but I can't know everything he knows. Was it ego, the desire to have at least a few survivors who could bear witness to his death? Yes, I think so. But there is much more to it than that. If he wishes he can control every facet of our lives. And our lives—yours and mine and Peony's, and thousands of others besides—have been thus controlled. We are part of a scheme by means of which he will someday come to dominate the world as Rossacher's book claimed he already had. So far, the instrumentality he's used to implement his scheme has been unwieldy, scattershot. He's made mistakes. Now that he is everywhere in the world, his manipulations will grow more subtle, more precise, and he will make no further mistakes. Eventually, I assume we will be unaware of him...and he will lose interest in us. It may be that this is, by necessity, how the relationships between men and gods develop." George fussed with his napkin and said in a reproachful tone, as if talking to a child, "You knew all this once. Have you truly forgotten?"

"Forgotten? Perhaps I place less value on the specific precepts of my belief than once I did, but no, I haven't forgotten."

George was silent for a while, silent and motionless, and I thought how restrained he had grown in his movements; yet he did not seem constrained or repressed in the least—rather it was as though he had become accustomed to stillness. He cleared his throat, took a sip of wine, and said, "Let us speak no more of it." He nudged the menu with a finger, turning it so he could more read the front page. "Shall I order something? The seaweed cakes are excellent here…and the cherries confit would go well with your port."

WHEN IT CAME time for George to leave, I felt strong emotion— we had been through an ordeal together and our conversation had, despite his coolness, brought back fond memories I did not think I had—I would have liked to acknowledge the experience with an embrace and I expected George to feel the same way, but he performed a slight bow, collected Peony, and left without a backward glance.

I have not yet broken the glass in which the scale is encased, yet I know someday I will, if only to satisfy my curiosity about George. I ran into him and Peony once more before returning to Teocinte. Two days following our meeting at Silk, I took the morning air on the promenade, looking at the boats in the harbor, their exotic keels and bright, strangely shaped sails giving evidence of Port Chantay's international flavor, and caught sight of George and Peony by the railing that fronted the water, engaged in what appeared to be a spirited conversation…at least it was spirited on Peony's part. I ducked behind a small palm tree, one of many potted specimens set along the promenade, not wishing to be seen. We'd said our farewells, as belated and anti-climactic as they were, and I felt rejected—I'd come to the meeting prepared to rebuff George's advances and had not expected to be treated with diffidence. If his cool manner had been studied, I would have chalked all he said and did up to hurt feelings; but his dismissive behavior had seemed wholly unaffected.

His back to the water, George leaned against the railing, his hands braced and his face tipped to the sun like a penitent at prayer, while Peony moved about him with quick steps, almost a dance, pacing to and fro, making graceful turns and exuberant gestures. I imagined her to be describing an event that had thrilled or elated her; but as I watched, though there was no overt change in their physical attitudes, I started to view them differently and perceived sexual elements in the dance—it reminded me of Griaule's temple in Morningshade and how some of my sisters in the brothel would circle the dragon's statue, caressing it from time to time. There is a sexual component in every young girl's connection with her father and I'm sure that was all it was between George and Peony...even if not, she was twenty-one, old enough to do as she pleased. Like most people, I needed to think meanly about something I valued in order to walk away from it, especially something I had neglected for no good reason and such a stretch of years; so I chose to think about George and Peony as having an illicit relationship and told myself it was none of my business what they did or which god they worshiped or how they went through the world, because they were unimportant to me. Perhaps those feelings and memories that surfaced during our meeting were, as are many of our recollections, born of a marriage between false emotion and a lack of clarity concerning the facts. Perhaps our lives are contrivances of lies and illusions. Yet when I think now about George and Peony, none of this seems relevant and scarcely the day passes when I do not call them to mind.

THE SKULL

I

THIS MUCH IS KNOWN:

Following the death of the dragon Griaule, after his scales had been removed, his blood drained and stored in canisters, his flesh and organs variously preserved, his bones pulverized and sold as a remedy for cancer, incontinence, arthritis, indigestion, eczema, and much else…after all of this, Griaule's skull (nearly six hundred feet in length) was maneuvered onto a many-wheeled platform and hauled across eleven hundred miles of jungle to the court of Temalagua. The history of this journey, which lasted two decades and featured dozens of pitched battles, a brief and nearly disastrous passage by sea, and cost many thousands of lives, would require several volumes to recount. Perhaps someday that history will be told, but for the purposes of our story suffice it to say that by the time the skull reached its destination, a tract of land outlying the palace grounds, King Carlos VIII, who had purchased it from the city fathers of Teocinte, was dead and buried, and his son Adilberto the First had ascended to the Onyx Throne.

Adilberto's obsessions were not those of his father. He spent the bulk of his reign pursuing wars of aggression against neighboring states and the skull became a roosting place for birds, home to monkeys, snakes, and palm rats, and was overgrown by vines and fungus. His son, a second and lesser Adilberto, restored the skull to a relatively pristine condition, transformed the land around it into an exotic garden, bronzed the enormous fangs and limned its eye sockets and jaw with brass, jade and copper filigrees that accentuated its sinister aspects and inspired the creation of tin masks that years later came to be sold in the tourist markets. He adorned the interior with teak and ebony furnishings, with gold, silk and precious stones, and therein held bacchanals that established new standards for debauchery (murder, torture, and rape were commonplace at these revels) and contributed greatly toward bankrupting an economy already decimated by the excesses of Adilberto I and Carlos VIII.

Upon his death (under circumstances that even a lenient observer would term suspicious), a third Adilberto known as *El Frio* (the Cold One) seized power following a protracted and bloody struggle with his elder brother Gonsalvo. *El Frio*, a religious zealot and occultist, intended to destroy the skull, but received warnings from his fortunetellers that such an act of desecration would not have a felicitous result. Instead, he devoted his energies to the systematic slaughter of his enemies, whom he apparently saw under every rock, for during his reign he put to death over two hundred thousand of his countrymen. His heir, a fourth Adilberto, was so ashamed of his father's legacy that he changed his name to Juan Miel, a name whose proletarian flavor embodied his proto-Marxist view of the world, and abolished the monarchy, thereby ushering in a period of tumult unparalleled in the tumultuous history of Temalagua. Fortyfour days after initiating this radical reform, he was hacked limb from limb by a crowd of cane workers whom he had been addressing—they were inspired to take action by his chief rival in the nascent presidential campaign, a wealthy plantation owner who had suggested that were they to act otherwise, they might lose their jobs. Thenceforth the country was governed by a succession of generals and politicians who had all they could do to combat innumerable revolutions and the economic incursions of more powerful nations to the north. The palace burned to the ground during the early years of the twentieth century and by the 1940s the gardens built by Adilberto II had merged with the surrounding jungle and the skull was hidden by dense vegetation, though it maintained a significant place in the public consciousness and was considered to have been the root cause of Temalagua's fall from grace…if, indeed, grace had ever prevailed in the region.

Travelers occasionally visited the skull—many would pose for photographs inside the jaws, standing next to one of the brass-covered fangs, sheathed now in verdigris, and then they would hurry away, oppressed by the atmosphere of foreboding generated by the huge bony snout with its barbarous decorations protruding from epiphytes and tree ferns and the shadow of the thick canopy. Those who camped overnight at the site reported disquieting dreams, and several adventurers and scientists who had undertaken longer stays went missing, their number inclusive of a herpetologist who was discovered years later living with coastal Indians and had no memory of his former life. In the 1960s the city (Ciudad Temalagua) mushroomed, growing out and away from the jungle that enclosed the skull in much the same fashion that Teocinte had spread in relation to Griaule, as if obeying some arcane and relativistic regulation. No attempt was made to clear the land or destroy the skull, and the area was accorded the status of an historical site, one deemed essential to an understanding of contemporary Temalagua, yet was neglected by historians who preferred to ignore it rather than to risk their lives by studying its central relic (a tactic frequently employed in places whose history is dominated by villains and villainy). Slums sprang up along the western edge of the jungle, creating a buffer zone between the city and the skull, and producing a steady stream of abandoned and abused children who wandered off in one direction or another, into the urban sprawl or the vegetable, there to meet a fate that, although it could be guessed, was rarely verifiable. Over the next forty years, as the country declined toward the millennium, impoverished by corporate greed and narco-business, the slums became a breeding ground for fierce criminal gangs that contended for control of the streets with death squads composed of extreme right-wing factions within the army; yet even they were reluctant to enter the jungle and confront the strange cult purported to flourish there.

It is at this point that our story becomes the story of the woman who came to be called La Endriaga, and veers away from historical fact, entering the realm of supposition, anecdotal evidence, and the purely fictive, which are, after all, the most reliable forms of human codification. Her birth name was Xiomara Garza (though she was more widely known as Yara) and she was born in Barrio Zanja, a desolation of shacks and streets without names situated on a hillside overlooking the jungle. During the rainy season, mudslides intermittently cut wide swaths through the barrio, killing dozens of people and leaving hundreds more homeless; but since the shacks were flimsily constructed of plywood, cardboard, and so forth, and because moving to another location was not an option for the majority of the survivors, within a week or two a new and equally fragile settlement would be established. By many accounts Yara was a happy child, yet this might be doubted—Barrio Zanja was not an environment conducive to happiness and other accounts testify to her sullen temperament and stoicism. In sum, far more people claim to have been familiar with her as a young girl than lived in the barrio at the time, so it is probably safest to say that her early childhood is cloaked in mystery.

Images of an eleven-year-old Yara were among those discovered in a digital camera belonging to an Austrian pedophile, Anton Scheve, whose body was found lying in a pool of blood on the floor of his hotel room, his chest punctured by multiple stab wounds. In the pictures Yara, a lovely dark-haired girl with a pellucid complexion, can be seen supine on a bed (the same beside which Scheve breathed his last) in various stages of undress, her eyes heavily lidded, this somnolence attributable to the glue-soaked paper sack crumpled on the mattress next to her. As these images were the last recorded by Scheve, the police put forth a sincere effort to locate Yara—sex tourism, while officially discouraged, constituted a sizable portion of Temalagua's tottering economy. Yara, however, was nowhere to be found and so, prevented by her absence from demonstrating their egalitarian approach toward the prosecution of murder, no matter the despicable character of the victim, the government printed Scheve's images (with black bars obscuring her genitalia) in the capital's largest newspaper alongside an article decrying the moral contagion that had been visited upon the country.

The next we hear of Yara comes in the form of a partial memoir published in *An Obscure Literary Journal* (both a description and the actual name of the publication) by George Craig Snow, a strikingly handsome young expatriate with dirty blond hair and weary-looking blue eyes and a wry manner who lived in Ciudad Temalagua between the years 2002 and 2008. As a child he never thought of himself as "George," a name he associated with dweebs, wimps, and insurance adjustors, and so he went by his mother's maiden name, Craig. During the first years of his stay in Temalagua, he worked for a fraudulent charitable interest called Aurora House as a correspondent—his job was to write letters in clumsy English, in a childlike scrawl, that pretended to be the grateful, semi-literate messages of the children supported by Aurora House. These were mailed to gullible contributors in the United States who donated twenty dollars each per month in order to sponsor a Pilar or an Esteban or a Marisol. Included with the letters were pleas for more money and photographs that Snow snapped at random of happy, healthy children in school uniforms, proofs of the good effect that the contributions had on the malnourished children shown in photographs previously sent. To be clear, no child so depicted ever received a dime of charity from Aurora House, nor did any child whatsoever benefit from the enterprise. The majority of the monies collected went into the pocket of Pepe Salido, a lean, gray-haired man who put Snow in mind of a skeletal breed of dog with a narrow skull and prominent snout. The remainder of the funds were doled out in minuscule salaries to the Aurora House staff, among them several gringos like Snow, slackers who were cynical enough to find the swindle bleakly amusing, understanding that even if the money had been donated to the cause, twenty dollars a month paid by however many well-meaning housewives and idealistic students and guilty alcoholics was insufficient to counter the forces arrayed against the children of Temalagua.

Snow lived with a woman of Mayan heritage, a leftist teaching assistant at San Carlos University by the name of Expectación (his memoir was entitled *He Lives With Expectation*), who made her home in Barrio Villareal, a working class neighborhood in process of decaying into a slum. When not on the job, his two preferred activities were having sex with Ex (his lover's nickname) and smoking heroin, the latter serving to cut into the frequency of the former. Evenings he would sit on his stoop, high, shirtless, and shoeless, scuffing up dirt with his toes, studying the stars that emerged from a pall of pollution above the low tile roofs, and taking in the pedestrian parade: shop girls scurrying home with their eyes lowered and bundles clutched to their breasts; short, wiry workmen who carried machetes and nodded politely in passing; dwarfish, raggedy street kids holding paper sacks with soggy bottoms drifting along in small, disheveled packs—on occasion, sensing a kindred spirit, they would hover beside Snow's stoop, gazing up toward the rooftops and tracking things he could not see. One evening as he sat there, joined on his watch by a wizened-looking kid who could have been ten but was likely fifteen and, except for stringy, dark hair, resembled a tiny old man in grungy shorts and a faded Disneyworld T-shirt...one evening, then, he spotted a teenage girl approaching through the purpling air. Slender, leggy, pale. Black curls cascaded down over her shoulders, an opulent architecture of hair at odds with her overall Goth-punk aesthetic: black jeans, black kicks, and a long-sleeved black turtleneck. Black fingernails, too. Heavy make-up. She walked with an unhurried step, yet her movements were crisp and purposeful, and she had about her such an aura of energy, it seemed to Snow that he was watching the approach of a small storm. He pictured a funnel cloud of dirt and masonry chunks flying up in her wake, an image that prompted him to grin goofily at her as she came alongside them. She did not seek to avoid his scrutiny, but stopped in front of the stoop and gave an upward jerk of her head that spoke to him, saying, You got something on your mind? Spit it out.

"*Buenas noches*," said Snow.

The kid stuck his face into his paper sack and huffed furiously, and the girl asked him in Spanish, "Who is this asshole?"

"He lives here," said the kid groggily.

"I speak Spanish," Snow said. "You can talk to me."

The girl ignored him and asked the kid why he hung out with this *pichicatero*. The kid shrugged.

"*Pichicatero*? What's that?" Snow asked the kid.

"A fucking drug addict," said the girl in lightly accented English.

"He's the addict." Snow gestured at the kid. "For me it's just a hobby."

With its mask of mascara and bloody lip gloss, her face was trashy, beautified not beautiful, yet once he had wiped away the make-up with a mental cloth, he realized the basic materials were quality. A casual observer would perhaps have judged the face too bland, too standard in its perfection, like a schoolboy's rendering of his favorite teenage angel vampire slut, but to Snow, a connoisseur, it was exuberantly and idiosyncratically feminine, a raptor's purity of purpose implied by the way her lips curved above a slight overbite, the delicate molding of the tiny, tapered chin, and beside the nose flare of a nostril, the necessary flaw, a pink irregularity, a scar that, had it been treated properly, would have required but a stitch or two to close. Her skin seemed to carry a faint luminosity. Her irises and eyebrows were such a negative color they might have been cutaways in her flesh that permitted a lightless background to show through. She was, Snow decided, scary beautiful.

"Dirty feet," she said to him. "Dirty fingernails. Dirty hair." She gave him a quick once-over. "Dirty heart."

Though too stoned to be offended, Snow felt that he should offer an objection and said mildly, "Hey. Watch your mouth."

She switched to Spanish and addressed the kid. "Be careful! You don't want to wind up a shriveled soul like him."

"Bet you used to be an emo girl," said Snow. "Then you hooked up with some Goth guy and crossed over to the dark side."

"That's right," she said. "Come see me and I'll introduce you to him. He loves to meet new people."

"Sure thing. Give me your address"

Her face emptied and her eyes lost focus, as if she were hearkening to an inner voice. She was silent for so long, Snow waggled a hand in her face and said, "Hello!"

She turned abruptly and strode off without another word—a man passing in the street gave her a wide berth.

"That was weird," Snow said.

"Yara." The kid fingered a tube of glue out of his pocket and began squeezing it into the paper sack.

Snow said, "What?"

"Her name is Yara. She's crazy."

"How's that make her different from anyone else?"

Snow thought he would have to explain his view that human beings were no more than a collection of random impulses bound up in a net of societal constraints, but the kid may have had an innate awareness of this, because he asked for no clarification and said, "Yara's not monkey-crazy. She's snake-crazy." He started to bury his face in the fume-filled sack, but then offered it to Snow, and Snow, moved by this unexpected display of etiquette, accepted.

II

Excerpted from *He Lives With Expectation*
By Craig Snow

...EX KICKED ME OUT OF the house again. It was for the usual reason, an inability to balance her radical politics with having a boyfriend who espoused no political view more complex than "Yeah, America sucks, but so does everywhere else." As usual I checked into the Spring Hotel, so Ex would know where to find me once she had time to rethink her position, and spent the next few evenings playing video games in an arcade off Avenida Seis and drinking at the Club Sexy, a gay bar frequented by the wives and girlfriends of right-wing military types, women notable for their hotness and the monumental triviality of their conversation. You could hang out there all night and not hear a serious concern mentioned, though now and then things would get heated when the talk turned to hairstyles.

The club was a great place to go should you want to commit suicide-by-babe—a big room with frigid air conditioning and subdued lighting, round tables of bamboo and glass, and a childlike mural of a tropical beach with a starry indigo sky and coco palms painted on the walls. Most afternoons this old daisy in a tux would totter onto the bandstand and play Latinized arrangements of Beatles tunes and similar shit on a Casio, his silver-gray head nodding to the whispery samba beats. If you qualified as a cute guy, the women would have sex with you, no problem, but then you risked winding up in a basement with a Col. Noriega look-alike clamping electrodes to your dick. To be on the safe side I would sit at the bar, blending in with guys who were fans of the owner of the club, Guillermo, a pale youth of approximately my age with exciting hair and the look of a male ingénue.

LUCIUS SHEPARD

About four PM each weekday, "*La Hora Feliz*," the ladies would come breezing in, all bouncy in their low-cut frocks, sunglasses by Gucci and make-up by Sherwin-Williams. If you stared at them through slit eyes, it looked as though a couple of dozen spectacularly vivid butterflies had perched beside the little round tables. They were two-fisted drinkers, mainly tequila shots washed down with orange juice, and before long they'd be gabbing away happily, their chatter drowning out the Casio. I had an on-again, off-again relationship with one—Viviana, a perky blond with fake tits—and on the Thursday after Ex kicked me out I met her in the rear stall of the men's room for a quickie. It wasn't that I was eager to die. We'd begun our relationship before I fully understood the situation and after I became aware of what was going on...well, I had a self-destructive streak and a corresponding nonchalant attitude toward personal safety, and these qualities, allied with my American sense of entitlement, were sufficient to make me lower my guard. The thought of all that available pussy was too tempting to resist. Early on during the affair Viviana and I were caught exiting the women's john by her boyfriend, a typical death-squad-loving psycho army captain. She leaped to my defense, screeching at the bewildered young sociopath, demanding that he stop beating me, claiming that I had been helping with her hair and saying, "Can't you tell he's a faggot?" Thereafter I felt relatively secure in bending her over the toilet, though afterward I would have to re-establish my gay bona fides by acting femme and flirting with Guillermo.

That Thursday, once we had finished our business in the ladies' room, she joined me for a drink at the bar. I told her about Ex giving me the boot—she offered sympathy, stroking my hair and murmuring encouragement, though she did so without much sincerity. Her gaze drifted about the room and locked onto a table close to the stage.

"That filthy cunt!" she said venomously.

The Goth girl who had insulted me on my stoop the week before, Yara, was talking to a woman named Dolores for whom Viviana had a thing (her infidelity was by no means gender specific—she had explained that many of the women, like her, felt imprisoned by their relationships and would fuck anything that moved so as to express their frustration and cause psychic damage to their significant others—Club Sexy provided them with

THE SKULL

a perfect cover). She started up from her barstool. I caught her arm and asked what was wrong, but she shook me off, bee-lined for the table and proceeded to chew out Yara, who regarded her with an impassive expression. When Viviana paused for breath, Yara spoke briefly. Whatever she said must have been potent, for without further ado Viviana went off to sulk at a corner table. I watched the girl for a while. Her gestures were slow, calm, languid, as if she were explaining a serious matter, taking her time, being patient. Several women at other tables watched her as well—dotingly, I thought. Intently. The way you'd stare at a movie star. This girl had a definite presence. In a room full of beautiful women, she was the one who stood out, who drew your eye.

"Oh, Guillermo!" I beckoned him over. "Could you make one of your elegant mango mojitos for Viviana?"

"Of course."

I put my elbows on the bar and interlaced my fingers, using them as a chin-rest, watching him prepare the drink.

"I believe I'll have one, too," I said. "Extra sweet." Then, leaning close, I added in a whisper, "Why's Viv so upset?"

"She thinks La Endriaga is hitting on Dolores."

"You mean the girl in black? She's La...what was it? La Endriaga?"

He poured lime juice. "Aren't you familiar with the story? La Endriaga's supposed to be a creature part snake, part dragon, part female. The girl's real name is Lara...or Mara. Or something. You know how I am with names. But people call her La Endriaga because she lives in the jungle, near the skull."

"I thought that was just a story...the skull."

"I've never seen it myself." Guillermo gave his hair a toss. "But Jaime Solis...you know, the boy who dyes his soul patch all different colors? He told me it's real. He offered to take me to see it, but I said, 'Why would I want to look at some nasty old bones? There are better ways to impress me.'"

I had drained the larger part of my mojito when Dolores passed Yara a fat envelope, the kind that in the movies often contains a payoff. Yara stuffed it into a straw market bag, presented her cheek to be kissed, and headed for the exit. Curious, I followed her outside. It was almost eight o'clock and the sidewalks were crowded, the street dressed

— 317 —

in neon, choked with clamorous traffic, the night air steamy and reeking of exhaust. Music from radios and storefronts contended with the crowd noise and the squeal of arcade games. Grimy children, mainly pre-teen girls of the sort Aurora House was purported to help, plucked at my sleeve, held out their hands and made pleading faces. I surrendered my pocket change and shooed them away. Yara had been swallowed up by the crowd, but I spotted the psycho army captain's Hummer, its hood decorated by red and purple smears of reflected light. He was hunting for a parking place, leaning on his horn—instead of a honk it produced a grandiose digital fanfare. We had long since made our peace, but I thought it best to move on. I went west along Avenida Seis, uncertain of my destination, pausing to look in shop windows, and caught sight of Yara in an otherwise empty electronics store, talking to a clerk, her black figure as slim and sharply defined as an exclamation point under the bright fluorescents. The clerk—a tall, stringy guy with a shock of white in his forelock—appeared upset with her, making florid gestures, but he cooled off when she passed him the envelope Dolores had given her. He inspected the contents, glanced about as if to ascertain whether anyone was watching, then removed a few bills from the envelope and handed them to her. She stuffed them into the hip pocket of her jeans and headed for the entrance. I turned my back and pretended to be studying a window display of cell phones, but she walked up to me and said cheerfully, "I wondered when we'd meet again."

Put off by the dissonance between her tone now and that she had employed during our first encounter, I said, "You wondered that, did you?"

"Don't you want to know how I knew we'd meet again?"

"Sure. Whatever."

"I always know that sort of thing."

I waited for a deeper analysis and when none was forthcoming I said, "Well, this is nice, but I've got to be stepping."

"Don't go." She linked arms with me and did this little snuggle-bunny move against my shoulder. "There's something I want you to see."

"Whoa!" I disengaged from her. "Last week you treated me like I was a fucking STD and now…"

"I'm sorry! I was in a terrible mood."

"And now you're coming on to me in this retarded way. What's that all about?"

She took a backward step and said soberly, "I'm not sure we're going to have a relationship. You're an attractive man, but I think it'll just be sex with us."

"Okay," I said. "Enough crazy talk. I'll catch you later."

She gave me a pouty look. "Don't you want to see where I live?"

"Why should I? What do you have in mind?"

"Americans are so paranoid," she said. "I guess you've a right to be. There's a lot of anti-American feeling down here. A girl might invite you to dinner just so she can chop off your head."

"Damn straight."

"You could take preventive measures," she said. "Notify a policeman. Give him your name and destination. That way if you go missing they'd come after me. I'd be forced to control my murderous impulses."

"Now I really want to go with you," I said. "Because you saying that, wow, it makes clear what a paranoid asshole I am for thinking your invitation is suspicious."

Four boys wearing designer jeans and polo shirts, expensive watches on their wrists, rich kids just into their teens, came pounding into the entrance-way of the electronics store from the street, laughing and breathless, as if they had just played a prank on someone and made a narrow escape. One of them noticed Yara and said something about whores. For some reason, this infuriated me. I told him to fuck off. The boys' faces grew stony, all the same face, the same soulless, zombie stare, and I had a shocking sense of the seven-billion-headed monster of which they constituted a four-headed expression. I spat on the sidewalk at their feet and took a step toward then. They cursed us and scooted off into the crowd, re-absorbed into the body of the beast.

Amused, Yara said, "You were really angry with those kids. You hated them."

I became aware of the street sounds once more—radio music, car horns, the gabble of shouts and laughter—as if the curtain had been raised on a noisier production.

"What's not to hate?" I said. "They'll grow up to be fascist dicks just like their daddies."

She seemed to be measuring me. "I think you're a nihilist."

I laughed. "That's way too formal a term for what I am."

She didn't reply and I said, "You have a thing for nihilists, do you?"

"You should come with me. Seriously."

"Give me a reason."

"You'll like what I've got to show you. If that's not enough of a reason…"
She shrugged. "You'll miss out on the fun."

"What kind of fun are we talking about?"

"The usual. Maybe more."

Yara leaned against me, her breast nudging my elbow, and, though I
remained paranoid, my resistance weakened.

"Come with me, man," she said. "If you die, I promise you'll die happy."

WE TOOK A taxi to the rain forest. If we walked, Yara explained, if
we went down through Barrio Zanja, we would have to traverse almost
two miles of jungle terrain—this way we would only have to walk for fifteen or twenty minutes. The taxi whipped us around Plaza Obelisco, past
the unsightly concrete monument to Temalaguan independence, some
despot's idea of a joke, and past the Flame of Liberty, which had been
installed to memorialize the overthrow of the very same despot, and before
long we were bouncing along over a dirt road that grew ever more narrow
and dead-ended in the isolated village of Chajul on the verge of the jungle,
set beneath towering aguacate trees. Yara gave the driver the bills she'd
received from the electronics store clerk. I asked if the money had been a
pay-off and she said, "They're contributions. Funding."

"Funding for what?"

"I'm not certain," she said.

Away from the city I could see the stars and the glow of a moon on the
rise behind hills to the east, but once we entered the jungle it was pitch-
dark. Yara shined a flashlight ahead and held my hand, warning me against
obstructions. Insects chirred; frogs bleeped and tweedled. Rustlings issued
from every quarter. Smells of sweet rot and rank decay. Mosquitoes whined
in my hair. It felt hotter than it had in the city and I broke a sweat. Shuffling

along in the dark, passing among unseen things, twigs and leaves poking, brushing my skin—I imagined vines forming into nooses over my head, spiders scurrying up my trouser legs, vipers uncoiling from branches above, pointing their shovel-shaped heads and darting their tongues. Yara may have sensed my apprehension because she told me we'd be there soon, but I didn't buy it, I knew she was leading me into a trap. I gave thought to taking her hostage in order to forestall an attack by whoever was lying in wait, but I glimpsed a ruddy glow through the leaves and caught a strong fecal odor and shortly thereafter we emerged into a clearing the approximate length of a soccer pitch, though narrower, overspread by a dense canopy and bounded by walls of vegetation—you could have fit the upside-down hull of a mighty ark into the space described by those walls and that canopy. Among tree stumps and patchy underbrush lay a jungle squat that spread out across the clearing, a settlement combining the harsh realities of Stone Age life with those of brutal urban poverty. Lean-tos, tents, thatched huts, and a handful of shacks with rusting tin roofs. Campfires generated a smoky haze and as we passed through the settlement I saw shadowy people stirring, all moving about with what struck me as an excess of caution. Some acknowledged Yara with a wave, but no one called out her name. I estimated that several hundred souls lived in the squat and would have expected to hear a conversational murmur, the odd laugh or shout, music and such, yet the place was as hushed as a church and there was a corresponding air of pious oppression, one comprehensible when you considered the enormous reptilian skull, yellowed with age, illuminated by torches, that occupied the entire far end of the clearing, looming high into the canopy.

I had left the States five years previously, discouraged by the quality of my life, bored by the drabness of the American tragedy, with the consumerist mentality and the market forces that bred it, with celebrity scandals orchestrated to distract from more significant trouble, with every element of that carnival of lies—I had hoped a more vivid landscape would serve to pare away the rind that had accumulated over my brain, yet everywhere I went it seemed I brought drabness and boredom with me, and my life remained tedious and uninvolved. The skull was the first thing I had seen to put a crack in my worldview. Its size and uncanny

LUCIUS SHEPARD

aspect, the barbarous embellishments added by man and nature over the centuries, scribblings of moss and fungus, inlays of milky jade and black onyx, the fangs coated in verdigris, the snout covered by painted designs, much faded, that had been applied by some long-vanished tribe, all of it visible in the erratic light...at one second it seemed a clownish, grotesque fake, a gigantic papier mâché Mardi Gras mask, and the next I grew terrified that it would return to life and roar. Vegetation hid the greater part of the sloping brow and a thick matte of vines obscured one of its eye sockets, but apart from a few clusters of epiphytes the snout was unencumbered, reaching a height of forty feet above the jungle floor. Propped against the side of the jaw, its topmost section resting against a portion of bone adjacent to a fang, was a telescoping aluminum ladder. When I realized we were heading toward the ladder my anxiety peaked—I was insecure with the idea of climbing into the mouth, but Yara displayed no sign of trepidation and I kept my worries to myself. A disquieting atmosphere of the sort that gathers about ancient ruins enveloped the skull, an absence of vibration that causes you to listen closely, to attune yourself to the possibility of vibration, so that you may feel something where, perhaps, there is nothing to feel...except this particular vacancy had an inimical quality, as if it retained a residue of its former contents, like a glass that once held poison.

Yara scurried up the ladder with the quickness and confidence of someone accustomed to the ascent, whereas I, less certain of my footing, lagged behind, pausing to steady myself and to rethink the wisdom of this excursion. But on reaching the top, standing beside the wicked bronze-green curve of the fang and gazing down at the squat, I had an unwarranted sense of power. It was as though I'd scaled some hithertofore unscalable peak and was for that moment master of all I surveyed. Yara took my hand and her touch boosted the sensation. I felt heroin high, the way it is after your rush has dissipated and you seem in complete harmony with every part of your body, the slightest movement (the twitch of a finger, the curling of a toe) signaling a joyful competence. She led me deep into the skull, past volutes and voluptuous turns of bone, then upward along a narrow channel into the cavity that once had housed the monster's brain, the far end of which was brightly lit by groups of candles and furnished with

— 322 —

a much-patched waterbed, a desk, a table and three wooden chairs, and an antique steamer trunk that served as both filing cabinet and chest of drawers—the rest was empty, pale curves of bone lost in dimness. Seeing this collection of thrift shop artifacts crammed into a corner of a cavernous skull sponsored the thought that I had stumbled into a child's bedtime story about a lost girl who dwelled in an abandoned palace of bone. I noticed that the candles had not burned down very far and asked who had lit them.

"The adherents." She opened the bottom drawer of the trunk and removed a couple of towels. "They always seem to know when I'm going to return."

"You mean the people down below?"

"Yes. They take care of me."

"Why would they do that?"

"They're extremely nurturing."

"Yeah? You must do something for them."

"I perform an equivalent service." She tossed me a towel. "They'll be bringing food soon. We'd better hurry if we want to wash up before dinner."

BEHIND THE SKULL, at the entrance to the gateway of splintered bone that had once sheathed part of the spinal chord, with thick tree trunks, leaf clusters, and ferns crowding near, stood a wooden tub, large enough in which to host a modest pool party and filled with water. A dripping pipe depended from the darkness overhead and, since there were no leaves adrift on the surface, I assumed the adherents had drawn Yara's bath a short time before. She lit torches mounted beside the tub, igniting reflections in the water, and proceeded to strip off her clothes. Her body was perfectly proportioned, her pubic hair trimmed into a neat landing strip. I had presumed her to be heavily tattooed, but she sported only two: a tiny soaring bird of blurry blue ink above her right breast, not the work of a professional, and a diamond-shaped pattern of dark green scales positioned like a tramp stamp on the small of her back. These were of recent vintage and marvelously detailed. I joined her in the tub and watched her scrub away make-up (she had previously removed some of it with tissues) and city grime, revealing prominent cheekbones that added exotic planes to her face. After she finished scrubbing she sank down so that only her eyes and nose were visible. Serpentine tendrils of hair floating on the water were lent the impression of undulant movement by the flickering reflections with which they merged, making it appear that fiery snakes were swimming toward her, joining their substance with hers.

The jungle pressed close around and the chorusing of frogs was loud, which might have explained the absence of insect—yet I could recall no insects inside the skull. I mentioned the fact and she made a so-what face, watching me with eyes aglint with torchlight.

"Do you want insects?" she asked.

"Can you arrange for some?"

"I can try."

I moved my hands in semicircles, sending ripples toward her. "Did you bring me out here just to take a bath?"

"I'm a creature of impulse."

"Why won't you tell me what's going on?"

She rested her arms on the edge of the tub, facing me, and let her feet float up. "I'd prefer you reach your own conclusions. That way you won't be able to accuse me of manipulating you."

"Is my opinion that important?"

"It's difficult to say."

"This woman-of-mystery shit," I said. "It's not working for me."

"You're not giving it a chance."

Torchlight lapped at the trees, quick tides of orange radiance illuminating leaf sprays and sections of trunks, and flared along bone interiors. From above came the long, stuttering trill of a bird chortling over its live supper. *National Geographic* Primitive, I told myself, trying to blunt my reaction to the place. But the presence of the skull overwhelmed me once again and I had an apprehension of danger.

"Know what I think?" I said. "I think you must be running some sort of game on those people back there. The adherents."

"You're not the first to say that."

"Well, are you?"

"Sometimes I wonder."

"This kind of answer, it's all you're going to give me?"

"For now."

The tops of her breasts showing above the surface distracted me—whenever she stirred her nipples bobbled up into view, pastel pink, an after-dinner mint color, centering perfect circles of slightly paler, delicately pebbled skin. I speculated on how it would be, screwing in her bone bedchamber, and compared her physicality to Ex's heavy-breasted, thick-waisted body, her areolae large and oblate to the point of appearing misshapen. Though Ex had thrown me out, though we both slept with other people, I trusted that we would get back together. The relationship was too comfortable for either of us to discard. I had a trickle of guilt because Yara was prettier than she, yet guilt was not strong enough to prevent me from swimming over and putting an arm beneath her thighs to support her legs. Heat streamed off her. With my free hand I cleared strands of damp hair away from her face and started to move in for a kiss, but she held me off and leaned back further, as if hoping for a better perspective.

"I want to be lucky for you," she said.

I mustered a glib response, something about getting lucky, but kept it to myself—there was nothing playful in her face, no indication of banter in her delivery and, with desire thickening my voice, I told her I could use a little luck.

WHILE OUR SUPPER (chicken and saffron rice) grew cold, we went at it hard on the waterbed. Yara was energetic and inventive, alternately demanding and giving, but the sex was merely good, merely proficient, and not great. As sometimes happens there was an element of performance art to our little exercise that diminished its other qualities and hampered emotional involvement. Her moans and cries were sweet to hear, but I recognized that she was in part emoting. Not faking it, exactly. Just throwing in a few extras to make sure I knew that she was having a grand time, and my execution was the masculine equivalent of hers. What surprised me was that instead of the usual pillow talk we discussed this afterward, analyzing our lovemaking in terms of its authenticity.

"When attractive people hook up," Yara said, "narcissism sometimes gets in the way of things."

"I don't consider myself a narcissist," I said.

"Be honest!"

"Actually I'm more of a self-hater."

She blew air through her lips, a disparaging puff. "You don't think it's possible to be a self-hating narcissist?"

"I guess you could say self-hatred is an extreme form of narcissism."

"It's the soul of narcissism. Self-love and self-hatred aren't mutually exclusive. In fact, one's a precursor to the other."

I clasped my hands behind my head—the play of light across the ceiling gave the bone a creamy, cheese-like appearance.

"How old are you?" I asked.

"Seventeen. Did you think I was older?"

"I didn't think much about it, but yeah, maybe a couple of years."

"And now you think I'm too young for you? Is that it? I should hope not, because I've been with guys older than you. A lot older!"

It was a peculiar conversation and her part in it seemed sophisticated for someone so young, but this digression made me aware that her personality was mostly posture and an occasional blurt of teenage defensiveness. I told her age didn't matter to me and that mollified her.

"It's strange," she said, returning to the topic at hand. "I think self-love is decaying into self-hate in your case. Usually it's the other way around."

"I don't know if that's true. I've been afflicted with a mixture of the two ever since I was fifteen."

"Since the girls got interested, eh?"

"Nah, it was when I began using them to get at their mommies...that's when the self-hate kicked in."

"I don't understand."

"The girls I knew had some hot moms."

"You had sex with them?"

"A few. Rene...my first mom. She came on to me while her daughter was out running errands. It made me a big deal in high school."

"You told your friends about it? What an asshole!"

"I was fifteen, an idiot. And Rene told *her* friends. She even set me up with one of them. No one got hurt and I learned a few things."

"About sex?"

"Sex…and women."

Yara sighed—a sigh of forbearance, I figured. "The moms must have been bored with their husbands."

"I didn't think about them. They were targets to me. I suppose they were bored. With their husbands, and themselves. But I don't believe that's what motivated them. It was the idea they were corrupting me that got them off. They needed that kind of excess in their lives. So I played the innocent and let myself be corrupted. It got to be a thing with me, bagging mothers and their daughters. When the moms found out their little Madisons and Brooks were fucking me, too, they were deeply pissed. But after they cooled down, a couple of them suggested threesomes."

"You must have thought you were a wicked boy."

"I was wicked."

"In an innocent way, maybe."

Channeled through some complexity of bone, a warm breeze penetrated the chamber, producing a mournful whistle.

Yara turned onto her side, facing me. "I wasn't interested in sex until last year."

"You got a late start, huh?"

"Oh, I've had my share of experiences, but they were unpleasant. Most of them, anyway. I quit having sex when I moved out here. Then about a year ago I took a lover, but we didn't communicate well in bed. We had chemistry, but it never came to much." She did a finger-walk across my stomach, coming to rest on my hip. "But you and I communicated very well. We understood each other's signals."

"Yeah?"

"Your time with the mommies must have taught you to be aware of a woman's desires, because you knew what I wanted and when I wanted it. And I'm certain I knew what you wanted…which is unusual. I've never been adept at reading men."

"Give me an example."

"You remember what happened."

"Refresh my memory."

"You just want to hear me talk dirty."

I smiled. "If you don't mind."

"All right. At the end, when you were battering away at me, I knew you were close and I wanted you to finish in my mouth. And you did, without my having to tell you."

"It seemed like the thing to do."

She peered at me. "Am I embarrassing you?"

"No."

"I am, aren't I? You're embarrassed!"

"No, really. I'm not. I just think it's weird, talking like this."

"Why is it weird?"

"People tend to be gentle with each other after they hook up. They whisper sweet nothings. They say stuff like, 'When did you know?' and 'The first time I saw you I was rocked.' Or they tease one another, they're playful. They don't start breaking shit down."

"That kind of talk is generally insincere on some level."

"Not always."

"No, not always."

The wind had grown stronger. Wheezy flutings came with increasing frequency over the bone channels of the skull, like an old calliope giving up the ghost.

"It's good to get all this out in the open," Yara said. "It'll rid us of unnecessary baggage."

"You think? It's making me more self-conscious."

"Probably that's how it'll be at first, it'll help in the long run."

The notion that we might have a long run started me thinking about Ex. I saw her in the entryway of our house, taking off the old army coat she wore in winter, smiling at me over her shoulder, her glossy hair braided into a thick rope.

"You know, until recently I've been living with someone," I said.

"What of it?"

"We've been together on and off for almost four years. I'm not sure it's over."

THE SKULL

"She won't have anything to do with how things work out for us."

"That's an arrogant thing to say."

"It's not arrogance if you're certain about something, and I'm certain about this."

Yara dozed awhile, lying on her stomach, but I lay awake, highlights from the previous hour or so flaring up in my head. Bored, I propped myself on an elbow and kissed her shoulder, ran a hand along the slope of her back, and studied her tattoo. She stirred and made a pleased noise. I touched the middle scale of the diamond pattern and was astonished to find that it was hard and had a distinct convexity. Before I could examine it further, she swatted my hand away and sat up.

"Don't!" she said angrily.

"What is that? Some kind of implant?"

"Yes, an implant. Leave it alone."

"How did they do it? I didn't think it was possible to do something like this."

I stretched out a hand and again she knocked it away from the tattoo, saying, "I don't want you to touch me there!"

I laughed.

"It's not funny!" She swung her legs off the bed, as if preparing to bolt. "I mean it!"

"I've heard women say that before, but they were referring to another part of their bodies."

She picked up a flimsy robe from the floor and put it on. I asked what she was doing and she said she was going to eat.

"It'll be cold," I said.

"It's good cold."

She sat at the table and dug in, forking up a bite, chewing, swallowing, forking up another bite, making of the meal an act of mechanical ferocity.

After a minute I stood and stepped into my boxers. Yara continued chowing down, not sparing me a glance. Despite the breeze I felt hot, my thoughts stale and repetitious. The unbroken eggshell-smooth surfaces of the chamber oppressed me.

"This place could stand a window or two," I said.

I SLEEP TOO deeply and wake too abruptly to remember my dreams, but during the week that followed, though I retained nothing of their substance, I woke with a sense that my dreams had been disturbing, and not in the customary sense, not due to anxiety or stress. I had the feeling that something had been picking at the shell of my consciousness, trying to insinuate itself into a crack, to find a way in. When this feeling persisted I mentioned it to Yara. She said it was a common reaction.

"Reaction to what?" I asked.

"To being here," she said, and headed off to the tiny chamber set forward of the brain box, where she commonly passed an hour or two each morning.

I spent a portion of the following day exploring the skull, negotiating channels that often led to other channels, but occasionally to small chambers, all so scrupulously clean that I suspected someone must have snuck in and done the sweeping. Nothing was out of the ordinary about the majority of the chambers (aside from the extraordinary fact of their existence), but the chamber to which Yara went each morning had a soporific effect on me, making me drowsy whenever I entered it. I would have asked Yara about this had she given me reason to anticipate a straight answer—as things stood, after determining that the drowsiness was not the product of my imagination, I marked it down as an anomaly, a minor mystery in the midst of a greater one.

My initial impression of the adherents had been that they were timid, sullen, and ignorant, dimwitted in some instances, and that they represented the disenfranchised, their lives ruled by poverty and informed by delusion. Yet though they lived rough, and though I continued to believe that the foundations of their community were based upon a significant delusion, I came to acknowledge that I had mistaken distraction for temerity, self-absorption for sullenness, and that a majority of the approximately five hundred people dwelling beneath the canopy were upper middle class: educators, doctors, artists, researchers, and professionals of various types. Of course there were also a good many laborers and shop clerks, and a number of ex-derelicts, reformed drunks and addicts, but these were counterbalanced somewhat by the presence of people like Major General Amadis de Lugo, who inhabited a shack close by the skull. A smallish man in his seventies, with a time-ravaged yet still handsome face, ragged white hair, and an untrimmed beard, customarily dressed in fatigue pants and a white T-shirt, he was nonetheless an imposing figure, at least to me. When I first arrived in Temalagua he had been the titular head of Department 46, the country's notorious internal security unit, and thus had been responsible for the deaths of several of Ex's colleagues at the university, not to mention thousands more deemed politically untrustworthy by the government. I was shocked to see him (I recognized him from newspaper photos), astonished that he could survive in the community. Someone in the camp must have lost a friend or relative to de Lugo's death squads—I presumed that they would seek to exact vengeance, but the cult made a point of ignoring all sins committed before joining, even those of a villain like de Lugo, and the policy had not thus far been contravened.

Four days after I moved in with Yara, she spent the morning sequestered in her little bone chamber and in mid-afternoon she went about the encampment, conversing with the adherents. They were less conversations than counseling sessions—she did the lion's share of the talking and the adherents were limited to nods and affirmations. I tagged along behind her and from what I could hear she appeared to be offering advice designed to shore up their commitment to some nebulous goal, generic hogwash of the kind that enraptures the fans of asswipes like Tony Robbins and Dr. Phil. She had a ways to go before she perfected her spiel, but she had Tony and Phil beat all to hell in the looks department and I thought with proper management and a team of make-up people and hair stylists, she could be coached up into a serious money maker. She had a terrific back story: the abused street urchin who had learned life's secrets from the rain forest swamis and was engaged in hauling herself up from society's rat-infested basement to become every loser's dream of success, a Rolex-wearing, couturier-clad, self-help diva striving to reach a platform that would enable her to sell the world some perfumed brand of bullshit. I imagined myself her advisor and complicitor. I'd warm up the audiences, an Armani-wearing stooge delivering a well-rehearsed message of non-denominational love, toothless liberalism, and capitalist greed, yielding the stage to Yara in order to seal the deal with a double shot of the same rendered in her charmingly accented English, all the more charming for having been polished so as to achieve a desired effect.

It was a humid day, the air heavy with the smell of rain. Smoke from the campfires lay close to the ground, thickening the usual haze to a roiling smog, so that people who were not close at hand acquired a ghostly aspect, their indefinite figures fading in from the murk and then dematerializing. Tired of listening to Yara mold her constituency, I staked myself out on a makeshift bench near the ashes of a fire and began sketching in my notebook, adding brief written descriptions of each subject. I'd been at it for perhaps twenty minutes when someone cleared his throat in an attention-getting way and I glanced up to find General de Lugo standing beside me, leaning on a cane, partially blocking my view of the skull. Seeing this emblem of death's human expression superimposed against that vast iconic figure unsettled me, but de Lugo smiled—not the most assuring of sights—and indicated that he wished to sit down. I made room and he lowered himself onto the bench, groaning as he completed this arduous process.

I looked at him expectantly, waiting for him to speak. His hair was exceptionally silky and his clothes reeked of mildew. The flesh beneath his eyes looked bruised—from lack of sleep, I assumed. "Go on," he said, pointing at the notebook. "I will watch."

He beamed at me again, a beacon of his approval, but when I continued to sketch he tsk-tsked and grunted as in apparent pain, as if displeased by my work. I sketched a pink umbrella tree at the edge of the clearing, a shriek of color like an exposed vein, a more vital territory laid bare behind the smoky green vegetation, and he snorted impatiently. I asked if I was doing something wrong.

"You draw trees, shadows, people." De Lugo gestured at the skull—it towered above us some sixty or seventy feet away. "But not the dragon. Why? It is the only thing worth drawing."

"You want me to draw the skull? You got it."

After a couple of false starts, using a pen with a fine point, I managed to get going on a miniature of the skull protruding from its cover, focusing to such a degree that once I finished I was startled to discover that three other people had joined us and were sitting on the ground about the dead fire. A young couple, student types, the guy's hair longer than his girlfriend's, and a middle-aged man with a salt-and-pepper beard, wearing shorts and a worn, dirty dress shirt with rolled-up sleeves. De Lugo took the notebook from me, studied it a moment before passing it to the girl. She shared it with the two men and they murmured their appreciation.

"Very good." De Lugo patted my arm—I could not help but flinch. "Perfect! You have captured him."

Ignoring his personification of the skull, I asked him and his friends what had drawn them to the camp.

The girl—rather plain, with a complexion the color of adobe brick, she appeared to have lost a great deal of weight recently—introduced herself as Adalia and asked in a dusty contralto if I knew why I was there.

"I'm with Yara," I said.

"I am with Timo." She leaned into her boyfriend's shoulder. "But that's not why I am here."

"You tell me, then. Why are you here?"

The middle-aged man, a lawyer, Gonsalvo by name, said, "We are the ingredients."

"The ingredients for what?" I asked.

"A miracle," said Adalia.

I repeated her words quizzically and she added, "A miracle that will change the world."

The others nodded and Timo, putting an arm around Adalia's shoulders, said, "He will perfect us."

They had bought into Yara's craziness, perceiving her to be the key to a numinous mystery, and I doubted they knew any more than I.

"You expect him to do all this?" I asked, waving a hand at the skull.

"With Yara's help," Timo said. "Yes."

"Are you familiar with his history?" Adalia asked.

"All that crap about being paralyzed in a mystical battle, his mental powers becoming godlike? Sure, everybody's heard that fairy tale."

"You do not give him his due," Gonsalvo said solemnly. "For thousands of years he lay on the plain at Teocinte. His mind grew to be a cloud that enveloped the planet, controlling every facet of our lives."

"Well, he's dead meat now," I said. "He doesn't control jack."

"Jack?" Gonsalvo said. "Who is Jack?"

Adalia explained it to him.

A silence rolled out over our little group and I became aware of two people stepping past, a snatch of soft talk, a man coughing. Gonsalvo intoned some tendentious garbage about how the dragon, having survived death, had been reduced to a shade with a fraction of his former prodigious power and now he required our assistance in order to be reborn and restored to primacy.

"How're you going to work that?" I asked. "CPR? Give him a heart massage? No, wait! His heart's in Minsk, Shanghai, Las Vegas, all over the place...in a zillion fucking pieces."

"We will contribute our energies," de Lugo said grandly.

I tried to resist the impulse toward further sarcasm, but failed. "How does that work? When the moment's right you chant? You think pure thoughts in his direction?"

De Lugo nailed me with a stare that would have weakened my knees at another time and place. Timo scowled and Adalia said, "You haven't answered my question. Why are you here? Be truthful."

"Curiosity," I said. "And chance. I'm a leaf blown to your door."

"And Yara? What of her?"

"I enjoy fucking her, but she's a little young for me." I tapped my forehead. "Too young in here, you understand."

"He doesn't know," said de Lugo,

Adalia leaned back into the crook of Timo's shoulder. "Perhaps that's all he is, a leaf. One day soon the wind will take him."

Irritated, I said, "The least you can do is wait until I've gone to talk behind my back."

They gazed at me with the placidity of stoners, impervious to amazement, as though we were guests of the Mad Hatter and they were waiting patiently for me to turn into a camel.

"What the fuck are you talking about?" I asked. "What don't I know?"

"Why you're here." De Lugo prodded the ashes of the dead fire with his stick. "Please don't take offense. It's something all of us wonder about now and then...with regard to ourselves as well as others."

Still vexed, I asked why he was here and he replied that of all the "ingredients" gathered beneath the canopy, he might well be the most essential.

"Griaule will require ruthlessness to achieve what he must," he said. "And, God help me, I have been ruthless in my day."

Adalia put a hand on his knee to comfort him. Gonsalvo offered consoling platitudes. I thought they might burst into a chorus of "Kumbaya." De Lugo's "day" was scarcely a year in the past, an incident wherein seven priests had been found with their brains cut out, excavated from their skulls in a side chapel of the National Cathedral, following which he been forced to relinquish his post. I wasn't about to buy his penitent act and withdrew from the conversation, paying it marginal attention, and sketched their faces, their physical attitudes, anything else that caught my eye. Not until they left me, de Lugo being the last to go, patting my shoulder in an avuncular fashion...not until then did I think about the questions they had raised. Why was I there? Was I, too, an element essential to the dragon's rebirth? Had I been drawn to the community not by the Yara woman, but by the dragon's proxy? And what had they meant by their use of the word "ingredient"? The word had an ominous sound in context, implying the surrender of one's individuality to a grim purpose.

Dusk blended the shapes of the leaves and branches, but the skull appeared to gain sharpness and detail and vitality, standing out from an indistinct backdrop, gray and granitic in the half-light, as if it were the only real thing in the picture. I envisioned the muscles of the face and jaw reforming over the bone, the packed masonry of green and gold scales reassembling, and I could have sworn that I glimpsed movement in the oily shadows filling its eye sockets, the flickering of a membrane, a glint of reflected light, evidence of life harbored within, still potent after centuries of dormancy. I felt its shadow heartbeat on my skin like the reverberations of a gong. My susceptibility to suggestion, I thought. Yet I couldn't rid myself of the suspicion that the skull was the source of danger and a catastrophe was about to occur, that a more terrible visage would surface explosively from beneath that illusion of bone and fungus, and the dragon would shrug off its vegetable shroud and move against the city, mistaking Temalagua for Teocinte, the city where it had been imprisoned for millennia...or perhaps any city would serve as an apt target for his vengeance.

This was nonsense, sheer fantasy, but the idea had fastened onto me and I stared at the skull for such a long time, I became convinced that my watchfulness was all that prevented the transformation. When fatigue caused my concentration to falter I worried that the change had begun without my notice. Infinitesimal changes. Fluctuations on the sub-atomic level. Subtle shifts that we would not register until too late and a shattering conclusion was already upon us.

FROM THAT DAY forward I more-or-less accepted that some fragment of the dragon's anima clung to the skull and what skepticism I retained derived from my feelings for Yara, feelings that had magnified in intensity and scope over the weeks. I knew I was falling in love with her and love was something I had hoped to avoid—she wasn't the sort of girl you gave your heart to unless you were looking to get it back FDA approved and sliced into patties. In many ways she was the female version of me, efficient in her cruelty where I was casual. More political and less cynical, but no less a manipulator, not someone in whom you would place your faith. I tried to equate loving her with my revamped attitude toward the skull, countenancing them both to be symptoms of mental defect, of weakness induced by exposure to a spiritually toxic environment. She was still the child-woman I had met in Barrio Villareal—I knew more about her than I had, but nothing that would alter the basic picture, and yet her flaws had diminished in my eyes and her strengths had become pre-eminent. This idealization, I told myself, was patently a distortion, a by-product of love's madness, but I couldn't so easily label and dismiss my emotional and physical responses to her. And, further, while I had my doubts about Yara's sanity, her honesty, I didn't really want those doubts to prosper.

Often I would pass an hour or two in the early evening sitting in the eye socket (the one not overgrown by vines), where I would pretend that my presence counterfeited the dragon's missing pupil and was staring out over his kingdom, as it were. At full dark the clearing was a black field picked out by a scatter of dull, redly-glowing patches, like embers left over from a great burning whose smoky smell infused the air, with here and there the backlit, lumpy shapes of huts and tents, and silhouetted figures moving along sluggishly, appearing to struggle with their footing, as if walking in thick ash. Despite this infernal vista, my thoughts tended to be upbeat, consisting of flash visions of Yara, pieces of memory, a look, a cunning smile, a touch. One humid night she joined me there, kept vigil with me, and after a silence said, "This place was so much different when I arrived."

"Oh?" I said.

"There were only eight or nine people and most of them were crazy. Homeless guys. A couple of old women. The clearing was very small. Not even a quarter of what it is now."

She left a pause and I did not try to fill it. This was the first time she had spoken in a nostalgic tone and I was afraid of spoiling the moment, hoping for a revelation. Birds rustled the foliage overhead, a last flurry before sleep.

"It's strange," she said at last. "I never thought any of this would happen. When I came here I was miserable, full of anger. All I wanted was to die…and to injure people by my death. I still have anger inside me, but now that seems irrelevant."

She fell silent again and I felt the need to prompt her.

"Some of your adherents tell me…"

"They're not *my* adherents," she said sharply.

"The people down below tell me they're here to help with the dragon's rebirth."

"Did you laugh at them?"

Two people appeared to be dancing down below, silhouetted by a campfire, but I could hear no music. I felt Yara's eyes on me and said carefully, "I'm less inclined to laugh than once I was."

"They have dozens of theories," she said. "I don't subscribe to any of them."

"What theory *do* you subscribe to?"

"I have no theory."

"But you advise them, you're their guide, their mentor."

Her sigh seemed to ignite a chorus of cicadas. "Each morning I go into that little chamber…you know the one."

"Yes."

"I'll have a nap. When I wake I go to the clearing. I'll see someone… not the first person I see, but a specific person. I'll be moved to speak to them. I realize I have something to say, but I don't have any idea of what it will be. The message comes to me as I speak. Usually it's a positive message—you've heard me. At other times I'll give them a chore to do."

She reached back and gathered her hair into ponytail, held that pose for a beat, as if trying to think of something else to say.

"That's it?" I said. "That's all you got?"

"I know the idea of a renewal is involved. An alchemical change, a marriage of souls. And I know Griaule is behind it. I've been here so long I can feel him. Like how you feel when someone's behind you, watching what you do."

I thought she would have a complex rap explaining the great good news coming from beyond the sky. This sketchy recital didn't mesh with my assumptions.

"He compels me to do things I don't understand," she went on. "The money, for example. There's so much of it, more than we could ever use, and I keep on collecting more. He has me meet people in the city and give them money. It frustrates me, not being able to understand everything."

"Who are they, the people you give the money to?"

"Young men, mostly. Some are military, I think. I tell them things, but I don't have any recollection of what was said, just blank spots in my memory."

I stopped short of asking how much money she had collected and said, "He must have big plans for you."

"For me? Maybe."

She lay back and plucked at my arm, urging me down onto the cool bone surface beside her.

"Why'd you wait so long to tell me this?" I asked.

"I don't want to talk anymore," she said, fiddling with the top button of my jeans.

I pushed her hand away. "Was it the dragon? Did it feel like a message, as if he wanted you to tell me now?"

"Un-uh. Don't you want to fuck?"

"One more question. Say you're right about everything, about the dragon. How can you trust him? A beast, a giant lizard that has a *really* good reason to hate us. How can you think any change he brings will have a good effect?"

Even as I asked the question I suspected her answer would be the same that I had received from Ex when we argued about the value of revolution some months earlier:

"You've been here how long? Four years? Five? Long enough to realize that any change is welcome in Temalagua. Any chance that things will improve, however slight, is welcome. You can't impose your American logic on us. You people are smothered by the media, by lies, by silk sheets and fatty foods. Most of you don't notice how fucked you are. Here the government doesn't bother to hide things from us. Savagery, poverty, and injustice are shoved in our faces every day. We're fucking desperate! If change makes things worse...so what?"

Yara's answer was more succinct, yet no less to the point. Once she had spoken she pressed her body against mine and said, "Come on! I don't want to talk." She kissed my neck, my mouth and eyes, and though I had further questions I allowed myself to be converted from inquisitor to lover.

That night was as close as I came to complete intimacy with her. I put my lips to her ear and told her I loved her, yet I didn't whisper the words, I merely shaped them with my mouth. For one thing I was leery about what saying the words out loud would portend, but I suspect more devious motives were in play. By this inaudible, irresolute declaration I may have been hoping to convince myself that I wasn't just a victim of sexual infatuation, but a real boy capable of real love, and so I pretended to be afraid that if she heard me, she might react badly, she might throw me out or something of the sort...because I had no clue, really, as to how she felt about me or about love or any of it. Then again, I may have been daring her to hear me, making said declaration so close to the range of the audible that she might hear the slight popping of my lips and deduce from this that I had spoken and conclude that "I love you" was the most likely message, thereby leaving it up to her aural acuity and emotional state as to whether or not we would go to the next level. Someone once wrote that love is the drink that does not kill thirst, meaning that one's thirst for love is inexhaustible, or that love is an addiction that demands more and more of it in order to satisfy the lover, and yet, like an opiate, has less and less effect, so that in the end demand outstrips supply. While these interpretations are congruent and both undoubtedly true, in the case of Yara and myself love became a perverse psychological competition, a power struggle wherein we used our attitudes and our principles (such as they were) to deconstruct the very thing we desired before it could disappoint us, because we knew the game was fixed.

III

SNOW'S NARRATIVE CONTINUES FOR ANOTHER
156 pages, many treating of the tedious day-to-day life in the camp, an
almost equivalent number constituting a disquisition on the nature of love,
also tedious and overly analytic (as the preceding paragraph foreshadows),
and some few detailing and explaining ("justifying" might be more precise
a word, for he appears to have borne a heavy burden of guilt) the circumstances under which, four months after initiating a relationship with Yara,
he sneaked away from the clearing, intending never to return. He cites as
the root cause of his abandonment the ominous atmosphere that accumulated about the place and goes on to describe the event that precipitated
his escape.

"One morning," Snow writes, "Yara went to stand in the mouth of the
skull, at the point of the jaw, and there she stayed for several hours, saying nothing, motionless as in a fugue. Over a span of fifteen minutes the
adherents gathered beneath her. They were perplexed at first, calling out
to her and conferring among themselves, but then they grew as silent and
still as their queen…as their god. They remained standing in a loose assembly for nearly four hours, rapt as though compelled by unheard voices.
The air grew warmer—substantially warmer, it seemed to me—as if this
act of devotion, of pathological immersion, were somehow increasing the
spin of their constituent atoms and generating heat…though it's probable
my anxiety led me to misapprehend a slight elevation of air temperature.
Throughout the episode I was close to panic. The gloomy space under
the canopy, the rundown camp, the zombie-like connection between the
adherents and their queen: it was an eerie spectacle that evoked images of
Jonestown. That I had been excluded from the group, cast in the role of
onlooker or tourist, someone unworthy of participating in the experience,

amplified my sense of alienation. I didn't belong here, I told myself. I was a leaf blown by chance to their door and not party to this insanity. If I were I would be as mindless and mute as they, as the creatures of the jungle (they, too, had gone silent), receiving instruction from a woman who channeled the wishes and whims of a gigantic reptilian skull.

"When Yara turned away from the assembly, the jungle erupted into a clamor of croaks and screams, and the adherents shambled off, resuming their normal activities. Yara claimed to have no memory of what had transpired, yet she was not in the least disconcerted to learn of it, and this as much as anything convinced me that the disaster I feared was days if not hours away. I begged her to put some distance between herself and the skull, but when I told her the scene in the clearing had reminded me of Jonestown, she flew off the handle and accused me of subverting her work and otherwise distracting her.

"That night I lay in bed wondering what to do, feeling wrecked, staring at yet not focused upon Yara's naked back, pinpricks of actinic brilliance popping and fading before my eyes like miniature flashbulbs. And then I observed that the skin bordering her implant was inflamed, a distinct redness suffusing the colors of the surrounding tattoo. The implant itself appeared less regular in shape, its convexity more extreme, and I thought perhaps her body was rejecting it. I gently pressed my forefinger against the skin at the edge of the implant and her hips began to roll and jerk, a slow, grinding torsion, as if she were having sex with an invisible lover. I snatched my hand away, startled by her reaction, and the movements subsided. Lately she had encouraged me to touch the implant while we made love, but I had been too intent on my own pleasure to notice whether there had been a marked increase in hers…though it seemed then, in the unreliable archives of memory, that she displayed a measure of reaction. "Yara!" I said, and repeated her name, but she was out like a light. I pushed down on the implant with the heel of my hand—her hips thrashed as if she were on the verge of an orgasm. Once again I tried to wake her, shouting at and even shaking her, all to no avail. Horrified by her comatose state, by her erotic reflex, I was too rattled to think, yet a portion of my brain must have been functioning, a batch of neurons excited by dread must have sparked and transmitted a warning, for as the sky grayed I concluded that I needed to save myself."

THE SKULL

The disaster anticipated by Snow did not occur, at least not within the time frame he expected, and when nothing had happened after a month he was tempted to revisit the clearing, but shame and fear combined to negate this impulse. For a time he moved back in with Ex, yet it quickly became evident that the relationship had gone sour, as had his relationship with Temalagua, and he returned home to Concrete, Idaho, where he lived for free in an apartment owned by his father and landed a job in a local bookstore. He had intended to regroup there, to earn a little money and go off again, perhaps to Thailand, but was seduced by the lazy, listless patterns of existence in Concrete and stayed for the next ten years, maintaining a desultory lifestyle dominated by affairs with unattainable women, either married or disinterested in him as other than a pastime. The one noteworthy achievement of those years was the publication of his partial memoir, which remains unfinished to this day. (This may not be ascribed to a lack of effort, to youthful lassitude, but to the fact that it is an immature work to which he had only a passing attachment.) His infatuation with Yara developed into a full-blown obsession and, though when called upon to do so he would describe love in terms that accorded with his previous statements on the subject, he grew to think of Yara in terms more consistent with a romantic ideal. He searched the Internet for news of her and, finding none, he scribbled in his notebooks, dredging up memories, striving to piece together a coherent narrative of his four months in the jungle. He had done nude studies of Yara, but in them her face was either turned away or partly hidden by her hair—he could not recall why he had posed her this way, if it had been her idea or his, but the sketches seemed emblematic of their inadequate commitment to the relationship. He tried drawing her face from memory and was able to create accurate renderings of her features, but they were devoid of vitality and character, like better-than-average police sketches. He perceived this to be emblematic of what they had lost—an opportunity for emotional brilliance, for the transcendence of the ordinary. The conflation of time and an erratic memory presented him with the certainty of what he had heretofore merely imagined—that he had been in love with Yara and she with him, but they had not taken the final, necessary step to confirm those feelings.

One evening while netsurfing he chanced upon an article dated two years earlier about unexplained Central American mysteries that devoted a few sentences to a Temalaguan religious cult whose membership, some eight hundred strong, had recently vanished along with their object of veneration, a skull belonging to an immense specimen of the genus Megalania (this last assertion was without scholarly basis). The leader of the cult had been, the story said, "a charismatic young woman." And that was all. There was no mention whatsoever of the incident in the Temalaguan press at the time of the disappearance, a fact Snow found disturbing, and he could find no other online stories that referenced the event. Based on this sliver of information, however untrustworthy, he chucked his job, bought an airline ticket, and a week later arrived in Temalagua.

The city was more polluted and poverty-stricken than Snow remembered, though he wondered whether he had been too self-absorbed to notice how bad things were ten years before. Perhaps it had always been a smoky, slum-ridden slice of Mordor, Detroit with less industry, brighter colors, and hills crawling with the poor, the anonymous-as-roaches poor, some carrying their shelters on their backs. Beggars rushed at him in platoon-strength, displaying deformities, amputations, and open sores. Child prostitutes, some as young as eight or nine, called to him from alley mouths and doorways, and in piping, playground voices offered to perform the most deviant of perversions. Widows in black dresses and shawls sat on the curbs along Avenida Seis, their heads down, mere inches away from the stream of traffic, as if they had given up hope and were waiting for a car to swerve and put an end their misery. Many of Snow's old connections were dead or otherwise defunct. Ex had lost her taste for revolution and married the proprietor of a department store who called her his little Commie and delighted in pinching her now substantial ass—she was pregnant with their fourth child and was reluctant to speak with Snow. The offices of Aurora House had been taken over by a travel agency, Pepe Salido had been murdered in a gambling dispute, and Snow's colleagues in the charity had drifted away to parts unknown. Club Sexy hadn't changed that much. They had put in track lighting above the bar and added a karaoke machine. Miraculously, the old man still played his rickety Beatle tunes against the same chintzy backdrop of silver glitter, moonglow, and palms. Expensively attired women thronged the tables—Snow failed to recognize any of them, yet they were of a type similar to those he did recall, and the fabulous Guillermo was still pouring drinks. Aside from the start of a double chin and a questionable goatee, he looked none the worse for wear. On seeing Snow he rushed out from behind the bar to embrace him.

"You look wonderful! Fantastic!" said Guillermo, pulling back. "How do you do it?"

"You look pretty good yourself," said Snow.

"Me? I'm an absolute disaster! But it doesn't matter anymore. I have a husband now, I can let myself go to seed."

He steered Snow to a corner table and told the other barman, Canelo—a young black man with a light, freckly complexion, close-cropped reddish hair, and diamond piercings in his cheeks—to bring a bottle of tequila. Snow realized that he had forgotten to employ gayspeak and began to shade his inflections, subtly (he thought) re-acquiring his verbal disguise. Guillermo laid his hand atop Snow's and said, "Please! There's no need for that."

Baffled, Snow asked what he meant.

"Your act." Guillermo poured him a shot of tequila. "It never fooled anyone, you know. Some of us were angry—we thought you were mocking us. But when we realized you were using us to get close to the ladies, we understood and we laughed about it. Since you were a nice guy, we played along."

"I wasn't a nice guy," said Snow. "I was a total asshole."

"Well, you looked nice, anyway. And you acted nice. That's what counted most back then."

They drank and reminisced for a while and then Snow asked about Yara.

Guillermo lowered his voice. "Did you hear about what happened to her?"

"Only a little. I just read about it last week. I'm hoping to learn more. That's why I came down."

"You must be careful who you talk to about this. Very careful."

"Why's that?"

"The PVO." Guillermo refilled their glasses. "The Party of Organized Violence." He knocked back his shot. "They showed up about fifteen years ago, but they didn't make much of a splash and no one took them seriously until the elections last year when they gained a plurality in Congress.

They're thugs. Scary right-wing thugs. Extremely scary. If they win a majority in the next election, and everyone says they will…" He affected a shudder. "They don't like gays. Joselito, my husband…he thinks we should relocate to Costa Rica."

"What's this have to do with Yara?"

"After she vanished a reporter got into Chajul. You know, the village out near the skull? This one guy got in, but soon the PVO sealed off access to that area of the jungle with their militia."

"They have their own soldiers?"

"Nobody fucks with them. They might as well be running things already. But like I was saying…" Guillermo knocked back a shot—it looked as if it hurt going down. "I have a friend who knew the reporter. The guy said most of the villagers had already fled, but he talked to one woman who told him there was a big spill of heat from the jungle. Hot enough to make you cover your face, she said. Then rippling lights appeared over the treetops. All colors. She assumed it was a religious thing, Jesus was coming down on a rainbow carpet, so she went into her house to pray to the Virgin. She heard people in the street and swears they had come out of the jungle, but she didn't see them—she was afraid and hid. That's all she had time to say before the PVO turned up and carried her away. The reporter beat it out the back window."

The ancient keyboard player announced he was taking a break— the sounds of the Casio were replaced by Latin pop.

"Can I talk to him?" Snow asked. "The reporter."

"He disappeared," said Guillermo, giving the word "disappeared" a certain emphasis.

Snow covered his glass to prevent Guillermo from pouring him another shot. "I guess I don't get it. Why were the PVO so interested in a screwball cult?"

"You'd have to ask them…but that's not something I would recommend. You don't want to attract the attention of those guys."

Guillermo was called away to settle some issue at the bar and Snow, glancing around the room, caught a thirty-ish brunette at another table checking him out. She wore an orange-and-yellow print frock with a tight bodice that accentuated her cleavage and she permitted herself a half-smile before saying something to her companion, a plump blonde. The blonde cast a quick look in his direction and the women shared a laugh. Snow had an impulse to make a move, to indulge in his old life again, if only for nostalgia's sake. Guillermo rejoined him and nodded toward the brunette.

"Stay away from that one, man," he said. "She's Juan Mazariegos' mistress."

"He's a bad guy?"

"The worst. He's a bigshot in the PVO. Half the women here are PVO."

Snow asked him whether it was safe to visit the encampment.

"Yes, I think so," Guillermo said. "But there's no point. You know how quickly the jungle comes back. It's all overgrown in there. Nobody lives in Chajul nowadays and Yara…" He made a gesture of finality. "She's gone."

Snow didn't want to believe that and had nothing to say. With an inquiring look, Guillermo held up the bottle—Snow shook his head.

"Man!" said Guillermo. "Drink with me. Who knows when you'll be back again?"

"I might stick around," Snow said. "I don't really have anywhere else to go."

"Then we'll drink to you staying. I'll fill you in on all the gossip. Ten years worth."

With reluctance, for he was not that much of a tequila drinker anymore, Snow let Guillermo pour him a double.

Guillermo raised his glass. "Old times!"

Snow hesitated before touching glasses and said, "La Endriaga."

GUILLERMO HAD BEEN right. The site of the camp was overrun with new vegetation and all Snow managed to unearth were a few sections of rusted tin. Despite the witness report of extreme heat, there were no charred tree trunks, no scorched areas. Nothing. He poked around for an hour, but couldn't even find ashes. What kind of fire could have vaporized the skull and left tin unmarked? The absence of the skull, of any evidence as to the cause of its destruction, started to make him jumpy and he soon returned to his hotel.

Snow had saved his money over the past decade and could have survived for quite some time in Temalagua without a job, but he thought it prudent to find work and secured a position teaching English at a private school in the suburbs. Each morning he would ride the bus from the city center, where he had taken an apartment, and spend the better part of his day preparing the spoiled teenage sons and daughters of the wealthy—who, chauffered by armed bodyguards, arrived in Hummers and town cars and limousines—to deal with their equally spoiled peers in the United States. They were arrogant little monsters, for the most part. Sullen and disrespectful even to one another, they treated Snow with a polished contempt that, if one didn't examine it too closely, might be mistaken for civility. He entertained fantasies of walking into a classroom with an explosive device strapped to his mid-section. He met regularly with their parents, advising them of learning disabilities and behavioral problems, and it was during such a counseling session that he encountered Luisa Bazan, a zaftig brunette of thirty-five years, mother of Onofrio, a lizard-like youth with a penchant for upskirt photography, a pursuit for which he had been threatened with expulsion (this threat unlikely to be acted upon, since Onofrio's father was Enrique Bazan, in line to become the PVO's defense minister after the elections).

Approaching his thirty-ninth birthday, Snow had retained his youthful good looks and thus he was not greatly surprised when Luisa requested increasingly frequent parent-teacher conferences and that during these sessions they discussed Luisa's personal life more than they did Onofrio's scholastic failings. Luisa complained about her husband's cavalier treatment of her, his mental abuses, his rudeness to her family, his lack of concern for her concerns, and hinted at more heinous offenses. Snow offered a sympathetic ear, he understood the implied invitation and was tempted to accept it—although she would soon fall prey to obesity, sublimating her womanly desires with sweets and starches and bi-monthly shopping trips to Miami, where she now (according to her) satisfied her every appetite, Luisa was still exceptionally attractive and her desperation to employ her physical charms before age and indulgence further eroded them was as palpable and alluring to Snow as an exotic perfume. But he held firm and, when one afternoon she flung herself at him, rather than rejecting her out of hand, an act that might have antagonized her and sent her running to Enrique, complaining that Snow had committed an impropriety...on that afternoon he told Luisa he was grieving for a lost love (only half a lie) and that she was the first woman in years to have pierced the shroud of his grief and touch his heart. He asked for time to clear his head, to adjust to this unexpected change—he did not want to come to her encumbered by any shred of the past, he said. She deserved better and if she could wait but a little while for him to purge himself of old feelings, then all things would be possible. Due to his experience with such women, knowing that what they wanted was something excessive in their lives, some form of drama to break the comfortable tyranny of their marriages, Snow anticipated that a make-believe drama would be enough to suit Luisa's purposes and in this he proved correct. From that day forward their conferences were models of comportment, marred only by incidental brushes of skin against skin, as happened when he helped her on with her jacket or handed her paperwork, and smoldering looks redolent of their unrequited passion.

If you had asked Snow why he stayed on in Temalagua after learning what he could about Yara's fate—that is to say, very little—he might have answered because the cost of living was cheap and the weather temperate, but in truth he remained obsessed and began to make discreet inquiries about Yara's activities during the period leading up to her disappearance. Over the next two years his life acquired an unvarying routine, teaching by day and by night and on the weekends pursuing his investigation via the Internet and in the various establishments (offices, shops, bars) mentioned in passing by Yara as places where she had collected or delivered sums of money. Yet for all his efforts, the sole result of his investigation came to him by chance. Some twenty months after his return to Temalagua, while leafing through the Sunday newspaper, he ran across an article on page six of the front section concerning the murder (by terrorists, the paper suggested) of one Hernan Ortiz, an official of the PVO. Accompanying the article was a headshot of the victim that showed him to have been a lean, cadaverous fellow with a distinctive shock of white hair in his forelock. Further photographs found on the Internet depicted a lanky man dressed in army fatigues. Snow thought instantly of the electronics store clerk to whom Yara had given the envelope stuffed with currency. He hadn't gotten a close look at the clerk's face, but given the PVO's interest in Yara's cult, her statement that some of the men to whom she had given instructions and money were military, and now this photograph of a man with an identical streak of white in his hair...he refused to believe it could be a coincidence.

That same morning, a warm spring morning, Snow met Guillermo for coffee at Mocca's, a popular sidewalk café on the Avenida with a façade of tinted windows and heavy glass doors. Snow did not make friends easily. A serial manipulator, he mistrusted the validity of his emotional investments in other people and as a consequence he mistrusted the people as well—yet if forced to characterize his relationship with Guillermo, he would have said they were friends. In addition to feeling comfortable around Guillermo, he envied his openness, his ability to discuss freely every aspect of his life, and thus their Sunday meetings had become a semi-regular occurrence. They sat in the shade of an umbrella that sprouted from the center of their table, emblazoned with a Flor de Cana logo, one among several dozen identical tables from which arose the laughter and chatter of over a hundred upper class Temalaguans. The traffic stream was less heavy and less clamorous than usual, and the smell of coffee contended with that of gasoline fumes. Waiters in red T-shirts and dark slacks glided about, bearing trays loaded with food and drink, and chased off beggars who had infiltrated the tables, where they were being pointedly ignored by people so at variance in aspect from themselves, so well nourished, richly dressed, bedecked with gold, jewelry, and expensive sunglasses, they might have been of a different taxonomic order, sparrows among peacocks.

Guillermo dominated the conversation, commenting cattily on the scene, pointing to this or that local celebrity, tossing out bits of gossip, but when Snow showed him the photograph of Hernan Ortiz he had clipped from the newspaper and inquired about the man's connection with Yara, Guillermo's airy mood dissolved. He covered the photo with a napkin and said, "What is it with you? You live with this girl a few months, you leave her, and now, years later, when she's dead, you want to know everything about her."

"Curiosity," said Snow. "The road not traveled and all that."

"Get yourself another hobby. This one could get you killed."

"Did you know Ortiz? Back in the day, I mean?"

Guillermo made an exasperated noise.

"Come on, man," said Snow. "You knew everyone on the Avenida in those days."

"Yes, I knew him. He was a punk. He used to run with a gang who hung around the bus station. They ripped off street vendors returning home at night to their villages. They'd beat the hell out of them for a few *quetzales*. They beat the hell out of people like me for fun. A couple of years later he turned up looking clean and presentable, working at the electronics store. Word was he'd joined up with a big organization…but he was still a punk."

"A big organization? The PVO?"

"Keep your voice down!" As Guillermo sipped his coffee, he darted his eyes left and right. "Yes."

"Why didn't you tell me?"

"I'm telling you now."

"But why didn't you tell me when I first got back? Or when I got involved with Yara?"

"The PVO" (Guillermo whispered the acronym) "weren't that big a deal when you hooked up with Yara. It didn't occur to me to tell you then. When you returned, well, call me sentimental, but I don't want to see you dead." He dabbed at his lips with a napkin. "The reason I'm telling you now is to stop you from pursuing the matter. If you keep it up you're going to make the acquaintance of some very unpleasant people and stir up a lot of trouble for your friends."

"Yeah, you keep saying that, but nothing ever happens."

A weary-looking Indian woman with an infant in one arm, clad in a dress gone gray from repeated scrubbings, its printed pattern all but worn away, stopped by an adjoining table and dangled four or five necklaces in the face of a man with chiseled features, wearing aviator sunglasses and a crisp, pale yellow guayabera. He looked off to his left, surveying the tables, and his companion, a pretty woman with a *café-con-leche* complexion, carmine lips, and rhinestone-studded sunglasses, exhaled a jet of cigarette smoke and said something that made him smile.

"For your lady," said the Indian woman, gently shaking the necklaces, an enticement. Her voice barely audible, she murmured a litany of afflictions—the child was sick, they were hungry, they needed money to return home.

The Indian woman noticed Snow was watching and moved toward him, an ounce of energy enlivening her face on having spotted an American. Guillermo looked away, but Snow, before the woman could begin her pitch, gave her ten *quetzales*, at least twice what she could have asked for, and selected one of the necklaces, a piece of poor quality jade upon which the design of a bird had been scratched, strung on a loop of black twine.

"Why do you encourage them?" asked Guillermo as the woman hurried off, a few paces ahead of a grim-faced waiter intent on evicting her.

"The poor need to be encouraged, don't you think?" Snow slipped on the necklace. "And don't tell me that I can't give them all money. That's a rationalization you use for not giving money to any of them. Besides, I was angry and I knew it would piss you off."

"*You're* angry? Why's that? Because I'm trying to keep you from getting into trouble?"

"You're not keeping me out of trouble. All I'm doing is asking questions of people I trust. And that's basically you. I won't take it any further."

"You're a liar! Do you think I don't hear things? People come up to me all the time and say, 'That gringo friend of yours was in last night asking questions.' It's a wonder you haven't been picked up."

"Well, that's my business, isn't it?"

Guillermo shrugged, as if to imply that Snow's survival was of no importance to him. He had plainly taken offense at Snow's characterization of him as an uncaring sort. True or not, he liked to think of himself as egalitarian and not class conscious in the least.

"Look, I apologize," said Snow. "I told you I was angry."

Guillermo pretended to be interested in the goings-on at another table.

"Stop this shit, man!"

"What shit?" Guillermo dug out his cell and checked for messages.

Already bright, the sunlight brightened further, bespeaking a break in some thin pall of pollution.

"Okay," Snow said. "How about next time we come out I'll buy you a necklace? Will that put the roses back in your cheeks?"

THE SKULL

Guillermo's struggled to maintain his indifferent pose, but the façade crumbled and he smiled. "Joselito will be *so* jealous!"

Snow touched the black twine about his neck. "Maybe I should just give you this."

"Oh, no!" said Guillermo. "It'll have to be something much more fashion forward. I'll help you pick something out." He shifted in his chair and sighed. "It's such a glorious day I can't stay angry. I think I'll have a glass of wine. Do you want one?"

"I'll take another coffee."

"Days like this I feel I could fall in love with everyone." Guillermo laughed and patted Snow's forearm. "Even you." He signaled a waiter and then looked soberly at Snow and said, "You do know I love you, don't you?"

His machismo enlisted, put off by this expression of sentiment, Snow said in a sardonic tone, "Oh yeah, sure."

Guilllermo shook his head sadly. "What an asshole you are! I thought you'd grown up, but I'll bet you still think about love as something that makes you dizzy."

Two Sundays later when Snow dropped by Club Sexy to meet Guillermo, the place was empty except for a pair of solitary drinkers. Even the old keyboard player was absent. Snow asked Canelo, the black bartender with freckles and reddish hair, where everyone was and Canelo said, "Haven't you heard?" And when Snow said he had heard nothing, Canelo, who had recently grown a Van Dyke that, along with his piercings, his red skullcap of hair, and downcast manner, gave him the look of a sorrowful devil, told him that Guillermo and Joselito had been found dead in a *barranca* outside the city. Both had been tortured. He went on to say what a shock it had been to everyone and the club had been closed for three days out of respect, but now business was picking up again, especially at night, and some of the ladies had started coming back in. He might have said more, but Snow ran from the club, burst through the front door, and stood in the entranceway, letting the city's polluted roar explode over him, a wetness in his eyes blurring the light, turning passersby into colored shadows. Canelo followed him out and told him to come back inside and have a drink.

"Who killed them?" asked Snow.

Taken aback by the question, Canelo said he didn't know.

"It was the PVO, wasn't it?" Snow came a step toward him.

"In this life, the sort of life Guillermo lived, a man makes a great many enemies."

"What are you fucking saying?"

Canelo spread his hands to demonstrate his helplessness. "I wasn't there. How can I know who killed them? It might have been a jealous ex-lover, a madman. The cops said the bodies were horribly mutilated. Their cocks were in each other's mouths."

"Guillermo was terrified of the PVO. He said they hated gays."

"That proves nothing. Hating gays is all the fashion down here."

Frustration overrode Snow's sense of loss. His emotions crested, over-flowing their confines, and he shoved Canelo in the chest, knocking him back against the wall. "You know damn well it was political! If it wasn't why are people staying away from the club?"

"Calm down, man! Okay?" Canelo inspected the rear of his jeans for stucco dust. "Let's go inside. I'll tell you what I know."

He held the door open and Snow, his temper cooling, went through. The instant the door swung shut behind them, he heard a complicated snick and Canelo slung him face-first into the wall. Something cold and sharp pricked his throat. Canelo pressed his mouth to Snow's ear, his funky breath overpowering the smell of his cologne, and said, "Don't you ever put your hands on me again!"

Snow held perfectly still. "Yeah. Okay."

"If you weren't Guillermo's friend I'd open you up. But don't get the idea *I'm* your friend. To me you're just a stupid fucking gringo who doesn't know his ass."

Canelo stepped away and Snow, hearing another snick, turned to see him pocketing a butterfly knife.

"You want to know who I think killed Guillermo?" Canelo asked. "It was you. You didn't cut him, but he died because of you."

"That's crazy," said Snow.

"You don't understand where you are, man. None of you fucks have a clue. You go blundering about, thinking you can solve any problem because you're superior to the pitiful, fucked-up Temalaguans, but all you do is make more trouble for us."

"I think it was the PVO," Snow said weakly.

"Maybe. It might have been political. The PVO could have done it, or some other political party. See, what you don't seem to understand is that in order to stay in business Guillermo had to be an informer. All these bitches with their bigshot husbands coming around...the husbands asked him questions. He tried to be cool. He'd give them some information, nothing serious, enough maybe that someone would get slapped around now and then. But nothing more. He didn't want anyone to get their head chopped because of him. He walked a fine line. But when you started asking about La Endriaga the line got even finer. He should have handed you over. We tried to tell him, we said if you give up the gringo the pressure will ease off, but he wanted to protect you. 'He's my friend,' he'd say. 'I'm not going to betray a friendship.'"

"He should have told me!" said Snow. "If he'd told me about his predicament, how bad things were..."

"Get real, man. Think about it. He warned you constantly. You simply didn't want to listen."

"He didn't tell me the whole story. I never understood...he never conveyed to me how serious it was."

"Maybe he thought you were smart enough to fill in the blanks. Or maybe he believed you were as much a friend to him as he was to you. Maybe he thought you respected him and actually paid attention to what he said. Big mistake, huh?"

Snow stood mute, absorbing what Canelo had told him.

"It was casual with you," Canelo said. "You thought it was cool to have a fag who owned a night club for a friend."

"That's not how it was!"

"Sure it is. You're like a half-ass method actor, man. One who almost buys into his character, but can't quite get there." Canelo gestured at the door. "Get the fuck out."

Snow balked at leaving. "It's not like you say. Maybe I've made some missteps, but I..."

"*Maybe?* Fuck!" Canelo's scorn was a physical force. "Nobody cares how you see the situation. Your viewpoint doesn't mean dick. Now beat it! If I were you I'd leave the country. Guillermo wasn't good with pain. He probably ratted you out when they tortured him. Even if he didn't, I'm getting an urge to tell the next cop who comes in that you were talking shit about the PVO. I'm not kidding. Nothing's stopping me and I may not be able to resist the temptation."

IV

FOLLOWING HIS SET-TO WITH CANELO, Snow returned to his apartment and packed his bags, shaken by what the bartender had told him and frightened not just by his threat, but by the world of threat, a world of maniacs and bloody politics of which he had, of course, been aware, yet never thought would menace him. He intended to catch the first plane north, wherever it was bound, but as he waited for the taxi and afterward, on the way to the airport, his guilt concerning Guillermo elbowed his paranoia aside and he wished for some way he could make a stab at redemption. He had nary a clue of how to go about this, but perhaps fate conspired to assist him, for on reaching the ticket counter he discovered that the destination of the first available flight was Miami—that provided the platform for the germ of an idea. An hour later, en route to that city of second-rate glitterati and leathery, sun-dried MILFs, he debated whether or not it was worth the risk and concluded that he could safely take a first step and pull back if things went badly. And so, upon landing in Miami on a humid Wednesday afternoon, Snow rented a cheap motel room in Coral Gables and prepared to initiate an affair with Luisa Bazan.

Every second Friday Luisa would check into a suite at the Bon Temps, a boutique hotel in the heart of South Beach, where she would reside until Sunday night. She had invited him to meet her there several times, offering to pay his airfare, and he had made his excuses. Now he hoped she would be amenable to an encounter (lately she had been testy toward him, impatient with the unconsummated relationship) and he also hoped that he could get to her before she secured the services of a cabana boy for the weekend. On the Friday evening after his arrival in Miami he staked himself out in the hotel bar, the Tres Jolie, and waited there without result until after midnight. He had steeled himself against this possibility (her

LUCIUS SHEPARD

schedule was governed by her husband's whims) and he was certain she would come eventually—but waiting for another week to pass was more difficult than he presumed and he nearly abandoned his scheme. What, after all, could he learn from Luisa in one weekend that would alter the situation? She would likely have no salient information about the PVO and, even if she did, how could he use it? It was a crazy idea that had seemed for a moment wonderfully crafty and wise, one of many similar strokes of genius that had misdirected the meandering course of his life. The only consideration that stayed him from leaving Miami was that he had nowhere to go. He had blown his job at the private school, he had no friends to speak of in Temalagua, what with Guillermo dead, and no support system now that he had been banned from Club Sexy. No purpose, no real direction. He refused to contemplate the horror of returning to Idaho. That left him with the image of an addled, gray-bearded Snow drinking the dregs of his life away in some misbegotten Central American hell, with "Margaritaville" and "The Piña Colada Song" dominating the soundtrack and a tattooed female lizard by his side, watching for symptoms of terminal weakness that would allow her to rifle through his pockets for money and drugs. This picture in mind, the prospect of a weekend with Luisa Bazan acquired a fresh gloss.

At half past seven on the next Friday evening, Luisa flounced into the Bon Temps, spike heels clacking on the marble floor, her impressive rack rendered more impressive yet by a ruffled blouse that exaggerated every jiggle, blond streaks in her beautifully coiffed hair, and clingy slacks that made her ass seem iconic, like the majestic rump of a horse cast in bronze and mounted by a heroic warrior with a plumed hat and sword. Were she to put on ten or fifteen pounds more she might be able to pose for a fetish magazine, but for now she resembled a voluptuous sexual cartoon. From the reception desk you had an unobstructed view into the Tres Jolie—the bar was crowded with a group of yelping and whooting twenty-somethings having a starter drink before hitting the clubs, and Snow had positioned himself so Luisa would be likely to notice him, hanging his jacket over an adjacent stool to prevent anyone from sitting beside him. He watched out of the corner of his eye as she chatted up the receptionist, a bellboy, the manager. When she spotted him her face emptied and she took a step toward the elevators, as if intending to sneak past the bar without acknowledging him, but then she adopted an expression of haughty reserve and approached to within an arm's length and said, "Craig?"

Snow glanced up and smiled—a well-rehearsed smile of boyish delight to which a dash of sadness was added.

"What are you doing here?" she asked. "The school…they told me they didn't know what happened to you?"

He persuaded her to sit and told her an equally well-rehearsed story consisting of half-truths and outright lies. He had, he said, experienced an emotional crisis. Thinking that he would never be able to exorcise the residue of feelings for his old flame, he'd decided that the most honorable thing he could do for Luisa was to remove himself from the picture and, obeying an impulse, he bolted. It was an act of desperation, perhaps of cowardice, for which he apologized. He had wanted to say goodbye, but she was a woman whom you did not say goodbye to easily. If he had come to her, her beauty, her spirit…they would have been too great an allure and he would not have been able to sustain the courage of his convictions. En route to Miami, however, he experienced an epiphany. He couldn't think of anything other than Luisa. Her scent, her mouth, her sensitivity, the very sum of her pervaded his thoughts and nowhere could he find a trace of his obsession with his former love. It was a consummate irony, he said, that by running away from the object of his desire he had dissolved the bonds that prevented him from attaining it, though it was characteristic of the ironies that seemed to rule his existence.

Snow did not believe Luisa had bought into his story. She maintained a cool and disaffected mask throughout and he had been planning to amp up the emotion, to say that he expected nothing of her, he realized how badly he must have hurt her, and he would go his own way if that were her wish, etc…but at this juncture she drew him into a passionate kiss, drowning him in perfume, engaging him with tongue and breasts, eliciting cheers and approbative comments ("Fuck, yeah!" and "Dude, if you don't hit that, I will!" and the like) from the nearby twenty-somethings, some of whom had been eavesdropping. Luisa blushed and led Snow from the bar, accompanied by a smattering of applause, and into the elevator, where unrestrained kissing and fondling supplanted the need to speak, and thence to her suite on the ninth floor, an interior decorator's wet dream of "travertine floors, faux-zebra-skin rugs, Calcutta marble counters, and petrified wood accent tables…" (Out of boredom he had read and re-read the hotel's brochure while waiting for Luisa.) Amidst this hideous thousand-dollar-per-night splendor the evening held few surprises, yet Snow was unsettled to discover how demanding Luisa was in the bedroom. He felt like a German Shepherd being put through his paces. Harder, faster, deeper. Heel. He supposed her aggression and dominance were due to her enforced docility at home. Thankfully he had procured a supply of Viagra and was able to perform up to her standards, emerging from the training run unscathed apart from a bite mark or two and a sore tongue.

Around noon they went shopping for lingerie, a brief excursion that saw her buy a variety of peignoirs, bra-and-panty sets, and a number of more risqué costumes. Upon their return to the Bon Temps, Luisa put on a fashion show, modeling each and every item, breaking from the process for bouts of coitus interruptus. Their involvement had been so all consuming that it had frustrated Snow's desire to extract information from her about the PVO, but the fashion show afforded him an opportunity to ask his questions. He had thought that he would have to be subtle in his interrogation, but once he got her started Luisa spoke freely about her husband's lack of character and his nefarious activities. One typical exchange went as follows:

Luisa (from the next room): Here I come, baby!

Snow: Okay!

(an interval of several seconds)

Snow (hushed): My God.

Luisa: It's pretty, no?

Snow: That's not the word I'd use. You look…incredible. Amazing. There are no words. Enrique's eyes are going to bug out when he sees you in this.

Luisa (sternly): Enrique never see me like this. Never. These clothes… they are for you. No one else.

Snow: Don't you have to show him stuff that proves you went shopping?

Luisa: I buy some junk at the airport…at the duty free shops. Here. You like me like this?

Snow: Oh, yeah!

Luisa: You ready for me?

Snow: What do you think?

Luisa (giggles): Look. I can slide this over like so. And then I can sit like…Ohhh! That's so nice!

(a minute or two of strenuous breathing)

Luisa (playful): Let me go, baby. I don't want you to come yet.

Snow: You're going to fucking kill me.

Luisa (laughs): I'm going to try.

During a viewing of the next outfit:

Snow: I don't get it. Won't he be able to tell you bought lingerie from the receipts?

Luisa: Enrique don't ever look at the receipts. He don't do nothing. I take care of the receipts, the bank, everything. That's how I know where he goes on and the presents he buy for women. *Puto pendejo! Lambioso!* He don't care if I know about them!

Snow (casually): Where's he go on these trips?

Luisa: Mexico, sometimes. But mostly he goes to Tres Santos.

Snow: Tres Santos? That's a little speck of a village. At least it used to be. What's he do there?

Luisa: It's where he meets the Jefe. The guy who runs the PVO. How's this?

Snow: Very sexy. Beautiful. So what's his name?

Luisa: Jefe. They just call him Jefe 'cause he's the boss, the chief. He don't like names. He got lots of secrets and he don't ever leave Tres Santos. Enrique says he's a really weird guy. He spend all the time flying inside this big building.

Snow: I've never heard of anything like that—flying in a building.

Luisa: I don't know nothing about it. That's what Enrique says.

Snow: What's Enrique do? Does he fly, too?

Luisa: He fucks whores. I can smell them on him when he come home. And I can tell there are many because of the clothes he buy for them. Clothes like this. Different sizes.

Snow: I don't recall there being any whores in Tres Santos. The population couldn't support them.

Luisa (impatiently): Well, they got some now and Enrique buys them presents. Why you care? You want to talk about Enrique or you want more of this?

Snow: It's just I can't believe he goes with whores when he has a beautiful woman like you.

Luisa (coyly): You like these, eh?

Snow: When you shake them like that, I can't think of anything else.

And again:

Snow: Maybe he's a fag. You ever think about that?

Luisa: Enrique?

Snow: Maybe the reason he goes to see the Jefe so often is because they're fucking.

Luisa: No, not Enrique.

Snow: You say this Jefe's a weird guy. And powerful. Power can be sexy. Enrique wouldn't be the first person to switch teams in that kind of situation.

Luisa (uncertainly): Jefe's got a woman, but...

Snow: But what?

Luisa: She's sick or something. I don't know.

(a pause)

Luisa: I'm going to try on that black lace thing. What you call it?

Snow: A peignoir.

Luisa: Yeah, I'm going to try that on.

Lastly:

Snow: If you wear that tonight, I'll rip it to shreds.

Luisa: You can rip up anything you want. We buy more next time.

Snow: You make me so crazy, I might hurt you. Accidentally, of course.

Luisa: You hurt me last night, baby. Did I complain?

(she hums absently)

Snow: You know, the more I think about it, the surer I am that something weird is going on with Enrique and Jefe. You say Jefe lives alone, unprotected? No guards, no soldiers?

Luisa: He don't need them. Everyone is scared of him. Every time they walk around in the village, the people hide. Enrique say Jefe laughs when he sees that.

Snow: Right, and yet you're telling me there are a couple of dozen whores in the village. It doesn't make sense. Maybe the presents Enrique buys, maybe he does that to cover up what's really going on. What's he tell you he does with Jefe?

Luisa: They talk about the elections, about they going to get the country back on the right track. Make the army stronger.

Snow: (mutters unintelligibly)

Luisa: Huh?

Snow: Nothing.

And so it went. Sex, driblets of information extracted, more sex, the sole interlude an excursion out onto Collins Avenue and the Mynt Lounge, an exclusive club whose doorman dropped the velvet rope for Luisa, glanced suspiciously at Snow, and ushered them into a surprisingly drab room with black theater carpeting and spacious booths with Mynt green lighting and black walls painted by video projectors (at the moment they were playing what looked to be clips from the Sea World aquarium—manta rays and sharks and barracudas, oh my), presided over by a high priest DJ wearing robes adorned with Illuminati-type symbols, mystic eyes, ankhs, radiant objects, who spun anthemic techno at ear-bleeding levels, the dance floor jammed with cavorting models in micro-minis and drug dealers and their clients butt-shaking their way to Jesus or, more likely, the Big Red Dude, and a swank of celebrities, foremost among them in terms of personal power, a black-clad movie director named Brett (a purveyor of cinematic dog shit, in Snow's view), the Annoying Ego-monster Incarnate with a Van Dyke that reminded him of Guillermo, who swaggered over to their table trailed by his personal assistant, a diminutive clean-shaven imp or familiar also dressed in black and bearing a bottle of designer vodka and three glasses (the imp was not permitted drink, apparently, lest he grow great with self-importance), and following an exchange of cheek kisses with Luisa, the Bearded One inquired of Snow his place in the world, a shouted conversation that evolved into a tiresome supercilious put-down once Brett ascertained that his place was lowly, though Snow wasn't altogether sure whether or not he had fallen prey to paranoia, because Luisa had earlier that evening slipped him a large blue capsule whose contents wreaked havoc with his judgment and caused the inside of his eyeballs to itch and filled the air with lime spiders and their dark, astonishingly complex webs in which Snow could detect patterns revealing of both past and future, presenting him with the once-in-a-lifetime ability to anticipate the onset of consequential events, but that he wasted on foreseeing the approach of a model with icy eye shadow and breasts like highway emergency cones who slithered up shortly before they headed back to the Bon Temps, insisting that Brett and Luisa do jello shots off her lovely, tanned tummy, as an afterthought including Snow in the invitation, though not the imp—thoroughly disoriented at this juncture, he complied, pretending to be flattered, delighted, eager, but found the experience unpleasant, like licking puke off a still-convulsing corpse, and then lifting his head from this ghoulish feast he saw that the legion of the beautiful damned on the dance floor had broken out sparklers and were waving them around, setting fire to the webs, sending the spiders scuttling for cover, and a booming female voice exhorted everyone to "…feel free…while there's time to be free!", words to live by, advice Snow took to heart and went out into the soft warm air lit by the glowing, buzzing, neon cuneiform sign language of the Bauhaus hotels just off the strip, the noise from Collins Avenue—whooping groups of revelers, the purr and growl of muscle cars, sexy and dangerous, dripping with reflected light—a relief by contrast to the din of Mynt, and as they walked he tried to recall a clever phrase he had come up with, something about performing a glitterectomy on the nation, but removed from the environment that had bred and nurtured and defined it, the fundamental relevance of the phrase fizzled out, and Snow along with it.

THE SKULL

SUNDAY EVENING, AFTER a final copulation, a bouquet of tearful goodbye kisses, Luisa limo-ed off to the airport, promising to return in two weeks time. She had paid for the suite until Monday morning and told Snow that he should stay the night and charge whatever he wanted to the room, but cautioned him about over-tipping and, semi-playfully, advised him not to bring up any girls. The admonition was unnecessary—Snow was whipped. He ordered a thirty-dollar cheeseburger, fries, and two Cokes from room service and sat on the balcony, eating, watching combers rolling in, reduced to wavelets by the time they hit shore. Too tired to think, he lay down on the bed around eight-thirty and slept until one. South Beach would be still going strong and he briefly considered rejoining the party. Ten years before he would have, but now he went to the refrigerator and opened a bottle of water and stood at the kitchen counter, attempting to concentrate on the big issues: what next, whither, and so forth. He noticed a shadowy bulk at the end of the counter and switched on a light. A striped gift box—inside was a camp shirt he had admired in a shop window and a pill bottle containing about twenty blue capsules and a note. The note was in Spanish and read:

I can't carry this through customs. For God's sake, don't take more than one at a time.

It was signed with a lipstick imprint and a cartoon drawing of a tubby little heart.

Snow pocketed the pills. He was still getting dark webs in the corners of his vision from the previous night. Distended or broken capillaries, he figured. But there might come a time when a blue pill would seem an appealing option. Feeling vacant, lethargic, he rode the elevator to the lobby, staring at his reflection in the mirrored walls, and went out to the deserted pool area and lay back in a lounge chair. A thin layer of clouds diminished the stars. The rectangle of placid aquamarine water lit by underwater spots and surrounded by empty white chairs complemented his mental state. He closed his eyes and thought about Yara, Guillermo, Tres Santos, redemption, but arrived at no clean answer to the question they posed. Now that he knew something, it seemed he understood less than before. One thing was clear, however. None of his passions were American and perhaps he was no longer an American but a citizen of some international slum, a country of losers without borders or passports or principles. The idea that he had wasted his life brought forth a self-pitying tear. He supposed everyone felt this way at one time or another, even people with lofty accomplishments to their credit, yet they had some basis for redemption, a foundation upon which to build a new life, whereas he did not.

"Hey!" said a voice above him.

A skinny kid of thirteen or fourteen in baggy swim trunks and a navy blue T-shirt peered at him through strings of long brown hair. "Is it too late to go in the pool?"

"I think so, but I don't know for sure," Snow said. "You could dive in and find out."

"My dad'll kick my ass if I get into trouble."

"You down here with your folks?"

"My dad and his girlfriend." The kid flopped onto a chair beside Snow—his lugubrious, bored-shitless look was the same that had dominated Snow's expressions during his teens, and he had a cultivated flatness of affect that armored him against potential human interactions...and yet he appeared to want company.

"How's that going?" Snow asked.

"It fucking sucks."

The writing on the kid's T-shirt was in small lower-case white letters and read:

i went with my father to south beach, the home of wicked, beautiful, diseased women with unnatural desires, and all i caught was this lousy t-shirt

"I like your shirt," said Snow.

The kid glanced down at his chest and sniffed. "My dad had it printed. He thinks it's funny."

"But you don't, huh? Why you wearing it?"

"Because if I wear it long enough, like every day, it'll start pissing him off."

The water in the pool lapped against the tiles, the distant surf hissed, and a breeze stirred the chlorine smell.

"How come you were crying?" the kid asked.

"Huh?"

"You were crying when I came over."

"Oh…yeah."

"How come?"

"I was remembering this old movie."

"Which one?"

"*Bladerunner.*"

No sign of recognition registered on the kid's face.

"You ever see it?" Snow asked.

"Nah. What's it about?"

"These people, they're called replicants. They're clones, they only have a lifespan of a few years. Twelve, I think. Which makes them angry. They do all this dangerous work in outer space, in the far-flung corners of the galaxy. They fight humanity's battles. They're better than people. Stronger and better-looking. So like I said, they're angry, and a few of them return to earth to try and learn if they can get an extension. Have a longer life, you know."

"What happens to them?"

"I don't want to spoil it for you."

"I probably won't ever see it. I'm more into games."

"They die," said Snow. "There's no cure, no remedy, and the bladerunners, these special cops who hunt runaway replicants, they kill them."

The kid thought this over. "You'd think they'd name the movie after the replicants."

"Yeah, you'd think. I guess Bladerunner sounded sexier."

"It's kind of sad," said the kid after a few beats. "But I wouldn't cry about it."

"The saddest part is the replicants aren't just stronger and better-looking. They live more intensely than regular people, even the cops that shoot them."

"I knew a guy who got shot by the cops once, but he was an old sleazebag." The kid stripped off his shirt. "Fuck it!"

He did a racing dive into the pool and swam furiously yet efficiently, showing off several strokes, with an especially strong butterfly. Snow refocused on his troubles, but his thoughts kept returning to Rutger Hauer, tears in rain, and when Daryl Hannah killed the toymaker. Romantic bullshit. He wondered if the book was better. The kid hauled himself out of the pool, dripping, and sat down, gathering his hair into a ponytail and squeezing water from it.

"You didn't stay in long," said Snow.

The kid acted surlier than he had before swimming, as if his nifty strokes had proved a point. "I didn't want to get caught."

"You're a pretty good swimmer."

"I'm all right."

He picked up his T-shirt and slung it over his shoulder, preparing to leave.

"I've got a problem," Snow said, struck by the irrational notion that the kid might have answers, that he had been sent by God or fate or a controlling interstellar agency. "A decision I'm struggling with. That's why I was so emotional earlier. It wasn't about the movie."

This put the kid on the alert. "Yeah?"

Without going into much detail, Snow sketched out his problem.

"You're joking, right?" said the kid snottily. "Take a shit job in some dead-ass place or go have a big weird adventure in another country? Where's the decision? I'd be down there already."

Snow didn't care for the kid giving him attitude. "If your old man let you go, you mean."

"Fuck you, you pussy!"

The kid hurried away toward the hotel.

"Some oracle," said Snow.

V

UNDER A THREATENING SKY, WITH the bumpy, leaden underbellies of the clouds passing low overhead, winded from altitude (eight thousand feet) and exertion, Snow sat on a ridge top high above Tres Santos, eating a chocolate bar and peering at the village through binoculars. Except for two striking additions, the place was as he remembered—an impoverished outpost of humanity whose sorrows were obscured by distance, lent the illusion of tranquility by a lack of definition. Tres Santos was laid out on a relatively flat stretch of ground bounded by two rocky hills, their lower slopes forested with pine, the boughs ghost-dressed with rags and streamers of morning mist. A red dirt road with ruts brimming with rainwater angled away between the worn hills, leading toward the village of Nebaj. Whitewashed one- and two-room houses ranged a cross-hatching of muddy streets, many having a vegetable plot and banana trees for a back yard, and there were wandering pigs, goats, a cantina with a hand-lettered sign above the entrance, Cantina Alhambra, and a couple of dinged-up mini-trucks, Toyotas, both painted a bilious yellow. Surmounting the hill to the east stood the most impressive of the additions—a stubby white building without windows or doors or any feature whatsoever, jutting up from the summit like a strange, geometrically precise tooth from a moldering green jaw. At the base of the hill, about one hundred feet from the edge of the village, was a long single-story structure of pink concrete block with multiple doors and windows—it brought to mind an elementary school annex.

He replaced the binoculars in their case and finished the chocolate bar. An updraft made him shiver. He pulled the cowl of his sweatshirt over his head and zipped up his windbreaker, wishing the overcast would lift. He'd forgotten how cold it could get in the highlands. He shouldered his backpack and started down the hill, losing sight of the village once he was among the pines. With every step he felt lighter, more buoyant, as though the stupidity of what he was doing, the sheer pointlessness, somehow allayed his fears. Near the bottom of the hill he caught sight of Tres Santos again and his resolve faltered, yet not until he set foot on the dirt streets did his pace slow and weakness invade his limbs. He felt as though he were going against an invisible tide flowing in the streets, striving to bear him back among the pines. From his previous visit he surmised that the men of the village were working in the fields that terraced the gentler slopes on the opposite side of the hills, but now their absence seemed evidence of desolation. The women, who normally would wave or peek from their doorways, hid behind curtains and the one person who came forth to greet him, a naked toddler gnawing on a pulped mango, was snatched back into the shadows by his mother. No music, no chatter. Tension was a stench into which the smells of ordure and diesel fuel and cookery were folded.

The Cantina Alhambra was dingy and cramped, with plaster walls adorned by a religious calendar and the framed photo of an elderly Mayan man in a shabby suit coat posing stiffly for the camera—a black crepe ribbon cut diagonally across a corner of the frame. Three wooden tables and eight chairs were scattered about, and fencing off the rear of the room was a crudely carpentered counter behind which stood a pretty girl of fifteen or sixteen with an impassive air, glossy wings of hair falling down her back, and strong Mayan features. She wore a white *huipil* with a pattern of embroidered roses across her breasts. At her rear was a doorway covered by a red-and-white checkered plastic curtain. She spoke neither English nor Spanish, only Mam, the language of the region, and Snow was forced to pantomime his desire for coffee. She produced a bottle of beer and a dusty glass. Snow decided it wasn't worth the effort to attempt a more accurate definition of his needs. He carried the beer to one of the tables and sat with his back against the wall, looking out at the empty street, now and again glancing at the girl, who swiped idly at the countertop with a rag.

Sipping the tepid beer failed to improve his outlook. He'd wait here fifteen minutes, he decided, no more, and then walk about the village, see what developed. And then, depending on his state of mind, he would either approach the pink building—the whorehouse, he suspected—or he would get the hell out of Dodge. At the moment he leaned toward the latter. He had satisfied his commitment, he told himself. It had been without any real purpose, a romantic gesture, a sop to his conscience, a token idiocy. Now that he had come to Tres Santos and found nothing of consequence, seen nothing that bore upon Guillermo or the skull or anything in his past, he could go home with a clear conscience.

Wherever home might be.

He lifted the bottle to his lips and a slim, pale, diminutive man emerged from the back room, pushing aside the plastic curtain. In his early thirties by the look of him, the same height as the girl, at least a head shorter than Snow, with barbered dark brown hair and a loose-fitting, button-less white shirt woven of coarse cloth. He had a TV actor's plastic beauty, a clever symmetry of feature that appeared to be the work of a surgeon whose intent had been to create the face of a male doll with sharp cheekbones and a square jaw, yet one capable of simulating a feminine sensibility, this implied by the largeness of his eyes and the fullness of his lips. He brushed the girl's hair aside and kissed the side of her neck, putting a stamp on the nature of their relationship. He nodded pleasantly to Snow, rested his elbows on the counter, and said, "Doing some exploring, are you?"

Snow, flustered by the man's sudden intrusion, aware of who he must be, said, "I'm sorry. What?"

"Exploring." The man indicated Snow's backpack. "Hiking. Taking in the scenery."

"Oh, right. I'm heading for Nebaj."

"Nebaj? What's the attraction? Nebaj is a shithole."

"There's a bus…to the city."

"Ah!" The man stepped from behind the counter and, without invitation, joined Snow at his table. Snow was alarmed to have him so near. The cantina seemed more cramped than before, as if the man occupied a much greater space than in actuality he did. His movements were deft, precise, yet theatrical in their precision, and his eyes looked to be set at a peculiar angle within their orbits, canted slightly downward, investing his stare with an unnerving flatness. He flicked his hand toward Snow's bottle and said, "A bit early for beer, no?"

"I wanted coffee, but I didn't know how to ask."

The man spoke peremptorily to the girl, who vanished into the back room, and then said brightly, "Coffee's on the way. Care for some eggs, some tortillas?"

"No, that's...I'm fine."

"Itzel can fix you something. It's not a problem."

"I'm not really hungry."

"Well, if you change your mind, it's no problem."

"Thanks."

Snow couldn't place the man's accent. It was definitely not Temalaguan. Possibly some place farther to the south. Argentina or Chile.

"You know," the man said. "You look familiar."

"I don't think so."

"You don't think you look familiar to me? That's quite a presumption."

"I meant, I don't believe we've met."

"I didn't say we'd met." The man's voice held an ounce of irritation and Snow had the impression that he was seething with anger, that anger was his base emotion.

Itzel returned with a tray bearing a jar of instant coffee, another of Cremora, a cup of hot water and a spoon. Chickens squabbled out in the street. A pig trotted by, emitting soft, rhythmic grunts. The coffee restored Snow somewhat and he hunted about for a conversation starter, something that would lighten the mood.

"You've been in my head," the man said.

Snow was caught off guard, perplexed by this peculiar phrasing.

"You or someone very like you," the man went on. "I've been trying to remember."

"I've no idea what you're talking about."

"Of course not. Why should you?"

Snow's sense of unease spiked. "Look, I..."

"You know who *I* am, don't you?"

"Maybe," said Snow, uncertain whether or not he could pull off an outright lie.

"So who am I?"

"I figure you're the guy who lives in the big house on the hill."

"And you believe that because…?"

"You're obviously not from around here and yet you act like you're in charge."

The man chuckled. "I believe you know more about me than that."

Sitting up straight, Snow said, "I'm not sure what you think I know, or why you're fucking with me. I'm just going to drink my coffee and move along."

"That's a real shame. Visitors are at a premium here."

Snow's eyes went to Itzel. She stood with her head down, hands spread on the countertop, unmoving, as if bracing herself.

"You ought to stay a while," the man said. "I'll put you up at my place."

"That's kind of you, but I can't afford to miss my bus."

"Tres Santos may not look like much, but it offers a variety of attractions for the casual tourist. Of course the main attraction is…" He performed a florid gesture, as though presenting himself to an audience. "Me. People come from all over to ask for my advice. I counsel them, and sometimes I put on a little show. An entertainment. It's only an exercise routine, but I'm told it's unique."

"Yeah, well." Snow gulped down coffee. "Wish I had the time."

Without warning, the man hauled Snow's pack over to his side of the table.

"Hey!" Snow made a grab for the pack, but the man fended him off. "What're you doing?"

"Having a peek inside."

The man unzipped the top of the pack and began to inspect the contents.

Snow froze—then, thinking a lack of response would lend substance to the man's suspicion that he, Snow, knew more than he had admitted, he reached for the pack again. The man caught his wrist and squeezed until the bones ground together, causing Snow to cry out. He struggled to break free, but the man's grip was irresistible.

"Please don't do that again," the man said, letting him go.

Snow put pressure on his wrist to quell the pain and gazed out into the street. The gray sky and reddish mud, the puddles, the houses and the portion of the hillside framed by the doorway seemed to flutter, as if all the air and every object within view were made of the same inconstant stuff and troubled by a single disturbance. He was in deep shit, now. A thrill passed through a nerve in his jaw.

The man riffled through Snow's passport. "Snow," he said, and repeated the word a couple of times, as if amused by it. "George Snow."

"Craig," said Snow, speaking out of reflex.

"It says here, George."

"I don't like George. My middle name is Craig. That's what I go by."

"I think George is better for you," said the man indifferently.

He pulled out a filthy work shirt from the pack, deposited it on the floor, and extricated a pair of jeans.

"It's just dirty laundry," Snow said, and rubbed his wrist.

"So it would appear." The man searched the pockets of the jeans. "What's this?"

He fingered out a pill bottle, opened it, and shook three blue capsules out into his palm. "These aren't prescription, are they?"

Alarmed, first by the fact that he had brought the pills through customs unawares, and secondly because he feared the man would force him to take them, Snow finally said, "A woman gave them to me in Miami. I didn't realize I had the bottle with me."

"It's contraband? Drugs? Are they any good?"

"If you like to hallucinate."

The man studied the pills and then popped them into his mouth. After a swift internal debate, realizing that if the man felt he had been poisoned he might punish him, Snow elected to err on the side of caution.

"If I were you I'd bring those things back up quick," he said. "The woman who gave me them, she said not to do more than one."

The man shook out two more pills and gulped them down.

"Jesus! You need to stick a finger down your throat. Trust me, that shit will fuck with your head!"

"Don't be alarmed. Nothing will happen to me."

"I don't know. I've done a shitload of drugs and one of those pills messed me up for a more than a day."

The man seemed to take offense at this statement and said defiantly, "I have a strong resistance to drugs. I could swallow them all and it wouldn't hurt me."

Despite the man's confidence, Snow was unconvinced, but there was nothing for it other than to hope he knew what he was doing.

"If they don't affect you," Snow asked, "why take them?"

"Sometimes they affect me—they just don't harm me." The man lost interest in the pack, pushing it aside with his foot. "Your coffee must be getting cold. Would you care for more?"

Anything to delay, thought Snow. He needed time to think how to deal with this teensy fucker. He said he would and held up his cup to attract Itzel's attention.

"I have better coffee at my place." The man scraped back his chair. "Bring your pack. I'll have someone wash your clothes."

Hoping for guidance, Snow glanced at Itzel once again, but her eyes were glued to the countertop...perhaps a message in itself. He thought about taking a swing at the man, catching him by surprise, but doubted that would end well. Despite his stature, the man's strength hinted at extreme physical competence, so running was probably out of the question.

The man preceded him into the empty street and established a brisk pace, heading for the pink building, but stopped abruptly and, putting a hand on Snow's chest, said, "You know who I am. Don't deny it."

Snow believed that if he admitted to any knowledge, it would be a fatal misstep. He could feel his heart beating against the man's palm. "I've never laid eyes on you before today."

The man struck him in the face—it was a light slap of the kind used to wake someone up, but his hand felt like solid bone and the blow twisted Snow's head around and made him take a backward step.

"I think you have," said the man.

"I swear, I've never seen you! I don't know anything about you!"

The man seemed dispirited, as if he had been seeking not an admission, but rather had hoped to learn something. He started walking again, The gray light flattened things out—the hill with its two buildings resembled a painted backdrop.

"You can call me Jefe," the man said. "That's what everyone calls me, but it's not who I am."

WOMEN PEERED FROM the windows of the pink building as they approached—one of them beckoned, soliciting a visit—yet Jefe paid her no mind and entered a door with an intercom mounted on the wall beside it. Beyond lay a tunnel with concrete walls and a ceiling less than a foot higher than Snow's head, lit for its entire length by fluorescent fixtures. He pictured electric carts rolling along the tunnel, conveying grim uniformed men with side arms and secret orders and missile codes toward a command center. He kept an eye on Jefe, watching for a sign that Luisa's pills were having an affect, but the man's walk held steady and his conversation was terse and on point.

After three or four minutes, by Snow's estimation, they came to a large paneled room with indirect lighting, a burgundy carpet, and three doors leading, he assumed, to bedrooms, kitchen, and so on. Its central feature was a long banquet table set about with high-backed chairs, the dining surface fashioned from an ancient church door carved with a complex scene that illustrated a typically Temalaguan confusion of cosmologies—anguished men and woman supplicating the angels who hovered just beyond reach, appearing both disinterested in their suffering and unaware of the doings of the less well-defined beings above them who looked to be doing a portage across the heavens with some kind of solar vessel. A mahogany sideboard stood against one wall, supporting an array of liquor bottles, ice buckets, and glasses, and mounted above it was a flat screen TV. Four photographic prints in aluminum frames hung on the opposite wall, each depicting a spectacular cloud formation. For all the luxuriousness of its appointments, the room stood two-thirds empty, far too spacious for such a paucity of furnishings, and this indicated to Snow that while its primary inhabitant might have an awareness of interior decoration, he was seriously myopic as regarded an overall aesthetic.

Jefe told him to have a seat at the table, spoke into an intercom mounted on the wall, and then said to Snow, "I'm going upstairs for an hour or two." He opened the door to reveal a stairwell. "Yara will bring coffee and whatever else you require."

Snow had nurtured a faint hope that Yara had survived the disappearance of the cult, but that had been wishful thinking and now, hearing her name, her presence alluded to so casually, it was as if a bomb had gone off in his head, obliterating his ability to reason. Once Jefe had gone he stood up from the table and immediately sat back down, dizzy to the point of passing out. He stared at the two doors at the far end of the room, shards of memory falling through his mental sky, and when a woman entered, wearing a shapeless gray smock (a nightgown, his initial impression), moving stiffly, slowly, her hair close cropped, a monastic look, lines of strain on her face deeper than those he would have predicted a thirty-year-old to have...and when he recognized her to be Yara, *his* Yara, miraculously alive and still beautiful despite the attrition of time, he started up from his chair again, intending to embrace her, a great joy building, enfolding him like a garment he had prepared in anticipation of this day yet never thought to wear...but then he halted his approach. Her expression betrayed no trace of any kindred emotion, not an ounce of welcome or happiness. She wrangled a chair back from the table and collapsed into it, breathing shallowly. After collecting herself, she said, "You have some things to wash?"

"Yara," he said. "It's me...Craig."

"I know who you are. Show me your clothes and I'll wash them."

Baffled by her response, he asked what he had done to anger her.

"Apart from running out on me?" She sniffed. "Nothing."

"I tried to persuade you to come with me."

"You should have tried harder. You could at least have told me you were leaving. You didn't have to sneak away."

"You don't..."

"I hunted for you everywhere. People thought I was demented, I went on about you so. You should have told me. I wouldn't have tried to stop you and we could have said a proper goodbye."

"It was all..." He gave his head a frustrated shake. "You don't understand how much I beat myself up for abandoning you, but I was afraid. I didn't know what else to do."

"I guess I shouldn't blame you for being yourself."

That stung him, but he reminded himself that these emotional post-mortems unfailingly began with a litany of bitterness.

"You're not truly at fault," she said. "You weren't a part of what was going on. But it hurt and I hated you for a long time. Seeing you again brings back a great deal of anger and heartsickness, but I suppose it's just residual emotion."

"Yara, listen. I…"

"Don't bother. It's all in the past."

"Maybe for you. It's been my present for the last thirteen years."

She laughed humorlessly. "Don't tell me you're a romantic at heart!"

"Listen to me for a minute, okay?"

"If you've come here thinking you can rekindle our affair, forget it. That part of my life is over."

"How can that be?" he asked. "You're still young, you're a beautiful woman."

She liked hearing that, he could tell, yet tried to hide the fact, thinning her lips in disapproval.

"I didn't come here for any reason I can name," he said. "I assumed you were dead. I may have hoped to see you again, but the hope wasn't real. It was…"

"Stop it!"

She slapped the table and, as if cued by that percussive sound, a mechanical grinding issued from the stairwell, growing louder with each passing second, impeding their conversation.

"What the hell's that?" Snow asked.

"He's flying. Shut the door."

Snow did as instructed, reducing the noise by half, and returned to the table.

"Did you notice there aren't any men in the village?" Yara asked, cutting off his unspoken question. "Within a month after we came to Tres Santos, Jefe had killed them all. Some tried to run, he seemed to know when they ran, and where, and he hunted them down. He kills every man who comes here except for the PVO guys, and he'll kill them once they've outlived their usefulness. I actually believe he gets along with men better than he does with women, but it's like he's obeying some beastly imperative, wiping out the competition." She paused. "He's probably going to kill you."

Snow wanted to make light of what she had told him, but could not.

"Don't look so shocked," Yara said. "I don't know how you found this place, but you knew about the PVO, didn't you? You must have realized you were taking a risk by coming here."

"There must be some way of dealing with him. What should I do?"

Yara's face, which had softened a little, walled over again. "I can't help you."

Snow was hard put to think of anything to say.

"Do you want me to explain?" Yara asked. "Can you listen without interrupting, without telling me I'm being ridiculous? I don't have the patience for that anymore. There's a lot I don't understand, but what I know, I know."

"How long have I got?"

"Chances are you're safe for today." She brushed strands of hair from her eyes and, with no small degree of malice, said, "Even if I'm wrong, we have time. He'll be flying for hours."

"AS YOU RECALL," Yara began, "when we were together I used to go into the city to meet with various men, passing along Griaule's instructions and delivering the money I'd collected from Club Sexy and other sources. I recalled little of those meetings, because I was under his thrall. But soon I realized the money was being used to establish the PVO, to fund their arms purchases and recruitment campaigns…even the construction of this complex. It was completed years before Jefe and I took up residence, and built according to a design I imparted to the architect. Of course I have no recollection of this, but I've been assured that was the case.

"As the party grew in strength and numbers, the job of fund-raising was taken over by men who could operate with more efficiency than I, but I continued to serve as a conduit between the dragon and the party. It might seem odd that a woman could function as the putative leader of a male-dominated organization, especially once the party was on a solid footing. At any rate, it seemed odd to me. Yet I came to understand that extremist groups depend on a mystical element, an occult component, to lend gravitas to their actions. I was for the PVO that mystical element, the Virgin Mary who in effect gave birth to their messiah, so I was granted immunity from their prejudices, protected from their violence. Whenever a man crossed the line with me, as happened more than once, the party dealt with him mercilessly.

"When you lived with me I wasn't altogether certain about things. There were times I doubted my sanity and your doubts, your accusations, affected me more than I let on. Had you stayed, I might well have fled with you, because I was having a crisis of faith. I questioned the dragon's reality and, in moments during which I was satisfied that he *did* exist and was not simply a function of my madness, I questioned his plan. Getting involved with the PVO was the antithesis of what I wanted for myself, for the country. After you left, however, my communication with the dragon sharpened. Previously I went into that little bone chamber, I went to sleep and emerged with vague messages. Now those messages came into my head while I was awake and were more defined. I could sense their flavor and configuration. It became evident that the PVO was only a step in Griaule's plan. They would protect the dragon reborn until he no longer needed them. For a while I believed he had brought you and me together for some purpose. To test my faith, perhaps. But I know now that was a conceit. Disembodied, his will was weak and he required years to shape people to his purposes. I overestimated his influence where we were concerned.

"Along with sharpened communication I experienced painful side effects that limited my mobility. Before long I was unable to venture into the city and I concentrated my efforts on the adherents, lecturing them on my enhanced appreciation of the dragon's nature, counseling them and presiding over events like the one that frightened you away. You had a right to be afraid, as it turned out, but after each of them I felt enraptured, understanding that someday they would result in the achievement of our goal. We had additions to our community, and subtractions. Colonel de Lugo died, but not before he recruited his replacement. That was the way of it. Some left, others arrived, and little by little we approached the right mix of people that would enable the miracle to occur. I became so involved with the dragon, I was scarcely aware of my own life. One morning I woke to the knowledge that this would be the day. Everything was so sharp, so clear. I knew precisely what to do. From the first moment when the dragon touched my mind, I recognized that I would be the instrument of his renewal, but not until then did I fully comprehend the nature of that renewal, the act of transubstantiation it demanded. In this regard, the adherents had been closer to the truth than I. He may have whispered a promise to them, a guarantee that they would live on in him, and for all I know they do live on. But he made no such promise to me and I thought I was to die that morning.

"I gathered the adherents in front of the skull and brought them into a trance state. The dragon's mind and my own were in perfect unity, interpenetrating. His thoughts were mine, and mine his. What was about to happen might be seen as horrific, an event to rival Jonestown, as you had said, but all I saw was the perfection of Griaule's design and I felt exalted to be part of it. The air grew warm, uncomfortably warm. Several people fainted—I remember fretting about them, but my main worry was whether they needed to be conscious for the miracle to take place. And then my clarity went away, my mind clouded over. When I regained my senses I discovered that I was wandering in the jungle, far from the skull. It was still hot and seconds later a burst of heat boiled through the trees, like the heat from an explosion, knocking me off my feet. I made my way to the clearing as rapidly as I could manage. The shelters had been flattened and the adherents were gone. The skull, too, was gone, yet the trees and the bushes were virtually undamaged, and there was no sign of scorching or charring. I was distraught. The deaths of hundreds of people, no matter I had anticipated this outcome…how could I feel otherwise? But my feelings may have been due less to grief than to the fact that I had not witnessed the miracle. All those years laboring to create it, and I had missed it! Where was the result? Had nothing happened apart from a mass disappearance? I looked around the clearing, hoping to find some evidence as to what had taken place. I think I was on the verge of losing my mind. I stumbled about, going first one direction and then another, beating aside the brush, becoming frantic, until at last I spotted Jefe. He lay curled up on a patch of emerald moss, close to where the jawbone had rested. A beautiful little man, naked and perfect. I had believed the dragon would be reborn in his original form, but I knew him at once. The sight was so serene and lovely, it was like a balm to me. It had the quality of myth. His milky skin against the oval of vivid moss, his fists clenched like a newborn infant's. I went to him and cradled him in my arms. He woke to my touch and gazed about in confusion, unable to speak, clinging to me. Once he was able to stand

I helped him out to the road. Shortly thereafter the PVO showed up and brought us to Tres Santos."

Yara drew a deep breath and released it slowly.

"In the years since," she continued, "he's made unbelievable progress. He's learned to speak and perform as a human. It wasn't learning, really, I don't think. I'd teach him one thing and within a day or two he'd display a complete spectrum of behaviors. As if we'd given him a key and he unlocked a door behind which a store of knowledge was hidden. Yet his instincts are different from ours and he doesn't understand us very well. He assists the PVO with their schemes—he has an amazing grasp of politics and is a brilliant tactician. He has no memory of his life prior to his rebirth, yet he does recall the plan for political dominance he developed and he knows something is not as it should be. He talks about a recurring dream, a vision in which he stands in an arena before thousands of people and says that when that dream becomes reality he will undergo a change—from what I gather he's referring to a second alchemical act, a more radical transformation, one that will enable him to regain his original form and fly as once he did, without the need for mechanical aids." She laughed merrily, a laugh that seemed misplaced to Snow. "He'd spend all his time flying if I let him. Neither the PVO nor I have been in a hurry to illuminate him about his past. Rushing the process would damage him, I believe, and their concern is fueled by a desire to keep him ignorant and under their control. They think that once he's done his duty for them, they'll get rid of him. They haven't accepted the fact that their control is limited…if it exists at all."

Yara winced as she adjusted her posture. "That's the story in brief. It sounds mad, I know, but…" She shrugged.

It did sound mad, classically delusional, and Snow would have liked to pass it off as madness, but sufficient evidence existed to suggest that it was not and he believed to a certainty that he was in imminent danger. He had only half-listened to much of her account, consumed by worries about his future, but one sentence in particular had attracted his notice: "He'd spend all his time flying if I let him." From this he deduced that Yara was capable of influencing Jefe.

"So your position here is…what?" he asked. "Surrogate mother?"

"In the beginning, yes, that would have been an accurate description of my function. But as he's matured I've become more of a nurse, a servant. He turns to me for advice now and then, and he trusts me. I doubt that'll change."

"Isn't there anything you can tell me that'll help with my situation? You must know some way of playing him. What buttons to push."

"Flattery," she said. "He responds to flattery, but he's so mercurial, so volatile…it may prolong things, but sooner or later he'll turn on you."

"Then I guess my best bet is to run."

"Don't!" She stretched out a hand as if to hold him back, and then seemed flustered by her show of concern. "When someone tries to escape him, he's spectacularly cruel. They, the PVO…they set snipers in the hills to watch him. He found out and chased them down and tore them limb from limb."

"You saw this?"

"I saw what he did to the man who gave the snipers their orders. Two other PVO officials witnessed the murder as well. And yet they still believe they can control him."

"Can he be? Controlled?"

"You're asking if *I* can control him? I don't want to. He's the only chance we've got."

The old political argument again—any change is good, whatever the risk. It was proof against logic, but nonetheless Snow said, "What about the cost? He's already slaughtered the men in the village and who knows how many more. Next he…"

"What do you know about costs? I've got more than eight hundred souls on my conscience, and many of them friends. I've known for years that I'm damned. I want him to go through another transformation, even if thousands are killed in the process. He has no real depth of interest in us. Once he's able to fly he'll go his own way and leave us to sort things out. The PVO won't survive his absence—they're incompetent. I know this for a fact because I helped to recruit their leadership. The country will explode, the army will be in chaos, without direction, and we'll have the opportunity for reform in Temalagua."

"If things are as you say…"

"They are!"

"It's a shaky goddamn premise. What if you're wrong? What if he doesn't go his own way, or if this second transformation is a fantasy? You'll be handing over your country to a fucking monster."

"We've had worse." Her voice became less strident and a note of tenderness crept in. "You don't know him like I do. He doesn't care about any human thing, about revenge or politics. They're a means to an end, that's all. Admittedly it's an end he can't yet see, because he's in the dark about his past. He doesn't remember the centuries he spent paralyzed on a plain, or much of anything before that morning when he woke in the jungle—but he's obeying his instincts, acting out the behaviors he learned when he was a dragon. All he really wants to do is fly about and fuck female dragons. You of all people should understand that."

Ignoring the dig, Snow said, "He's going to be pretty pissed off when he discovers there aren't any female dragons."

"You don't know that there aren't."

"You're talking about those old wives tales? The ones that claim dragons are still living in Argentina?" He made a derisive sound, expelling a jet of air between his lips. "Or maybe Oz."

"You see? This is what you always do. We can't have a conversation without you ridiculing me. You're right! I don't have all the answers and I may be proved wrong in the end. But I've been right so far, haven't I?"

The mechanical noise overhead rose in pitch and they sat for half a minute without speaking.

"You could help me if you wanted," said Snow churlishly.

Yara sighed impatiently and said, "What did you do after you left me?"

"What's that got to do with anything?"

"Humor me. Where did you go after you left Temalagua?"

"Home."

"And what did you do there?"

"I got a job. Wrote a little."

"I imagine there were quite a few women in your life. And drugs."

"Yeah, you know. But mainly I thought about you. I realized…"

"So you had a job, probably something that just allowed you to get by. You wrote some things no one ever saw…"

"I published some stuff!"

"And you fucked around. You lived the same kind of life in Idaho you lived here. That's the man you expect me to sacrifice everything for? If I could help you, which I can't, that's the man I should give up…"

"That's not fair!"

"No? You just admitted it."

"Superficially, yeah. That's how it was. I was accustomed to that kind of life. But there were other things going on with me."

"You've got hidden depths? Is that what you're telling me? You've grown a soul? Who cares? You expect me to toss aside the one chance we have of getting rid of the real villains? And I should do this because of the way you once made me feel?" She waved her hand about as if dispersing a swarm of gnats. "Fuck it! Enough! I have to wash your clothes!"

She levered herself up from the chair, biting her lip, and stood, wobbly, trying to stabilize herself. He took hold of her elbow and, obeying an old reflex, she leaned into his shoulder. He slipped an arm about her waist—despite her infirmity it was supple as ever. She tensed, her breath quickened, and he found himself wondering how long it had been since she'd had a lover.

THAT EVENING YARA ushered Snow into a narrow corridor off the dining area ranged by a series of small bedrooms—like cells, really—each with plain concrete walls, a bath, and no lock on the door. She installed him in one of these and told him she was down the hall if he needed anything. He started to say that what he needed was her honesty, her help, but if her help were forthcoming, a direct approach was not the way to achieve it. Subtle pressure such as he had been applying ever since their initial conversation, reminding her of their golden moments years before, touching her as often as possible and sowing doubts about Jefe whenever he saw an opening, yet doing so slyly, indirectly—that was his best hope of influencing her. He knew he had made some progress, but how much longer could he afford to be subtle?

Lying in bed, he gave the situation a turn or two, but soon dozed off, waking some time later (an hour or two later, judging by his stupor) with the impression that someone else was in the room. He slit his eyes and saw a man standing beside the bed—just his trouser legs—and pretended to be asleep. The seconds slogged past. His circulatory system whined, his heart thudded and then he felt the man's breath warm on his cheek. Recalling Yara's talk about Jefe's savagery, picturing him squatting beside the bed, sniffing out his fright and deliberating his fate, it was all he could do to refrain from shouting and scrambling away—yet he kept his eyes shut and his respiration normal until he heard the faint click of the door closing. Still terrified, he went over to the sink and splashed cold water onto his face. The mechanisms of his thought were gummed up, gears clotted with a sludge of fear. He pulled on his jeans and, after making certain the coast was clear, with no plan in mind, a frightened man making for the known, the familiar, he padded along the hall toward Yara's room. Her door was open half an inch. He eased it wider.

She sat naked upon her bed, applying ointment to her pale skin, to the edges of what appeared in the dim yellow light of a reading lamp to be dark green slashes (not unlike a tiger's stripes in form) that curved along her legs and torso and back. She was fleshier than she had been in her teens, her breasts larger and more pendulous, her pubic hair unruly, yet she was still beautiful, exquisitely proportioned, and thus after understanding that the dark green areas were some sort of growth, a hard, unyielding substance similar to the diamond-shaped convexity centering her tattoo, her tramp stamp, the likeness of a dragon's scale, an implant she'd said…after understanding this he felt a mix of revulsion and sympathy and arousal. She set the tube of ointment on the bedside table among a phalanx of medicine bottles, opened a plastic container, and squeezed a dab of lotion into her palm. The diamond shape of the original scale (Snow now assumed it to be a scale) had lost its integrity and become a blotch occupying much of her lower back, the epicenter from which this apparent contagion had spread—as she reached behind her with the lotion, twisting her neck about so she could see to apply it, she caught sight of Snow. She gasped and fell onto her side, dropping the container and scrambling to cover herself. Snow entered the room and she said, "I don't want you to see! Please!" He perched on the side of the bed and laid a finger on her lips to mute her speech. Her eyes brightened with tears. "Please," she said again. He had questions, but knew what she needed from im. He picked up the plastic container and began to rub the lotion in, concentrating on places where the scale merged with the skin. She covered her face with her hands and sobbed, but he continued his ministrations, kneading the lotion into her skin, and felt stress draining from her body. Once he finished with her back, he turned her toward him and focused his attention on the stripes (he viewed them now as veins of a strange mineral) crossing her abdomen and fettering the slopes of her breasts, gripping and partly supporting them as would some cruel instrument of bondage. She searched his face, searching it (he suspected) for some twitch that would trigger her detectors, an aberrant expression conveying an excess of pity, a delight in the perverse, anything apart from an acceptable devotion. He maintained a calm, dutiful exterior, intent upon his task, and she surrendered herself, she closed her eyes and let him work. Before long, sighs escaped her lips, musical and daft, like the delicate sounds a contented infant might make. An urgency in her flesh manifested as a shudder, an arching of the back. Careful not to jostle her, he lay down and cupped her face in his hands and kissed her. Her mouth was slack, but soon she responded and when he broke from the kiss he saw that the lines of strain around her eyes and mouth were less deep, as if years had fallen away. He touched her belly, her nipples, the soft places between the stripes of her affliction—she caught his hand and whispered, "I want you, but you can't come inside me. It'll hurt me if you do." He was too riveted on her to explain that this act, born of empathy, had evolved into one of desire. His decade-long obsession had been given release and he was redeemed by her pleasure, he needed nothing else. He eased his fingers into the heated damp of her, eliciting a cry, but not one of pain. As he guided her through a prolonged and convulsive orgasm, he pressed his face close to hers and said, "I love you." He kept on repeating the words, a counterpoint to her moans, as if this inculcation were a proof of love, until her thighs clamped together, trapping his hand, and she lay with her head tight against his chest, trembling, enduring the final aftershocks.

"Are you okay?" he asked.

She nodded, but gave no further reply, her breath coming in shudders.

It began to feel awkward, holding her that way and not speaking, and he asked if she wanted him to leave. Another nod. She must be, he decided, ashamed of what had happened, or confused by it, or both.

He got up and adjusted his belt. "Will I see you in the morning?"

An affirmative noise.

He started to tell her once again that he loved her, but thought she might not want to hear it. He went to the door, peeked out into the hall.

"Craig."

She had pulled the sheet up so that her head and shoulders were visible, and—separated by an expanse of the white cloth, appearing to be part of a separate body—her right leg from the knee down, marked by dark green striations.

"Tomorrow," she said. "If not tomorrow, soon…he'll bring the women from the pink house."

"The prostitutes?"

"Yes, and others. He'll throw a party. The women will be dressed provocatively. Whatever you do, don't flirt with them. Ignore them. Act as if you're offended by their interest in you."

"All right."

"It's a test, something he does in order to discover whether or not you're interested in his women. If you don't show interest, that will buy you some time."

He expected her to say more, but when nothing was forthcoming he peered out into the hall again.

"Craig."

"Yeah?"

"I…never mind."

"What about you and me?" He turned from the door. "Will that piss him off?"

Time became elastic, stretching out into a single un-demarcated moment. At long last she said, "I'm not his woman."

OVER THE NEXT days all Snow's questions evaporated, those dating from years before as well as those arising from his encounter with Yara. It was obvious she had been correct in her belief that there was magic in the world, albeit of a dire sort. The striping of dark green scale that defiled

her body could not be explained by any means other than her contact with
the dragon. It had to be a physical consequence of their unnatural spiritual
union, a punishment levied upon her for consorting with beasts, a curse
she had accepted in order to achieve her ends. He was nearly persuaded to
her opinion that Jefe might be a force for good and, left to his own devices,
would allow Temalagua to determine its destiny—but the recognition that
he would be long dead by the time such a future came to pass diminished
his enthusiasm for the idea.

As Yara predicted, on the night following their encounter Jefe herded
a group of approximately twenty attractive women into the dining room,
all clad in lingerie. Judging by Luisa Bazan's story, Snow accepted that her
husband Enrique had purchased every scrap of silk and lace that adorned
them, but that Luisa's accusations of infidelity were without merit, or else
(if he were to believe Yara) Enrique would be dead. Among the women
was the girl from the cantina, Itzel. Jefe thrust her at him and, expres-
sionless, she attempted to fondle his genitals. Snow, as instructed, rejected
her. Before long the room was aflutter with drunken, chattering, under-
dressed women who came at him singly and in pairs, making much over
him, cooing and caressing, while Jefe watched icily from a doorway. Snow
was impervious to their tender assaults, affecting boredom, brushing them
off, winding up alone in a corner and thinking that Griuale's legendary
subtlety must have gone glimmering along with his memories, because
Jefe was nothing if not unsubtle. He felt he would have been able to see
through this deception without Yara's help, and he speculated that Griaule
may never have been a subtle creature, that his reputed prowess in this
regard had been exaggerated due to his bulk (even a gross manipulation
would be perceived as a subtlety when the manipulator was roughly the
size of a county in Rhode Island) and to the ease with which people could
be manipulated, thanks in large part to their eagerness to absolve themselves of responsibility and shift blame for their behavior onto an outside
influence, as if they were at the mercy of forces beyond their control.

Coincidentally, there were moments during the ensuing week when
Snow saw himself as a master of calculation and guile. Because he was
consumed by the prospect of death, these moments were fleeting, and
yet they seemed of critical importance, crucial to his self-awareness, his

self-worth, his entire sense of self inclusive of his will to survive. Each night, a male Sheherazade, he visited Yara in her room and made love to her, each night extracting information from her (a tip, a tendency, an allusion) that would enable him to prolong his life. Afterward he would have a flash of satisfaction, a not-quite gloating appreciation of his canniness. Yet at the same time his emotional connection with her deepened, as did his desire to please her, to ease her burdens—it injured him to watch her move about the complex, she was so frail and had so little stamina. These two strains of behavior appeared intertwined like the coils of a double helix, neither of them having primacy over nor pre-dating the other, neither seeming more authentic, but he felt certain that one of them concealed a fathering principle. He sought to sneak up on himself, to catch himself unawares and snatch a glimpse of the bottom of his soul, hoping to discern whether selflessness or self-interest was the ground from which all else sprouted, or if they were an embodiment of an essential duality, two sides of the same coin. He failed to reach a conclusion, of course, and it seemed to him that his fear of death was not much greater than the fear that he might never acquire the slightest knowledge of his own heart.

One night toward the end of the week, Yara came astride Snow, allow-ing him to penetrate her. Her movements were rickety and it was appar-ent some pain was involved, but she went past the pain and seemed to lose herself in the act. Snow held her by the hips, guiding her, helping her move, yet he wasn't as active as he would ordinarily have been, not wishing to hurt her. The striping on her body generated a fantasy that he had been transported to a cell in a Tibetan temple lit with the glow from a butter lamp, and she was a woman sprung from one of the legends illustrated by the tapestries that hung about the place, the handmaiden of an obscure god or herself the female incarnation of an elusive archetype, her ritual markings symbols in a perfected language known only to nine bodhisatt-vas that pointed up rather than detracted from her beauty. She flowed like honey around him and he, too, lost himself in the moment, in the old con-fusions of their relationship and the new. Yet once they were spent, as they lay quietly together, his mind began to run its usual circuits and he asked why she had chosen this night to make love to him.

"'Make love,'" she said teasingly. "You never said that when we were first together. It was always, 'Let's fuck.' You've become so gentlemanly."

Impatient with her, he said, "Okay. Why did you fuck me?"

"I couldn't bear not to any longer."

"It wasn't like a pity fuck? You weren't saying goodbye?"

He expected a denial, but she said, "I don't know."

"What's that mean?"

"It means I don't know!"

He waited for an explanation.

"In the morning Jefe may invite you to watch him fly," she said. "He'll..."

"I should say, 'No,' right? Pretend to be sick or something."

"No. You have to accept. And you have to flatter him constantly while he's flying. I'll come with you if I can, but he may send me away. If that happens, you have to cheer and applaud...applaud fervently no matter how long he flies. Be prepared for him to fly a long time. Several hours."

Half-formed thoughts crowded one another aside in Snow's head— a cold spot bloomed beneath his breastbone.

"I have to do something," he said.

Yara pressed herself against him.

"I can't just sit around here waiting to be executed."

She flung an arm across his stomach, resting her head on his chest so he could see nothing of her face.

"Yara?"

"I'm here," she said.

EVERY MORNING AT TEN AM Jefe ate his single meal of the day, consisting of four roast chickens. He would sit at the head of the dining room table, tearing off strips of meat, chewing methodically, gnawing clean the bones, reducing the birds to skeletal remains while Yara and Snow observed from their chairs. At Yara's prompting Snow would offer absurdly fawning statements such as "You're looking fit today" and "I wish I had your appetite," and Jefe would cut his eyes toward him, grunt, and then cast his gaze toward another portion of the room, as if he found there something of greater interest. From time to time he would address himself to Yara, reminding her of some obligation, but otherwise he ignored her presence. On this particular morning, however, his eyes never wavered from Snow, transmitting a steely neutrality. As the number of chickens dwindled, believing his life could be measured in bites, he experienced a predictable cycling of conflicting emotions (fear, love for Yara, regret, anger at Yara for being complicit in his decision to stay, self-recrimination over that anger, fear...etc.) and at length decided that he'd had enough and would do or say something to bring matters to a head. The question of whether he would have acted on his decision was rendered moot by a loud buzzing that issued from the TV. A grainy picture appeared on the screen showing three men beside the pink house, at the entrance to the complex, one a boy of college age with a stubbly scalp, wearing a shiny rayon jacket embellished by the signature NY of the New York Yankees, and two fleshy, prosperous-looking types in their forties, also wearing jackets, but of leather. Jefe's aloof manner did not change, but anger streamed off him. He walked over to the TV, half a chicken in his hand, and continued to eat, watching the men shift about.

The largest of the three spoke into the box mounted beside the door. "Jefe! We need to talk with you!"

Without turning from the screen, Jefe waggled a hand at Yara—she made her way haltingly toward the intercom, keyed the speaker, and said, "What do you want? You know he doesn't like surprise visits."

"We have an urgent matter to discuss," said the man. "We called, but there was no signal."

Jefe put his finger on the screen, touching the young man's image.

"Who's the kid?" Yara asked.

"Chuy Velasquez. He's one of us," said the other man. "We had car trouble and he volunteered to drive us."

"It's an honor..." Chuy began, but the big man shushed him.

Yara asked Jefe if she should have Chuy wait outside. Jefe bit off another mouthful of chicken.

The intercom squawked. "Yara?"

"He's thinking it over," she said to the men outside.

"This is intolerable," Jefe said without emotion, as if the intolerable were merely a fact of his existence. "Ask them what they wish to discuss."

THE SKULL

Yara did as instructed and the big man said, "We're having difficulty with Ortega. We could use force, and we will should it become necessary, but that will complicate our future dealings with him. The shipment is due in tomorrow and I didn't want to move without consulting you."

Jefe made a hissing nose and pointed at the door leading to the stairs. "Wait for me there."

"Both of us?" Yara asked.

"Just him." He glanced over his shoulder at Snow. "You don't mind, do you? Private business."

The stairwell was unheated and, after hovering for ten or fifteen minutes, unable to hear what was going on in the dining room, feeling the bite of the chill, Snow ascended the stairs. His spirits had been lifted by his banishment—it stood to reason that since Jefe did not want him to hear private matters discussed, this could be interpreted as a sign that Snow's survival was guaranteed. For a while, anyway. If Jefe wasn't merely being cautious. If his actions were governed by a logical scheme approximating reason, which of course they were not. By the time Snow had climbed four flights of stairs, his natural pessimism had been restored. Preoccupied with worry, he pushed through the door at the top of the stairway and went several paces onward before he understood that he had penetrated to the heart of Jefe's complex and perhaps to the essence of his dragon-soul.

He stood in the depths of an enormous, well-lit shaft, one wide enough to encompass three or four good-sized barns, a structure whose terminus, he realized, had to be the white, windowless building surmounting the hill. The top of the shaft, five or six hundred feet above, was the blue of a deep autumn sky and spread across the walls were photomurals of the four framed prints in the dining room: cloudy, pristine Himalayas pierced by diamond rays of sun; tiers of parchment-colored, painterly clouds edged with peach and golden-white, complexities of dust and light that called to mind an elaborate music; a Turner-esque chaos of smoky stuff drenched in red and gold, yielding a brassy radiance redolent of a war in heaven; pale billows of cloud shading to indigo, some of them resembling figures and faces that were nearly recognizable, like the ghosts of Great Identities dissolving into dusk. Hundreds, maybe thousands of fine-linked silver chains strung ten feet apart were suspended from the ceiling, stretched taut, running the length of the shaft and vanishing into curved tracks on the concrete floor. Snow made to slide one of the chains along its track, but it wouldn't budge. He thought there must be some controlling mechanism and, as he searched for it, he spotted a discoloration on the floor out among the chains. On closer inspection it appeared to be a dried-up pool of blood. Feeling like a child alone in a forest of skinny silver trees that offered neither shade nor protection, he hurried back down the stairs and sat on the bottom step, trying to equate the grandeur and strangeness of the shaft with the vicious killer in the next room, imagining that if a dragon-become-a-man had the slightest refinement it would have something to do with the sky...and yet it was difficult to believe a minimal creature such as Jefe deriving pleasure from anything apart from the exercise of power. Worn down by stress, he gave up analyzing the situation and rested his head on his forearms, his mind drumming with a single dread thought.

A half-hour later, more or less, Yara invited him back into the dining room. Flanked by his two friends, the big man stood partway out the tunnel door—he had a thick, glossy head of hair and a mustache trimmed to a straight line above an arrogant mouth. Belly flab overlapped his belt. His image on the TV had been too grainy to identify, but Snow knew him now: Enrique Bazan. He'd run into him once or twice at the school. Hoping that Bazan would not remember those meetings, Snow took a seat next to Yara and gave no sign of recognition, but Bazan said in a demanding tone, "What's this prick doing here?"

"Mister Snow is a guest." Standing between the table and Bazan, Jefe glanced back and forth between the two men, his face sharp with interest. "Do you know each other?"

With bad grace, Bazan said, "He's my son's teacher."

Jefe's eyes swerved to Snow. "Small world, eh?"

"I *used* to be your son's teacher," said Snow. "I resigned from the school some time ago."

"Is that so?" Bazan's voice surged in volume. "Then why does Luisa talk about you all the time? Tell me that!"

Yara said, "Don't you have business elsewhere, Enrique?"

"Indeed," said Jefe. "I suggest we leave this for another day."

Bazan's face grew flushed. "Fuck that! I want to ask him some questions."

The elder of his companions, a man cut from similar cloth, same mustache, same belly flab, but shorter and with a receding hairline, moved in front of Bazan, or else he might have come at Snow.

"The son-of-a-bitch has been fucking my wife!" Bazan tried to throw the smaller man aside, but Chuy helped restrain him.

"Is this true?" Jefe's enjoyment of the moment was evident in his tone of prim amusement. "Have you been trifling with Luisa's affections?"

"Hell, no!" Snow made as if to stand, willing to let his anger rip after so long an enforced repression, but Yara dug her nails into his arm.

Bazan shook his head furiously, like a bull swarmed by bees. "What the fuck is he doing here?"

"I was hiking in the hills," said Snow. "Jefe asked me to stay. As for your wife, I've never had so much as a cup of coffee with her."

"Calm yourself, Enrique." Jefe joined the two men who had Bazan backed against the wall. "Whoever's been at your wife, I'm certain you'll get to the bottom of it."

"It's him! I can tell by the way she talks about him!"

"That's your proof? Luisa talks about him? It's hardly convincing."

"Man, I've been married to her fat ass for eleven years! I know the signs!"

"It doesn't matter who's been staining your bed sheets," Jefe said. "The real crime has nothing to do with your wife. Right, Chuy?"

Jefe patted Chuy on the back, shifted a hand to the nape of his neck, and Chuy, responding to this amiable gesture, looked to him over his shoulder, a smile aborning on his face...and then the smile, before it had fully established itself, dissolved into an expression of befuddlement, and thereafter into one of shock and pain. His right leg began to shake. Spittle flew from his lips.

"The real crime is you bringing someone here who wasn't invited," Jefe said to Bazan. "Someone I don't know."

Chuy clawed feebly at Jefe's hand and loosed a warbling note that thinned into a keening. His shoes were not planted on the floor, but drifted across the carpet, their toes grazing the burgundy nap.

"Jefe, don't do this." Bazan eased away from him. "He's a good kid."

Chuy's shoulders hitched violently, his arms went rigid, held out to the sides like a marionette whose elbow-strings had been yanked.

Yara heaved up from her chair. "The boy's done nothing. Let him go!"

Startled, Jefe turned on her, rag-dolling Chuy.

"No one's harmed you." She pried at Jefe's fingers, trying to loosen his grip. "He did you a favor by driving them. Or would you prefer to have been kept in the dark about Ortega? Let him go. Let Enrique get on with his business."

"Keep out of this!" Jefe said.

"This is how leaders treat their friends." She pried at his fingers again. "Presidents, generals, kings. Whatever title they give themselves, they're pigs. Villains. You have to be better than that."

So much fury was concentrated in Jefe's face, Snow thought it might explode.

Yara's words took on a blathering tone, as if she were counseling a disobedient child while straightening his collar. "You swore you'd pay attention to my advice. Well, I'm advising you now. You mustn't lash out every time someone does something that doesn't please you. You have to use some discretion."

Jefe backhanded her, striking her side, releasing Chuy at the same moment. She reeled back against the table, shrieked and clutched her hip, and sagged to the floor. Yet after the briefest of intervals she sat up and continued her scolding, as though the shove had been but a trivial interruption. Jefe went toward her and Snow, thinking he was going to hit her again, came out of his chair and said, "Well done! A man has to maintain order in his house."

Jefe's head snapped toward him.

"Without discipline at home," said Snow, "you can have no discipline. Who are these people to think they can rule you while you rule their country? It's absurd!"

"You should act from the standpoint of reason, not emotion." Yara managed to get to her knees. "You can't simply react to events."

Jefe turned back to her.

"Reason, yes. But you can't tolerate an insult to your authority." Snow began to understand where this byplay might lead. "There has to be a price."

Helped by his friend, Bazan hauled the semi-conscious Chuy erect—his feet scrabbled for purchase on the carpet and he groaned. Hearing the commotion, Jefe whirled about, but was distracted once again by the dialogue between Yara and Snow.

Yara: "It's important you keep things in balance…"

Snow: "Showing you have a temper has a certain value."

Yara: "…or else you'll lose control of the situation."

Snow: "You can't govern effectively unless people are afraid of you."

An indecisive expression stole over Jefe's face as they continued in this vein, and he became agitated when Bazan asked for permission to leave.

"First and foremost, you have to learn self-control," said Yara. "You can't expect people to respect someone who constantly yields to impulse."

"Chuy needs a doctor," said Bazan.

"I agree with her," Snow said. "But the idea that you might be erratic, that you pose a threat, the iron fist in the velvet glove, that sort of thing…"

Bazan: "Please, Jefe!"

"…that's what'll keep them in line."

Jefe nodded in Snow's direction—it seemed an acknowledgement—and headed for the stairwell, his composure restored.

"The past is the past," said Yara. "We can't afford to repeat it any longer."

"Neither should we utterly renounce it," said Snow.

"For the love of God!" Bazan.

Jefe dropped into a crouch and roared at him, an open-throated scream delivered with such ferocity that Snow feared it was prelude to an assault—but Jefe merely said, "Take your garbage and go. And don't call me for a while." He slammed the door behind him.

Chuy's head lolled back. Thick, dark blood eeled between his lips.

Snow pointed this out, saying to Bazan, "Your boy's leaking."

Though shaken by Jefe's outburst, Bazan had recovered enough of his macho to curse Snow.

"There's a clinic in Nebaj," said Yara. "I think it's open."

Bazan might not have heard her. "I'm going to have your balls, man!"

"Are you crazy?" She limped toward Bazan. "Get out of here! Go! Before Jefe changes his mind!"

The men started down the tunnel with Chuy in tow. Bazan looked back and Yara flapped her arms at him shouting, "Go! Go!"

Once their visitors were on their way to Nebaj, to a roadside ditch or wherever Chuy's destiny might bring him, Yara sank into a chair.

"That's the guy you're going to put in charge?" said Snow. "Really?"

Yara rubbed her hip, tipped back her head, and closed her eyes—her skin held a waxy pallor.

Scattered, unsteady on his feet, Snow sat down. "That prissy little fuck's going to make Hitler seem like a day at the beach!"

She rubbed her hip again, glanced down at her hand.

"Okay," he said. "Okay."

He worked to slow his breath, his heart rate, but his anger boiled over.

"Do you actually fucking think he'll be an upgrade?" he asked. "A creepy teenager with the morals of Caligula? This sure as hell changes my view of dragons. I mean I figured them for noble beasts, at least to some degree, but they must have been like a gang of kids armed with flamethrowers, torching shit and getting off on it. Of course..." He laughed scornfully. "I bet you're going to sling some crap about how the act of transubstantiation squeezed his soul and it came out all scrunched and malformed like a balloon animal. Once he has his dragon body again, hey it'll snap right back into shape! He'll be the fucking lizard version of the Lion King!"

His head fizzed with adrenaline. In quick order he envisioned Chuy's feet dangling, a tiny figure superimposed against a godlike immensity of clouds, and a vastness hung with silver chains.

"The place with all the chains," he said. "Is that the..."

"Can you help me back to my room?"

Rankled, he said, "How about answering my question first?"

The grinding noise kicked in upstairs.

Yara held up her right hand, showing the palm and fingers smeared with red.

"I'm bleeding," she said.

WHERE THE EDGE of the table had impacted Yara's hip, blood seeped between her skin and one of the dark green lesions. Snow stopped the bleeding with compresses and then sat in a chair by the bed. She rested on her uninjured side, holding his hand, giving it a squeeze each time she experienced a fresh twinge of pain. It felt as though a colloidal weight, a gel compounded of hopelessness and something darker, colder, were shifting about inside his skull, forcing him to lower his head in order to stabilize it. When he looked up he found her watching him. Her color had improved.

"How you doing?" he asked.

"I'm all right."

There followed an awkward pause—it felt awkward to Snow, at any rate—after which they both spoke at once.

"You go," he said.

"No…you."

"I don't have anything specific to say. I was just going to make comforting noises."

She wetted her lips. "I can help you, I think."

A match head of bright emotion flared up inside him.

"The lair…the place with the chains," she said. "It's where he does the preponderance of his killing. He uses the chains to fly. It's not flying per se—it's acrobatics. But it's amazing to watch. There are ledges on the walls where he…"

"I didn't see any ledges."

"Most of them are high up, too high to see, and the ones lower down blend in with the mural. You wouldn't notice them unless you were looking for them. They're where he perches. Where he rests between flights."

"This was part of your design, the ledges, the clouds…you gave them that kind of detail?"

"It's Griaule's design," she said. "I only added one thing. In case of a malfunction, the chains can be disengaged from the ceiling tracks. There's a separate code for each chain that permits them to be replaced. When we moved here, while Jefe was still too weak to fly, we had an engineer and some workmen in to make sure everything was ready to go."

She took a sip of water and replaced the glass on the nightstand.

"After I'd been with Jefe a few weeks, caring for him twenty-four seven, I realized how willful he could be and I began to worry he wouldn't turn out as I hoped."

"There's a shocker," said Snow.

"I wanted a means of stopping him, so I bribed the engineer to provide me with a code that would enable me to bring down the central section of the chains all at once. At first I asked for a code that would bring them all down, but he warned there would be a splashing effect—if all the chains fell they'd likely kill everyone in the room. I've been tempted to use the code several times, but until now I always trusted my original decision."

He could guess what had changed for her, why she was now willing to act, and he wanted to be sure, to ask, Why now? because he doubted it had much if anything to do with Chuy—but he bit back the question, worried that if he pressed that particular button it would enlist a negative emotion and she might rethink her decision.

"What's the code?" he asked.

"In the lair there's a panel at eye-level just to the left of the door. Inside there's a keypad. Punch in seven-one-three-nine-one. It's my birthday. Seven, thirteen, ninety-one. When it's the right moment, you press Enter and down he'll come. But I'll be the one who enters the code."

She sat up in bed, a process that required his assistance, and once she had resettled with pillows behind her, she said, "It's best I do it, anyway. If he stays true to form, he'll take you up to one of the perches and leave you there while he flies. I know the precise section of chains that will drop and I'm used to watching him fly—I know his timing and you don't. But he may not allow me to go upstairs with you. In that case…he might leave you on the ground and have you watch him fly. Maybe you can use the code then. We have to make certain he brings me up with you. The way to ensure is to act like we're angry with one another and keep on arguing about how he should govern."

"How's that?"

"He was interested in what we said. If we can hold his interest, when it comes time to kill you, he'll want me there to watch him end the argument."

"I'm not good with heights," Snow said after an interval.

"You're going to have to be." She rolled her neck to loosen the muscles. "There's one more thing. You might have to finish him off."

"Wait," he said. "I thought the idea was to make him fall from a height."

"The fall may not kill him. When he first started to fly he took a number of falls—they laid him up for a day, but that's all."

"How long a fall are we talking about?"

"The longest was fifty or sixty feet."

"He fell sixty feet onto a concrete floor and lived?"

"This time the chains will come down on top of him—that should do the job. But we have to prepare for the possibility that he'll survive. I'll bring a machete, but you'll have to use it. I'm not strong enough."

"Can you get a gun?"

She shook her head. "No guns. Since the sniper incident, he hasn't let anyone near him with a gun. He sniffs them out."

"He doesn't worry about machetes?"

"He sees me with one every day. I have to kill chickens and chop weeds in the garden. He's not concerned about anyone killing him at close range."

"Jesus fuck!"

"You can do it! If he's not dead he'll be stunned, chewed up in the chains."

"How about making him fall from higher up?"

"He wants his audience to see everything. Generally he'll strand whomever he's going to kill on a perch close to the floor. Then he makes this tumbling run across the center of the lair that brings him in at around thirty or forty feet. He plucks whomever it is off the wall and carries them higher before he drops them. I'm familiar with that run, I can time it. Otherwise he flies erratic patterns, and the odds against my being able to time him go way up. We can discuss it, but that's not the path I'd choose if my life were in the balance."

Something about the plan, her sudden conversion to his cause, seemed flimsy and too facile by half. Of course it hadn't been that sudden, the conversion—it had taken him more than a week to work this change, to make her reflect on her feelings for him, yet nonetheless it was a quick turnaround.

"You look funny," she said. "Is there something wrong?"

"I was thinking...visualizing."

They went over details. The chains, she told him, slid up or down, back and forth along their tracks, and their movements could be modified by means of the keypad, but usually Jefe keyed in a code that initiated a pre-choreographed sequence. The trucks, the old yellow Toyotas parked on the streets of the village, belonged to the PVO. They looked like wrecks, but were kept tuned up and gassed, and could be counted upon to get them as far as the border. They could not stay in Temalagua once Jefe was dead—they'd be hunted. If they could reach the States, they could sit down somewhere and decide what to do next. And so forth. A multitude of ifs, ands, and buts attached to the plan. No matter how carefully it had been worked out, they would need to be very lucky. One thing in particular kept nagging at Snow, causing him doubt, and he finally asked why she had risked involving the engineer.

"It wasn't much of a risk," she said. "I had no choice, and I knew the PVO intended to disappear everyone who worked on the project."

"Yeah, but he might have blurted out your secret before they could execute him. He would have betrayed you if he thought he could save himself."

A grave look veiled her features. "Give me some credit. I killed him before he had the opportunity to betray me. As soon as I was certain the code worked, I stabbed him. I explained to the PVO that he had tried to rape me."

Snow, nonplussed by this admission, by the cool authority in her voice, ducked his head and scratched the back of his neck to hide his reaction.

"You see?" she said. "I told you I was damned."

OVER THE NEXT few days Snow concocted elaborate paranoid fantasies about Yara. His favorite, the one he kept returning to, was that her plan was a cruelty meant to extract the last drop of torment from him, a lie that would insure his docility as he was led to the slaughter. He imagined her taunting him as he waited to die, and her insistence that they sleep in separate beds in order to reinforce the notion that they were feuding, played into the fantasy. Now she was through with him, the trap set, and the distasteful (to her) act of intercourse was no longer necessary—thus her ploy. He stopped short of believing this, yet when he recognized how dependent he was on her and thought of everything she had done to guarantee the dragon's survival, he was tempted to think the worst of her.

"You probably think it's weird I haven't told you I love you," she said the following night when Snow dropped by her room to wish her good night.

He thought she must have told him and searched his memory, wanting to remind her of the occasion.

"I'm not sure why I've been so reticent. I think I know why, but…" She pretended to punch the side of her head. "Sometimes things get all screwed up in here. Anyway, it must be obvious."

"What's obvious?"

"That I love you."

Her voice carried no conviction. She had draped a blue scarf over the lampshade, dimming the light, making it difficult to read her expression.

"I don't mean to sound tentative," she said. "I had to decide about Jefe first and then I wondered whether you really wanted me. And there were other considerations, other pressures. I do love you, but saying it has just seemed awkward."

He sat down on the bed. "I know you have trust issues."

"It's not that. You've changed so much from how…"

"I haven't changed. Basically I'm the same post-hippie I've always been."

She chewed that over. "Have I changed? Aside from physically?"

"Yeah. You're more worldly now, more in control. Less moody."

"That's what being a murderer does for you—it either derails you or works wonders for your poise."

"I don't think that's to blame. You'd already killed someone when I met you."

She looked at him in surprise.

"The Austrian guy," he said. "The child molester."

"How do you know about that? I didn't tell you, did I?"

"Guillermo told me."

After a few beats she said, "I don't recall killing Scheve. I remember him bleeding, but I'm not certain it's a real memory. I was always stoned when I was a kid and a lot of things happened that I'm not too clear about. Anyway…" She dismissed the subject of her childhood with a flip of her fingers. "In my head I feel more-or-less the same as I did when we met, and yet you say I've changed. And I bet it's like that for you. So if I've changed, you have to admit to the possibility that you have, too."

"I suppose."

She lay without speaking for several seconds. "I forget what I was going to say. You made me lose track with that talk about Scheve."

"Sorry."

"It'll come back, maybe." She pressed her fists to her temples. "Even if I can't remember how I wanted to link things up, I do remember the point I was going to make. We're both of us pretty fucked-up."

Snow chuckled. "You think?"

"Listen! What I'm saying isn't funny."

"All right. I'm listening."

"We're fucked-up people. Me, because my life was a mess from day one. And you because…"

"Being fucked-up was kind of my ambition," he said, but she acted as though she hadn't heard.

"…because the world disappointed you in some way I don't understand. Whatever.

"When we were together back then we never used the word 'love' much. I don't know if we ever used it, but we both knew there was something there. Something strong. But we didn't deal with it, we skated around it. The night you got here, when you said you loved me, I knew it wasn't totally sincere…but it wasn't totally insincere, either. It was the most you ever gave to me. I felt that, and that's why I responded."

Her words had come in a rush, but now she faltered. "And…it got better after that.

"Every night it's better…" She stared at him helplessly. "I wish you hadn't mentioned Scheve. Now I've got these images in my head. I can't think."

He lay down beside her and she turned to face him—he kissed her forehead and felt her relax.

"I'll just make my point," she said. "We could be dead in a couple of days, maybe as soon as tomorrow. There's no way to avoid what's going to happen, but there's an opportunity here. If we can get through this, if we stand up for one another and do what has to be done, we have a chance to turn all our fucked-uppedness, all our imperfections into strengths. That's little enough to hope for considering everything that's happened, the terrible mistakes I've made, and your mistakes…but if we can salvage that much, the relationship, love, potential, whatever you want to call it, maybe it's something we can build on."

Her pause lasted no longer than a hiccup.

"God, that sounds lame," she said. "I had it worked out, exactly what I wanted to say, but then you brought up Scheve and…poof! It's out of my head."

Snow told her to take her time and she closed her eyes for a minute.

"I remember bits and pieces of it," she said. "How if we can kill Jefe, we have an obligation to the people we've destroyed to take advantage of the opportunity. And how if we do kill him, it'll change us. It'll be our alchemy. But without logic behind it, you know…without the proper order, the way I planned to say it…it sounds like straight bullshit."

Her inability to remember was persuasive in its authenticity and Snow felt guilty for having doubted her.

"It's strange how just mentioning that bastard's name can screw me up," she said. "I don't recall many details. About being with him, you know. Just this sick, detached feeling, like it was in a dream. Like that movie you took me to in Antigua, remember, where I freaked out? His face was all blurry and distorted, moving in and out of frame, very close, like the guy in that movie. And that's it. That's all I remember about him. But if you say 'Scheve' I start to fall apart."

"I'm sorry I brought it up." He kissed her again. "Are you going to be all right?"

"I'm just mad at myself. I'll be okay."

"Then I guess I should go."

She traced the veins on the back of his hand, studying them as if they were a puzzle she needed to solve, and then said, "No, really. You shouldn't."

WHENEVER JEFE CAME within earshot they would resurrect their argument, debating conflicting styles of governance, and Snow, perhaps due to his dependency on Yara, the sense of helplessness it engendered, derived a trivial satisfaction from his ability to argue the right-wing point-of-view, one with which he did not agree in spirit, yet had to admit was the more pragmatic of the two political stances. He derided as a "leftist fairy tale" Yara's insistence that firmness tempered with altruism would bring about a peaceful and prosperous Temalagua, and suggested that it was odd to hear such drivel issue from the mouth of someone associated with the PVO since its inception.

"What she's saying is great for kids to hear," he said. "That is, if you want your kids to grow up without a spine. It's moral pablum that weakens them, programs them to cling to their mothers' skirts. A leader, a man who would rule, he has to rid himself of such naivete. He has a country to think of—every day he'll have to resolve issues that will cause pain and anger whichever way he decides them. He has to see beyond that sort of morality, a morality whose function is solely to curb one's instincts, to limit one's behavior. His role demands he be capable of wider judgments."

Jefe no longer seemed distressed by their contentiousness. In fact, he acted as if he relished these exchanges and would signify hs approval whenever Yara or (more frequently) Snow said something with which he agreed. Then at breakfast one morning, the fifth day following the incident with Chuy, he invited them to watch him fly. His manner was casual, genial, as if he were asking them to join him at a movie. Snow was unable to conceal his dismay.

Jefe clapped him on the shoulder. "Man, come on! I promise you'll enjoy this."

Yara picked up the machete from beside her chair and he told her to leave it, saying with heavy sarcasm that he doubted she would find any chickens upstairs.

A diversion from their plan so early in the game did not augur well, yet as they mounted the steps, though Snow knew the fearful incredulity of a condemned man going to the gallows, he nevertheless felt a corresponding sense of relief, one springing from the knowledge that they would soon have a resolution. Jefe stripped off his outerwear and stood before them clad only in black tights, his chest and arms plated with unusually smooth muscle, only the balance muscles in his back and those protecting his joints exceptionally defined. He opened a panel in the wall camouflaged by a section of indigo cloud and punched in a number on the keypad, initiating the grinding nose and starting the chains to slither up and down, to and fro in their tracks, some rapidly, some slowly, the light rivering along their silver links. He then pulled on a pair of thin black gloves and caught hold of a chain that carried him aloft.

Yara squeezed Snow's hand and shouted into his ear: "Once you get back down to the floor, run and get the machete!"

When Jefe reached a height of around twenty feet he launched himself into the air, catching another chain, then whipped himself about, swinging higher, and caught yet another chain and swung again, repeating this process, going higher and higher until all Snow could see of him was a minute figure hurtling through a moving forest of silver chains and against a cinematic backdrop of brassy light and clouds like battle smoke. He descended in like fashion, performing a sequence of loops and somersaults, sudden shifts and reversals of direction that brought him, after several minutes, to within a few feet above them, whereupon he ascended again rapidly, arrowing from chain to chain, crossing spaces of forty feet and more before redirecting his course, throwing in spins and tumbling maneuvers and other elaborate stunts. Yara applauded wildly and shouted her praise, despite having scant hope of being heard. She elbowed Snow, enjoining him to do the same and, though he was not so inclined, he followed suit and was partly sincere in his applause, for he had never witnessed such a display of stamina and strength and coordination. He lost sight of Jefe among the chains and clouds, and inquired of Yara where he had gone—she pointed to a speck superimposed against a spray of golden light, perched on an invisible ledge. And then he was off again, soaring amongst the chains, not appearing to utilize their stability and momentum to alter his course, but scarcely touching them, as if gliding on updrafts, diving and banking, aerials too fluid and graceful to be other than flight.

How long Jefe flew, Snow could not have said. An hour, surely. Long enough so that his motivation for clapping and cheering waned and he stood silent and motionless until Jefe descended to the floor of the shaft and walked over to them, a light sheen of sweat the only register of his exertion. Yara congratulated him, patting his shoulder and smiling, but Snow, incapable of participating in this charade any further, looked off as if distracted, fighting panic, going over the list of things he needed to focus upon. Jefe smirked, stepping to him with a swaggering walk, rolling his shoulders, and gave him a push, moving him toward the wall covered with smoky clouds. Snow scuttled away and Jefe gave him a harder push that sent him reeling backward. As Snow toppled, windmilling his arms,

Jefe sprang after him, snagging his belt, and lugged him toward the wall, kicking and twisting like a living satchel. He seized a chain, wrapping it once around his arm, and let it bear them upward.

Watching the floor shrink beneath him, Snow ceased his struggles and shut his eyes, clinging to Jefe's leg, dizzy and sick with fright. After an interminable time he felt himself lifted. He screamed, convinced that this was the moment he had dreaded, but instead of plummeting downward he found himself pressed back against the wall, held there by Jefe's hand at his throat and by something solid underfoot. A ledge. He slid his left shoe forward, feeling for the edge, and found it after two or three inches.

"Don't worry," Jefe said in his ear. "I'm not going to harm you."

Snow squinted at Jefe, who stood beside him, facing the wall, and then glanced down at the floor of the shaft. Their elevation was so great he could not be certain he saw the floor, only a chaos of glittering, slithering chains, bright clouds on the wall opposite, and, as his eyes rolled up, the autumnal blue of the ceiling near to hand. His stomach flip-flopped, his knees buckled, and if Jefe had not tightened his grip, half-throttling him, he would have fallen.

Jefe gave him a gentle shake. "Didn't you hear me?"

Mind trash erupted from a shadowy place in Snow's consciousness, like a gusher from a vent in the sea bottom, resolving into a silt of childlike prayers and wishes.

"Calm yourself, my friend! It's okay!"

If you fell far enough, Snow had heard, you would lose consciousness before the impact.

"I know you don't like it up here," said Jefe. "But I've got you, see? Try to relax."

Jefe's face was too close to read, only an ear and part of his cheek and neck visible. He had an arid scent, slightly acidic—like the smell of an alkali desert. Snow released breath with a shudder and closed his eyes again. The grinding of the chains gnawed at the outskirts of his reason.

"Your advice strengthens me," said Jefe. "I value it greatly. I want you with me. This is a joke. A little joke I'm playing on Yara. Nothing more. Do you understand?"

Snow did not understand.

"She deserves it, don't you think? You were right about her."

There were voices in the grinding noise, like those you hear in the humming of tires while resting your head against the window glass of a fast-moving car—hypnotic, hyper-resonant, trebly voices eerily reminiscent of Alvin and the Chipmunks, voices at once sinister and cheerful that sang a simple song advising him go with the flow, go with the flow, go with…

"Look at me!" said Jefe.

He pulled back, permitting Snow to see his entire face, a face composed so as to illustrate the quality of assurance, and then came close again. "Everything's going to be fine. You've won."

Snow couldn't think of anything to say—he essayed a grin, but wasn't sure he had pulled it off.

"We haven't had much chance to talk," said Jefe. "That's my fault. I apologize. When I found you in the village I assumed you were a spy. I very nearly killed you the first night. But over the past days I've come to appreciate your insights into my situation. Others might say fate brought you to me, but someone like myself shapes his own fate. I must have sensed you and called you to my side, so you could give voice to what I know in my heart."

He removed his hand from Snow's throat and patted his cheek. Snow felt the pull of the gulf below and tried to sink into the wall.

"I'm an intuitive sort," Jefe said. "I know you can help me access the portion of my life that's closed off. I think I knew that the instant I first saw you, but I understand now that you were afraid. That's why you refused me. You needed time to adjust, to acclimate to my presence. I tend to forget the effect I have on people. I can't always be expected to notice it. Obviously I don't have the same effect on myself."

Snow would have preferred to tune him out and concentrate on his footing, but Jefe kept on bellowing nonsense into his ear, inducing him to listen. He had the cogent, albeit somewhat hysterical thought that he might have been onto something when he berated Yara after Enrique Bazan's visit—maybe when translated into human form dragons were reduced to prattling twits with superhuman powers, yet once returned to their natural state they expanded into their bodies and became the mysterious cosmic beasts of legend. Or not. Maybe they were assholes, whatever their shape.

Jefe gave him a hug and kissed him on the cheek, a move that made Snow cringe. "We've been up here long enough," he said. "We can talk more later. Let's go down, shall we? Let's finish the joke. Yara will be surprised to learn she has lost. We'll show the bitch, won't we?"

Snow had a presentiment of what was about to occur, but the idea that he might be carried down from the wall swept all else aside.

Jefe winked broadly at him, grabbed his belt and, before Snow could react, he leapt for a nearby chain, Snow hanging from his left hand. There was a split-second when he thought Jefe had lied and the joke was on him, but he felt a severe jolt that stopped his fall, the belt buckle digging into his gut with such force, he couldn't breathe. Once he recovered he saw that they were descending at a rapid clip, the floor growing larger and larger. This time he didn't shut his eyes—he yearned for the floor, he wanted the floor above all things, he willed it to rise to meet him, and when Jefe deposited him on the concrete, when the rough surface abraded his cheek, he almost wept with relief and lay there soaking up its beautiful wideness and firmness. He remembered Yara and looked for her. Spied her thirty feet above on a ledge, on the wall that portrayed clouds at dusk. She stared at him—he couldn't make out her expression, but a bolt of terror shot through him, as if she had beamed it into his heart. Jefe flew in swoops and ascensions high above, sticking close to the wall, and then went higher yet, out into the center of the shaft. Something was different about his flying. It was less dervish, less spectacular than earlier, having a languorous air that reminded Snow of a trapeze artist doing lazy somersaults, relaxing, gathering momentum for his next show-stopping trick. Panicked, realizing what that trick must be, he sprinted to the panel and started to enter the code, but blanked on it. Her birthday. Seven...seven something, he thought. Fuck! He racked his brain. Seven thirteen ninety-one. He put in the numbers and his forefinger hovered over the keypad as he tried to locate Jefe among the chains. Spotted him descending from the heights, from the wall across from Yara, tumbling and twisting, a mad Olympic diver committed to a suicidal plunge, already halfway to her, more than halfway...Snow jabbed the Enter key, knowing he was too late.

Had he thrown in one less tumble, one less frill or flourish, Jefe might have saved himself. As it was, his momentum almost carried him out of danger. The grinding noise stopped abruptly and his graceful run became floundering and disjointed high above the concrete floor. His fall lasted two or three seconds, no more, but the replay, when Snow summoned it, took much longer to unwind. Jefe flung out a hand, snatching at a chain still attached to the ceiling, his fingertips grazing the links, and he went down without kicking or flailing his arms, his body describing a simple half-roll onto its side. He gave no outcry and impacted with a sickening crack, a leg touching first, as if he had made an effort at the end to land on his feet. He sagged onto his back so that, if he were still aware, he would have seen the chains collapsing, appearing as they descended to coalesce into a cloud of silvery serpents with long, lashing tails, their lengths all entangled. They smashed into the concrete with a clashing sound, dozens of them striking out in every direction as they hit, one leaping straight at Snow, cobra-quick, missing him by inches. Then it was quiet. An ominous quiet despite the happy result it represented. The lair had been made over into a piece of Gothic art, a stage set for the final scene in a surrealist play, a grim medieval fable whose ending was open to interpretation. A considerable fringe of chains remained connected to the ceiling, curtaining the huge photomurals, and a pall of concrete dust was suspended throughout the lower third of the shaft, a lunar fog partially obscuring the mountainous heap of chains that lay dead center of the floor, like a burial mound intended to confine some immortal monster.

Yara called out to Snow, telling him to bring the machete, and he shouted, "Not until you're down!"

"The machete!"

Stubbornly, Snow asked what he should do to help her down.

She stood pressed flat to the wall on the narrow ledge, arms outspread for balance. He knew she must be afraid to do so much as nod for fear of toppling off the ledge, yet she briefly lifted a hand to point at the mound of chains. He saw nothing and said, "What are you pointing at?"

"He's alive! Look at the chains!"

"Where? I don't see anything!"

"The pile of chains! The section nearest me! Just look!"

He could detect nothing, no trace of blood, no sign of a living presence, but came forward, stepping over outlying snarls of chain shaped like the ridged and twisted roots of a metal tree, like crocodile tails, like the spines of antediluvian creatures whose heads were buried beneath the spill of silver links. The mound was three times higher than his head and shed a cold radiance. He began to circumnavigate it, pacing slowly, warily, alert for movement, yet seeing none.

"Where do you mean?" he shouted, and then saw chains slither down across a slight convexity at the edge of the mound where they were piled only four and five feet deep. His heart jumped in his chest, but there was no further movement.

"The mound's settling, that's all!" He glanced up to Yara. "How do I get you down?"

"Are you sure?"

He waited a bit, watching the mound, and said, "Yeah!"

"Go to the panel—key in nine-nine-nine! That'll start the chains moving down!"

"Don't you want me to come up?"

"I can hang on long enough to reach the floor!"

A rattling at Snow's back—the chains shifted, the base of the mound bulged, and then a bloody-knuckled fist punched out from it and Jefe's fingers clawed the air.

Galvanized with fear, Snow ran for the stairs. He pounded down the steps, grabbed the machete, and raced back again, pausing on the landing to gather his courage, and his breath, and then re-entered the lair. Lengths of chain were draped around Jefe's torso and legs, but he had fought mostly free of them and gotten to his knees. Blood welled from splits on his chest and arms—it was as if his skin had not been torn or abraded, but rather had cracked like a shell. He stared balefully at Snow, yet spoke not a word and made no threatening movement. Yara shouted, "Kill him! Kill him!" Jefe did not react to her, continuing to watch Snow, who approached with trepidation, holding the machete behind his head, poised to strike.

He assumed Jefe would lunge at him when he came near, but he closed to within a few feet, just beyond reach, and Jefe had not moved, merely tracking his progress. This gave him confidence and he aimed a blow at Jefe's head. Jefe flung up his arm to block it and the blade skimmed along the inside of the arm, taking with it a shaving of skin. Not human skin, but a rind of sorts, a thick sheath protecting his flesh, and Snow, as he retreated, remembered how hard Jefe's hand had felt when he slapped him.

"Don't let him stand up!" Yara shouted. "If he stands, he'll be harder to get at!"

Snow did not believe Jefe *could* stand and he was uncertain whether or not Yara's statement was accurate. The mound made it impossible to get behind Jefe and his range of motion enabled him to defend attacks from every available angle. On his feet and badly wounded, he might be vulnerable to a range of attacks—in his current posture there was no option except to try another frontal assault. Snow stabbed with the point of the blade and Jefe deflected it with ease. He feinted a backhand slash, shifted his stance, and swung the machete straight down at the top of Jefe's head—but he strayed too close to his target. Jefe clubbed his wrist, sending the machete skittering across the floor, and snatched at his shirttail. Snow broke free and hurried to retrieve the weapon. As he stooped for it, Yara shouted a warning. Jefe had clambered to his feet and was heading toward the stairs, dragging his right leg, his torso bent to the right, staggering, going off-course and having constantly to correct it, a crooked man on a crooked path. Snow darted after him and took a swing at the side of Jefe's good knee, hoping to cut a tendon, but due to the awkward angle at which he delivered it, the blow had little force and did no discernable damage. Moving with an old man's stiffness and deliberation, Jefe turned to him and gave a hissing cry, like that of an enraged cat. His face had lost every ounce of humanity, revealing it to have been a cunning mask behind which some odious and repellent thing had hidden, and now that the tissues of the mask were dissolving, a corrosive anger shone through, directed not only toward Snow, but toward all things not itself, a vicious, wormy hatred that had kept it alive for millennia and become its sole reason for existence. All of this conveyed by a mere glance. It was as if a germ of the dragon's vileness had spanned the distance between them and infected Snow, breeding of an instant its semblance in his brain and inspiring in him a consonant anger. As Jefe labored toward the stairwell, Snow let that anger spur his actions and guide his hand.

Leaping forward, sensing the truth of the blow as he swung the machete, he sank the blade into the side of Jefe's neck, the tip transecting the hindward portion of his jaw. Jefe made a cawing noise and jerked away, tearing the machete from Snow's grip, so firmly was it embedded in meat and bone. Blood seeped from around the edges of the blade. Jefe stumbled out onto the landing, his step grown discontinuous. He slipped, clutched ineffectually at the railing, and then pitched forward, bumping down the stairs on his belly and onto the landing below, dislodging the machete. He picked himself up and kept going, blood fron the wound cape-ing his back with a darker crimson.

An unusual calm, sudden in onset, was visited upon Snow. Not unusual as regarded its emotional basis, for he knew to his soul Jefe was dying and a menace no more, but in that it seemed to proceed from an inner resource he had not known he possessed. He stood calmly, then, watching Jefe totter from view before returning to the lair. Yara called on him to finish Jefe, but Snow walked over to the panel by the door, keyed in nine-nine-nine, and set the chains to rattling downward. The noise drowned out her cries. Once he knew she would be safe, he went downstairs at a leisurely pace, scooping up the machete, and entered the dining room. He stopped by the sideboard and, taking a minute to make his selection from among the whiskeys and tequilas, he poured a double shot of single malt and sipped it appreciatively. A tremor palsied his hand. He downed the scotch and strolled off along the tunnel, following Jefe's blood trail.

He had not been out of the complex for almost two weeks and the sight of daylight at the tunnel's end disoriented him, as did the wideness of the world and the hills enclosing the grassless stretch whereon the village had been established. Under a dreary sky eight or nine women—two of them dressed in filmy peignoirs, the others clad in shawls and long colorful skirts and embroidered blouses of coarse native cloth—had gathered at a point midway between the village and the pink house, and were staring with grim fixity at something Snow could not see from his perspective. On stepping from the tunnel mouth, he spotted Jefe to the right of the entrance—he still dragged his leg, yet made a doddering run across a stretch of sloppy ground, hitching his shoulders repeatedly as he went, going about ten yards before losing his footing and sprawling, splashing down into a puddle. It took several tries for him to stand. A commingling of blood and brick red mud slimed his chest and back, and he wore an expression of abject stupefaction. Appearing to have no awareness of Snow, he made a second and shorter run back toward the tunnel, adding a little hop at the end, but with no better outcome. Snow recognized he was attempting to fly and wondered whether he knew that he did not possess a dragon's body.

A voluptuous black woman with blond spiky hair, holding the neck of her peignoir shut against the cold, approached Snow, circling away from Jefe. She touched the handle of the machete and said, "You did this?"

"Yes. With Yara's help."

"Yara? I don't know this Yara."

"La Endriaga."

"La Endriaga is not Jefe's woman?"

"She was his prisoner. Like you."

As Jefe made another effort to fly, the woman shouted excitedly in Mam to the others—Snow understood only the words "La Endriaga."

One of the village women shouted in response and the black woman asked Snow if Jefe was mortally wounded.

"Yes," he said. "He's lost a lot of blood, but he may still be dangerous."

She reported this to the group and two of the women ran for the village, most likely to spread the news.

Jefe fell again—he lay on his side for a long count, his breath venting in gasps.

Snow's calm had eroded into a mood as gray and energy-less as the sky above Tres Santos. The clouds looked to have the inert weight and solidity of battered armor plate, though thunderheads with dark bellies had begun pushing in from the north. As Jefe gathered himself for a further attempt, Yara limped from the tunnel. She stood at Snow's side and watched Jefe perform his miserable trick. Her eyes brimmed with tears. This must be for her, he thought, like watching someone who had once had promise, with whom she had invested her precious time, and was now reduced to an addled derelict with half a functioning liver, putting on a show of his degeneracy and decrepitude in a parking lot, hoping his audience would throw quarters at him so he could buy a pint of fortified wine.

The black woman tapped Snow's arm and whispered in his ear: "If she is not Jefe's woman, why is she crying?"

"She was Jefe's prisoner for most of her life," Snow said. "When you've lived with someone that long, even as a captive, your emotions become confused."

She nodded at this lie, or half-lie, as if she understood him, but her expression was perplexed.

More women joined the group, swelling its ranks to four times its former size. Some carried garden implements, others pointed sticks and fist-sized rocks—a young girl in chartreuse satin pajamas brandished a pair of sewing shears. They seethed closer to Jefe, their voices a chorus of vituperation, yet did not attack, wary of their tormentor, though he looked to be done with flying. Positioned on all fours amidst a large puddle, his head hanging down, slathered all over in reddish muck, his hair caked with mud, blood oozing from splits and gashes, strings of ruby-colored drool depending from his lips—he might have been an animal of the village, a pariah dog gone rabid, exhausted by fever, his world narrowed to a hideous reflection in murky water. Snow had no pity for him, no disgust, no anger. If he felt anything it was the temper of a functionary compelled to discharge an unpleasant duty. He stepped forward and rested the edge of the blade on Jefe's neck. The women fell silent and Jefe's guttering breath could be heard. He sought to lift his head, perhaps to inquire of Snow, perhaps simply alerted by the blade, but either his head was too heavy or else he lacked the will to see, to know what this cold, sharp object was. Perhaps he knew and no longer cared. Summoning his strength, Snow swung the machete in a savage arc. The blade sliced deep, burying itself to the bone, yet Jefe's reactions were minimal—he gave forth with a grunt and shuddered and listed a degree or two, but remained upright. Frustrated at his inability to finish the job, Snow yanked at the blade, but once again it was stuck. He planted a foot between Jefe's shoulders, pushed down and wrenched the blade free, shoving him face-first into the puddle. A tide of blood sluiced from the wound.

As Snow prepared to strike again Jefe's breath blew a bubble in the mud and, with a choking cough, he flipped onto his back, his entire frame coming off the ground and twisting in mid-air—it was such a physically adept movement that Snow feared Jefe's strength had been miraculously restored, but then he understood that it had been a lizard-ly reflex, a final surge of vitality, for Jefe was clearly close to death. His limbs jerked and twitched, and a horrid slackness overlay his features and from his throat there issued a repetitive glutinous clicking, indicative of a disruption in some internal function and not an attempt at speech...though his eyes yet held a glint of the poisonous hatred that had infected the world for thousands of years.

The women descended upon him, first Itzel with a hoe, blood welling from the trench she dug in his chest, and then the rest, stabbing and cutting and pounding, exacting their vengeance for rape and murder and innumerable humiliations. They swarmed over the body, blocking it from view, and shoved one another aside in their eagerness to share in his destruction, announcing their fury and delight with orgasmic cries, until a puff of heat and rainbow-colored light (no more impressive to see than the flash powder of a second-rate magician) bloomed from the rags of meat and splintered bone, causing them to fall over backward, to scramble and crawl away yelping with fright, spattered by the same amalgam of mud and thick, dark blood as their ancient enemy, some bearing slashes and bruises received during the melee, inadvertently gotten at the hands of their sisters, and some nursing curious burns they seemed to obtain from some melting process, deriving from the paltry magic of Jefe's death. Snow glanced up at the sky, fearful that rippling lights would manifest in the clouds like those seen above the village of Chajul thirteen years before, the beacon of the dragon's rebirth—but none materialized. Jefe was dead. Utterly and irrevocably dead.

At the last an elderly woman brought a gasoline can and emptied its contents upon his corpse, which had been rendered unrecognizable as life of any kind, like a red meal that had proved indigestible and been spat forth by the thing that consumed it. She lit a twist of paper and dropped it thereon. The flames yielded were low and of a ruddy translucence in the decaying light, and were whipped about by a cold north wind that soon would bring the storm. An oily smoke arose and was quickly dispersed. All the women of the village had come forth, and those of the pink house as well, and they huddled together in small groupings, somber and silent in that shabby, inglorious place, occasionally exchanging whispered comforts and assurances. When the blaze had burned down some retreated to their homes, but more gasoline was brought and many stayed to watch a second burning, and to stir the coals now and again so that a wisp of transparent flame licked up, signifying the immolation of a crumb of intestine, a scrap of cartilage. The sky darkened. Drops of icy rain began to fall, yet the women covered their heads with shawls, violent nuns at a ritual observance, and kept to their sentinel stations until they were shadows and the wind stiffened, carrying the taste of grit to their mouths, and all that survived of the dragon Griaule and his human avatar were nuggets of charred bone, which they would later collect and grind into meal for a mystical supper, and a cinereal residue indistinguishable from the dusts that had blown across those hills since time was in its cradle and the sky still bright with creation fire.

VI

IT WAS RAINING STEADILY BY the time they drove out from Tres Santos in the late afternoon, heading for Nebaj and the north in one of the battered yellow mini-trucks. The women of the village expressed no interest in having them join their celebration. They wanted a swift return to normalcy, to their traditions, and they treated Snow and Yara, despite their service, with disdain, there being no place amongst them for a gringo and his pale, crippled woman. As for Snow, he had no desire to linger in Tres Santos a second longer than was necessary. He suspected that these women would be forever at their burning, whether in dreams or by means of some surrogate or effigy. Their new husbands, if husbands they took, would be lucky to survive such passion.

Yara had barely spoken since Jefe's death and she was not given now to speech. As they jounced over ruts and potholes, Snow jamming the gears in order to gain traction in the mud, she rubbed his leg every so often—whether to reassure herself or him, he could not have said—and offered neither commentary nor advice. In truth, he would have had little in the way of response, preoccupied by the gusting wind and the rain driven sideways against the windshield, and by the precipitous drop-off to the right of the narrow road. They were past the halfway point to Nebaj when the storm broke full upon them. In those regions it would not have been considered either an especially fulminant storm or one of great duration, unremarkable as to its apparitions and thunderous concatenations and lurid bursts of lightning that illuminated sections of the pine forest, bleaching the separate trees to bone-white and shrouding them in purple-haloed effulgence like sainted relics set to burn on the mountainside, charms and admonitions against some ghastly form of predation. It sufficed, however, to persuade Snow to shut down the engine and switch off the useless wipers. He cracked a window to prevent the glass from fogging over with their breath. Rain washed down in spills thick as gray paint, its drumming increased to deafening measure. He had wanted to talk to Yara, but now he thought the storm with its progeny of light and sound was a blessing, for there was too much to be sifted through and digested and mulled over before they could begin to discuss what had happened and what would be. And yet to sit there encysted in that musty cab, blind to the world, surrounded by spirits real and unreal, separated one from the other by silence, by a gearbox and a divider with receptacles for drinks and maps and such, that was no better solution to the moment. His mind pulled ahead, worrying about how they would negotiate the border crossing and where they could live and what he would do with a woman as damaged as Yara at his side, all the demeaning practicalities and shameful concerns that would inevitably dissolve the bond they had forged anew, a bond already once broken. He wished he could resist these dour thoughts, but they were ingrained in him—he had too long cohabited with the idea that love born of illusion would never prosper, and the principle that every truth could be fashioned into the lie of itself. It seemed to him all they had undergone and felt and done would one day be diminished and relegated to mere narrative, its heroes oversimplified or their heroic natures overborne by the mundanity of detail, a story so degraded, so shorn of wonderment by telling and re-telling that—despite love and redemption, suffering and loss, mystery and death—it would be in the end as though nothing had happened.

The rain abated and the worst of the storm moved toward the lowlands. Snow started the engine. Yara reached a hand across the divide and he warmed her chilled fingers. In her face was a serenity he could not fathom. He thought she must be drawing upon some secret female provenance to which he had no access, but something stirred inside him, sparked to life by her expression, and he had then a fresh recognition of what they had accomplished together, the destruction of a monster, the killing of a thing that could not be killed. And although it went against every negative of his former faith in nothing, he submitted to belief and believed...believed in alchemy, in the marriage of souls, in accomplishment and noble obligation, and believed also that he would never fail her again, nor she him.

THE SKULL

Static spat and crackled on the radio, *salseros* lamented about injustice and pop divas celebrated the endlessly trivial. In a thin voice Yara sang along with those songs she knew and they talked of inconsequential things, favorite bands and bad movies, touching one another often to reaffirm their connection, for they were their own country now. When they turned onto the highway they lapsed into silence, Yara gazing out the window and Snow focusing on the traffic, each alone with their thoughts, each striving to ignore the outposts of doubt and fear that flashed at them from the darkness, as vivid in their enmity as the gas station-hotel-brothel where they stopped to fill the tank—a big, ugly, raw building englobed in lemony radiance, like the local headquarters of evil and sons, and out front a string of six short-skirted women standing brazen and hipshot along the road, shadowy figures who bared their breasts for speeding cars, watched over by a chain-smoking devil with gold incisors, who strode back and forth, cursing the cars, the women, cursing everything in sight, pimping the apocalypse. Some drunken teenage soldiers, Indian kids with AK-47s, lounged by the entrance, giving people a hard time. In a spirit of playful menace, one lifted the hem of Yara's skirt with his rifle barrel—upon seeing her disfigured legs he let the skirt fall, made the sign of the cross, and held conference with his friends. Snow hustled her into the truck before they could decide to investigate further and drove away quickly. After that they kept to the back roads, to blue highways and unmapped trails, driving north and west into the realms of the ordinary, ordinary monsters and ordinary seductions, past towns whose sole reason for being was a refusal to die, making for a land of cynical enchantments and marathon sales, of lap dancers for cancer and political doctrine based on new wives' tales, the Great American Salmagundi in all its glorious criminal delirium, with nothing to sustain them, nothing certain, only the strength of their imperfections and hope reborn a dragon in their hearts, while behind them the old world trembled and the light caught fire and roared.

STORY NOTES

THE MAN WHO PAINTED
THE DRAGON GRIAULE

THE SEMINAL IDEA FOR GRIAULE occurred to me when I was stuck for something to write about while attending the Clarion Writer's Workshop. I went out onto the campus of Michigan State University and sat under a tree and smoked a joint to jog my brain. I then wrote down in my notebook the words "big fucking dragon." I felt exceptionally clever. Big stuff, I thought, is cool.

The idea of an immense paralyzed dragon, more than a mile in length and seven hundred feet high, that dominates the world around him by means of its mental energies, a baleful monster beaming out his vindictive thought and shaping us to its will…this seemed an appropriate metaphor for the Reagan Administration, which was then busy declaiming that it was "Morning In America," laying waste to Central America, and starting to rip the heart out of the constitution. That likely explains the political content carried in one degree or another by the stories. So in a sense, the Griaule stories concern two mythical beasts, a dragon and an addled president whose avatar is an undying monster…or vice versa.

I don't know what it is that has brought me back so many times to Griaule. Generally speaking, I hate elves, wizards, halflings, and dragons with equal intensity. Perhaps it's because I saw a list once of fictional dragons ordered by size and mine was the biggest. This caused me to think that I might make a career of writing stories about the biggest whatever. The biggest gopher, an aphid the size of a small planet, a gargantuan dust bunny, and so forth. Fortunately I never followed up on the idea.

When I returned home to Ann Arbor from the workshop I asked my brother-in-law, James Wolf, an artist and the guitarist in my band, if he would make me a drawing of the dragon—I wanted something to meditate upon while working out the story. I expected something rudimentary, but he did the dragon in water colors on flimsy, oversized sheets of paper and taped them together, thereby creating a rendering eight feet long and three feet high, complete with all the vats and ladders and etcetera that were part of my conception. I tried to preserve it as best I could, but eventually it became tattered and unsalvageable. Anyway, I stared at the painting for a year or so, endured a thoroughly unhappy love affair that formed the emotional core of the story, and eventually wrote it all down.

THE SCALEHUNTER'S
BEAUTIFUL DAUGHTER

THIS STORY HAD its genesis in the notion that Griaule might be infested with parasites. It was an interesting notion and I envisioned the plot to be more-or-less an excuse for doing a taxonomical survey of the dragon's interior, something that would have suited a more novelistic approach to the subject. Indeed, "The Scalehunter's Beautiful Daughter" was initially intended to be a portion of a novel, or rather a series of stories linked by excerpts from fictive works about the dragon, but I soon realized I had little desire to read such linkages and even less to write them.

Then, too, I wrote the story during a stressful time. My mother was dying and I was living in her cramped Ormond Beach condo, assisting in her care, a grim business. The movie theater in the mall close by showed nothing I wanted to see (*Yentl* had played there for more than a year). I had no friends in the area—I was the youngest person in the condominium by three decades—and I had no money to speak of, no car, nowhere to go for a break except for the Denny's down the street. Thus I was inclined to write a sunnier story (by my lights, anyway), more of a straight-ahead escapist fantasy than I might have done otherwise.

I roughed out the story while drinking coffee at Denny's, usually in the early morning hours, writing in bursts of fifteen, twenty minutes and then running over to the condo to check on my mom. Not a lot of happy people come into a Denny's at three o'clock in the morning, at least this was my observation. Most of the ones who seemed happy were drunks whose happiness would be short-lived, and the rest were loners, addicts, insomniacs, hookers, cops, sour-looking old men who'd had a bad night at the dog track, and losers of various stripe.

The star of the graveyard shift at this particular Denny's was Fred the short order cook, a swarthy black-haired guy about my age who cracked wise-ass jokes through the serving window and carried on a sardonic and often amusing dialogue with the regulars. When cops stopped by for take-out he would surreptitiously mimic their radio calls—he did this with such authenticity, static and tinny voices and all, the cops would grab their walkie-talkies and respond. One night two cops went back into the kitchen and gave him a stern talking-to. Thereafter the fake radio calls ceased and, possibly as a result of this restraint upon his comic stylings, Fred's commentary grew increasingly hostile and embittered. He started yelling at customers and soon was let go. He was rehired a couple of months later following a breakdown and a stay in a mental health facility, or so I was told. Whatever the facts were, he had lost his edge. His jokes provoked polite laughter, not legitimate mirth, and he took to offering advice that was patently the product of time spent in group therapy and was not well received.

The world of Denny's became my world and, as tragedies like Fred's (seemingly minor compared to my own) played out around me, I sat there drawing dragon heads on napkins, scribbling in my notebook, canoodling with one of the waitresses, living as best I could in the jaundiced light… the kind of light that might have shone from a cracked and dusty lantern that illuminated some claustrophobic and hermetic fissure deep within Griaule's mountainous bulk.

LUCIUS SHEPARD

THE FATHER OF STONES

I REMEMBER LITTLE about the creation of this story, mainly because I was under the influence of the neighborhood where I wrote it. I lived during the early and mid-eighties in the Georgetown area of Staten Island, the neighborhood closest to the ferry terminal, on Westervelt Avenue, a street that aspired to be a crime wave and was populated by drug dealers, hookers, small-time monsters, a few brave souls who considered themselves the vanguard of a movement toward gentrification and would talk rebar with you for hours, and, oddly enough, a handful of genre folks: the horror writer Craig Spector, Beth Meachem and Tappan King (at the time, editors at Berkley and *Twilight Zone* respectively), me, and Maureen McHugh, all living within a block of one another.

Two townhouses down from me was a crack house, its front yard littered with rusted lawnchairs and motorcycle parts, run by a fake Rasta guy from Brooklyn, Nicky, who had dropped a dime on someone higher up the food chain and in exchange had been given carte blanche by the cops. Every morning the schoolkids would stop by for their rocks and sometimes the cops would pass the house and wave to Nicky, who—the soul of expansiveness—would return the salute. He also ran an illegal taxi service and maintained a string of hookers who operated out of the abandoned cars along New York Bay, and most nights would get into screaming fights on the street out front of my house. Drug dealers wearing Just Say No T-shirts made plaintive cries beneath my window at every hour of the day. I hand-wrote most of a novel called "Kingsley's Labyrinth," stopping only when I realized I had filled eleven notebooks with an indecipherable script that resembled seismograph readings, and I hung out with people whom I would normally run from—Uzi-toting Cubans and so forth. There were frequent gunshots and each morning when I walked out, my footsteps crunched due to the empty crack vials littering the sidewalks—it was as if a kind of glassine hail had fallen during the night.

My downstairs neighbor, a beautiful black transsexual named Renee, constantly fought with me over her right to play Connie Francis albums on her deck beneath my bedroom window at 6 AM, an argument ended when someone cut her throat, broke all her LPs, slashed her pretty blouses, and put bleach in her fish tank. These and other neighborhood tragedies came to occupy my attention, and I grew increasingly paranoid and unsound. The then-New York City mayor, Ed Koch, would once a month herd together a bunch of the most deranged homeless people in Manhattan and ship them over to Staten Island on a late-night ferry—his way of cleaning up the city. We'd wake the next morning to find a fresh crop of schizophrenics wandering the streets, talking to the CIA, to aliens, making phone calls to heaven. Most drifted back to Manhattan, but a few took up residence, including this one guy who was given a home by someone and built a life-sized, authentic-looking electric chair and every Fourth of July weekend would drag said chair out onto the traffic island on Victory Boulevard, strap himself in, and grin at the commuters. No one to my knowledge tried to stop him—it was as if the authorities accepted this as an appropriate commentary. To top it all off I began dating a businesswoman who appeared at the outset to be level-headed, stable, but three weeks into the relationship started breaking into my apartment to clean it and one night announced that she was a ninja and capable of starting fires with her eyes. We didn't make it very long. In my mental state, the last thing I wanted was a woman who could incinerate me on a whim.

Good times.

Somewhere in the midst of all this was a dragon, but it seemed quite mundane when contrasted with the vivid weirdness of the gangster fantasy in which I lived.

LIAR'S HOUSE

FOR MUCH OF the '00s I lived in Vancouver, Washington, essentially a bedroom community for Portland, Oregon, a gigantic strip mall with an endless supply of unprepossessing, unattractive people embarked upon the consumption of corn dogs and reality TV. This was my initial take on the town, at any rate, because, having grown up in a suburb, having steeped in its flavorless juices, I tend to loathe such places. But at the same time I firmly believe that the human species does not encompass a great range of intelligence, that the difference between an Einstein and an idiot is much less than we might imagine, and I am certain that people who are inarticulate and stolid and apparently thick often have interior lives every bit as complex and eccentric and rich as those of showier models. "Liar's House" received some criticism at the time of publication for the literate interior life of its ox-like protagonist. The criticism may have been deserved, yet this narrative tactic is not without precedent—there have been countless incidences of savant narrators throughout literature and, for my part, I've known plenty of uneducated people who were incapable of expressing themselves in precise language, yet had other means of self-expression and were extremely precise in their comprehension of the world, of what was going on around them. In any case, the character of my protagonist was informed by the people with whom I was surrounded. I suppose you might think of him as the personification of Vancouver, WA.

Even a paralyzed dragon must grow and change, and for this story I decided during the course of writing it that Griaule would want children—how then would he go about it? I assumed that he wanted children due to the natural desire to procreate, to create a legacy, but it might have added to the story if I had thought the matter through, because when I did so several years later I came up with an idea that would have made the link between this story and the last more apparent. I was tempted to go back in and rework the story, but decided to let things stand, figuring that it would be more honest, more illuminating as to how a writer's style evolves, to let the story stand as written.

Then perhaps I was just being lazy.

THE TABORIN SCALE

THIS STORY WAS a premature attempt to kill off Griaule, but the odd thing about these stories is that each one seems to breed a multitude of possibilities...and even in the final story, *especially* in the final story, it seemed every few pages there was the germ of yet another story. It was as if the dragon didn't want to die and was offering up intriguing possibilities, tempting me to spare him. Now I suspect that Griaule won't be done until I am.

I began writing these story notes while saddled with an apocalyptic case of the flu, and so had no clear idea of what I was about…though it seems that a main thread running through the notes is the relationship of writing to environment. However, in the case of "The Taborin Scale" I have nothing salient to say on the subject. I was living in Portland, Oregon, where I now reside. My life was basically untroubled, comfortable, the writing went easily, the story just popped out. The only thing remotely interesting about the story from a background perspective is the guy upon whom the main character, George, was based—a spindly punk rocker I knew casually in New York City who made a living by going to garage sales in upstate New York, searching for antique collectibles, which he then resold. This struck me as a very organized activity for someone who by night wore his hair in spikes and howled demonically into the mike and would spit up into the air and try and catch a loogey on his face. I'm going to have to assume that this is the way writers feel who have an office and a regular home and don't leave their possessions in storage lockers scattered across the country—I live in constant anticipation of seeing my stuff on one of those reality shows that focus on a small group of auction buyers who bid on abandoned lockers, watching the winning bidder paw through my junk, gazing with perplexity at a Hugo or a Howard or some such, wondering about what kind of loser bothers to store empty cigarette packs in a box of scribbled-in books and dirty laundry.

Takes all kinds, I guess.

THE SKULL

ONE NIGHT I was playing pachinko in a crowded arcade on Avenida Seis in Guatemala City and, as sometimes happens, I got so into the game that I lost track of what was happening around me. When I looked up I discovered that not only was the arcade deserted, the proprietor preparing to roll down the metal door, but the street was devoid of traffic, with only a few frightened-looking pedestrians scurrying for cover—Avenida Seis was like Broadway in New York City, busy at every hour, and I knew something bad must have occurred to clear it so quickly. (Unbeknownst to me, a group of left-wing students and Indian activists had taken over the Spanish embassy, where an ex-president of Guatemala was being feted, and were holding him and the embassy staff hostage, their purpose being to initiate a dialogue on land reform.) I began running, heading for my hotel, seeing military vehicles (Jeeps, armored anti-personnel carriers, etc.) moving along the side streets—but my hotel was a long ways off and, since I was a gringo and paranoid, fearful of being picked up and beaten, or worse, when I saw a man slip into a doorway I ducked in after him and found myself in a gay nightclub. In addition to a lot of young guys ranging the bar, there were several dozen attractive women seated at the tables. They were all partying as if nothing untoward were happening out in the streets and so, feeling relatively secure, I stuck around for the next several hours, learning from the bartender that the women were "*loritas*" (parakeets), upper class wives and mistresses who cultivated triviality as an armor against reality, and that their presence in the club served to protect the gay men from harassment. He went on to say that if I were so disposed it would be easy to get laid—many of the women were promiscuous to a fault—but there would be risk involved, since their husbands and boyfriends were mostly right-wingers and/or associated with the military.

The left-wing group holding the embassy was reacting to the fact that when the owners of immense ranches in the north of the country found that Indians had settled on their land and lived there long enough to establish legal rights, they did not take the matter to the courts, where they were certain to lose, but simply hired the military to massacre the Indians and destroy their settlements—the left-wingers hoped by taking action to initiate a dialogue about land reform. The government's reaction was to fire-bomb the building several hours after the takeover, killing everyone inside, including the Spanish ambassador and the ex-president, and thereafter to shut down Guatemala City for a week, closing the airport, burning all the buses that attempted to leave or enter the city, making a show of power. It was an extremely nervous time, people jumping at the least unexpected sound, a heavy military presence on almost every street corner day and night. I'd been planning to leave for Honduras the following day and, prevented from this, I spent a good bit of time at the nightclub during the week. Though I wasn't as adventurous as my protagonist with regards to the women who habituated the place, I did have a number of conversations with some of them, and it was on these that I based the character of Luisa Bazan and the dynamic that serves a key plot point in the story.

Of all the Griaule stories, this is the most grounded in my life experience and in the political realities of Central America, a place where I've spent a considerable amount of time. Temalagua is, of course, a scramble of Guatemala, and the Party of Organized Violence was an actual Guatemalan entity, very much on the ascendancy when I was first there. I could point out a dozen other correspondences between fiction and my Tru-Life Adventures in this piece, but that would be overkill. The important thing, at least to me, is that writing "The Skull" returned me to my original motivation in writing about Griaule, and if there are to be further stories about the dragon and his milieu, I think they'll be more focused upon the central theme, the political fantasy, than those that preceded it.